Celeste & Chris

CELESTE
& CHRIS
Manjula
Lisa Stokes

For Shannon, Nayana, Zoë, Indigo, Cecily, Cy,
Corwyn, Carson, Harris, Josh. With all my love

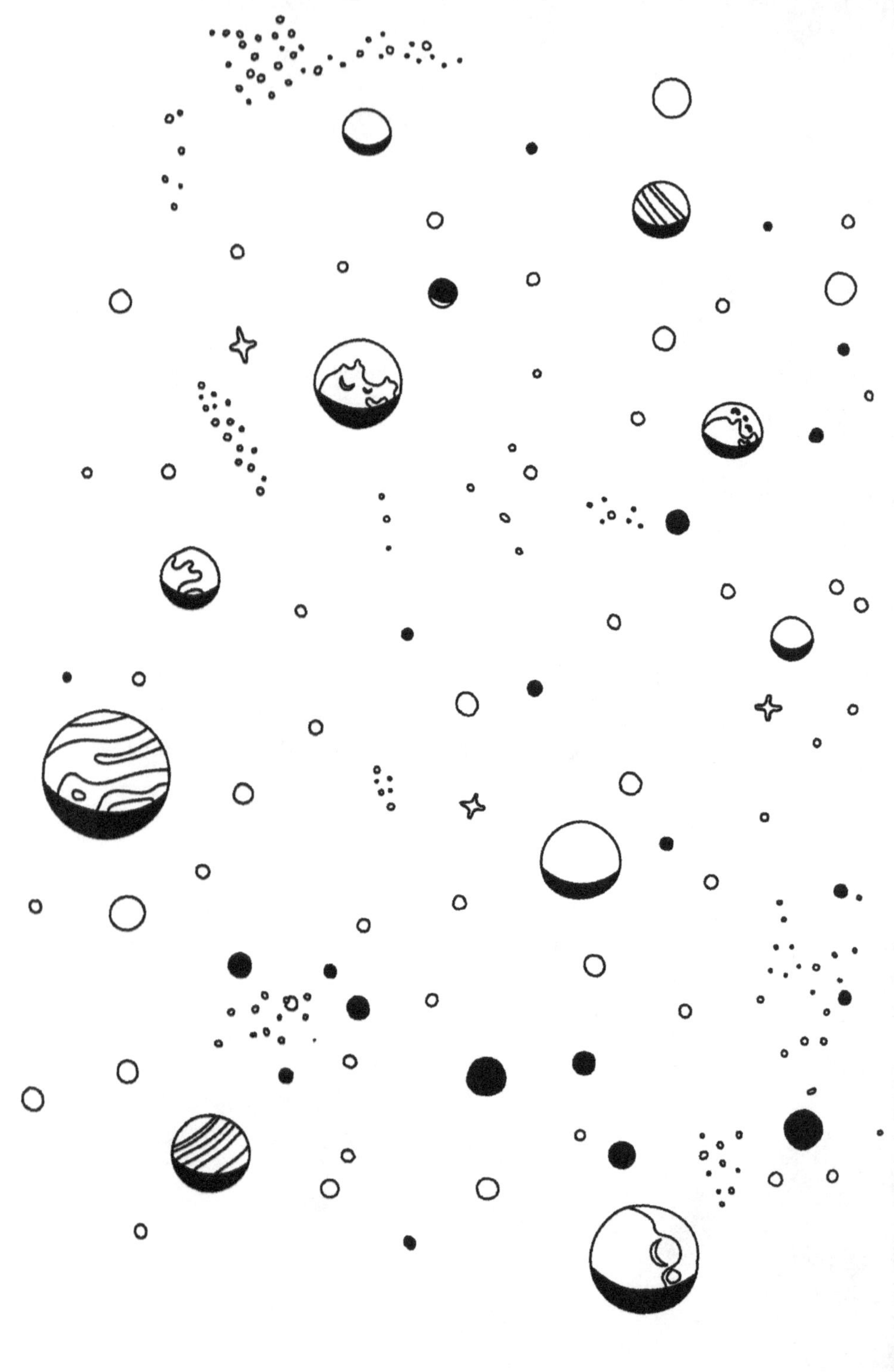

PART ONE

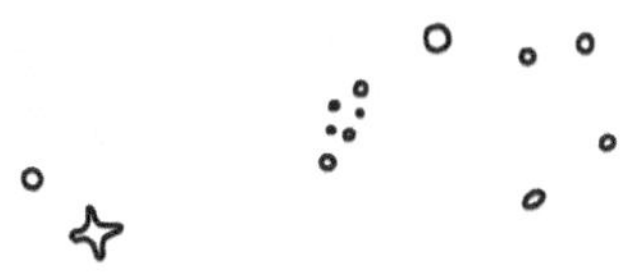

Celeste used a red rubber ball as a demonstration model for the rocket ship Mercury. On the surface, she'd drawn a chimpanzee strapped into a seat behind a control board. "Animals in Space," she announced. She'd memorized her report but didn't think the details important, relying mostly on drama for effect. Carrying the ball throughout the room, she let everyone see the chimp's brave face. As she moved, her starch pinafore brushed against the sides of desks, its whoosh the sound of a launch.

A boy named Chris raised his hand. Although he was usually shy in class, this time he spoke before being called on. "What's the chimpanzee's name?"

Celeste shrugged. "He doesn't have a name."

Chris asked, "What about Jacques?"

"Jacques?" she asked. "Fancy name for a chimp."

The students giggled. Chris blushed.

"Fine. I'll call him Jacques," she said.

"All right, Mary Celeste, please conclude your report," the teacher said.

"Endless space. Mercury. Chimp at the controls." Without warning, Celeste bounced the ball hard. "Crunched on impact. That's what happens to pets up there."

Chris jumped from his seat and caught the ball before it bounced again.

The teacher frowned. "Sit back down."

Chris complied with the teacher's demand but held Mercury in his lap, refusing to hand it back. Celeste felt annoyed at this boy's interference but appreciated his concern.

"I'm going to be a chimp vet in space," she said. Passing around a bucket, she requested donations to fund her education to NASA. She got a few milk nickels. Even her teacher dropped in a quarter.

"You're mean," Chris said. He pushed the donation bucket away.

She pointed to the smiling chimp. "Did you know about all those dead monkeys before I told you?"

"No, and I don't want to," he said, wrapping his arms around the ball and holding on tighter. "I like animals."

"Monkeys and mice and dogs are dying out there. Sizzling, suffocating, starving."

He covered his ears. "Stop talking."

Noticing he'd released his grip on the ball, she grabbed Mercury. "I'm going to orbit the earth and take care of the creatures before anything bad happens. That's why I need money. Astronaut school is expensive. I'll be Mary Celeste, the first vet in space."

"Celeste's a better name for an astronaut," Chris said.

"Why? Why is it better?" The chimp peeked from the crook in her elbow.

"Celeste sounds celestial." He pointed out the window into the bright noonday sun. "Like stuff in outer space."

"Stuff?" She emphasized the word stuff with a tone of disdain. "What kind of stuff are you talking about?"

"Like comets and constellations and galaxies."

"Celeste." The name held infinite possibilities. Mary had the tether of Jesus. She did not want to be tethered to Jesus. Mary lived her life as a long-suffering mother. She did not want to live her life as a long-suffering mother.

"I have a book on Mars," he said.

The teacher told them to stop talking and get back to work.

During lunch, Celeste saw Chris sitting alone near the back fence. Most of their class played kickball or jumped rope, but he often chose the isolation of the sandbox. Approaching him to discuss what else he knew about the universe, Celeste threw Mercury, hoping he'd catch it. He didn't. The ball bounced, rolling into the grassy field. She scooped it up, wiping dirt from Jacques's chin. She called, "You're not good with balls, are you?"

"Isn't it supposed to be a spaceship?"

"Can I see your book about Mars?"

"It's from the public library," he said. "My mom won't let me bring it to school." He scooted away from her. Peering into his lunch sack, he said, "See you later."

"Have you got cooties? Because if you do, you should tell me now." She set Mercury in the sand, making sure the chimp's smile faced him.

"I don't have cooties. I like being way out here. Nice and quiet. Alone."

Celeste sat beside him. "When I'm an astronaut, I'll be alone. The first thing written in the official NASA handbook is, 'Like yourself best because that's who you'll be spending lots and lots of time with.'"

"You've got the handbook? A real one?" he asked, sounding both skeptical and in awe.

"Rule Number Two, 'Enjoy the company of primates and dogs because they want attention and sometimes their backs need to be scratched.' There's ten rules all together. The rest are way too technical," Celeste said, squinting in the sunshine. "I'd need a blackboard and a few recesses to teach you. If you want to learn them. Do you?"

"Maybe."

Using a twig from the magnolia tree overhead, she drew stars in the sand. "Number Ten is confidential, but if you confess a secret, I'll tell you."

Chris took out a package of pink snowball cupcakes. "I don't have a secret."

"Are you going to eat both of those? Can I have one?"

He hesitated but reached over to hand her a treat. "My mom tells me I have to share."

"You'd be a compatible astronaut if you memorized all ten rules."

Peeling the marshmallow crown from his cupcake, he pinched a piece and popped it in his mouth. "I like life down here on earth."

Celeste noticed a cord dangling from his jacket. "Is that a weapon? Are you a Russian spy? Being a quiet kid is a good cover. No one would suspect you."

"I'm not a spy," he said.

"If you show me what you've got in your pocket, I'll confide the tenth and most important rule," she said. "You can trust an astronaut. We take an oath. Protect. Serve. Be a good sport. Loyalty matters most of all."

Chris took a swill of milk from his thermos. "No, you can't see what's in my pocket."

She said, "I named the chimp Jacques after your suggestion, didn't I? Also, I'm calling myself Celeste, not Mary Celeste. I'm Celeste the Astronaut."

He eyed her with suspicion. "You named him Jacques, then killed him."

Celeste pointed to the chimp. "He's alive and well and ready for another mission."

A slip of whipped cream oozed from the middle of his cupcake, dropping onto the ground.

She continued, "I'm not a snitch. I can keep a secret."

"If I show you, you have to promise you won't make fun of me," Chris said.

Celeste crossed herself. "I swear I won't make fun of you. I won't tell anyone. Jesus will slug me if I do."

Chris pulled the cord—the tail of a stuffed toy rat. "Her name is Juliet of Provence. I made her myself." Crafted from white cloth and sewn with tiny stitches to bind her cotton stuffing, Juliet had green embroidered eyes, a pink embroidered smile, brown embroidered freckles, and yellow yarn hair pulled into a tight ballerina bun.

"Boys don't play with dolls," Celeste said.

Juliet danced along the wooden railing of the sandbox and twirled in the air. "I do."

"Aren't you scared of getting teased?"

Chris slid the doll into his pocket, then back out again. "That's why she's small. I can hide her if I want."

Celeste peered closer. "Can I hold her?"

"The tutu's scratchy," he warned. "I cut apart an old window screen to make it."

Cradling Juliet of Provence in her palm, she frowned. "Russians send rats into space. Imagine this poor thing crashing and burning in a ball of flames."

"Juliet won't go into orbit. She'll stay on this planet and dance." Chris rattled a list of French terms. Arabesque. Fouette. Cabriolet.

"The final top secret NASA rule, 'If you ever meet a Martian, don't invite them home. The last thing we need are aliens running around eating up our food. Martians are constantly hungry.'" She handed Juliet to Chris. "Sounds rude to be unfriendly, but can you picture our school filled with green Martian children? They'd always want to be first in line for everything."

Chris tucked his hair behind his ears. Curls bounced free. "Then let them."

Celeste thought, Chris looks like a girl. Pretty with his galaxy of freckles, rosy pink lips, and blond curly hair. Not like the other boys with their stupid faces and crew cuts. "You're not afraid of Martians, are you? Well, neither am I. That makes us friends," she said.

Before meeting Chris, Celeste had often played with a girl named Molly, who wore her long black hair in pigtails tied with ribbons to match her blue eyes. Molly dripped with goodness, smelled like lilacs, and had the voice of a songbird, but was also unkempt—stained dresses, dirt beneath her fingernails, and frilled socks that slipped below her Achilles, disappearing into the heels of her shoes.

The last time they spent together, Celeste and Molly left a game of checkers on Celeste's kitchen table and went upstairs to play Queen for a Day. Pretending she'd won a new washing machine, Celeste curtsied to accept the towel cape Molly knotted around her shoulders.

"Why do you want to be Queen for a Day?" Molly asked, imitating the television host of the show.

"Who wouldn't?" Celeste adjusted the cape and continued, "I need a new washer because I've got six kids and a husband who's a lumberjack in Siberia."

Molly placed a paper crown on Celeste's head. "The Applause-O-Meter shows you told the saddest story of all our contestants. Congratulations. You're our favorite Queen."

Yelling came from downstairs. "Mary Celeste!"

"What's wrong?" Molly asked, her eyes widening. "What's wrong with your mom?"

Celeste threw the cardboard scepter aside and sprinted two steps at a time. Molly followed close behind.

In the kitchen, Bernadette pointed a meat cleaver at the unfinished game of checkers. Stepping forward, she used the blade to wipe pieces from the table, sending black and red discs reeling across the floor. "I'm your mother, not your servant."

"We were going to clean up," Celeste said. The theme song from Queen for a Day went round and round her head.

Bernadette slapped a breast of chicken onto the cutting board, chopping the bird straight down the middle with one enormous whack. "I need an organized kitchen while I'm trying to make dinner for your father." Her voice grew calmer as she spoke. The thud of the cleaver against the chicken did not. She cubed the meat, rolled the chunks in cornflakes, and threw them into the pan of sizzling lard. "Would the Kennedy children treat their mother this way?"

Celeste knelt and pinched a checker between her fingers. The sight of Molly's scuffed shoes angered her. Molly had a mother who didn't make her polish her saddle shoes before church and reapply if they got even the tiniest scratch.

"Mary Celeste was winning," Molly said with a honeyed smile. "It was my fault we left the game and didn't put it away. I wanted to play Queen for a Day. You'd be a good Queen, Mrs. Roderick. You're beautiful like one. You cook and clean. You should go on the show. You'd win."

Celeste hated Molly for her efforts to placate Bernadette. She wanted Molly to tell Bernadette if the mess bothered her so damn much, she should pick up the pieces herself. Celeste told Molly to go home and never come back. On the way to the front door, Molly tried to comfort Celeste by mentioning that her mom shouted too. Celeste knew the comparison wasn't the same. Molly's mom yelled a tired, worn-out yell. A too-many-kids yell.

Days after Chris showed her Juliet, Celeste hurried to the sandbox with a present she made during arts and crafts. "Being alone out here with you as my copilot lets me practice how life will be once I'm shot into space to fix sick monkeys and dogs and rodents."

"I don't want to be a copilot," Chris said. "Did you know Russians send puppies into orbit? Strap them in and blast off. They're given a hero's welcome when they return. Confetti. Ticker tape. Bowls of beef. If they return."

Chris stroked Juliet's tail, wrapping the cord around his finger. "Celeste," he said with irritation, "go away."

Celeste shook her head. "You and I have the same birthday. Did you notice that on the teacher's bulletin board? June first. We're twins."

"That's nice, but I want you to leave me alone," he said.

She handed Chris the gift she'd crafted, a rocket ship made from a toilet paper roll and covered with glittery red tissue and streamers. "It's called Astro. This new design will soar to the outer reaches of the universe. With the help of Astro, if anyone sees your doll, they'll think she's an astronaut rat, not a prima ballerina."

Chris eyed the contraption. "Juliet of Provence doesn't want to be a space explorer. I already told you."

"Without gravity, she'll have the chance to leap and twirl, and never come down."

Chris scratched his upper lip. "Leap and twirl without gravity? She'd like that."

They sat in silence, watching their classmates jump rope and play hopscotch.

"Can I bring her home for the night?" Celeste asked.

"No. You'll stuff Juliet of Provence inside this rocket ship and throw her across your room," Chris said.

Celeste promised she'd also let Juliet dance. She described how her floral bedspread would be the stage and Juliet would have a huge audience of stiff-limbed dolls forced into thunderous applause, even if their sockets popped.

Glancing from Celeste to Juliet to Astro, he repeated, "No."

Celeste said, "I'll treat her like royalty."

Chris put Juliet in his jacket. "No."

"You don't want me to treat her like royalty?"

"I want you to go away."

"I'll go away and leave you alone for the rest of your life if you let me bring her home tonight. Just one night." Celeste put her palms together, closing her eyes as if in prayer. "Astronauts keep their promises."

The bell rang, signaling the end of recess. Chris stood. "You'll never bother me again?"

"If that's what you want," she said.

Chris reached into his pocket for Juliet. "Don't let anything bad happen to her."

"I'll treat her better than anything I own."

He kissed the doll goodbye before placing her into Celeste's open palm. "I'm trusting you."

"I'll miss being out here with you, but a promise is a promise," she said.

That night, when Bernadette tucked Celeste into bed, she pointed to the tip of window screen poking from beneath the covers. "What's this?" Bernadette said, reaching for Juliet. "Where did you get this darling little doll?"

"My friend Chris let me borrow her." Celeste had to stop herself from grabbing Juliet back.

"What a lovely friend to entrust you with such a delicate ballerina. Do you suppose she'd like a change of clothes for after her performance?"

"I guess," Celeste said, but thought differently. All Juliet ever did was perform.

She fell asleep listening to the hum of her mother's Singer. In the morning outfits appeared next to Celeste's placemat, perfect replicas of her own clothes. A brown-and-plaid pinafore; a simple dress with yellow stitching meant to recreate smocking; a fancy dress with a frilled, tiered skirt and very large bow at the back; plus a tutu made from an old crinoline slip, soft and a dozen layers thick.

On Friday, in the grocery store, Celeste spotted Chris down the cookie aisle. She shouted his name and waved.

Bernadette swatted Celeste's arm, saying, "Shhh, we're in a public place, Mary Celeste. Church volume."

Chris hurried over. "Mrs. Roderick, thank you for sewing Juliet's clothes. I love them so much." Pulling her from his sweatshirt pocket, he made the rat fouette across the handle of the grocery cart.

"She's your doll?" Bernadette flipped open her cigarette case. Sliding a Cavalier from the narrow strap holding them in place, she struck a match. "Yours?"

Celeste stared at a box of cereal, noticing the ridges of shredded grain, the splash of unnaturally white teardrops, the blue pitcher. She wondered what kind of family uses a pitcher to pour their milk.

Bernadette lowered her voice, her lips pressing Celeste's ear. "Boys play with swords. Girls play with dolls. Where's Molly been lately? She's a fine, normal child." Bernadette went to the produce aisle to select a bag of oranges, another of apples.

Celeste whispered to Chris, "Invite me over for dinner."

"Why?"

"I like your mom."

"You've never met her," Chris said.

"She buys you snowball cupcakes."

"Yeah," he said. "Yours doesn't buy sweets?"

"If you invite me, I'll bring another outfit for Juliet."

Bernadette dropped produce in the cart. "Fruit. Fruit. Fruit," she said.

"Chris invited me for dinner tonight," Celeste said, nudging him with her elbow. "Can I go?"

Chris said, "We're having spaghetti and meatballs. My mom's around here. You can meet her."

Bernadette's waxy orangish lips clenched the cigarette as she inhaled. The tip sizzled red. "Christopher, what a lovely invitation; however, we already have plans for dinner." Stopping in front of the meat counter, she put in her order.

The sound of the butcher's blade screeched toward them: the bone saw cutting apart a rack of lamb. Scents of blood and flesh nauseated Celeste. She held her breath, silently begging Chris to put Juliet back in his pocket.

Bernadette turned to Chris and said, "Perhaps another time we can arrange something appropriate."

"Celeste won't be a problem," Chris said. "My mom likes company."

Celeste said, "I love spaghetti and meatballs. It's my favorite food in the world."

"Not tonight, Mary Celeste." Bernadette's nostrils flared when she emphasized Mary. "Goodbye, Christopher. I'm glad I had the opportunity to meet my daughter's little friend with the darling ballerina doll." She moved toward the checkout, unloading the groceries onto the conveyer belt, smacking each item down as if she didn't care that eggs break.

Celeste glanced back at Chris, but he'd disappeared in the afternoon crowd of shoppers. "I really want to go to Chris's house for dinner."

"Absolutely not." Bernadette tossed a pack of peppermint gum on the pile.

"His dad's a doctor. If anything bad happens, he'll be able to save my life."

Instant mashed potatoes, a can of tuna, condensed milk.

Bernadette whipped toward Celeste, the smoke from her cigarette curling from her mouth to her nostrils. "Something bad has already happened." Dropping the filter on the scuffed floor, she ground the butt with the toe of her pump.

"What?" Celeste asked. "What happened?"

Hamburger, stroganoff noodles, Wonder Bread.

"Jesus, Mary, and Joseph. Be quiet for once in your life."

Frozen peas, iceberg lettuce, Collins mix.

Bernadette stooped low, cupping Celeste's chin in her palm. "Meatballs on a Friday? That's a mortal sin. Do you want to commit one?"

"I would've rolled them off my plate."

Bernadette wrote a check and handed her payment to the cashier.

"I simply don't understand what kind of mother lets her fat fruity boy play with a doll."

"I play with her, too," Celeste whispered.

Taking the strip of green stamps, Bernadette stuffed them in her purse and snapped the clasp. "The Devil knows the boy's heart and the temptations harbored inside of him."

"What temptations?"

"Shh," Bernadette said.

On the way home, she stopped at church to light a red votive and pray to the Virgin for Chris's salvation. "Because," she told Celeste, "he is a child, after all."

Celeste held in her urge to blow the candle out. The only other people Bernadette ever lit votives for all ended up dying.

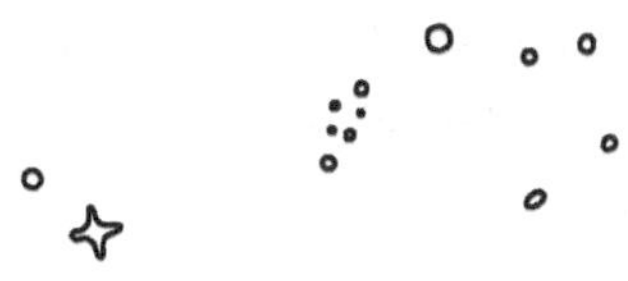

Before Bernadette unlatched the front door, she glanced at Celeste. "I fell in love with your father because he was a Protestant." She was on her third Limestone, tipsy enough to need the doorframe to lean against.

"He still is a Protestant, isn't he?" Celeste said.

George had been on the road for three days, and Bernadette insisted Celeste dress up for his homecoming. The bow in her hair stood upright, starched and scratchy on her scalp.

Bernadette said, "You look fine today, Mary Celeste," and opened the door.

Her father stood on the welcome mat, his fedora beneath his arm. When he flung the hat toward the coatrack, Celeste imagined the pheasant feather stuck in the band demanded the chance to fly again. George kissed his wife on the cheek.

Celeste said, "Welcome home."

"Didn't see you standing there, Mary Celeste. You look pretty," he said, patting the top of her head.

Bernadette helped him take off his coat. She slid her hand into the deep pockets, pulling out a dozen receipts, a carton of cigarettes, coins, and a few wadded bills. "Where on earth did they send you this time?"

He opened his satchel, handing her a tube of lipstick. "A new shade of coral. Try this beauty on," he said.

Tapping the orange color against her lips, Bernadette rubbed them together, puckering. "How do I look?"

"Like Mrs. Jacqueline Bouvier Kennedy on her wedding day." He set his satchel on the floor beside the coffee table, took a tin can of furniture polish, twisted the lid, and poured. With a flick of his wrist, a chamois spread wide open. "Another present for you, Bernie. A miracle product." He wiped the puddle around the reclining figurine of St. Bernadette.

"Be careful of my saint." She moved the sculpture out of the way.

"Girls, swipe the table's surface, then inspect your fingertips for signs of dust." He paused a moment before adding, "Squeaky clean," his words spoken with care.

"No mumbling," Bernadette said. She pulled a compact mirror from his array of beauty products and held it in front of her mouth as she modeled the proper way to pronounce Sq and K.

He stared at her lips, watching the phonemes sail effortlessly.

"Now you try," she said, handing him the mirror.

"Sq. Sq. K. K. Sq. Sq. K.K," he obeyed, repeating into his reflection.

George was a Fuller Brush man, but as Bernadette often mentioned, traveling door to door reciting the canned line, "The best products of their kind in the world," couldn't have been easy for a man with a stutter.

Celeste wondered what her gift would be. Usually, George brought something useful for her, like a whisk broom or a stainless-steel sponge or a comb.

As if cued, George tossed Celeste a nail-and-hand brush. "To make an impression, keep your fingernails clean and tidy," he said.

Removing the brush from the box, Celeste stroked the bristles with the pad of her thumb. "Soft."

"And here's a lipstick sample for you to play dress up with." He handed Celeste a small tube. "Rose."

Celeste twisted the lid. Pink. She wasn't particularly fond of pink but swiped it across her lips anyway.

"George, make us Limestones, Catholic strength," Bernadette said.

"Aye aye, Captain." He saluted.

Bernadette said, "You forgot to tell me you're here to sweep me off my feet." His standard joke whenever he came home from a Fuller Brush trip.

He pushed the rolling bar toward her, used tongs to retrieve ice cubes from the bucket, dropped two in each glass. "I'm here to—"he paused, puckering his lips and taking a breath before continuing with the difficult Sw sound—"sweep you off your feet."

"Bravo. Hardly a mispronunciation." Bernadette lit a cigarette.

Celeste wanted to tell her father she'd stocked the rolling bar in preparation for his arrival. She'd emptied the ice cube tray the moment his car pulled into the driveway. She'd refilled the decanter with Heavenly Hill. All Bernadette had done was deplete the supplies. "I used Fuller Brush metal polish on the silver tray," Celeste said. "Best product of its kind in the world."

"Nice and shiny. Keep up the good work." George mixed the cocktails and handed one to Bernadette. "Protestant strength. Then we can have two," he said.

Bernadette curled her fingers around the tumbler. She tapped the rim with one polished fingernail at a time.

Popping the lid from a ginger soda, George poured it over ice, squeezed in a bit of lime. "Child strength, Mary Celeste," he said, clinking his glass against hers.

The zing of ginger tasted grown up, but not at all like the flavor of bourbon. Once or twice, she'd snuck a sip of Heavenly Hill. Her throat had burned. Eyes teared. Nose dripped. Head spun.

Bernadette fluffed up her coif of hair. "Notice anything?" Cigarette smoke trailed her lips as she spoke, creating the illusion of a thin veil across her words.

He said, "Your Uppity Do looks lovely, Bernie."

"Just don't touch it, George."

Those coils of starched strands sat on top of her head all week until Thursday when they unraveled and curls fell free. Celeste thought Bernadette looked the prettiest like this. George seemed to feel the same, because those were the nights he brought home cartons of Chinese take-out and offered to rub her shoulders, and later, music floated from their bedroom.

Celeste sat on the floor near the coffee table, unfurling the sample tube of rose-colored lipstick. The salve elongated, hovered, toppled over, breaking in half. Celeste stuck the two parts together and twisted until the stick slipped back into the tube.

Wooden crosses hung on every wall of their house. Statues of saints cluttered the shelves and windowsills. On the console stood a porcelain Madonna, her arms gesturing toward the candy dish. Alone, Celeste held her by the waist and danced her around, tilting her lips to heaven, mouthing the words, "Hey Daddy-O, mints again? Where are the Hot Tamales?" Even their car had a Mary glued to the dashboard. Celeste wanted her hips to sway like a hula dancer she saw once in a passing sedan, but this Virgin was frozen stiff.

Celeste tried to be religious. She built a shrine in the front yard beneath the bottlebrush hedge. The spindly red petals pointed upward like hands raised to heaven. Bees hummed as beatific as a choir. She stacked driveway pebbles for an altar and twisted colorful electrical wire into a crucifix, then opened a box of Licorice Babies and shook one into her palm. The size of a bean, the candy had the image of a body imprinted into the gummy surface. Spearing the baby through the center with a safety pin, Celeste secured him to the cross, then propped the rest of the box of licorice against twig pews. The candy resembled a congregation brought to their feet.

While gardening, Bernadette wielded her rake, pulling the black licorice church onto the driveway. She bent over and plucked the crucified baby Jesus between her fingers, inspecting it and the cross. "Black people are Baptists. Baptists are pagans, and pagans are no better than sinners." She emptied the dustpan of candy into the garbage.

"What do you mean?" Celeste asked.

"Black. Baptist. Pagan. Don't bother me anymore."

Celeste pulled Jesus and the parishioners from the rubble and shoved them into the pocket of her pinafore. She had no idea what a Baptist was and needed to find out. "Can I go to the library?"

Bernadette nodded. "You never have to ask me that."

Celeste ate the candy congregation as she walked down the street. Despite flecks of dirt stuck in the soft sides of the black licorice, she chewed. By the time she arrived at the doorway of the library, she had swallowed Jesus Himself.

The local librarian Mr. B, which stood for Mr. Books, wore cardigan sweaters all year long and smelled like cherry tobacco. If anyone could help her understand Baptists, that man would be Mr. B, the most educated person Celeste knew. She stood on tiptoe at the checkout counter and repeated what Bernadette said.

"Baptists and pagans?" Mr. B rubbed his hands together and tilted his head to the side. "I believe you're asking to expand your mother's worldview of people and religion? Do I have this fact correct?"

Celeste wiggled a fleck of candy stuck between her teeth. She didn't particularly like the taste of black licorice, but she wasn't going to leave the faithful Baptists and their Jesus in the garbage.

Mr. B said, "To begin, Baptist is a Christian religion."

"My mother says black Baptist babies are sinners."

"Well, shall we prove her assumption incorrect?" Mr. B flipped through the card catalogue, yanking library indexes as if weeding a garden. He weaved up and down the aisles, gradually loading her arms with books. "There are also white Baptists. Most importantly, babies, black or white, can't be sinners." He left her alone to read.

Fanning the selections across the library table, Celeste studied each one. She eventually made her decision based on the cover illustration and title. *Invisible Man.*

"Good choice for your mother. This should help her understand people with different backgrounds than hers." Mr. B stamped the card with the due date and slipped the book across the counter toward Celeste. "Powerful writing from an important author."

Arriving home, Celeste said, "I've got a good book."

Bernadette looked up from weeding the flowerbed. "Only one this time?" She set her rake against the garage door, took *Invisible Man* from Celeste, skimmed the opening paragraph, flipped through the rest of the pages. "This is much too advanced for a child. What was that idiotic man thinking giving you an adult book? Return it before it's lost in your room, and I have to pay an exorbitant fine." Bernadette tossed a handful of dandelions into a bucket. "The librarian obviously didn't listen to your request. Don't wander past the children's section. Look for books with pictures."

On her way back to the library, Celeste opened to the first page and read, "I am an invisible man... I am a man of substance, of flesh and bone, fiber and liquids — and I might even be said to possess a mind. I am invisible, understand, simply because people refuse to see me." She didn't get farther than those opening lines—the language was too difficult—yet the description thrilled her. Celeste understood how it felt to be invisible, especially around Bernadette and George.

At school on Monday, Celeste told Chris about the passage.

He said, "Invisible? Sounds fun."

"Only if you want to be. Not if you don't." She paused a moment before adding, "George's gone a lot, so when he's home, he only cares about Bernadette. I could build a rocket ship in the middle of the living room and they wouldn't notice."

"I'd notice," Chris said. "I'd be impressed."

"You would?" Celeste's heart fluttered.

Digging into his pocket, he pulled Juliet's cord tail. "If I was invisible, I'd play with Juliet of Provence wherever I wanted, and no one would know she's my doll. They'd only see a magical dancing rat."

During the Pledge of Allegiance, Celeste stared at the stiff flag propped in the corner of the room and wondered if they used Fuller Brush starch to make it stand straight. Next to the flag, the presidential portrait of John Kennedy, with his kind eyes and smile, reassured her everything would be fine with the space race. She whispered to Chris, "Are you a Catholic or a pagan?"

Chris shrugged. "My dad says our family's Jewtheran."

"I never heard of that religion."

"My dad's Jewish and my mom's Lutheran."

"I want to be Jewtheran."

At the competition of the pledge, their teacher sat behind her desk, took a stack of papers and a red pen, and said, "Get to work, kids." She didn't bother to look up.

Half the class, the ones who'd gotten lower than a B on a math test, stood in the front of the room writing equations on the blackboard. Chalk dust floated in the sunlight and settled across their shoulders, eyelashes, desks.

Celeste asked Chris to be her partner for their report on African elephants. She pushed her desk next to his. As she opened a folder, her elbow bumped the edge of the encyclopedia, knocking the book to the floor with a bang so loud the girl next to them dove for cover. "A Russian spaceship didn't crash to earth," Celeste said to her, adding, "but a catastrophe like that could happen. Good you're prepared."

The teacher wagged her finger in Celeste's direction. "Quiet."

Chris picked up the encyclopedia and flipped to a page, tracing the words with his fingertip. "People kill elephants for their tusks to make ivory."

"Disgusting," Celeste said, looking over his shoulder to read the paragraph he was pointing to. She frowned. "Brush handles are made from ivory? That means Fuller Brush brushes, too?"

Chris illustrated a large bull elephant grazing. "Hunters sneak up on them while they're eating savannah grass."

"Elephants are dead if they stick around to eat grass, and they're dead if they run away from hunters and head to the hills where they'll starve. Sounds like God's trying to trick them."

"God wouldn't do that," Chris said. He sketched a tree. In the background, zebras and giraffes galloped by.

"Jewtherans don't know much about God do they?"

"Do you know about God?" he asked.

"If Jesus is God, then yes, I do." Celeste noticed Chris hadn't reacted to her saying, If Jesus is God. Everything Bernadette taught her about religion hinged on Jesus and God being the same. Apparently, Jewtherans weren't judgmental of other's beliefs. Apparently, Jewtherans didn't equate Jesus with God.

The teacher announced the class had forty minutes until lunch. "Work wisely," she said.

Celeste wrote a list of objects made from ivory. Piano keys. Chessmen. Miniature tabernacles. "Do Jewtherans believe in the devil?"

Concentrating on his illustration, he glanced at her and frowned. "Maybe as a story."

"I've seen him under my bed, holding a vial of poison."

"No, you haven't."

"He wants me to drink every last ounce."

"No, he doesn't." Chris pulled his paper closer, coloring the hills.

"The more boys and girls he can get in Hell, the merrier he'll be," Celeste said. Bernadette often threatened her by saying the Devil stole weak-minded children and made them dance on hot coals. The Devil waited for the chance to infect them with a terrible childhood disease the moment they made a mistake. "Remember when we were marched to the cafeteria and forced to eat a sugar cube? That was the Devil's idea. Disease disguised as something kids would like."

Chris tapped his pencil on the desk. "My dad says that's called an inoculation. Keeps us from getting polio."

"The Devil wants me and probably wants you too, since you're Jewtheran."

"Shhh," the girl next to them said. She got up to tell the teacher.

"If you know all about him, what does the Devil look like?" Chris folded his arms across his chest. "Does he have a long red tail with a triangle on the end?"

"He's not like that."

"Pointed red horns?"

"Not that either."

"Well, is any part of him red?"

"No."

"Then you haven't seen the Devil. Everyone knows how he looks. Draw a picture of what you've seen." Chris pushed a blank sheet of paper toward her.

Celeste sketched a creature she supposed could be hiding in the shadows. A harbinger of evil.

Squinting at the picture, Chris shook his head. "You drew an imp. I have a book on English fairy tales. Imps like to make trouble."

"Imp? What's an imp?"

"They aren't even related to the Devil. Come to my house after school. I know a way to get rid of imps."

"Will it be okay with your mom?"

"Why wouldn't it be?" he said.

"My mom would demand a week's notice if you were coming over."

"My mom wants me to have friends."

From across the classroom, their teacher snapped her fingers. "Chris, since you're so chatty, tell us what you've learned thus far."

Chris said, "African elephants have bigger ears than Indian ones."

"Fine. Mary Celeste, what facts do you have to share with the class?"

"African elephants try to solve problems."

"Embellish, please."

"They kill hunters by holding them down with their feet, then ripping them apart with their trunks."

The class shrieked.

"Eeww!" Chris threw his hand over her mouth.

The teacher said, "Bequietrightnow" as if it were one word.

"They really do kill people like that." She'd heard this information somewhere.

Chris whispered, "Stop talking."

"Oh, Mary Celeste," the teacher said with a tone of resignation. As a punishment, Celeste had to stay in for lunch.

Alone at her desk, Celeste ate her sandwich and watched the teacher gently lift the leaves on her violets to water them.

Celeste sat beneath Chris's flowering dogwood and inhaled the sweet scent.

Dressed in a magician's top hat and cape, Chris wobbled out the front door and down the brick walkway. Setting a mixing bowl, wooden spoon, lemon juice, and honey on the lawn in front of her, he bowed. "Gather twenty-five blades of grass and seven rose petals, and while you're finding them, tell the imp to stay away. Put the plants in the bowl, add lemon juice and honey, mix one hundred times, and eat fast. My mom takes good care of her roses. They don't have aphids."

Celeste plucked petals and grass shoots, threw them in the bowl with the juice and honey. "Keep the Devil and imps away from me," she repeated as she stirred. The roses were chewy and flora-flavored.

A few blades of grass got stuck in her throat, tickling. Luckily, the honey made everything slide down easier. "Want to taste it?"

"Eating your spell would be stealing your magic," Chris said.

Although the concoction took less than ten minutes to prepare and eat, Celeste felt boundless relief as if the creature roaming her room, Devil or imp, had been banished to another child's house forever. "It worked," she said with a smile.

Chris rubbed his hands together. "Foiled by roses and grass and lemon and honey."

"Foiled by a boy in a magic hat."

He performed an elegant little bow, his hands pulling his cape like bat wings.

Mrs. Armstrong brought them lemonade and a plate of cookies. "The tree in the backyard is abundant with lemons. Enjoy," she said, and left.

The sun beat down but it wasn't hot or even warm; a cool breeze swept across his yard. Celeste tugged her ankle socks to cover as much leg as possible. Chris removed his cape and draped it over her lap.

She said, "Let's find a meeting place to leave each other messages. There's too much time between school one day and school the next. Too much time to go without the chance to talk to you."

"We have telephones," he said.

"Bernadette picks up the other line and listens in. She's suspicious of everyone."

"Should our hiding place be in your yard, since it's easier for me to sneak out of my house than for you to sneak out of yours?" he asked.

Celeste thought for a moment and agreed. "Beneath the Sacred Heart of Jesus statue. He's hidden in a corner out of view from our windows."

"You'll need to show him to me," Chris said.

"Never leave anything under St. Francis. Bernadette's always moving him around the garden."

"I'm Jewtheran when it comes to telling saints apart. I don't know what St. Francis or Sacred Heart Jesus look like." Chris put the ingredients and spoon in the mixing bowl.

"St. Francis is the guy with the birds sitting on his head. Jesus is holding his hand up like a crosswalk guard." She struck a similar pose.

"Crosswalk guard. Not bird guy."

"Jewtherans don't have saints or crosses or burdens to carry?"

"Half of me has a six-pointed star."

"Everyone loves stars," she said, and pointed at the sky. "I'm glad we're Gemini twins."

"Twins separated at conception." Chris mixed medical lingo into conversations the way Celeste evoked the grisly martyrdom of saints.

"Exploring Gemini will be my second mission after I cure the animals of antigravity illness and President Kennedy thanks me for being the one to beat Russia in the space race. I'll bring all the dogs and primates home and start a petting zoo in my backyard."

Mrs. Armstrong opened the front door. "Chris, time for homework," she called.

"Gotta go." Chris gathered the magic accruements, snack plate, glasses, and tray. "See you tomorrow," he said.

Celeste dug through her book bag. "I snuck the E encyclopedia from class since we can't work on our report together anymore. My fault," she said, and left the research book with Chris.

School had barely begun when the principal's voice boomed over the loudspeaker, "Go home, kids. Go home to the ones you love." He sniffled.

The hallway grew crowded with people wandering in all directions, bumping into each other, arguing and apologizing. Teachers cried and sobbed. The secretary collapsed against the counter and scolded everyone for lingering. Younger children ran around. Older students walked through the campus, dazed. Shadows appeared especially diabolical, the forces of good and evil battling. On that beautiful sunny, autumn day, nature remained oblivious to human suffering.

President Kennedy had been killed. Assassinated, everyone said.

The streets looked how she imagined the end of the world would look: Empty and eerie. Celeste couldn't find Chris anywhere. She went to his house. No one answered her knock. She ran home, not knowing where else to go, and left him a note beneath Sacred Heart of Jesus. Chris, "What are we going to do now that President Kennedy is dead? What's going to happen to the space race? What's going to happen to his wife and children? Your friend forever, Celeste."

Thehouse had no noise. No sounds of Bernadette cleaning or primping or watching the television. At the kitchen table, Celeste ate her lunch, even though the breakfast dishes hadn't been cleared. Putting everything into the sink, she rinsed and washed and dried.

Then Bernadette shouted from upstairs, "Is that you, Mary Celeste? I want George."

Away on the Fuller Brush Road, he wasn't due back until Saturday night. "He's coming any minute," she said, hoping the statement alone would comfort Bernadette.

"You should go to bed," Bernadette said. "Yes, go to bed."

Passing her mother's room, Celeste cracked open the door. "Can I help you until he gets here?"

"Our first Catholic President. Crucified. Those barbarians. Those pagans." She peered at Celeste from under the coverlet. The silk banding was damp and stained black from mascara. "Jesus abandoned us, Mary Celeste. He left us with a Protestant in charge." Bernadette rolled on her stomach, burying her face in the pillow.

Celeste wanted to remind Bernadette that as a Protestant, George would make an okay president. Deciding against bringing him into the conversation and making her mother sadder, she asked,

"Do you want a Limestone?" Celeste had watched George and Bernadette make plenty of cocktails because the rolling bar traveled room to room with them, and cocktail hour was an everyday, anytime occurrence.

Bernadette said, "Make it a double."

Celeste measured Heavenly Hill bourbon, Collins mix, and lime juice. She shook and poured over ice. "Here you are," she said, setting the tumbler on the bedside table.

"You're a wonderful helper," Bernadette said, sipping. "When you leave, close the door behind you."

In the den, Celeste switched on the television and sprawled on the couch, watching endless news clips about Mrs. Kennedy and her children. Celeste made Limestones for Bernadette and weaker versions for herself. Observing how the cocktail subdued Bernadette, Celeste decided that in a crisis like this, it was the best medicine. She liked the way the bourbon and lime complimented each other. Sweet and sour. Liked the way the cocktail made her head feel lighter than air. After her second drink, dozing and awakening and dozing and awakening, Celeste felt as if she lived and lived and lived forever.

She didn't phone Chris's house or head outside to check for messages beneath Sacred Heart of Jesus. The fierce loyalty she had toward her mother surprised her. Bernadette finally appreciated her. If the president had to die for a cause, this seemed like a good one. Immediately, she felt ashamed for that thought.

The following day, around noon, she carried a Limestone to Bernadette's room. "Are you awake?"

"You're a treasure for tending to me," Bernadette whispered. Hairpins lay scattered on her bed like an army of dead praying mantises. Sprayed curls stuck from her head. A halo of stiff coils. She'd missed her Friday beauty parlor appointment.

"Can I get you any food?" Celeste asked, sweeping the bobby pins into her palm and dropped them on the side table.

Bernadette said, "Sacrilege to even think about eating." She wiped her forehead with the back of her hand. "I'm sweating. I'm not used to sweating."

Celeste went to the bathroom and came back with a cool washcloth. "This will make you feel better."

Bernadette sat up, pulling her nightdress over her head. Closing her eyes, she ran the cloth across her torso.

Celeste had never seen her mother naked. Rib bones pressed against the skin. Her belly button protruded like the tied end of a balloon, small and round and slightly pink.

Bernadette lifted one round breast to scrub beneath, then the other. When she opened her eyes, meeting Celeste's gaze, she said, "You wicked girl." Dropping the washcloth on the carpet, she crawled back beneath her cover.

Celeste handed her mother a towel and backed out the door, wishing she had the chance to describe her pleasant memory of being born, taking a breath, then nursing from those welcoming breasts. Probably only one time, though. In all the photos of herself as a baby, Celeste had a bottle. Even now, she could feel the cold glass heavy on her cheek.

For a few days, the television flickered black and white.

Celeste took a cigarette from Bernadette's purse and stuck the filter between her lips. Sleek, powerful. A sliver of tobacco clung to her mouth. She flicked it off like she'd seen Bernadette do. She sipped straight from the Heavenly Hill bottle. Didn't bother with Collins mix or lime.

"George," Bernadette called. "Where is George? He hasn't phoned today, has he? I need him to come home."

Celeste refused to become a drab housewife like Bernadette or those stupid Queen for a Day types, content on waiting around for their husbands. She wouldn't become a mother, either. Wouldn't push a baby through her privates or force her nipple through its tiny lips. She'd be far away in her rocket ship, soaring through outer space.

Blitzed from bourbon and nicotine, and numb from hours of watching the television, she wasn't sure what she'd seen until a reporter's voice trembled and shook, making him almost indecipherable. "He's been shot. He's been shot. Lee Harvey Oswald's been shot."

"Turn the sound up," Bernadette shouted from her room.

Celeste did not move from the couch. She stared at the screen. Stinson hats. Crowd of men. Hood of a sedan. Someone's slumped body. Men tackling each other. The reporter's terrified face. The wobbly camera.

Bernadette ran down the staircase, saying, "Tell me everything that's happened."

Despite clumsiness due to the booze, Celeste hid her drink beneath the coffee table and snuffed her cigarette in a cereal bowl. "Lee Harvey Oswald was shot by a man with a gun."

"Is he dead?"

Celeste didn't answer.

"Jesus heard my prayers," Bernadette said. "I'll take a shower, then cook up a turkey dinner with everything except for the turkey because the one in the freezer doesn't have time to thaw. This is a day for rejoicing." She didn't make a single comment about the stench of smoke or the splash of Heavenly Hill puddled around the saintly figurine on the coffee table.

Celeste turned the television off, gulped her bourbon, and smoked another Cavalier. Her mind replayed the terrible moment a man pushed through the crowd and stuck a gun in Oswald's stomach. She couldn't block the shocked expression on Oswald's face, eyes squinting, mouth forming an O, his own initial. She'd become an accomplice to the murder because she'd watched as they paraded Oswald through the crowd of lawmen, watched a sheriff hold Oswald's rifle in the air, watched the man in the overcoat lift his pistol, aim, fire. The pop of the gun still echoed in her ears.

"Make me a drink," Bernadette said. She'd changed into her best, a scooped neck, navy dress with a pinched waist, and flounced skirt. Sprayed wet and shiny, her hair in a chiffon. "When you've got the Limestone made, come peel potatoes. Your father should be home soon. He promised the last time he phoned."

Celeste's head spun from whiskey and nicotine. She helped in the kitchen, and it was pure luck she didn't slice her finger off. She poured herself a glass of milk to coat her stomach and ate pieces of bread to sop up the booze.

While cooking, Bernadette didn't ask Celeste how she spent the past few days. Didn't ask if she had school on Friday. Didn't ask if she went to the library. Didn't mention the sponge bath. She hummed as she set platters of mashed potatoes, creamed corn, green beans, rolls, and pumpkin pie on the table. She and Celeste sat down to wait. "George told me he'd be here Saturday evening. It is Saturday, isn't it?" The food cooled, but they didn't eat.

Finally, when the front door opened, George called, "Bernie?"

"An eye for an eye," Bernadette said.

He dropped his satchel on the kitchen linoleum and held her in his arms. "You held up well, considering I've been gone during this ordeal." Pulling back, he sniffed the fragrant air. "You cooked?"

"It's a bit early for Thanksgiving, but today we have something to be thankful for, don't we?" Bernadette said.

"Bernie, I'm here to sweep you off your feet."

"Fine enunciation, George. Hardly a stutter," she said, patting his shoulder. "Please don't try to say the word assassin. We'll be here forever."

"I brought you something, Mary Celeste." George placed a black plastic letter opener on the table near her place setting. The top half appeared to be the outline of a Fuller Brush salesman. The bottom was pointed where his legs should have been. An advertising item. A promotional gimmick. "It's a letter opener," he said.

Celeste said, "Limestone?" Without waiting for their answers, she went to the rolling bar and mixed the cocktails. She used the Fuller Brush letter opener to swirl the ice in their drinks.

Bernadette toasted, "I hope Lee Harvey Oswald, the son-of-a-bitch, dies in agony."

"Long live Mrs. Kennedy," George said. "Terrible fate to be a widow."

Celeste said, "Terrible fate to be dead." Feeling nauseous, she pushed the food around her plate. She needed water. She needed Chris. She needed a bathroom. Covering her mouth, she ran from the table.

George said through the closed door, "Can I get you anything?"

Celeste retched and heaved, vomiting a day's worth of whiskey and tobacco.

"Let's get you up to bed," George said, but he didn't come help her.

Instead of kneeling to say evening prayers, she collapsed in a drunken stupor and pulled the covers over her head. What good to be Catholic if Jesus couldn't even protect His own? Tomorrow, she'd go to the corner market and buy a box of licorice babies and build them a new Baptist church. She'd find a better place than under the bottle brush. She'd hide the Baptists well.

In the morning, beneath Sacred Heart of Jesus, Celeste found a funeral notification for Juliet of Province. On it, Chris drew Juliet's portrait and put black x's for eyes. He wrote, "If Mrs. Kennedy can say goodbye to her husband, and their children can say goodbye to their dad, I can say goodbye to Juliet. Anyway, she's past mending."

Celeste appreciated the idea of a sober and serious ritual. She needed it. She needed Chris. She needed a way to feel connected to the grief that swallowed her while she cared for Bernadette.

At Chris's house, when she saw Juliet of Province, she cried. The rat's cotton stuffing leaked through unstitched seams like puffs of cartoon clouds.

Chris wrapped Juliet in one of Mrs. Armstrong's scarves, then set her in a hole in his backyard. "Dance with the gods, Juliet of Provence," he said, and covered her with dirt.

Celeste bowed her head although she didn't have faith anymore. Not in Jesus. Not in Mary. Her belief lay in the infinitude of the heavens and the joy of having a friend like Chris.

Atomic Bombs

The audiovisual boy wheeled a projector into their junior high classroom, and the teacher pulled the blinds to block out the daylight. A film usually meant a break from schoolwork, time to sit back and enjoy a cartoon character explain the three branches of the judicial system.

The boy set the projector in the center aisle, carefully threading the translucent film through a vertical maze of levers and slots, wrapping the end around a second, larger reel. He flicked a switch. The film whirled. Celeste held her breath, listening as the projector thumped clumsily, sputtered, and slowly started to spin. Often, when her class tried to watch a movie, the filmstrip broke, and they had to wait while the audiovisual boy spliced the ends back together. This time it moved through the projector with the effortlessness of an electric eel.

An image burst onto the screen: A puffy cloud, ballooning up from the ground and spilling into the sky. The title flashed bright: "How to Stay Safe When the Atomic Bomb Strikes Our Shores!" Kettledrums pounded. Trumpets blared. Violins screeched. The students and teacher gasped.

"Atomic weapons kill," the narrator said, speaking these words as calmly as if he were telling the class the chalkboard needed to be erased.

Twisting in her seat, Celeste turned toward Chris. They stared at one another. She said, "Damn."

The filmstrip boys and girls flew beneath desks and ducked beside buildings. With all those atomic bombs exploding and no parents to assist, the scene could have been total mayhem—the school's fire drills were more chaotic—yet these kids remained calm, even friendly toward each other. Sirens blared and people ran, but the film boys held the bomb shelter door open, gesturing the girls inside as if inviting them to a cotillion dance. The film girls adjusted their dresses before diving for cover, somehow maintaining a sense of modesty in the face of annihilation.

When the film ended, no one in the class spoke.

Finally, the teacher cleared her throat. "Okay, children, that's certainly food for thought." They filed out of their dim classroom into the overpowering sunlight.

On their way to the courtyard, Celeste held Chris's hand. "Crawling beneath a desk doesn't seem like the answer to a bomb that can melt skin and leave nothing behind but a shadow the color of dirty old lace." She'd stared at plenty of scarves on the heads of women in church and hated thinking her life would wind up as nothing more substantial than that.

Chris lifted the marshmallow dome from his cupcake and bit into it. "The teacher shouldn't have shown it."

"My parents say Russians don't like us. They say President Kennedy didn't like them either, because Russians went to space first. I'd like to pat Yuri Gagarin on the back and tell him that he did a good job."

"The Cubans almost bombed us once. Did you know that?" Chris said. "Bay of Pigs or something. Kennedy practically got us killed."

"But he didn't. He didn't get us killed," she said. Shielding her eyes to glance overhead, she continued, "If the Russians or Cubans drop the bomb from way up there, we won't even see it coming."

Chris unfolded his wax paper and took out a cheese sandwich. "The tree's kind of in the way."

"I don't know where any bomb shelters are, do you?" she asked.

He threw his crust to the dozen sparrows hopping around their feet. "These birds are so small they hardly have a shadow."

"If the atomic bomb gets dropped, will anyone in history know we were even born?" She tossed a piece of marshmallow onto the ground and watched as the sparrows pecked at the gooey blob. They squabbled and shook their beaks to loosen the sticky sweet.

"Don't feed them that. Their beaks will get stuck together," Chris said. A stellar jay landed on the sandbox railing beside him, eyeing his sandwich. "If a bomb shelter is in our neighborhood, there'll be a stampede to get in."

"If you're locked out, be sure to cover your face. It would be better not to have arms and hands than not to have a face." She twisted the stem of her apple until the brown twig split and broke off.

"Let's talk about something else."

"This is about surviving, Chris. We have to find a way to keep each other alive." Celeste's apple rolled from her lap onto the ground. Sparrows scrambled. The jay squawked. "I save you. You save me. We have to think of everything."

"Just because I don't want to talk about death doesn't mean I'm not thinking about how to live."

"We've got to figure out what to do when the stupid Russians or stupid Cubans attack and we don't have time to get anywhere safe." Celeste's tone sounded a mixture of panic and anger. A character in a horror film. An A-Bomb filmstrip girl.

Chris said, "My dad's a doctor. We'll be okay."

"Dummy, we'll be zapped to oblivion." She snapped her fingers in his face.

He dropped more crumbs for the birds. "If that happens, I hope we're together."

"One day, I'll have the power to fly in a rocket ship and disable all atomic weapons before they destroy everything." She squeezed his hand and tried to convey a Morse Code message of camaraderie.

Metal locks dangled like dead weight on both sides of their school's hallway, reeking of boy's sweat and girl's dime-store cologne. The principal blocked the entrance. He clenched a tangle of keys in his fist as he yanked a teen magazine from a girl's binder. "Illiterate trash not meant for the minds of our future," he said.

Celeste liked him for his facetiousness, because the only magazines truly worth reading had to do with space exploration. She stopped to share her thoughts. "The universe is the future. If we're lucky, we can find another planet to live on before bombs destroy everything."

"I couldn't agree more," the principal said.

Nearby, a group of girls laughed. They laughed before, too, when she used the words supernova and nebula.

Celeste approached them. "I'm president of the Yuri Gagarin Fan Club, if you have any questions about the cosmos."

"Yuri? Who's that?" one of the girls asked.

"The first man in space," Celeste said. "His mission was President Kennedy's incentive to build NASA."

"He's Russian," another girl said. "You can't be friends with a Russian."

"I can. I write Comrade Gagarin letters all the time. He answers back."

"The post office won't deliver mail to Russia," the girl said, her mouth a smirk.

The other girls giggled.

Celeste wished she didn't care if popular girls made fun of her, but she did. She envied their chic bubble cuts, collared shirts, cable-stitched cardigan sweaters, and A-line skirts in woven plaid. Bernadette still sewed most of Celeste's clothes, adjusting her own patterns to fit her daughter's small frame. Celeste looked too groomed, too old, too dated, especially when Bernadette used beaver fur to line the collars and cuffs.

The girls pressed their backs to their lockers. One said, "Comrade Celeste, fly away."

Celeste said, "My pleasure," and left.

After school, beneath Sacred Heart, she found a note from Chris. Daily, he left messages, mostly cartoons highlighting adventures or misadventures. Torn at the edge, this paper looked as if earthworms had gnawed on it. Unfolding the note, she read, "I like boys. I like them a lot." His cartoon showed two boys. One obviously Chris, if judged by the curly hair.

He likes boys? she wondered. Likes them how?

The air was soaked with the scent of freshly cut grass as she ran three blocks to Chris's house. Alyssum, tea roses, and pansies lined the Armstrong's brick pathway. She stood in his yard and tossed pebbles against his bedroom window. When he peeked his head outside, she waved the note in the air. "You like boys?"

He slammed the shutters. The windows on his side of the house rattled.

After ringing the bell, she opened the door. "Mrs. Armstrong?" she called. "Dr. Armstrong?" No answer.

Hurrying through the foyer, she rushed up the staircase, hesitating outside his bedroom door to catch her breath. Opposite her were his school portraits. Soon his eighth-grade photo would be hung there, too, marking the year his life veered off track. She hoped Jewtherans weren't as conflicted about boys liking boys as Catholics were.

In his room, she glanced around, trying to locate him in the shade-drawn dimness. Next to his Dodgers banners, he had a new poster of the bare-chested and shagged guitarist, Jimmy Page. She took a deep breath and said softly, "He's a good musician." Should she comfort Chris? Leave him alone?

Chris answered for her. "Go away." He lay on the carpet holding a pillow over his chest, one arm slung across his eyes.

Years ago, if she had listened to him at the sandbox when he told her to go away, they wouldn't have this lifesaving friendship. Stalling for something wise to say, she ran her fingertips along Jimmy Page's face. "You know the Donovan album he plays on? There's a song called 'Celeste.' The lines were written for me, I'll have you know."

"Doesn't make any sense."

"Yes it does, if you think about what he's saying." She sang a few of the lyrics: "...why would anybody like to try the changes I'm going through?"

"The song should be called 'Chris.'"

"I'll write Donovan and tell him to change it." She forced a laugh, sounding insincere, and regretted making the situation worse.

He pressed his hands against his skull. "I'm a pervert, aren't I?"

Bernadette would agree with him. Celeste didn't want to be anything like Bernadette. "No, you're not a pervert at all." She hoped Bernadette was wrong about the Devil's temptations, but if there was any truth in those beliefs, Celeste would build a shrine to the Virgin. She'd promise undying devotion if Mary kept Chris safe.

Chris's fists balled like a boxer ready to hit. "I like boys so much."

Crouching next to him, she wondered what intelligent words he'd whisper to her if the situation reversed. "If you're a pervert, I'm a pervert."

Bangs, wet with sweat and tears, stuck to his temples. "I hate myself."

"Don't hate yourself." She rubbed his forehead with her thumb, imagining the power to erase his negative thoughts. "You can fall in love with anyone you want."

"Who will I fall in love with? There's no one like me."

"Maybe we don't know him yet." She kissed Chris's cheek. It felt different. His skin used to be smooth like the texture of a silk rug. Now, it was rough.

Chris sat up and hugged his legs against his chest. "What will my parents think?"

"Your parents are nice people."

"Because they think I'm one way when I'm really another."

Celeste felt horribly obtuse. His confession launched her into the great unknown, further than the darkest depths of space. How would she find her way back to earth? Who'd be waiting for her? If Chris liked boys, would he still like her? Even if he did like her, would he need her? Would he want to be around her? Her face flushed.

"You're not much help," he said.

Wishing for stellar advice to pop into her head, she said, "If you like boys, we won't be the first husband and wife astronaut team."

"I thought you'd have an answer." He chewed off a hangnail and spit the skin out.

"I don't."

"You usually know everything." He folded his arms across his chest. "At least you act like you do."

"Give me a minute," she said. Or hours or days or forever.

"I told you about me because I thought you'd help."

Maybe I can convert him, she thought. Before that moment, she'd never considered Chris a boyfriend. To protect the person she adored more than anyone else in the celestial spheres, she said, "What if we kissed and you found out you liked me that kind of way?"

"Dumb."

"You've never kissed a girl, have you?" She hoped she could cure him with one thoughtful swipe of her tongue. Ignite passion in both of them.

Leaning on his elbow, he rolled over to face her. "This isn't a joke."

"I don't think it's a joke."

"Kissing you is your solution?"

"Kind of," she said, shrugging.

He puckered his mouth. "Okay. Go on. Let's see if making out with you magically fixes me."

"I don't mean right now. Neither of us is in the mood."

"I'll never be in the mood, Celeste."

If he'd never kissed a girl, how did he know he wouldn't like it? That's what was in her mind that day.

The sky outside his window changed from blue to pink. Dr. and Mrs. Armstrong would be home from work soon. They'd probably invite her for dinner, but Celeste wouldn't be able to sit across from them and pretend everything was fine. Those other evenings when she stayed for a meal, she'd been at his house studying, reading, watching television. Not counseling Chris about how to stop liking boys.

Hugging him goodbye, she said, "Tomorrow I'll have a better answer."

"I guess this is the end," he said.

"The end?" Seeing Chris in despair unnerved her. Closing her eyes, she prayed harder to the heavens for help. "Not the end."

"I wish I wasn't this way," he said.

Conversion seemed the solution to his misery. Liking her, the only answer. Either that or fail. Fail him. Fail herself. Fail their relationship. "Meet me in the middle of the night at the elementary school sandbox." Midnight seemed the bewitching hour. The sandbox reminiscent of better days.

She set her alarm for 11:45 but didn't need a reminder. She was wide awake in anticipation of what kissing him would be like. Throwing a sweater over her nightgown, she slipped into her sneakers, tiptoed down the hall, and out the door into the night. Everything dark, except for the sputtering lamps illuminating the street.

When she arrived at the playground, Chris sat on a blanket he'd laid in the middle of the sandbox. His transistor radio balanced on the edge where Juliet once danced. Turned on, yet almost inaudible.

"You're here already." She twisted the transistor dial until the gravelly voice of the disc jockey drowned out the cryptic owl on the branch overhead.

"I thought about your suggestion," Chris said.

"Me too." She'd brushed her teeth in preparation for the kiss.

"I can't do what you want me to do."

She lay back on the blanket. "Pretend I'm someone really cute."

"You are cute," he whispered.

"Cuter." She pulled him beside her—a little too hard for the romance she'd intended—and lifted his wrist, placing his palm over her breast. His hand lay as limp as the paw of a sleeping dog. "You have to press and rub." She'd meant to say this seductively but sounded like the home economics teacher telling the class the best way to marinate a rump roast.

"I can't," he said, but didn't pull away, which gave her hope.

She prayed for strength as she put her palm over his fly. The rounded outline of his penis beneath the thin cotton pajamas felt soft.

"If you're going to cure me, you have to stroke it," he whispered. "You're sure this will work?"

It made sense there'd need to be friction, but her hand didn't move. Couldn't move.

"You feel like a jellyfish." He uncapped her breast.

"You're like a sea slug." She knew they'd never share a bed in a space capsule if they couldn't even feel each other up in the playground at midnight.

The magnolia's shadow stretched across the sand as the moon broke from behind the thin fog. The colors surrounding them were dove and sparrow, gopher and mole. Against the night, even her hot-pink nightgown turned as dull as the ragged bark of the trees.

The comment Bernadette once made while watching a musical—"Those fruity boys dance beautifully, although they're all going to Hell"—singed Celeste's heart into a crispy mess. She had to stop him from burning for eternity. "Let's meet here again tomorrow. I'll bring some of Bernadette's Heavenly Hill. Booze will help."

"Bring a gallon," he said. He yanked the blanket from beneath her, wrapped it around his shoulders. Together they walked home, neither speaking of anything important.

Celeste dabbed George's Brylcreem through her hair, because its advertisement promised instant appeal. If she smelled more like a man than a woman, she'd have an easier time seducing him. On the way to the sandbox, she sipped bourbon from her Lost in Space thermos. If she drank enough, she wouldn't have a worry in the world. Nothing would matter. Not an atomic bomb exploding on her head. Not President Johnson luring boys into Vietnam. Not this predicament with Chris. Swills of Heavenly Hill transforming her into a free bird.

Chris got to the playground after her this time. "You brought the alcohol?"

Handing him the thermos, she said, "What are we going to do about you and your problem?"

"I've no idea." He gulped, coughed, and covered his mouth before sipping more.

Unbuttoning her nightgown, Celeste prayed for a moonbeam to illuminate her breasts.

"What are you doing?" Chris covered his eyes.

She wanted to say, I'm saving you from the Devil. Instead, she told him, "Last time you couldn't feel anything through my nightgown."

"I felt them fine," he said. He gave her back the thermos lid.

"The booze will loosen you up. I promise." She wondered if he'd caught a whiff of the Brylcreem. Pointing to her chest, she said, "Touch them. You'll like how squishy they are."

Chris folded his hands in his lap. "I don't want to."

"Every normal boy wants to go to second base. Here's your chance." She gulped the bourbon.

"You think I'm not normal because I don't want to grab your stupid boobs?"

"They're not stupid."

"Don't tell me what normal boys wish they could do with a girl. Guys talk about this stuff all the time. It's all they ever talk about." He grabbed the Heavenly Hill, took a big sip, then dropped his head into his hands. "I hate how I am."

"If you hate how you are then let me help make you how you're supposed to be." She reached for the knot on the string of his pajama bottoms and pulled.

He slapped her hand away. "I am how I'm supposed to be."

"This will solve our problem. It has to."

"Our problem?"

"I want you to like girls," she said, sipping.

"Do you really think touching your boobs will solve anything? Because I don't." His voice sounded oddly quiet. He lay back on the beach towel, cradling his head with his arm.

"You'll stop liking boys and start liking me." I'll save you. I'll save you. I'll save you, she repeated in her head.

Chris reached toward the sky. "I don't want to stop liking boys."

In the starlight, she noticed the faint silhouette of an erection. "My stupid boobs are good for something."

He shook his head and rolled onto his stomach. "It's a mirage."

"You have a mirage boner?"

"I was thinking of someone else," he said.

"Who?" she asked. "Who are you thinking of? Does he know you like him? Have I met him?"

Chris shrugged. "Someone. Anyone. Nureyev, mostly."

Standing, Celeste danced along the sandbox railing, missed a pirouette, and fell into the sand. "Look at me, I'm a ballerina."

"Don't make fun of Nureyev," he said.

"Be my lawful wedded husband," she pleaded. "Let's zoom off in a spaceship and populate the moon."

"Do I need to say it again?" he said with irritation. "I want a boyfriend."

"So do I, but I'm supposed to and you're not."

"Thanks for nothing." He jumped up, storming away.

The sandbox, magnolia tree, playground spun out of control. She thought of the votive Bernadette lit the day she met Chris in the grocery store and hated her for her perception.

Chris taped a note to their locker: "Don't talk to me ever again."

Reading it, Celeste assumed he was exaggerating. Unaware how much the Heavenly Hill loosened her inhibitions, and ignorant of the insensitivity of her comments, she'd stumbled home believing she made progress toward coaxing him to like her.

The bell for first period rang. Chris hurried past her, his face turned away.

She grabbed his sleeve and yanked him close. Attempting her best imitation of a Soviet spy, she said, "Don't try to hide from me. I'll track you down and capture you."

"Leave me alone," he said, shrugging her off.

A boy in the hallway snickered. "Lover's quarrel?"

"No," Chris said.

"Yes," she said.

Chris's eyes narrowed. "You're not my friend anymore, Celeste. You were not nice last night. You were mean."

"What are you talking about?"

"Our friendship has expired," he said with such intensity it seemed he quoted Shakespeare.

"What did I do?" Her chest felt like something jagged was slowly being pulled from her heart.

"Don't act dumb. You know what you said to me." He left her standing there alone.

Their argument went on for weeks. The Sacred Heart of Jesus levitated from all her unclaimed apology notes. Without her conceptual twin, she became as lonely as the poor star Orion in its cold interstellar cloud.

Replacing her need for her only friend, she doused the apple juice in her thermos with Heavenly Hill. Although she wobbled walking to class, she was never caught, because being an average student assured she'd be ignored by teachers. Breath mints helped too.

She snuck fuchsia lipstick samples from George's Fuller Brush satchel. In the school bathroom, she rolled her skirts high, exposing her slips like a proclamation.

Chris said, "Eww," when he saw her.

"Don't worry," she said, her voice a snarl, "this isn't for you," but it was. Everything she did was for his salvation.

Finding a boyfriend didn't take long. On their first date, a boy took her to an expensive Italian restaurant and bent across the table to kiss her with his tongue. Above them, a travel poster of the Leaning Tower of Pisa slanted in her direction. When his mouth parted, she tasted basil. What a relief to be done with the milestone of her initial kiss, yet she wished his lips were Chris's and they were in space.

The boy didn't take her on any other dates. Instead, they went to his house. He'd lock his bedroom door, and they'd flop on his bed, wrestling and kissing beneath the blue-eyed stare of his fluffy Persian. Letting him touch her bra felt mildly pleasurable. Although not how she'd envisioned a love life should be. This boy lacked romance.

One day, he stripped down to his underwear, then stuffed her hand with toilet paper. "Use these after you stroke it."

"Stroke that?" she said, shocked how his penis popped from the slit in his boxers like a rocket ship ready for launch.

"Please," he begged. He pressed into her palm, his body twitching slightly, as though he were a martyr in agony.

Celeste grimaced as the boy's erection continued to grow. She wondered when it would stop.

"Curl your fingers around my dick," he instructed.

Tentatively, she followed his directive. It throbbed against her fingers. She felt his blood rushing through its veins.

"Rub up and down," he said. He kissed her.

She wanted to be adventurous and rub up and down. Wanted to be a girl with a boyfriend who told her to touch his dick. A girl who wasn't alone. Sliding her hand from the hairy shaft to the pink tip, she imagined her palm the piston. Imagined his hard-on, Astro.

A strange blob oozed from the slit on the head of his penis. The way he shook and groaned and thrashed about, she'd expected shooting stars.

The boy grabbed the tissue, wiped himself, ran straight to the bathroom, flushing the wad down the toilet. "Same time tomorrow?" he said with a wide grin.

She inspected her hands for residue. "Sure," she said. What else was there to do?

After a month of this, she feared she'd either sprain her wrist or be plummeted to death with the plunger his mom must have needed to unclog tissue from the pipes.

The next time he said, "Rub my dick," she told him no. He protested, his penis standing at attention, his face mushed in a frown.

Patting the blue-eyed Persian, she said, "It's more trouble than it's worth." Celeste left the boy with an erection he'd have to take care of himself.

At home, Bernadette was sprawled on the couch, smoking a cigarette and reading a copy of Hollywood Secrets Yearbook. "You're early today, Mary Celeste."

"My study partner fizzled out."

Bernadette peered over the top of the magazine. "I hope you don't fail."

She had failed. Completely failed. Failed the boy. Failed Chris's friendship.

Bernadette turned a page. Exhaling a plume of gray smoke, she said, "These women wear too much makeup."

If Chris was willing to put in the effort it took to please a boy, and if a boy was willing to put in the effort to please him, then she'd help Chris accomplish this goal. Boys liking boys seemed easier than a girl liking a boy who only wanted his penis rubbed.

Bernadette was already tipsy, but she asked Celeste to make her another drink. "Shame your study partner fizzled on you. What were you studying?"

"Male ballet dancers." Celeste measured and poured, less bourbon than usual. "Nureyev."

"Rudolf Nureyev may be fruity, but he's the greatest dancer who's ever lived." Bernadette kicked off her shoes and tucked her stockinged feet beneath her legs. She pointed to an advertisement for Yardley glamour products. "Fuller Brush doesn't stand a chance since the British Invasion. Poor George."

Celeste wanted to assure her mother Fuller Brush's fuchsia lipstick worked fine for attracting boys.

Bernadette sipped her cocktail and flipped to the back pages of the magazine. "Here are fan club addresses. Find Nureyev."

"He's Russian. Russians don't answer fan letters. I've written Yuri Gagarin for years."

"Because Gagarin hasn't defected from his Godforsaken country. Nureyev has," Bernadette said. She handed the magazine to Celeste. "If you find Rudolf Nureyev's address, use my good stationery. Make an impression. You'll get an A on your report."

Upstairs, Celeste skimmed through the magazine until she found a Nureyev fan club in New York. She unfolded Bernadette's monogrammed stationery and wrote,

"Dear Mr. Nureyev,

My best friend is smart and funny. He also likes boys. He likes them a lot. My mother tells me you do, too. I was wondering if you have any suggestions on how I can help him through this. One more question, in your opinion, can a boy who likes boys ever like a girl? If the answer is yes, how can I make something like that happen to me?

Sincerely, Celeste Roderick."

A week later, Celeste sat at the kitchen table and tore the seal on a manila envelope. She pulled out a glossy photo of Nureyev leaping through the air. The typewritten letter mentioned which cities around the world he'd be touring and where to write for tickets. She felt disappointed he didn't answer any of her questions or offer suggestions or say he wished he'd had a best friend like her when he was a small boy.

Bernadette peeked over Celeste's shoulder. "What a perfectly good waste of an eligible bachelor."

"He's got quite the wingspan," George said. He performed a comical pirouette across the linoleum.

Celeste scrutinized Rudolf's ecstatic expression, muscular legs, extended fingers, coiffed hair, tights and leotard, and bulging codpiece.

"Don't tell me you've got a crush on him, Mary Celeste." Bernadette stood at the counter, chopping onions. "You're not his type."

"Maybe I am," she said, thinking of Chris. "Maybe I could be."

George said, "We've got a fine-looking girl here, Bernie. Anyone's her type." George rolled the rolling bar into the kitchen. "Pre-dinner cocktail?"

Disguising her handwriting, Celeste wrote across the top of the photograph, "Dear Chris, Soar to your heart's content. Find love in all the right places. Yours truly, Rudolf. P.S. You're lucky to have a friend like Celeste."

The following morning, she taped the picture on the inside door of their locker.

Chris surprised her when he whispered, "How did you get Nureyev's autograph?" His hair smelled lemony, as if he'd stood beneath his citrus tree in his backyard and shook freshness upon himself.

She smiled when she said, "My presidency of the Yuri Gagarin Fan Club finally paid off. Rudolf and Yuri are good Russian friends."

"Juliet of Provence never soared through the air the way Rudolf does." He clutched the photograph to his chest.

"I'm a big ass and worthless," she said with sincerity coating her words. "I'm sorry for everything I did."

"You said some mean things," he said.

"I'll stop drinking Heavenly Hill."

"My mom asked why you weren't coming over anymore. I told her you have mononucleosis and have to stay in bed. My dad agreed that's the best cure."

"I miss your mom and dad. I miss eating dinner at your house," she said. Those evenings when Mrs. Armstrong fed her, Celeste felt comforted. "Mono was a good excuse."

"I agree you're an ass, but you're definitely not worthless. You got the greatest dancer in the world to send a photo with a personal note for me." Chris opened his binder and stuck the photo inside. "I'll keep him here so I can stare in private."

"I missed you," she confessed.

"I noticed you got a boyfriend right away. You weren't kidding about wanting me to kiss you."

"The idiot didn't want me. He wanted this." She held out her palm.

Chris covered his ears. "Don't tell me anymore. I don't need specifics."

"Our first date held promise. I was duped."

"Used by a teenage Casanova?" Chris said. "Did you have a good time, at least?"

"He made me hold toilet paper over his penis. It looked like a balding old lady in church with a lace scarf on her head."

Chris shook with laughter. "I don't want to know any more."

Smoothing back a few strands of his hair, loose from his attempt at a stylized shag, she grinned. "You can follow your dream, Chris. Boys are easy to seduce."

"Seduction and romance. Don't forget romance," he said.

"Start with the basics." She squeezed her palm. If Chris intended to have sex, she wanted his affair to be casual. Didn't want him falling in love and getting hurt. She'd share him—if she must. One thing felt absolutely certain—they'd never be separated again.

Boys in ninth grade, their first year of high school, didn't pay attention to Chris the way he paid attention to them. Celeste hated seeing his attempts at flirting. He chose the wrong kind of guy. Athletic and masculine and insensitive. Worried he'd be punched, she advised him to be more subtle around them. "Find a boy who's like you."

"A flamboyant fairy?" He exaggerated his walk, prancing around her in circles.

She pulled him against her chest to stop him. The hallways were filled with teenagers scrutinizing everyone to find someone to tease. Chris made himself easy prey. She said, "I mean someone shy and quiet. Someone small."

"If I want to be a flamboyant fairy, who'll stop me?" he said, but he straightened his posture, subdued his gait.

"The principal. Your parents. Other boys," she answered.

"You?" he asked.

"You can be as fairy as you want inside yourself. Not on the outside at school. Honestly, Chris, you're really cute. Stay away from boys who like to slug sissies."

"You called me a sissy," he said.

"I mean it from the point of view of a thug who likes to hit. The guys you flirt with who don't flirt back."

Chris said, "Sissy. Fairy. Flamboyant. Girly."

Celeste pointed to a guy, his hair fanning behind as he strolled past. "What about him? He looks like he could like boys."

"I'd like to feel his hair brush against my lips," Chris said. "Brush against my chest. Brush against my other parts."

Suddenly, jealousy riled her gut like an imp on hot coals. "He's a senior," she said. "He'll probably never go out with a freshman."

George aimed the camera toward Celeste and Chris, twisting the lens of his Kodak Pony. He'd hardly taken any photographs since the morning he got the present beneath the Christmas tree the year Celeste turned five. Probably had the same roll of film.

Bernadette sipped her cocktail, leaving a rim of coral lipstick on the glass. "Isn't this awfully generous of Chris to bring you a corsage?"

Chris lifted the gardenia from the box. "Smells really good."

"Like an entire garden of flowers," Celeste said. She showed him where to pin the flower.

The camera flashed. George said, "Wonderful."

"A gardenia's an aromatic blossom," Bernadette said. "Don't get your fingerprints all over the petals or they'll turn brown and a brown flower isn't as beautiful as a lily white one."

Chris looked handsome in his navy blazer and striped tie. Someday, she'd be forced to marry someone else, have children, and live a regular life, but what would happen to him? It broke her heart to consider he may be alone for the rest of his life.

George lifted the lid on the ice bucket. "What can I offer you, Chris?"

Before he answered, Celeste said, "We'd both like Roy Rogers, please."

"For goodness sake, if you're a girl, it's called a Shirley Temple," Bernadette said, waving her Cavalier in the air.

"Let the girl have her Roy Rogers," George said. He dropped cubes of ice into their glasses. "You two make a handsome couple."

Bernadette said, "I think they're just friends." The lipstick curvature on her glass shimmered.

"Friendship is a fine way to start a relationship," George said. "Look at us."

Chris folded his hands in his lap. "I'd love a Roy Rogers, sir."

"Are you sure?" Bernadette asked. "Wouldn't you rather have a Shirley Temple?"

Celeste stood, holding her hand toward Chris. "Let's go."

"Your first high school dance requires refreshments." George measured the spritzer and grenadine syrup, plucked cherries from the jar. "Stay."

Chris sipped the Roy Rogers, swirled the ice cubes around the glass, sipped more. "This is delicious. Thank you, Mr. Roderick."

Bernadette smiled. "You're as well-mannered as you were the day we met in the grocery store, Christopher," she said. "Are you the same sweet boy as you were back then?"

Chris inhaled, slowly exhaling before answering. "I am."

Bernadette said, "You're certainly honest."

Celeste finished her drink and encouraged Chris to finish his. The moment he set the glass down, she grabbed his hand and led him toward the foyer. Light flickered from the television console in the corner of the den. The newscaster spoke of the casualties of the Vietnam War, listing the number of deaths on both sides of the conflict as if reporting the score of a baseball game.

"Have fun," Bernadette shouted. "Be home by eleven. Twelve at the latest."

Celeste closed the front door behind them and stepped into the warm night. "My parents never turn the goddamn news off."

"Your mom scares me," he said, his eyes widening in mock terror.

"I'm sorry for making you come here. After my fiasco with Molly in third grade, I swore I'd never bring a friend home. I apologize for Bernadette."

"She's kind of entertaining," he said. He cocked his hip, waved an imaginary cigarette in the air, and slurred, "Get the boy a Shirley Temple, George."

Celeste laughed when she said, "Homo, and I don't mean sapiens, George."

"I do believe in fairies. I do believe in fairies," Chris said.

Spring perfumed the air. Roses in bloom. Gardenia corsage. Still, she couldn't shake the televised image of children running through burning villages while napalm exploded around them. It seemed impossible that anyone could make it through a war unscathed.

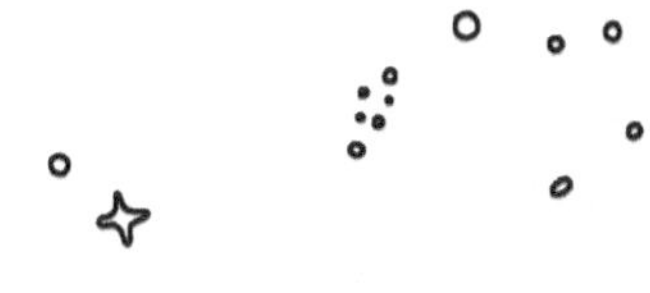

Chris's doughboy pool took up most of his backyard. The citrus tree hung heavy with fruit. Occasionally a lemon fell in the water, bobbing. On the other side of the yard grew miniature cherry trees. Easy picking.

Chris carried two glasses of lemonade and set them next to their beach towels. His swimsuit was a ribbed nylon short with a pretend belt buckle. Tight, highlighting his thighs and rear and groin. He rubbed oil across his chest. Hairless. Smooth. He'd been pretty as a boy, and he was pretty still.

"I like your new swimsuit. It shows off your goods," Celeste said. She wore a bikini. Blue cotton with white polka dots.

He posed like the Jesus statue. "Whenever I lift the Sacred Heart statue to leave you a cartoon, I feel like I'm looking up Jesus's robe."

"Maybe we should find a different place to leave our messages." She slathered baby oil and iodine over herself until her skin radiated like the underside of a sunset. She gulped the lemonade, pulp coating her upper lip.

Chris turned the pages of his library book. He'd recently discovered James Baldwin and spent hours skimming *Giovanni's Room* looking for what he called the "good parts." Lowering his voice, he read aloud, "'But I'm a man,' I cried, 'a man! What do you think can happen between us?'" Sitting down beside Celeste, he handed the book to her, his finger underlining the sentence where he'd left off.

"You know very well," she read in her best baritone, but she wondered what would two men do alone in a room once they got past the kissing and fondling part? The sun burned down on her stained skin, and the pungent aroma of iodine swirled around them. "Mr. B gave you a racy book."

Plucking a blade of grass, Chris twirled it between his fingers. "Sometimes I wonder if Mr. B is like me."

She shook her head. "He's married. He has a wife." Celeste had seen Mrs. B at the library a few times. A squat woman with butterfly glasses and pleated trousers. Not especially pretty, but strangely attractive. Like an exotic flower on a Formica kitchen table in a suburban house.

"He gave me *Giovanni's Room*. He said I'd enjoy the story."

"Because he's a good librarian," Celeste said. "Mr. B's got excellent taste in literature, and he knows his patrons well."

"The story is about two men getting it on."

"I'm sure it's deeper than sex."

"Two fags and a girl getting it on, to be specific."

Celeste covered her mouth. "The book uses that word?"

Chris shrugged, then stood, plucking leaves from the surface of the doughboy pool. "Baldwin's challenging readers to expand their way of thinking. By saying the word fag, he takes away the negativity. He's making it a part of his identity. Mine too, and everyone else like us." Chris tossed drowned leaves onto the grass. "If a word is derogatory and meant to put me down, I'll use it. Fruity, as your mom says. Queer. Fag. Fairy. Girly. Flamboyant. Homo. I could go on and on."

"But fag? Really?" Opening her book *Walden* to her favorite passage, she read, "Creeping along the endless beach amid the sunsquall and the foam, it occurs to us that we, too, are the product of sea-slime." How fantastic to consider she stemmed from the depths of the ocean and not Adam's rib.

"Sea slime?" Chris rested his arms on the edge of the pool. "No, thanks."

"Let's run away and live in the woods. I'm learning everything we'll need to survive." The day she'd checked out *Walden,* she also found books on edible plants and natural living, and told her parents she was writing an extra-credit report on California Indians. George had said, "Indians? Sounds informative." Bernadette responded, "Someday, they're going to have to stop blaming us for settling the land."

Chris shook his head. "Paris is the place to be. We'll go in search of *Giovanni's Room.* Also, a boy for me to tuck into bed."

"Acorn dumplings, not baguettes. Trees, not the Eiffel Tower."

"I've watched French films. Parisians like sex," he said.

"Everyone likes sex," she said with confidence.

Chris sat on his beach towel and sipped his glass of lemonade. "Everyone likes sex, but not as much as French men. They love it."

"You know a lot for someone who's never been kissed."

He lowered his voice and said, "Guess what? I met a neat guy."

"You met someone?" Her volley of questions came at a rapid pace. Who? Where? Name? Age? What does he look like?

"Yearbook committee," he said with a grin.

"But I'm a man. A man!" She plucked the waistband on his swimsuit, snapping the elastic against his skin.

Chris said, "Which one of us do you think will lose their virginity first?" He rolled onto his stomach.

The baby oil sizzled, pooled with sweat in the folds of her skin. She rubbed the lotion, then sprawled on the towel. "Me. I've had more experience than you." If by magic or miracle Chris followed the plotline of *Giovanni's Room* and decided to sleep with a girl as well as a boy, like the character who proclaimed, "I'm sort of queer for girls myself," she wanted to be the girl, and she wanted to be experienced.

Celeste decided to pursue Michael Paul, an altar boy from church. He could turn on an angelic smile sweet enough to seduce a nun, but also had a daring side, selling ten-dollar baggies of shake in the parish parking lot right under the priest's nose. Michael Paul's boggy brown hair and mud-brown eyes didn't make him handsome or even good-looking. His dangerousness was her aphrodisiac. She felt positive he would sleep with her if she asked him to.

On Sunday, she descended the church steps, approaching him. "Michael Paul, doing anything special on prayer Wednesday?" The most devout Catholics went to prayer Wednesday. His parents. Bernadette.

"Babysitting," he said, pointing to his two younger siblings running around the lawn, squabbling.

"Want me to come over and help?"

"Yeah," he said. "Sure."

On Wednesday, Michael Paul's mother set TV dinners on the kitchen table and a bowl of candy in front of the television console. "Be faithful, Michael Paul and Mary Celeste. Keep Jesus in your hearts."

Celeste nodded. She had faith she'd lose her virginity that very night. Faith in Michael Paul's willingness to take risks. Faith he'd toss her onto the bed, and they'd do it.

When his parent's car backed out of the driveway, Celeste asked, "Can I see your room?"

"Sure." Michael Paul clutched her hand and led her down the hallway, tiptoeing past his brothers' rooms. Bolting his door with a chair, he said, "Guarding against my nuisance siblings. They're annoying as hell." In the dimness of the room, he looked almost handsome.

She collapsed on the bed, lifting her hem as an invitation.

"These are pretty," he said, stroking her underwear. "Really pretty color blue."

Donovan's album "A Gift from a Flower to a Garden" played on his portable turntable. The needle slid across the vinyl, got caught in a scratch, turning the mellow song into a warbling mess. Michael

Paul thumped the table with his fist, and the record player's arm jumped. The song continued. Stretching beside her, he slipped his fingers beneath the elastic of her waistband, fondling her warm skin.

She squirmed away, nerves acting as her bodyguard.

"Don't be scared," he said.

"I'm not afraid," she lied.

"You're pretty," Michael Paul whispered. His gaze wandered slowly down her body. "Pretty."

The farther into her underwear his hand went, the more tingling she felt. She couldn't wait to leave a message for Chris beneath Sacred Heart of Jesus, telling him about her experience. Would he be proud or jealous or both?

"Your privates," Michael Paul said, "are precious." As he hummed along to the song "Little Boy Corduroy," his fingers stroked and found their way inside her.

She moaned, because he'd discovered a lost city of gold. "I like what you're doing, Michael Paul."

"If we ever have a little boy, we should name him Donovan."

Giggling, she said, "I can't get pregnant from your hand."

When he took off his pants, his erection remained lassoed by his tight briefs.

She prepared herself for what would come next. His penis jabbing and poking her insides, making her a real woman. She estimated they only had forty-five minutes before prayer Wednesday concluded and refreshments were served. Enough time to go all the way, then head downstairs, eat TV dinner meatloaf and cinnamon apple wedges.

Michael Paul unbuttoned her shirt. "Your bra is sexy," he said. The tip of his tongue poked from between his lips. "So sexy."

Her bra was plain white cotton, but she thanked him for the compliment and encouraged him to reach behind her back and unclasp the hooks. Instead, he opened the drawer on his side table and pulled out a stash box. Crawling beneath the sheet, she wiggled out of her bra, dangling it in the air like a welcome flag. She pulled the cover up to her chin. "I'm ready, Michael Paul." Her tone demanding. "I want to do this before we run out of time."

"Weed first," he said, striking a match. "Slow and steady wins the race, or haven't you heard what happens to rabbits?"

She twirled her bra in the air to get his attention. "I'm naked in your bed." She began to panic. Was there something wrong with her that he didn't seem to care?

Michael Paul took a hit and passed the weed to her. "Puff?"

She pinched the end of the paper and inhaled. Not because she wanted to get high—she'd had enough of altered bourbon states— she wanted to speed its burning. Her throat and tongue felt on fire. "Water," she begged. A cloud of smoke descended over her head like a lid. "Will the stench slip beneath the threshold and wake your little brothers?"

"Nope. They're used to it." Clasping the joint between his lips, Michael Paul climbed alongside her and took off his briefs. He rolled onto his back, taking long drags, coughing, exhaling, seemingly unselfconscious about his boner flopping around beneath the white sheet.

"Get on top of me," she said. "We're running out of time." Self-doubt and self-admiration ricocheted inside her.

"I love Donovan's psychedelic vibe." He offered her another hit.

Her brain became a helium balloon. "I want to have sex. You. Me. Please. Let's go, Michael Paul."

Hopping up to open the window, he used his pillow to fan the air. "Helps diffuse the stench." His penis stuck straight from his tangle of hair like a sword ready for battle.

"Stick it in me," she said. She admired and despised herself for her forthrightness.

He sucked on the end of the roach until it fizzled, then looked at her and grinned.

Stoned, she giggled, "Stick. Your. Penis. In. Me. M. P."

Kneeling beside the bed, he whispered, "Mary Celeste, my beautiful lady." His voice sounded oddly serious, suddenly old. "I have a question for you."

"Can you wait to ask me?" She lowered the sheet to her waist. Her head swooned when he stared at her breasts. "Prayer Wednesday refreshments usually don't go longer than half an hour. When do you think your parents will be home?"

"Your tits are beautiful. You're beautiful. I'm beautiful. Making love is beautiful," he said, lifting the edge of his mattress.

Truthfully, she didn't know much about sex. "What are you doing?"

Clutching a jeweler's box in his fist, he shouted, "Ta Da." Inside was a thin band of gold with a petite square diamond. "This used to be Nona's."

Celeste gasped and pulled the sheet up to her neck. "Oh, God."

The gem glistened impressively in the light, except his grandmother was dead. Celeste had been to the funeral. Was that what his family was doing up by the altar for so long? Wiggling this ring off Nona's stiff finger while she lay in her coffin?

"I offer this token on behalf of my admiration and gratitude for what we're about to do."

"Help," she whispered.

"Say you'll marry me," Michael Paul said. "Make me the happiest guy on earth."

"I can't marry you," she said, crossing her legs.

"You can if you want," he said. "Jesus would want this for us."

"Why? We're only fifteen."

He took the band from the box, forcing it on her finger. "Nona's ring fits you perfectly."

She held her hand up to show him the ring absolutely did not fit. It spun around her finger like a loose nut on a stripped bolt. "Sorry, Michael Paul, but I don't love you like a wife should love a husband." *I love you like a girl who wants to lose her virginity right now*, she thought.

"Someday, you'll love me like a wife loves a husband." He cupped her breasts in his palms. "They're so nice. I like them a whole lot. I like the way they feel."

Celeste stared at the diamond. Stared at him jiggling her boobs. The tingle she'd felt earlier faded. "Please, Michael Paul. Come on."

When he crawled under the sheet, his erection poked her hip, then her thigh. "I want all of you to be mine. Your body and your heart."

"Hurry. We don't want to get caught in bed having sex."

Rolling on top of her, he whispered, "The first Wednesday of the month, Mom stays to help clean the parish. Dad sits in the car and listens to the radio while he waits for her. We have time." His lips pressed against her lips. His tongue slipped into her mouth, resting on her tongue. He tasted like smoke.

She clasped him around the waist, anchoring him. "Let's get it on, Michael Paul. Let's go all the way." The ring slipped from her finger, settling in the imprint from his ass.

He scooped it from the mattress. "Before we make love, say you'll marry me."

"I like you, Michael Paul," she said. "I really do. I like everything about you."

"Commit to me," he said. His penis poked her, but didn't push in. "We'll do this for the rest of our lives."

"This isn't about love and… It's sex."

"You'd make love with someone you don't even love?"

"Not anyone," she said. "You."

Propping himself on his elbows, he frowned. "That's supposed to make me feel better?"

"I don't know. Does it?" She paused before adding, "All right. We can get married."

He rolled off her and flopped on the bed. His hapless erection bobbed about like it didn't understand what had happened.

"I'll marry you. I'll wear Nona's ring." She tried to kiss him, but his tongue sat in his mouth. "I want to get my deflowering over with. You're the one to do it, Michael Paul."

"Not if you don't accept my marriage proposal."

"I do accept. Didn't you hear me? I just told you I'd marry you." She held her left hand before him.

"You'll marry me?" Clasping her fingers in his palm, he bought them to his mouth, kissing them one-by-one.

"We can get married," she said, slightly disgusted by his lips touching her knuckles.

He put Nona's ring in the box and the box back under the mattress. "Next Wednesday. I'll get down on one knee. Make it romantic. You can wait a week, can't you?" He squinted at her like an animal in the forest daring another animal to surrender.

"No, Michael Paul, I cannot wait a goddamn week." Disappointment overwhelmed her. As she dressed, she called him a fag and instantly regretted her choice of word. Her head spun from the weed. Her heart coiled from embarrassment and rejection. Downstairs, she grabbed a fistful of Cherry Sours from the candy dish and fled.

Chris and Celeste sat on the planter at the edge of their high school quad. "You can't tell someone who wants to marry you that all you want to do is to bang him. You've got to have more compassion," Chris said.

"I tried to be reasonable," she said.

"Sounds like you were everything but reasonable."

"You and Michael Paul are sentimental fools. Why don't you marry each other?"

"Not my type. Too Catholic. Too dull white American. Not even close to being a James Baldwin hero."

"You make him sound so appealing," she said.

Chris opened his Pee Chee folder, showing her some photos he'd taken. "This is what I've been up to in yearbook elective. While you tried to seduce an altar boy, I became the official yearbook sports photographer." One picture showed rows of guys doing pushups.

Taking the photo from Chris, she looked closer. "I wonder if any of them are up for the challenge of taking my virginity. I'm probably the only girl in history who couldn't get a boy to sleep with her."

"At least you saw Michael Paul naked. That's a start."

"I wish I'd accepted his proposal, then waited until after we finished doing it to break off the engagement."

"Cold, cold heart," Chris said. "Love takes guts."

"Penises. Ugh."

"Obviously, you haven't seen a good one."

"You have?"

He nodded.

"Where?" she asked.

"Magazines."

She thought of the brown-paper-wrapped girly magazines at the newsstand. "Those are of nude women, aren't they?"

"One magazine has men."

"The sign says Adults Only," Celeste said. "How'd you get the nerve to ask?"

"The guy selling them likes me. Harmless flirting."

"He's a pervert," she said, swatting Chris's arm. "He used to give Molly and me free Chick-O-Sticks if we'd sit on his lap. Angelic Molly wouldn't, but I did. I always made him give me two for my effort."

"You're the perv," Chris said, grabbing his photograph from her grip.

"I guess I really wanted candy," she said, but was Chris right? Sex seemed to be on her mind a lot. "Am I a nymphomaniac?"

"You said it, not me."

She shrugged. "I suppose there are worse things to be."

Chris handed her a stack of notebook paper. "Changing the subject, look at these yearbook word searches I made as frames for the faculty photos." Pointing to the description around the principal's picture, he put an X over every third letter. A secret message emerged: "This school is a hellhole."

Celeste said, "Genius boy."

The vice principal's portrait had the hidden sentence: "I like punishing teens."

"Make love not war" for the history teacher's photo.

"Let's get it on" surrounded the sexy Spanish instructor.

Celeste patted Chris on the back. "You're bold."

"I'm trying to impress the guy in my electives class. His name's David. Super foxy."

"David's a stoner," she said, shuffling the notebook papers back in place. "The look in his eyes isn't horniness. He's dreaming of weed. Michael Paul has the same glazed expression."

"You're wrong," Chris said, flipping through the photographs. He found one of David in a baseball uniform, standing on the diamond, bat mid-swing. "We kissed."

"What? When did that happen?" Jealousy dangled above her like a morning star, poised to fall and stab her with its points.

"In the elective classroom, before everyone got there." Chris sat up straight, pulling his shoulders back. "He's got peach fuzz."

Celeste thought, What a relief he found someone he wanted to kiss and who wanted to kiss him. "I like the way his hair sweeps across his forehead like the wings of a bird."

"Or a rock star."

"But he's dumb," Celeste said. "We're in algebra together."

"I don't care how smart he is."

On a piece of paper, she sketched a log cabin with three stick figures dancing the perimeter. "Chris, David, and Celeste frolicking naked in the wilderness. A la Henry David Thoreau."

"I'm almost positive Thoreau wore clothes and didn't frolic," Chris said. He took her picture and drew erections on David and himself, then put the Eiffel Tower in the background. "The three of us will live together in a Parisian room. David and I will make love while you shop for baguettes and cheese, and find yourself a handsome, sex-crazed Frenchman."

"Thoreau didn't need Paris. Three chairs were good enough for him. One for contemplation. Two for company. Three for entertainment."

"Fine," Chris said. "We'll have three chairs in our French flat, and David will be the entertainment."

"I'm going to complain to Mr. B that *Giovanni's Room* has gone to your head."

"He'll be thrilled for me," Chris said, tucking the notebook back in his binder.

For Chris, she'd forfeit her dream of Walden and move to Paris. If this gave her the chance to be with him for the rest of her life, she could even learn to like David.

Michael Paul invited Celeste to the parish prom. Celeste accepted the invitation, thanking Jesus for a second chance to lose her virginity.

He wore a royal blue tuxedo with a shirt that rippled across his chest like the feathers of a prize rooster. "My mom made me ask you," he said as he held the car door open for her.

"I'm sorry for the way I treated you, Michael Paul." The taffeta of her gown stuck to the hot vinyl seat. Her corsage, a pink mum, smelled like hairspray.

In the driver's seat, Michael Paul pushed in the cigarette lighter. "I was an idiot." The knob popped out. He held the red tip against a Marlboro and took a long drag, exhaling smoke rings.

"You were being romantic, not idiotic," she said. She poked the rings with her finger.

"Romantic and idiotic, same thing," he said.

On the short drive, neither spoke. Celeste scooted across the bench seat, sitting close to him and resting her palm on his knee. He didn't push her away.

The church auditorium was decorated with tissue paper roses taped to the walls. Members of the marching band played Beatles tunes. Michael Paul danced the pony better than anyone. Soon a crowd gathered around, cheering him on. Celeste beamed with pride. Michael Paul, her date and the boy she'd be sleeping with after the dance. She'd put a roll of scotch tape in her purse, for fitting Nona's ring to her own size.

"We've made our appearance," Michael Paul said after an hour. "Father Murphy's seen us. Proof we were here. Want to split?"

"I do," she said. This is it, she thought. My final parish dance as a virgin. "Michael Paul, I'm excited about this."

"I'm not," he said.

"You will be," she said with confidence. His stern attitude didn't discourage her. Rather, it added importance. She'd done him wrong. He'd been hurt. She'd make it better. He'd seen and touched her breasts already. He'd put his fingers inside her. Those intimacy hurdles, done.

Michael Paul drove into the city, a half-hour way. He didn't speak until he parked, and then he turned to her. "The place we're heading has live music and the vibe is loose. I have a friend who'll sneak us in."

"We need to be snuck in?"

"It's a bar," he said. "A nightclub."

Although she hadn't had a drink in years, Celeste grinned. A bar meant alcohol. Alcohol meant inhibition. Inhibition meant that by midnight, she'd be a real woman.

He hopped out of the car and waited on the sidewalk for her to open her own door.

"That night at your house?" Looping her arm through his, she continued, "I was insensitive to your marriage proposal. I've reconsidered."

"So have I," he said.

The layers of taffeta kept them a safe distance from one another. He'd have to work hard to lift her hem. He'd get lost trying to find her underwear.

Tonto, his friend, met them at the stage door and offered a table up front. Tonto wore a mini dress and cowboy boots, and swung her legs high when she walked, as if she wanted everyone to see her underwear. "Your usual, Michael Paul?"

"My usual everything," Michael Paul said. "One for my mom's friend, too."

"I'm not your mom's friend."

Tonto served them a drink called Ride 'Em and Hold On. Whiskey and ginger ale. Familiar tastes. Celeste sipped hers. Michael Paul gulped his down and went to order another round.

Heading to the restroom, she passed Michael Paul at the bar. She pointed down the hallway to indicate her destination. He flashed her the peace sign.

The bathroom had one dangling lightbulb. Catching a glimpse of herself in the mirror, she frowned at the ridiculous gown.

A lady said, "How old are you?"

"Twenty-one," she said. "Old enough to be in this bar."

"Bridesmaid?"

Celeste said, "I sure was."

"Catch the bouquet?" the lady asked.

"Yes, and afterwards my boyfriend proposed." She excused herself to squeeze the prom dress into the stall.

Back at the table, she leaned close to Michael Paul and said, "I'm glad you brought me here." Drinking in a nightclub with a boy, listening to a musician on stage sing about searching for a woman, she felt her body tingling with expectation.

The place jumped with hippies and college kids but the beatniks in the dark back booth were the people she wanted to emulate. Hunched over their drinks, tapping feet and fingers, they made her want to rip off her taffeta gown, pull the bobby pins from her starched curls, shake her hair loose, tie a silk scarf around her neck, and make love in the alley.

Michael Paul ran his fingertips along her clavicle, tracing the neckline of her dress. "I'm glad you let me see your tits."

"You can see them again."

"You taught me what I want from life."

Smiling, she said, "Thank you." Her mind said whew.

He raised his hand to order a third round. "You like this Ride 'Em and Hold On?"

"I like my whiskey straight."

"Hip chick," he said. "Hip chick with sweet tits."

Tonto sat down at their table, put her hand over Michael Paul's. "You driving this girl home tonight?"

"I'm her chauffeur," he said.

"Slow down on the liquor." Tonto had a commanding tone.

"Too late, mate. I've been drinking since the second I slipped into this tuxedo." He pulled a flask from his jacket pocket. "This girl needs a shot of straight whiskey. She needs to catch up to me."

Tonto went to the bar and came back a moment later with two shots of whiskey and two glasses of water. "Give me your keys, Mikey."

Michael Paul turned to Celeste. "Are you sober enough to drive?"

"Yes, but I don't have a license. I'm not sixteen," she said.

Tonto said, "The girl's not even sixteen?" She reached for his keychain, a Saint Christopher medal, and stuffed it into her bartender apron. "How much time you got before your mom expects you home?"

"No hurry," Michael Paul said. "I can last all night."

"In the condition you're in? I doubt that," Tonto said. As she walked away, she removed her apron.

Michael Paul wrapped his arm around Celeste's shoulder, drawing her close. "You smell like flowers. I want to sniff you all over. Too bad you rejected me."

"I'm not rejecting you now," Celeste asked. She drank the whiskey in one gulp, squinting at the burn.

"You're the one who got me thinking about love and marriage and baby carriages. Also fucking. Mostly fucking. Fucking to my heart's content."

Celeste had never heard the word fucking spoken out loud. She found it vulgar and brutal, but also exciting. "I'll accept Nona's ring."

Pushing her chin upward with his finger, he kissed her, his mouth parting hers, his breath more whiskey than ginger ale.

Celeste imagined him parking his car at a lookout point, helping her into the backseat, the ruffle on his tux brushing her chest, the taffeta gown around her waist like a window-screen tutu, the zip of his trousers, his erection pushing into her, the voice in her head saying Bingo.

Tonto tapped his shoulder. "I'll drive you two lovebirds home."

"No," Celeste said. "We can manage."

Michael Paul said, "I'm really drunk."

"Come on, kids," Tonto said, looping her arms through theirs and guiding them to the car.

On the way home, Michael Paul sat in the middle. Celeste felt his thigh pressing hers, the heat of a drunken boy primed for sex. She wondered where they'd go to get it over with, considering Tonto's presence.

Tonto twisted the knob on the radio, never letting any song play from start to finish.

Pulling his flask from his pocket, Michael Paul handed it to Celeste. "Whiskey for the hip chick." He lit a cigarette.

Celeste sipped slowly. She didn't want to be too drunk for this episodic event.

Tonto asked for directions to Celeste's house. Celeste told her the long way home. She wanted Michael Paul to sober up. Wanted Tonto to get bored with the two of them. Drop them off on the side of the road. They'd find a bush and get it on.

When Tonto parked in front of Celeste's house, she said, "If your parents are waiting for you, don't mention me or the bar by name. If you're nauseous or hungover, say you've got food poisoning from the crap they served at the prom."

"I'd never tell them Michael Paul took me to a bar," she said. "They'd never believe it anyway."

Tonto elbowed Michael Paul. "Compliment her dress."

Michael Paul leaned across Celeste's lap and opened the passenger door. "You look pretty."

Celeste climbed out, Michael Paul following. She said, "You don't have to do whatever Tonto says."

Tonto smiled. "He doesn't have to and yet, he does."

Walking Celeste up the driveway, Michael Paul pushed her against the dark side of the garage. He kissed her and squeezed her breasts.

"We can do it out here," she said.

"I'd have to rip your dress." He chuckled, making a sound as if he were tearing the material.

"It has a zipper," she said, "and it lifts up."

"Fancy, fancy." His kisses traveled to her neck. Suddenly, he stopped, pulled back, and said, "Well, can't keep a gal like Tonto waiting."

"I'll come to your house on prayer Wednesday."

"Don't bother, Mary Celeste." He sprinted to the car and jumped in. Celeste stood in her driveway, waving goodbye. Tonto didn't drive off, though. She slid to the middle of the bench seat and bent over Michael Paul. The back of his head pressed against the passenger window. Had Tonto dropped her keys? Was she searching for the flask or a pack of cigarettes? Celeste waited for Tonto to rise, but she remained hidden from view. Michael Paul pressed his hands against the roof of the car as if he were keeping it from collapsing.

Celeste the Astronaut, peering from space. This unfamiliar universe spun and pulsed. In that moment she felt completely alone. She didn't want to be alone.

Smashed on Limestones and sprawled on the couch, a lit cigarette precariously clutched between her fingers, Bernadette didn't seem to notice how Celeste stunk of whiskey, tobacco, and disappointment. She said, "Was the parish prom everything you imagined? Did you remember to say hello to Father Murphy? Was Michael Paul the perfect gentleman?" Switching off the television, Bernadette headed upstairs before her questions were answered.

In the kitchen, Celeste tore a sheet from Bernadette's grocery list pad. She wrote, "Dear Chris, Michael Paul got even with me. My virginity remains intact." She ducked low, darting past Tonto's car, and slipped the note beneath Sacred Heart. Jesus stood in his frozen position and stared straight past her. Laying in the soil, Celeste's prom gown fanned around her like dirty angel wings.

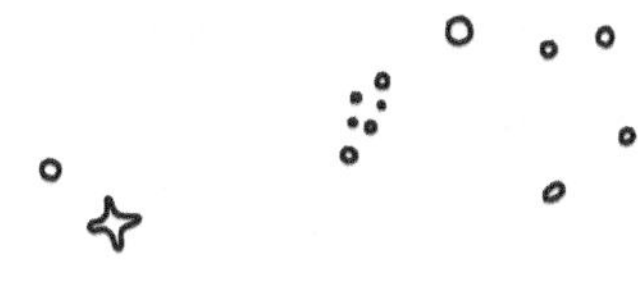

In the Reference section of the school library, crouching near the row of encyclopedias, Celeste searched for information on farming, canning, and planting an orchard, should *Walden* beat Paris or should they find a Walden in Paris.

The biology teacher, a lumpy man with thick-soled hiking boots stormed into her aisle. Celeste wondered if he noticed her squatting near the bottom shelf.

The English teacher squeezed into the row beside him. "What's so important you needed to see me right away?"

Waving a copy of the newly published yearbook in the air, the biology teacher shouted, "Look here. Rebel warfare."

"What am I supposed to be looking at?" the English teacher said. He squinted at the page.

Celeste assumed he was talking about Chris's hidden messages and had solved the one around his own faculty photo. (Sow plants. Sew pants.)

The biology teacher stabbed an illustration with his fingertips. "The frames, the ones around the student body photographs, are cannabis leaves. Printed in green. Can't erase. Someone drew marijuana on school property."

Celeste shifted her weight to avoid getting kicked.

The English teacher shook his head and said, "Those are Japanese maple leaves. I have a tree in my yard."

"I teach biology. I know the difference between marijuana and maple. Look at the tips of the cannabis plant," he said, thumping the yearbook against the reference shelf. Encyclopedias rattled. One fell over, making a clunk. "It's dope on these pages, my friend, and what will happen next? LSD and a personal invitation for Timothy Leary to give the graduation address?"

"Who'd do something like this? It's our duty to nab the little shits," the English teacher said.

Celeste had an inkling of fear that Chris had something to do with the prank. How did he even know what marijuana looked like? He didn't smoke. He barely drank. It had to be his crush, David.

As she hurried down the hallway to find Chris, the loudspeaker tinged and popped as the principal's voice boomed, "All students are requested to come to the gym for a school assembly. Immediately. Do not, I repeat, do not dally or delay. There will be severe consequences if you ditch."

Celeste got swept up in the stream of kids like lemmings to the sea. Or cows to slaughter. Or teenagers to a disciplinary hearing.

The boys were put on one side of the gym, the girls on the other. Celeste searched the crowd for Chris's blond curls. She wondered if he guessed what was about to happen to David.

The principal lifted a megaphone to his mouth. "If you have a preordered copy of the yearbook, hold them up so we can see."

Only a few students were organized enough to have put in early requests. Innocently and obediently, they lifted the books over their heads. Faculty charged the bleachers.

The principal held a piece of paper in the air. "I've got the yearbook elective class roster here in my hand. You can't pull one over on me. I fought in Korea. I know a subversive action when I see one." As he read their names, those yearbook students were yanked from their seats and escorted to the floor to stand alongside the faculty.

Shuffling like a convict in a line of prisoners, Chris nodded at her and smiled.

"What's wrong with you?" she shouted.

A girl beside her said, "Don't make this worse for him."

"I can't possibly make this worse," Celeste said. Helplessly, she watched as Chris and David and rest of the yearbook committee disappeared through the locker room doors.

The students were dismissed. Giggles and conversations bounced off the gym walls. If Chris had anything to do with this dangerous prank, anything, she'd slug some sense into him.

After school, she sprinted to his house. The dogwood tree, exuberant with pale blossoms— or bracts, as the biology teacher would define them—shrouded her. She rang the doorbell. She knocked. She shouted, "Chris."

Mrs. Armstrong answered the door. "Please come in, Celeste." Her voice sounded oddly quiet. "As Chris's girlfriend, this will affect you, too."

Celeste wanted to shout she was much more than a girlfriend. She and Chris were, as Homer describes, "Two friends, two bodies with one soul inspired."

Chris was slouched in a chair, seeming to concentrate on a rip in his bellbottoms. He'd embroidered the word Love with the same Harlequin green thread he'd used for Juliet's eyes.

Dr. Armstrong pinched the bridge of his nose and leaned against the fireplace mantle, his elbow pointed toward an array of framed photos of Chris. He cleared his voice. "I see the consequences of drugs all the time in the hospital, son."

Celeste willed Chris to look at her, but he didn't lift his head or turn in her direction.

"I see problems when I'm filing court documents." Mrs. Armstrong patted Chris's knee. "Last week the dregs of a marijuana cigarette, fished out of a toilet, no less, got a young man thrown in jail." Her mascara smudged across her cheek.

"This was Chris's idea of a joke," Celeste said. "He's a moron, not a drug addict."

"Drugs are serious business. With serious consequences," Dr. Armstrong said. He fiddled with his tie clasp.

Mrs. Armstrong added, "And serious ramifications."

Chris whispered, "It was a practical joke. That's it."

Celeste wanted to tell Dr. and Mrs. Armstrong it was Chris's way to get Stoner David to screw him. She'd never betray Chris.

"We have an important decision to make," his mom said.

Chris sighed. "I didn't think anyone would know what the plant was."

"This isn't Victorian England, dummy," Celeste said. "Marijuana leaves look like marijuana leaves."

"Should we be concerned for you, too, Celeste?" Mrs. Armstrong asked.

"Chris did nothing more than fail at a prank," Celeste said, glancing from Mrs. Armstrong to Dr. Armstrong. "The principal is acting like the entire student body plans to rip out the pages of the yearbook and light up."

"Light up? You know drug terminology?" Dr. Armstrong leaned toward her, sniffing.

Chris said, "Celeste is innocent in this. She's trying to protect me."

"Son, your drawing of cannabis is realistic, which indicates to me you've seen what the intoxicant looks like. If you have this knowledge, your girlfriend probably does too," Dr. Armstrong said.

"I don't," Celeste said with less conviction this time.

Mrs. Armstrong said, "We'll give your parents a call."

"I didn't have anything to do with it. I'm not even on yearbook. Chris is innocent. Call David's parents." She glanced at Chris.

"Shut up, Celeste," Chris said. His head dropped onto his knees.

"David?" Mrs. Armstrong gestured that it was time for Celeste to leave. She spoke as she escorted Celeste toward the front door.

"Another instigator?"

"David's the stoner. Not Chris." She despised that ridiculous boy, with his shag haircut and leather bracelets and fringe jacket and tight jeans.

Chris called from the other room, "David didn't do this."

Celeste hoped Chris understood that she'd tried to save him from the heap of shit he'd landed in. "Chris acted stupid. That's all," she said, and the door swung shut.

At home, Celeste hurried past the living room and snuck upstairs.

"Mary Celeste? Come in here right now," Bernadette called.

Celeste said, "Yes?" in her most innocent tone

Bernadette took a deep breath, exhaling long and loud. "I had the most disturbing conversation with Dr. Armstrong."

Celeste said, "You did? About what?"

"Seems your darling little acquaintance got himself into some trouble, and his father was worried you were also a part of the fiasco. I told him you are not morally bankrupt. Are you?"

On her way home from Chris's, Celeste had come up with a plan on what to say should she be questioned. "It's Michael Paul's fault."

"Michael Paul? How in the world is this his fault?"

"At the prom, I complimented a maple tree. Michael Paul described how similar it looks to marijuana. I mentioned this to Chris, because he likes to draw."

Bernadette took a sip of her Limestone and said, "I don't believe a word of what you're saying."

Celeste said, "Chris doesn't smoke marijuana. Michael Paul does. That's how he knows what it looks like." She'd easily sacrifice Michael Paul to save Chris.

"George," Bernadette shouted. "Come listen to the lies your daughter's spewing."

George's suit, wrinkled from the Fuller Brush road, had a smear of red across the lapel. He dabbed the stain with a damp chamois.

The scent of Italian spices wafted from the kitchen. He'd probably been tasting marinara. "Bernie?"

"Mary Celeste has gotten herself into the wrong crowd. She's trying to blame the problem on an innocent lamb." Bernadette patted a place on the couch for Celeste to sit.

"Who's the lamb?" George asked.

"Michael Paul," Bernadette said. "The clumsy altar boy."

"The one who swings the incense a little too high?" George asked.

"He didn't phone her after their prom date. She's getting back at him."

"Mary Celeste," George said. "Don't be vindictive."

Celeste rested her head on the back of the couch. "Chris acted cool to get a boy's attention." She covered her mouth. Oh Sacred Heart of Goddamned Jesus, she'd released the guillotine blade on Chris's queer virgin neck.

"Of course he craves a boy's attention," Bernadette said. Her lips stretched like a pink rubber band. "Haven't I been telling you this, George? Haven't I?"

"Getting a boy's attention could mean a number of things," George said.

"Like what?" Bernadette shouted.

"Maybe he admires the kid's ball skills. Wants tips on how to shoot or hit. Maybe he wants to be on a sports team and get a letterman jacket." Using the chamois he continued to wipe the marinara stain. The wet spot grew bigger.

"George, don't be an imbecile," Bernadette said.

George pushed the rolling bar into the center of the living room. The chandelier's light caught the etched glass, glistening in rainbow arcs. He snapped the tongs, digging into the ice bucket.

"Michael Paul let a cocktail waitress named Tonto give him a blowjob in our own driveway. He's not an innocent lamb. Chris is."

George froze, the ice dropping from the tongs onto the carpet. "My God, Mary Celeste."

"Vengeance is unbefitting of a lady." Bernadette held her tumbler in the air, rattling her cubes around like dice. "You've obviously been brainwashed by that ridiculous boy you call a friend. How you even know that filthy word is beyond me."

"Not from Chris. He's pretty stupid when it comes to sex."

"Mary Celeste," George snapped. "Go to your room."

On her route from the couch to the staircase, Celeste said, "You know who's ridiculous? A grown woman who calls herself Tonto and gives boys blowjobs, that's who." Celeste's anger overshadowed her fear of being grounded for the rest of her life. In her room, she drank from her old dresser drawer stash of Heavenly Hill. Getting drunk helped her fall asleep, but when she woke early, anxiety hadn't eased its stranglehold, and her head pounded.

The school lifted suspensions for everyone on the yearbook committee except Chris. He'd implemented himself by putting his initials in the center of the largest marijuana leaf on the back page. His guilt as clear as if he'd left fingerprints.

Newspapers sat on the Armstrongs' porch like unclaimed bodies. Chris didn't open his window after she pelted the pane with gravel. She looked beneath the planter where they kept the spare key, then unlocked the front door. Stepping inside, Celeste called his name and walked through the kitchen to the living room, praying she'd see him sprawled on the couch, eating a pink snowball cupcake and watching daytime soaps.

He wasn't.

She scanned the lawn around his doughboy pool.

Not there, either.

Heading upstairs, she prepared herself for a verbal onslaught. She deserved his wrath. She'd let him yell and wouldn't defend herself. They'd make up, and all would be well.

On initial glance, nothing in his bedroom looked out of place but the longer she stood in the doorway, the more she sensed the differences. His pillow, gone. Coverlet, gone.

"Redecorating?" she whispered, forcing herself to smile.

No answer.

Only a few clothes hung in his closet. His drawers nothing but cedar-lined emptiness. Chris had vanished. He could be anywhere in town or state or country or world. The last time she saw Chris, she should have sewn herself onto him like Wendy did with Peter Pan's shadow.

Outside, she returned the key to its hiding place and sat on the front porch, closing her eyes, waiting. The Armstrongs didn't come home. She went back the next day and the following few.

When their car finally pulled into the driveway, she shielded her eyes from the headlamps, trying to spot his silhouette in the backseat. Maybe he was lying down? She waved.

Dr. Armstrong carried a suitcase up the walkway. He stopped and said, "Wondering about Chris?"

"Where is he?" she asked, her voice like a mouse, not a lion.

Mrs. Armstrong unlocked the door. "Come in for a cup of tea."

The scene felt as calm and dignified as if she'd walked into a ladies' auxiliary luncheon and not the home of her missing best friend whose parents obviously overreacted to a flawed practical joke. She wanted to scream at them for being square, scream at them for not caring about her feelings, scream at them for sending Chris somewhere that wasn't his home.

Dr. Armstrong removed his watch, setting it in an ashtray. He dropped his cufflinks into another, his keys in a third. Chris once told her this was Dr. Armstrong's method for giving up smoking: fill the ashtrays with anything except ash and filters.

The clock on the mantle ticked loudly. The room smelled like dead flowers and furniture polish. Dr. Armstrong slid the window open. Celeste looked around at the floral drapes and checkered sofa, shag carpet, oversized chair. All familiar, yet everything had changed. Chris should be sitting opposite her. He should be home, grounded for his stupid prank. If his parents interrogated him about David, and he confessed the truth, would they have called him the same names Bernadette did? Tried to convert him to liking girls like she had? Celeste blushed, embarrassed of her rigorous and shameful attempt at seduction.

Mrs. Armstrong carried a serving tray into the living room, set it on the coffee table, and poured three cups of tea. The liquid inched toward a thin band of gold circling the rim. "Cream and sugar?"

Celeste said, "Where is he?"

"Military school," Mrs. Armstrong said, handing a teacup to Celeste. "He'll be back when he's learned his lesson." She dropped two lumps of sugar in her own cup then dabbed her eyes with the hankie Chris bought her on Mother's Day. It had been a plain white handkerchief before Chris embroidered roses in one corner and her initials in the other.

"You sent him to war?" Celeste's tea sloshed onto the saucer.

"Obviously our son's outlandish behavior proved too much for our lazy methods of parenting," Dr. Armstrong said. He picked up the creamer. "We failed."

"You've got this all wrong," Celeste shouted. "Chris is the best-behaved boy I know."

Mrs. Armstrong said, "If he's the best-behaved boy you know, then I hate to think who your friends are."

"I need him," she whimpered, putting the teacup down. "He needs me."

Mrs. Armstrong squeezed Celeste's arm. "I'm sorry, Celeste. I really am, but until he straightens up his life, you'll have to make do without him."

"Straighten up his life?" Celeste asked. Were they speaking in code?

"His mother and I are saving him from making more bad choices," Dr. Armstrong said.

Her chest felt like popcorn in a hot pan. Atoms exploding one by one. "Can I get his address? His birthday's soon. My birthday, too. Our sixteenth birthday. We had plans." A slow grind of loneliness edged its way into her being.

Mrs. Armstrong whispered, "Leaving him there is the hardest thing we've ever done."

"Why did you do it then? How could you?" She shook her head, as if that would change destiny.

Dr. Armstrong reached into his jacket pocket and handed her a pamphlet. "Here's the address. Happy early birthday."

Celeste studied the brochure. Basscombe Home for Boys: Where Bravery Meets Discipline. "Do you think he'll like it there?" Celeste asked, trying to quiz them on how much they knew about his life.

"It's a military school," Dr. Armstrong said. "He's not supposed to like it."

The cover photograph showed rows of boys standing in a field. Their gaze pierced the camera lens like bayonets. Celeste's only consolation was if Bernadette mentioned Chris's need to impress a guy, his parents wouldn't have sent him to a home for bad boys.

On the morning of their sixteenth birthday, Celeste dabbed George's new Debutante shade of red lipstick onto her cheeks and lips, then went downstairs to eat a bowl of cereal before dragging herself to school.

Bernadette lay slumped over the kitchen table, her head resting against an open cookbook. Recipe cards scattered alongside a decanter with bourbon the same color as her hair.

George stood behind her, rubbing her back. "Bernie, you can't be comfortable like this." Although dressed for work, he looked as tired as she appeared.

Bernadette lifted her head. Her eyes fiery, not dull from a night with a hardcover book for a pillow. "Would you like Quiche Lorraine for your birthday dinner, Mary Celeste?"

"Sure," Celeste said. She poured frosted cereal from the box into her mouth and twisted the faucet, filling a glass with water.

Bernadette had always loved Limestones, but lately—mostly on the days George was away on the Fuller Brush road— she had started drinking before lunch and not stopping until bedtime. Celeste ignored this escalation, because a drunk mother made sneaking from the house easier.

"Quiche is what you'll have." Bernadette pointed to the recipe in her new Redbook Cookbook. Celeste had been with her the day she bought it, the same day the book came out. She'd stood in line with other women, chatting about how happy they felt now that Betty Crocker could finally be retired. "They've added bacon to this recipe. You like bacon?"

Celeste didn't like bacon. Bernadette should know that by now. "Sure, I love eating strips of dead pig."

George said, "Bernie, the covers are turned down on our bed." He clasped her by the elbow, trying to lift her. "Come on, let's get you tucked in." His voice rose in pitch. Panicky, not angry.

"I want to make our daughter's birthday dinner." Bernadette swatted him. She stood on her own, wobbling.

"You have plenty of time to cook," he said, stuttering on the p and c. "It's only eight in the morning." He wrapped his arms around her shoulder, drawing her close to his chest.

Bernadette tugged free from his grip and steadied herself by leaning against the chair. "You're a liar, Mr. George Roderick," she said, pointing a shaky finger at him. "L.I.A.R."

He pointed to the window. "See? It's morning. I'm about to head off to work. Mary Celeste is leaving for school."

Bernadette whipped toward Celeste, fast enough to stumble, falling against the table. "Mary Celeste is not leaving for school. See the way she's dressed?"

The miniskirt was her home economics project. She'd purposefully bought less material than the pattern indicated. Didn't care if she got a D.

George whispered, "Go upstairs and put on something decent."

"She's off to fool around with boys," Bernadette said.

Celeste shook her head. "I don't want to fool around with boys."

"You look like you want attention. You look cheap." Bernadette's words slurred, but Celeste understood.

"The only boy I want is Chris."

"What a joke," she said, laughing in a way that didn't sound happy. "Hilarity ensues."

"You spent the whole night drinking Limestones and studying recipes. You passed out somewhere in the soufflés. Not the quiches."

George put his hands in the air, urging Celeste to stop talking. "Your mother did not pass out."

Rocking on her heels, Bernadette stepped toward Celeste. "Change your slutty outfit into the green dress I made for your birthday. I worked hard on the pattern, but you can't even be bothered to try the outfit on."

Correct. The design was an old pattern from the 1950s. Juliet of Provence probably wore the same one. "I did try the dress on. Doesn't fit. My boobs are too big."

George said, "Mary Celeste, let's not make this mole hill into a mountain." He gestured for her to stay quiet. More of a plea than a demand. "Nap time, Bernie."

"Invite that mamsy-pamsy boyfriend of yours for quiche," Bernadette said, leaning against George's chest. "We'll see what happens when he tries to smoke marijuana and sashay around the parlor."

Celeste grasped the handle of a pan. "Don't call him names."

Bernadette stumbled to the sink. "I'm going to clean up, then I'll make Quiche Lorraine for dinner." She jiggled a container of cleanser into the basin and shook the can over her windowsill of porcelain blue-eyed Madonnas until they looked like a forest of Virgins waiting in the snow. Dumping powder on the rubberized mat, Bernadette poured white across the instep of her bare feet, then swung the canister over the parquet floor in a wide, sweeping arc like a bleached rainbow.

George approached her, arms outstretched, his voice a stuttering mumble of whoas and calm downs and please dears as she brandished the can.

Bernadette wielded the container until the can rattled with the peculiar sound of an empty cleanser canister. The entire time, she shouted, "Goddamn, George. Goddamn it."

"You'll feel better when you've got some sleep under your belt." He yanked the cleanser from her grip. "Clean this up, Mary Celeste."

Celeste said, "School?"

"School for sluts," Bernadette said.

"You're a drunk. A bitter, mean drunk," Celeste said.

George frowned as he stroked Bernadette's hair. "You'll have plenty of time to cook the quiche. I can bring home Chinese if you'd like." Over his shoulder, he said, "How's this sound, Mary Celeste? Chow mein to mark your sixteenth?"

Bernadette said, "George, don't be ridiculous. The way she's dressed today, she's going to mark her sixteenth by letting a boy bed her."

"Letting a boy bed me?" Celeste's knuckles gripped the handle tighter. They began to tingle. "Bed me?"

George stuttered, "Write yourself a tardy excuse. Sign your mother's name."

Bernadette took a Cavalier from her pack, clenched the filter between her lips. Flicked the lighter. Clicked but didn't ignite. Repeating this, she finally gave up and threw the lighter onto the floor. "George?"

He picked it up, rolled his thumb across the wheel, and the flame leapt. He held it to Bernadette. "Light?"

"Bravo to you," Bernadette said, sticking the cigarette halfway through the fire. "You come through for me, darling."

George whispered to Celeste, "For your mother's sake, change your clothes."

"I want to cook, George. I want to goddamn cook." Bernadette stopped struggling as he led her out of the kitchen. The door swung back and forth, shutting with a bang.

The fry pan sailed through the air, knocking the crystal decanter. Glass flew across the cookbook, table, and floor. Bourbon spilled, soaking recipe cards and the pages of the cookbook. The only sound in the room was the drip of booze onto the linoleum.

Scavenging through the desk, Celeste lifted a sheet of paper and searched the margins of wet recipe cards to remind herself of the details of her mother's handwriting: the way she barely crossed her Ts; the way her letters leaned to the right as if giving up.

"To Whom it May Concern, Please excuse Mary Celeste for being late to school today. Mass ran longer than usual this morning. We were saying a prayer for the poor local boys shipped over to Vietnam. Sincerely, Mrs. George Roderick."

The time that Celeste had wasted on idiotic Michael Paul could have been spent persuading Chris from doing his subversive drawings. If she'd studied his yearbook sketches carefully and spotted the marijuana, she would have stopped him. Chris would still be here. With her.

Whiskey puddled. Shards of glass twinkled in the sunlight. Celeste stood in the center of the kitchen under a cloud of cleanser powder and a river of booze. Nothing in her house would ever change. Not the alcohol. Not the cruel words. Not the acquisitions. Celeste dipped the tardy excuse into the Heavenly Hill. The edges moistened and curled.

She opened Bernadette's purse and took all the bills from her wallet. In her bedroom, she packed a blanket, change of clothes, her copy of *Walden*, cash from her piggy bank, and the Basscombe brochure.

PART TWO

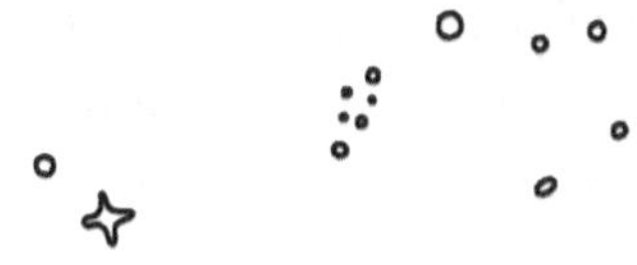

Living with Her Head in the Lion's Mouth

The Greyhound bus groaned to a stop, spewing exhaust, or as Thoreau would say, "The scent of miles." There weren't many passengers on the weekday in June. A few college students, two elderly couples, one family, and a young boy traveling alone, his destination pinned to his chest. People entered and exited, struggling with the overhead compartments, and walked down the narrow aisle, dragging baggage or small children. Celeste's seat stunk of sweat, desperation, anticipation. Stained with orange juice and coffee, the seat beside her remained empty. Soon, she'd arrive at Basscombe. She'd bust Chris from military school. They'd make their way into the wilderness.

Endless streets of suburbia slowly transformed. A stretch of shiny ocean; low, rolling hills flanking the highway; sparsely spaced oak trees providing shade for horses and cows. Celeste stared, astonished how unaware she'd been that farm animals lived only a few hours from the cement lands of her neighborhood. Bernadette and George never went anywhere, but why hadn't she bothered to explore on her own? She could have been brave and hopped on a bus.

Now, here she sat, watching animals huddled in pastures, flicking their tails. Here she sat, running away from home, her brain a scramble.

The gentle lull and roll of the bus rocked Celeste to sleep.

She awoke from dreams of snakes and worms. Drool tickled down her chin and wrist. Wiping it away with her sleeve, she glanced around to see if anyone noticed. Everyone else remained preoccupied with their own lives: reading, conversation, sight-seeing, naps.

Enormous redwoods, packed together like volumes of books on a library shelf, blocked the sun. Light streaked through the forest in feathery stripes of sun rays and fog.

Did Basscombe for Boys have a dormitory for girls or guests? If not, she'd stage a hunger strike in the dean's office, refusing to go until they built her one, because she would not leave without Chris. She'd fight for his freedom. She'd insist on his innocence. The Basscombe faculty would be wowed by this girl's love for her best friend and surrender to her wishes.

Had Bernadette woken up and found her note? Did she toast to her own independence? Bernadette and George wouldn't bother to send a search party. Good riddance, she could hear them say. They didn't care about her welfare. Dr. and Mrs. Armstrong would have gnashed their teeth and torn out their hair if they were her parents and she'd runaway.

The driver barked the name of her stop. When Celeste had bought the ticket, she'd asked for the station closest to the address on the brochure. "Miss?" the driver said, revving the engine. "Do you want to pay for another ticket? Go further?"

"This seems fine." She thanked him and stumbled down the aisle, the duffel held against her chest.

Unlike the stale bus air, the woods were saturated with aromas of tree bark, roots, moss, fern, loamy soil. At home, in the summers, it was impossible to take a deep breath without coughing, because a rind of smog enclosed the suburbs. Now, she inhaled, recharged. She'd never considered a place could house an abundance of oxygen. Thoreau must have understood this truth.

According to the map on the Basscombe brochure, the military school was off the highway, westward over a mountainous ridge, close to the sea. Celeste used the bus stop restroom, then sat on a bench and rearranged the items in her duffel bag as she decided what to do next. As frightened as she felt, she would not shed a single crybaby tear, because if she did, she'd forget about finding Chris and head home to her drunken mommy and pathetic daddy, change into her homemade birthday dress, and sit at the kitchen table, stuffing Quiche Lorraine down her gullet.

She stuck out her thumb, believing someone on their way to visit a bad son would give her a lift. Maybe they'd have aspirin. Her head throbbed from little food and no water.

A few cars zoomed past but didn't slow down. She started walking down a one-lane, forest-lined road. Her feet felt blistered from the sandals she'd left home in. Penance, she thought, and kept going.

Finally, a dusty truck approached, pulling into a small turnout. The driver leaned across the cab and rolled down the passenger window. "You look hot." He handed her a beer. "Need a drink?"

She took the can, because a refusal seemed slightly dangerous.

"Get in if you want." The truck was dented and decades old. "That's why your thumb's out, isn't it?"

"I'm heading to Basscombe. Can you take me there?"

"I'll take you anywhere you want to go." When he grinned, his teeth looked pearly white and perfectly straight.

The beer slid down her throat to her empty stomach, calming her nerves. "You'll drive me anywhere I want?"

He opened the passenger door. "I'll give you the ride of your life."

She studied his doe-like brown eyes, long blond hair, and beard; his colorful necklace and bare muscular chest. Beneath his hippiness he seemed fairly attractive.

"Last chance," he said, pulling a gum wrapper from his pocket and tossing it out the door. "Coming with me?"

"I appreciate the offer, but no thank you." She'd wait for a family heading to Basscombe. Not a hippie dressed in nothing but shorts and love beads. She waved goodbye and started walking.

"Make sure you don't get into a car with an asshole. There's plenty of them around these hills. You know how you can tell an asshole from a nice guy?" He paused a moment for her to answer. When she shrugged, he said, "Assholes drive new cars. Nice guys spend all their money on shelter, food, and girls."

Fear and curiosity wove around her chest like thorny vines. "You're saying you're not an asshole?"

"I'm as harmless as a puppy." He batted his eyes and stuck out his tongue, panting in a childish imitation of a dog.

"Thanks for the warning," she said, and started to duck into the woods, hoping for a shortcut to somewhere else.

"Careful," he called. "The forest is covered with poison oak."

"What does it look like?"

He put on the warning lights and climbed out of the truck. He pointed to a patch of shiny leaves and said, "Poison oak is gorgeous to look at but dangerous to touch." Standing in the rye grass, he reminded her of a centaur. Hairy chest. Sturdy legs. Long blond mane. Alert brown eyes. Fine form. "You can hike, but be alert. Also, bobcats and coyotes are shy but don't like to be spooked."

Celeste glanced from the poison oak to his truck to his smile. "I've changed my mind. I'll take you up on your offer." She set her duffel in the back of the truck and climbed in. The vinyl, ripped and torn, burned her thighs. Shifting her weight, she sat on her hands. On the car mat lay an adult magazine with a pouty, busty woman on the cover. The caption read, "Give Her What She Wants and She'll Want More." Celeste kicked the magazine under the seat.

"Careful. Don't beat up my girlfriend." Laughing, he opened another beer, offering it to her.

"Take me to Basscombe?" The cab of his truck stunk like burnt oil and weed. She sipped the cold beer.

"I told you I would, and I promise I will. Running away from home to see your delinquent boyfriend?" Despite zero traffic, he put on the blinker before pulling onto the road.

She lifted the can in a toast. "Today's my sixteenth birthday."

"Keep the brew low," he said, peering at her.

"I have to find Chris before my parents find me. Today's Chris's birthday, too."

"Sixteen is young to be on your own." He threw his empty can out the window. Liquid streamed through the air like the fuselage of a rocket ship. The can clinked and clattered. A squirrel scurried by, berating with its chatter.

"You shouldn't litter the forest." Her stomach rumbled and growled.

"Hungry?" He swerved the truck to avoid a pothole. "Fucking logging trucks ruin the asphalt." His fingernails, clean and buffed to a shine, tapped the dash.

"I haven't eaten all day." Besides the breakfast cereal she'd poured into her mouth.

"Come to my farm," he said with a smile. "I'll feed you dinner and dessert."

As tempting as eating sounded, she shook her head. "I've got to get to Basscombe for our birthday."

"Sorry to tell you this. You won't get there today. The school's nearby as the crow flies, but far by this road." He reached into his ashtray and pulled out a joint. "You smoke weed?"

"What do you mean Basscombe's far from here?" Enter, panic. Enter, terror.

"You took the wrong route." He brushed his hands through his hair. The smoky end of the joint smoldering. "Southwest instead of Northwest."

"The bus driver told me this was my stop." In the narrow canyon, light drained from the sky. Before that moment, she'd never hated seeing stars. Grabbing the door handle, she begged him to pull over. "Bus drivers don't lie."

At a bend in the road, he eased onto the shoulder and stopped. "The driver didn't know what he was talking about."

"But you do? You know the right way to get to Basscombe?" She absolutely did not believe this stranger knew more than the bus driver. Somewhere, a bird squawked. She felt positive it was telling her to run.

"Did the bus driver tell you this was the way to Basscombe, or did you tell him the stop you wanted, and he obliged you?" He sucked the end of the joint, held the smoke, exhaled in slow streams.

"When I bought the ticket, I showed the ticket seller the brochure map."

He took an atlas from the glove compartment. "Look up Basscombe's address."

She searched the index, turned to those pages, and found the road she should have taken. "Goddamn it."

"Listen, like I told you before, I'm harmless." He held one loop of his bead necklace in his hand, lifting it before letting it fall against this chest. "The forest isn't. Mountain lions, coyote, bobcats, assholes. In the morning, I'll make sure you get to the school safe and sound."

She'd never felt as alone as she did in that moment. "I'm an idiot."

Pinching the end of the joint with a roach clip, he offered it to her, but she said no. She needed a clear head to figure out what to do next.

"I understand. You're a girl out here by yourself. I'm a guy. You're cautious, and that's a good thing," he said, shrugging. He stubbed the joint into the ashtray, wiped his hands on his shorts. "I'll put you up for the night and take you to the school tomorrow. Don't worry about me. I won't bother you." He jumped from the car, sprinted to a plant, twisted a purple flower from the stem, and handed it to her through the open window. "Wild iris."

"I know karate," she said, feeling instantly stupid.

Laughing, he got back into the truck. "You can kick my ass if I'm not an honorable gentleman." As he pulled onto the road, he barely missed slamming into a large rock. The magazine slid from under the seat.

She glanced down at the two enormous boobs on the petite blonde lady. Cherry-red lips in an oval shape, as if all she wanted in this goddamned world was for someone to put a dick between them. "I hate her."

Bending over and pinching the corner of the magazine, he hurled it out the window. "Bye, sweetheart, you're making my guest uncomfortable."

"I hate litter."

"You hate a lot of things. Hard to please?" He slathered balm across his chapped lips, smacked them together.

She slouched next to the passenger door. "I don't think so."

A breeze blew hair into his eyes. It swirled when he shook his head, clearing his view. "We'll go to Basscombe in the morning." Holding up two fingers in a Boy Scout salute, he added, "Promise."

She wondered how dangerous a hippie could be. Everything she knew about them was they were antiwar, into love and peace. "You'll leave me alone tonight? It's been a long day. I'm sad and tired."

"If you want to be left alone, I'll leave you alone. You're too young for me, anyway." He angled the truck through a lane of black oak and onto a deeply pitted road. Whenever the tires got stuck, he revved the engine, backed up, then charged forward, hitting bumps hard enough for her head to knock against the roof of the cab. His expression determined and focused.

"Ouch," she said, rubbing the spot.

"I should have warned you. This isn't easy terrain." He drove along the gravel road until he pulled onto a long dirt driveway, stopping in front of a cabin. Turning the truck off, he left the key in the ignition when he got out. His shorts slid down, exposing the top of a nest of blond, wiry hair. When he caught her looking, he grinned and tightened the cord belt.

Embarrassed, Celeste remained in the cab. She could speed away if he tried to grab her. "Where are we?" she asked, looking at the emptiness of the place.

"Home. Otherwise known as Nowhereville. At least you're closer to Basscombe than you were an hour ago."

She spotted a rake she could use to smash in his head if she needed to protect herself. "My boyfriend's waiting for me."

He walked around to her side of the truck and opened the door. "I'll get you into his arms by tomorrow afternoon." A fragment of blue sky appeared from between the branches of oak. "All this effort for a boy?"

"Not just any boy," she said, and blinked, hoping he wouldn't see how close she was to crying. "The boy."

"Romantic," he said, and winked. Walking down a pathway, he passed a large, fenced garden. Chickens scattered around his feet, flying into the trees to roost. "I've got a fresh pot of vegetable soup ready to heat up."

The outside of his place appeared homey and lovely, which comforted her. Between the fight with Bernadette, bus ride, hitchhiking, beer, and lack of food, she didn't have an ounce of strength left. "Why do you live way out here?" She bent over, grabbing a twig and breaking the wood in half. If she had to gouge his eyeballs, she would.

"I'll let you have my bed. I'll sleep in the garden. Will that make you feel safe?"

"But why do you live so far away out here?"

"I don't like to talk about it with strangers. To show good faith, I'll share with you." He lowered his voice. "The draft begins in December. I'm resisting. I won't go. I refuse to fight an immoral war." He made a fist and raised it into the air.

"Chris has two more years before his number's called. He can't go to Vietnam."

"The government's trapping us. Let us get killed before they move down to younger, stupider ones. Military school is a step to brainwashing boys for battle."

"I need to get to Basscombe. I need to rescue Chris." She spun in circles, wondering if she should jump in his truck and drive there.

"Relax. Eat. Get a decent night's sleep so you can think straight. You have time." He held the cabin door open for her. Inside, he struck a match, lighting nubs of candlesticks stuck in beer bottles. The floor was littered with film canisters, a box of kindling, and stacks of old newspapers. He set her duffle bag on the unmade bed. "I'll make cookies later when we get the munchies."

"If I was home, I'd be eating Quiche Lorraine."

He said, "The bathroom's around the corner, second door, if you want to clean up from the road."

She hadn't peed since the bus stop. "Thank you. I'd love to wash my face." A mirror hung above the sink, but she avoided looking. Twisting the faucet, she splashed her face and underarms with cold water. Refreshed, she went into the main room.

He opened a small refrigerator and took out a bottle, hitting the top against the edge of the table. "I brew this beer myself."

The label showed a house, creek, dog, and one stick figure. Hand drawn. "Stony Brook Hide Out," she read. "How'd you come up with the name?"

"Dropped acid. Meditated. Had a vision." In the candlelight, the golden hairs on his arms appeared like fireflies.

She said, "Isn't acid dangerous?" In school, they'd had assemblies where guest speakers talked about LSD trips and people jumping out windows, thinking they could fly. No one ever mentioned meditating and coming up with a beer label.

"The feds want you to think it's dangerous, but it's mind expanding. Takes you on a journey to places you had no idea existed." He held a match to the burner and twisted a knob. The stovetop burst into flame. Setting a pot over the fire, he lifted the lid, sniffed, dropped in a sprig of rosemary. He plaited his hair into two braids and tied them with twine. Arms raised, as he reached for bowls on the shelf, his shorts slipped again, exposing the dimples on his lower back.

She sipped the Stony Brook. "You won't tell anyone about me?"

He nodded. "Not if you don't tell anyone about me. With this goddamn war waging, my options in life are limited."

"Mine, too, but I created my own war." She thought of Bernadette finding the shattered decanter and booze-soaked kitchen.

He stirred the soup as he spoke. "Resisters and outlaws are hidden in these hills. We don't have street addresses, so it's like we've stepped off the face of the earth. Disappeared."

"Young men shouldn't get killed. I hate seeing all those flag-draped coffins on the news." A cord ran from the base of a lamp to an outlet. He did have electricity. Leaning over, she pulled the chain, and the bulb flickered, lighting the clutter on the table.

"Turn it off. Wait for me to clean this place up. I had company recently, and they ransacked my cabin." He narrowed his eyes. "You aren't a narc, are you?"

"I'm a sophomore in high school. Or I was until today. Missing finals this week. Who cares, anyway. I'm not a narc."

He tasted the soup, added salt, then dished some into a bowl. He handed it to her and winked. "Eat."

Celeste slurped a carrot and a slice of ginger. Her stomach growled, demanding more. She asked for a second bowl.

Slicing into a pan of cornbread, he pushed a piece toward her. He dribbled molasses across the top of his own. It looked sticky as it oozed down his fingers. His tongue dabbed and licked the drips.

Celeste bit into the cornbread. She complemented the taste and dipped it in her soup.

While she was in the bathroom, he'd braided his hair and decorated it with crystalline buds of marijuana. He pulled a flower out and ripped it apart. A few blond strands became intertwined in the grass, but he rolled the joint anyway, moistened and sealed the paper before passing it to her. Striking the match, he said, "I grew this in my garden."

The burn slid and swirled through her lungs. Closing her eyes, she said, "I wonder if Basscombe for Boys will have a birthday cake for Chris."

He took the joint from her, pinching the end before inhaling. "He's how old?"

"Same as me."

"Holy shit," he said, laughing. "Kids."

Her head, buzzing with smoke and beer, bobbed to the sound of an owl's rhythmic hoot. "How'd you find this cabin in Nowhereville?"

"Some relative of a relative owns this place. Forty acres in the center of nothing," he said, exhaling smoke in half-rings and spearing them with his middle finger. "Ideal for getting lost."

Her world slowed to a crawl. She stared into space and opened another beer, sliced another piece of cornbread. "I don't even know your name."

"Truth."

The hair on his chest forms an inverted V, the bottom vertices disappearing into his waistband like an arrow on a treasure map, she thought, and giggled. "Truth? That's your name or what I said is the truth? You're lucky to have somewhere to hide."

"If you call being forced to leave friends and family behind lucky, well then, I suppose I am one fortunate bastard."

"This weed's strong," she said. Wiping crumbs from the table, she dropped them in an ashtray. "My last boyfriend sold baggies of shake." This pot helped numb her anxiety. Or mask it. She wasn't sure which.

"Another naughty boyfriend? Lame to risk jail time for selling leaves. I feed my shake to the deer. That joint in your hand is pure grade bud."

She nodded in agreement as if she understood. "Will you be able to go home after the war? If the fighting ever ends?"

Clearing their dishes, he dropped them in the sink, squirted it with soap, scrubbed, rinsed, and set them in a rack to dry. "Fuck if I know what Johnson's war regime government plans to do with me upon my return to the mighty civilization."

"I admire your dedication to resisting Vietnam and giving up everything to stay true to your beliefs. You're like a walking, breathing anti-war poster."

He grabbed a bag of chocolate chips from the shelf. "There's supposed to be a meteor shower tonight." Clasping her hand, he didn't let go as he led her through the house and into the garden. From up in the tree, a rooster crowed.

A million stars spilled from the darkness and spread across the sky. At home, streetlights blocked this brilliance, but in the garden, nothing stood between Celeste and the universe. "I'm in a spaceship soaring through the Milky Way."

Pouring chocolate chips into his mouth, he moved behind her and kneaded her shoulders. "You're knotted up."

Startled at his touch, she jerked away. "I rode on a bus for six hours," she said. "I walked with a duffel bag."

"You want me to rub away the pain?" His voice quiet and gentle.

She said, "I do and I don't. You're a conundrum."

"Big word for a little girl." He lifted her hair and began massaging her neck. His breath had the scent of chocolate, beer, pot, molasses.

"I read a lot." She tensed before relaxing.

"I like to read, too. Mostly cookbooks. I love to cook and bake."

His hands slid down her spine, loosening the stiffness in her lower back. If she wasn't slightly drunk and high, she may have worked harder to shake him off. Or maybe not. She liked it. She liked him touching her.

"Is there a library around here?" she asked.

"A bookmobile comes to town every two weeks." His hands moved to her hips, his fingers on her pelvic bone, his thumbs on her tailbone. "Want me to stop?"

"I don't want you to stop," she said. Afraid she'd collapse into a giant tangle of exhaustion and sadness, she leaned into him, keeping herself from tumbling down the mountain.

He whispered into her ear, "Free love is what we do around here."

"I love… the library."

"Love is all any of us are made for." His hands reached around to her stomach, his fingers circled her belly button. "We aren't our parent's uptight generation."

His touch stirred a mess of desperation and desire. Visceral and animalistic. Frightened of her feelings, she walked farther into the garden, following the fragrance of lavender.

"All those rules they inflict on us are bullshit. Adherence to them hasn't made our parents happy, has it?"

"My mom's a drunk." Saying this sentence while intoxicated made her double over in laughter.

"Not a bad way to go through life. Drunk. Stoned," he said, swaying his hips side to side as if he heard music. "Better than dying alone on the other side of the world, or rotting in jail for a crime gone haywire, or pretending you're someone you're not."

"My dad's her pet." She sat cross-legged on the pathway. Her miniskirt barely covering her.

"Monogamy's a screwed-up notion. We're not meant to be with only one person. We're meant to love as many people as possible. We're meant to enjoy ourselves in this short time we have on earth." Pointing through the pitch-black night, he said, "My business partner's on that ridge over there. Let's just say, we're not limited by definitions. We all like to fuck."

A blush spread across her body. "That's something I've wanted to do." He was a man, not a boy proposing with his nona's ring.

He plucked a lavender blossom and held it to his nose. "We're not dead yet."

She took off her shirt, unhooked her bra, wiggled out of her underwear. A beautiful, warm night, only a hint of a breeze. She felt free and high and drunk and uninhibited.

Smoothing a place between staked vines and twirling stems, he said, "Come to me, Little Girl," and kissed her.

She rested her head on her arm, looking up at the galaxies. The tongue she'd been watching lick molasses now began to lick farther than Michael Paul had dared to venture, farther than she imagined a tongue could go. "Take me past the moon," she moaned, lost in the most pleasurable universe imaginable. "Take me to the outer limits."

He untied the cord on his shorts, tugging them free. "I'll fuck you into oblivion."

"Into stardust," she said. A hard push. A painful break, and she wasn't a virgin anymore. Celeste, naked in the dirt, the tendril of a snow pea tickling her spine, the weight of a man pinning her to earth.

The morning light revealed a different garden bed. Without the India ink sky and scattering of stars, all she could see were shovels and trowels and buckets, ants marching by, daisies flattened, snail-laced tomato leaves, pea pods crushed from their lascivious weight, her rich red blood turned black in the soil.

A donkey's bray echoed throughout the hills.
He was not by her side, but she lay on a sleeping bag covered with a quilt. Sometime in the middle of the night, he'd climbed over her again. Both of them remained silent as if the darkness insisted on anonymity. He stroked and licked her until she came. When he climaxed, he cried. Confused by his emotion, but not wanting to ask, she'd touched his face with her fingertips, wiping his tears and shushing him with a kiss.

She hadn't expected to be sore, but her body ached. Still, she had no regrets about what she'd done. Free from the constraints of virginity, she couldn't wait to share this news with Chris. Walking through the garden, she stopped at the hose to rinse dried blood from her thighs, then headed to the cabin, where she found him beside the stove, cracking eggs into a skillet. He'd cleaned up the place, and it looked welcoming. "Hi," she said.

"Morning, Little Girl. You look refreshed."

"Don't call me a little girl."

"What should I call you?" He handed her a plate of buttered toast.

"Celeste."

"Then you should call me Matt. It's as good as any other name."

"Matt." Her head pounded from Stony Brooks and weed.

"I had a blast showing you my garden."

She tore her toast into pieces and dropped them in her mouth. "I had a blast seeing it."

Matt flipped the eggs. "You turn me on, Celeste."

She liked hearing those words. "I feel the same about you."

"Stick around," he said, handing her a cup of coffee. "Hang out a few more days. Rest. Eat. Fuck. Eat. Sleep. Fuck."

"I have to get to Basscombe." Unused to drinking coffee, her mouth puckered at the bitterness. "Do you have milk or sugar?"

Matt poured milk into a creamer, pushed that and a sugar bowl toward her. "We're civilized around here. No cartons on the table." He winked. "Eat. Drink milky coffee. Fuck. Sleep. Fuck."

"Hmmm—" she said. Part of her wanted to stay in the cabin, enjoying as much pleasure as she could before being caught at Basscombe, which seemed inevitable, and sent back home to die of heartbreak.

"If you're a runaway, the first place they'll look is your boyfriend's school."

"Yep, but I'll risk it," she said with defiance. "I need to rescue Chris."

"What are you going to say you've been doing while your boy's been locked up?" Matt turned the flame down on the stove. "When he discovers your cherry's popped, and he knows he didn't do it, he'll want to punch the guy who got to you first. Jealousy will be his incentive to break out of the prison school and beat me to a bloody pulp." He slid an egg onto her plate. "Worth it."

"I hope he's having sex, too." Although she doubted Chris had found anyone. "I hope there's another guy like him."

"You're saying he's queer?"

"I'm saying he likes boys." She stirred the sugar into the coffee. Tasted it, added more.

"If he's queer, he's in the right place." Licking his lips, he reached into his shorts, tugging his penis into view, rubbing as it hardened. "I bet all they do is jerk each other off."

"Jesus, put it away." By daylight, the sight startled her. The tip was octopus pink and smooth, with a myriad of veins like hidden rivers. Compared to Michael Paul and Persian cat boy, Matt's looked foreboding and too manly.

"Come on, Celeste. I'm hard. Let's ball one more time before you go."

"I haven't finished my coffee." She turned away from him, staring out the window at the chickens jumping down from their perches in the tree. "Why don't you have a coop?"

"A coop's constrictive."

She rubbed her temples and forehead.

"Hair of the dog," he said, pouring a shot of whiskey into her coffee. "Stay with me one more day, then I'll drive you straight to Basscombe." He slid his hand up her thigh. His palm callused, rough.

"Oh, Matt," she said, unable to ignore his erection.

Matt, a rugged man who worked the earth. Matt, a man with a cabin and a fertile garden and chickens. Matt, a man resisting an immoral war. Not a schoolboy who spent his days swinging incense in church and selling shake in the parking lot. Not a schoolboy who stuffed her hand with tissue. Matt, a man whose tongue educated her.

His fingers inched beneath the elastic on her underwear. "Don't tell a single person about me."

"I won't tell about you if you don't tell about me." What a relief to meet someone as desperate as she was.

Dustballs rolled across the pine flooring like fairy tumbleweeds. The scent of eggs in burnt butter and toast settled around them. He didn't take his time like he had in the garden. Didn't kiss her breasts. Didn't touch her where his tongue felt best. Matt, a hunter going in for the kill. She surrendered.

The erect pink flowers of the buckeye shrubs buzzed with honeybees. Following a trail along the river, Celeste wove in and out of black oak and laurel, stepped over watercress and duckweed. Poison oak grew vertical on tree trunks like renegade tinsel. Pausing under the shade of a tree, she drank water from the thermos Matt had given her. He'd also packed an extra blanket, a tattered down jacket, a pair of thick wool socks, and a hearty lunch.

A beetle sauntered past. Celeste knelt to examine its shiny, hard shell. She told it, "Soon, Chris and I'll come live in the forest with you." The beetle responded by tilting its rear in the air and letting off a terrible stink. She admired how something the size of an acorn had such a strong defense.

Ribbons of blue shimmered in the distance, rippling across the browning hills. Brushing past a thicket of flowering coyote brush, Celeste stopped to watch downy seeds sail in the breeze. What tactics were Bernadette and George doing to find her? Or not find her.

After walking for hours, she reached the Pacific. Redwood trunks littered the shoreline as if an entire forest had relocated horizontally. Wind kicked sand around her ankles. Without shade, the sun beat down. On that abandoned and uninhabited stretch of beach, she undressed and dove beneath a frigid wave. Floating, she searched for pictures in the clouds and spotted an elongated burst of white cumulus. When Matt dropped her off at the trailhead, he'd asked for a blowjob, telling her he'd come like a cannon. She'd refused, not only because it struck her as an embarrassing act, but because she hated anything to do with war, including metaphors. The fear of losing Chris to military discipline at Basscombe, then possibly to the draft when he turned eighteen, sickened and angered her.

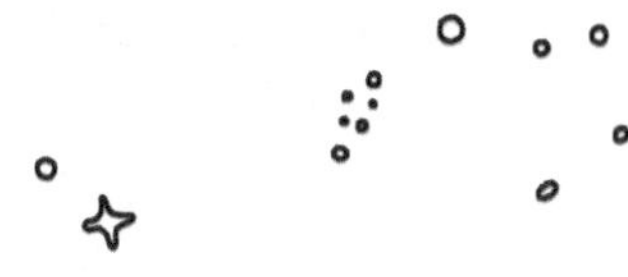

Basscombe was supposed to be a strict military institution, not a sprawling summer camp with a daisy-lined driveway and a charming three-story building with dozens of paned windows and a wraparound porch. Despite its enormity, the school blended well with the pruned shrubbery, ornamental trees, and tiered forest. An array of small cabins, each one painted a different shade of earthy pastels, disappeared into the wooded acreage.

Boys were everywhere. Boys. Boys. Boys. With all this testosterone, would Chris want to leave with her? It seemed doubtful that a boy who liked boys, submerged in a land of boys, would drop everything for a girl.

Students strolled, ran, rode bikes, planted in the garden, rocked in chairs, threw footballs, hit baseballs, groomed and rode horses, sat in the grass talking and reading. They seemed to be having a jolly good time, not toiling in a Dickensian work camp as she'd imagined.

Celeste used a hedge of thick, tangled, orange manzanita as cover. She wished she had on dull-colored clothing, not her vibrant plaid pantsuit. She took off the gaudy jacket, stuffing it in her duffel bag. She had no plan beyond the point of arrival.

Chris should have been easy to spot because of his bouncy yellow curls, but the boys, with their shorn haircuts, all looked the same. Plus, they all wore fancy uniforms of dark gray suits and burgundy ties. She'd expected khaki fatigues and trench helmets.

No iron wall, either. No guards with nightsticks. Not one authoritative shout, command, or bugle call. She'd envisioned Chris struggling with hours of KP duty, a backpack loaded with bricks, a canteen of muddy water, masculine boys beating the hell out of him for being girly. These guys looked healthy and strong. A homosexual boy's heaven.

She couldn't stroll to the office and ask to see him, not looking the way she did, a filthy, runaway girl who stunk of weed, beer, semen, fried eggs, and ocean. Even if she cleaned up, they'd take one look and send her home.

Behind the manzanita, she decided to wait until night closed in and she wouldn't be conspicuous. Ants nibbled her arms and millipedes crawled over her legs. She wrapped herself in Matt's blanket. A voice in her head—Virgin Mary, Jesus, God—coaxed her to forget Chris, Walden, and men like Matt, go home and become nunlike. "Shut up," she answered.

The hoot of an owl woke her to a black and foreign landscape. Rubbing the chill from her arms, she put on the tattered jacket Matt gave her, left the duffel tucked under a redwood tree, and dashed up the driveway. The crunch of gravel beneath her feet echoed like buckshot. Every inhale and exhale seemed as loud as breathing into a megaphone. The closer she got to the main building, the more she doubted her foolhardy plan to search every corner of Basscombe until she found Chris. Still, on she marched. The manicured lawn stunk of fertilizer.

Slowly, she turned the doorknob on the first cabin. Peeking inside, she whispered, "Chris Armstrong?" Someone stirred, and his breathing changed. She backed out, took a deep breath, persuading herself not to quit. She tried a second cabin, a third, and finally on the fifth, someone said, "He's probably in the shower house."

Neither steam nor light led her to him. Muffled voices lured her into a long, low building. A room of lockers and benches lined the hallway walls. Low, rhythmic drumming came from another room. She hesitated. Someone was in there, obviously, but what if it wasn't Chris? What if she walked in on the principal and teachers? She had to take the chance. What else was there for her to do? She opened the door, peeking into the dark, and saw the silhouette of a figure bent over another. He said, "Mon amour. Mon garçon beau."

A voice stammered, "Ahh, Luc."

"Chris," she whispered. She didn't see his face, but even in the blue-black of the room, she knew she'd found him.

The boy clutched Chris around his waist. Their bodies moved in unison, rhythmic. Their feet planted on the shower room floor. Chris's hand pressed against the tiled wall in support of their weight.

Despite listening to Chris read and reread sections from *Giovanni's Room*, she never went beyond imagining two men kissing and fondling each other. Observing Chris and this boy being intimate and erotic, her body tingled in the place Matt had awakened. Embarrassed, she mumbled, "It's you, Chris. It's you."

Chris's body reeled forward. He stammered, "Celeste?"

The boys scrambled away from each other, slipping on the slick floor.

Chris shielded his eyes, staring into the void where she stood. "How'd you get to Basscombe?" he said, his tone pitched high. "Are my parents here? Did they bring you?"

"Bus. Walked. Hitchhiked." Hearing the fear in his voice, she reassured him, "Your parents aren't here."

"Shhh," the other guy said. He grabbed a towel, wrapping the cloth around his waist. "Not too loud." He had an accent. French, of course. He towered over Chris.

French? Chris manifested a Frenchman for a lover? A black Frenchman? "I've come to save you," she said.

The other boy laughed. "Save him from what? Amoureux?"

Chris stepped forward and hugged her, pulling her against his bare chest. "You're crazy, Celeste. Nuts."

The touch of his softening penis against her thigh startled her. Long and thin and beautiful. How different in comparison to Matt's impressive bold erection that poked until her body gave in. "I guess neither of us are virgins anymore," she whispered into his ear.

Chris reached into a pile of clothing laying in a heap on the floor and slipped into his pajama bottoms. "Do Bernadette and George know where you are?"

She shook her head. "I left them a note saying I was leaving. I didn't tell them where."

"They'll call my mom and dad. They'll figure out you're here," he said. "They'll come get you."

The boy put his arm around Chris's waist. "Your parents must be terribly afraid."

"I don't care," she said.

"Thank God you were the one who walked in on us and not one of the staff," Chris said.

The boy buttoned his pants and slid a tee shirt over his head. Dressed, he held out his hand. "Now a formal greeting. Je m'appelle, Luc."

"Je m'appelle, Celeste," she said, embarrassed at her terrible pronunciation. She turned to Chris. "I've found the perfect meadow for us to live in. I'll make acorn dumplings from the oak trees. We'll drink fresh peppermint tea. Heal wounds with pennyroyal. Chew sap like gum. My California natural history books paid off. We can live off the land."

Luc whispered into Chris's ear, "Femme fragile?"

"Cuckoo, not fragile," Chris said. He whistled like a cuckoo clock striking the hour.

"It's not a crazy idea," she said. "We'll become hippies."

Luc kissed the top of Chris's head and smiled. "Hippies, oui."

Chris said, "You can't be here, Celeste. You'll get us in trouble."

"Isn't fooling around in a shower stall in the middle of the night what will get you two in trouble?" She signaled to Chris's half-naked body. "Someone in your cabin told me where to find you."

"My cabin mate won't tell on me," Chris said. "He can be trusted."

Luc rubbed Chris's back and said, "I'll leave you two alone. I'm sure you have much to talk about, oui, mon amour? Lovely to meet you, Celeste. Despite the intrepid timing."

"I didn't see anything," she said. Untrue. She'd seen everything except their facial expressions, but based on recent experience, she could deduce the ecstasy.

"Bonne nuit, Chris and Celeste," Luc said. He gathered his belongings and left, quietly shutting the door of the shower house.

She said, "A Giovanni character in flesh and bone?"

"My dream man. My one and only. I'm hopelessly in love." He crossed his palms over his heart, shoulders shimmying as if he were dancing.

"Really, Chris. Love?"

"Love," he said. "Explosive love."

"The sex I had felt explosive, but it wasn't love."

"So, you and Michael Paul finally did it? Where's the ring?"

"I didn't lose my virginity with that idiot. I did it with the hippie who picked me up hitchhiking."

Chris's eyes widened. "A stranger?"

"After last night and this morning, Matt isn't a stranger," she said with a smile.

"A guy who picked you up hitchhiking is a stranger. He could have taken you to the woods and—" he stopped mid-sentence. "Done something bad."

She hugged Chris, squeezing him tight. The scent of sex lingered on his skin. Pungent, like the core of the earth. "How long was Luc a stranger before you two had sex?"

"Luc's a visiting artist from Paris. One of my teachers."

"A teacher? The plot thickens," she said, rubbing her hands together dramatically.

"He's a man!' I cried. 'A man!" Chris said. "A real man."

"Matt, too." Her emotions skyrocketed up, swooped down, up, down. "A teacher, though?"

"A French artist."

Her skin felt salty and itchy from her ocean swim. "Do you think I can shower without getting caught?"

"I doubt if anyone else is awake at two in the morning. If they are, they'll think someone's too embarrassed to shower during the day when this place is hopping with naked boys. That sometimes happens. Luc and I have to be super sneaky." Chris turned on the faucet. The water spurted before flowing.

Celeste undressed, tossing the jacket and pants onto a nearby bench. She rolled a sliver of soap in her palm and over her thighs. Didn't care how many armpits it touched or penises it scrubbed. She'd found Chris.

Chris removed his pajamas, stepping in beside her. "If I get caught with you, I'll be a local hero," he said, laughing.

"Tonight your boner wasn't a mirage." She turned her face upward toward the spray. "Remember in the sandbox when you said that to me? It's a mirage boner?"

He squeezed shampoo over her hair, gently rubbing it into her scalp. "Tell me about the stranger who picked you up and gave you more than a lift."

"Matt fed me vegetable soup and cornbread. He brews his own beer," she said, leaning against Chris's chest as he washed her hair.

"Was the sex what you imagined?" He rinsed the shampoo, then turned the shower off, reaching into the dark for a towel.

"Better." She wanted to tell him what Matt had done in the garden but felt embarrassed to share this with Chris. What if only perverts licked genitals? What if only nymphomaniacs liked their genitals licked?

In the locker room, he twisted a combination. "My padlock number's the same as our old locker." He wrapped her in a robe, patting her dry.

This affection was home. This love, familiar. "I won't see Matt ever again. He's a war resister hiding in a cabin in the woods. Comfortable and free."

Chris said, "Why won't you see him again?"

"I'd never find my way back there. Plus, I'll be a recluse in a meadow. With you. Say you'll escape from here and come with me," she said.

Chris shook his head. "I can't leave Luc."

"You can't stick around Basscombe, screwing a teacher."

"You and I can't live in a meadow eating crickets and oak dumplings." When he spoke, his face pinched as if the taste of bugs was already in his mouth.

"We won't eat crickets." The disappointment Celeste felt overwhelmed her. How would she persuade him to change his mind? He'd manifested his dream. He'd manifested Luc. As she slipped into her clothes, she said, "I explored the perimeter of Basscombe. There's a secluded circle of redwoods behind the manzanita. Meet me there in the morning? We'll come up with a plan for our future."

Chris bent close, studying her face. "I have a plan, and it includes Luc."

Celeste frowned. Chris believed he was in love. As long as he lived in that state of euphoria, he wouldn't leave Basscombe. "We'll add him in, okay? Our woodsy remake of *Giovanni's Room*."

"Celeste, go home before you're caught."

"To Bernadette and George? Are you insane? No goddamn way am I going back to them."

"You'll get in a shitload of trouble when they find you. Maybe sent to juvenile hall," he said.

Celeste squeezed water from her hair, watching droplets fall on the floor. "You have a boyfriend. You want sex. I understand. What you've got to understand about me is I'm committed to making *Walden*. I'm going to live in the woods. You can join me. You can bring Luc. That part's up to you. I'm becoming a girl Thoreau." She slipped into Matt's jacket.

Chris finished getting dressed, threw her towel into the hamper, and leaned against the lockers. "I really appreciate what it took for you to get here."

"I've lived an entire life in the past two days. Like I'm thirty, not sixteen. Happy late birthday, by the way."

"My Gemini twin." Kissing her lightly, he added, "It'll be easier for me to meet you on Sunday. Most of the boys and teachers go to church. Afterwards, there's an enormous banquet. I'll have a few hours free."

"Cheers to other people's need for church. Cheers to Baldwin and Thoreau. Cheers to us living the themes of our favorite books. Cheers to sex. Cheers to hair regrowing." Rubbing his shorn head, she said, "See you Sunday," and kissed him goodbye before disappearing into the blackness of Basscombe's passages.

Spiderwebs, strung from oak to madrone, broke against her face as she walked the narrow path along the river looking for a habitable meadow. Mourning doves cooed. Water rushed by. Apart from these noises, the forest was perfectly silent. Sinking up to her ankles in damp silt and slush, she tugged herself free with each step. Shoreline changed to rock. Bay trees grew close to the river's edge. She climbed over gnarled roots, her feet plunging through patches of watercress submerged in the muddy slosh of mud and stems.

Sun and shadows turned everything whisper green. The river took a sharp twist to the left and formed small rapids. Boulders created a whirlpool, trapping sticks and leaves. The variety of birds surrounding her seemed as if they'd flown off the pages of an encyclopedia and into her life. Plovers, sandpipers, sea gulls, surfers, killdeer, rails.

After miles following this trail, she found her California *Walden.* "The same everlasting serenity will appear in this face of God, and we will not be sorrowful." Purple needle grass grew in clumps, and between those clusters, verbena, stalks of sand bur, tricolored lupine, and mock heather. Plants swayed in the breeze. A lovely, lush field of greens and purples and whites and yellows. Here was where she'd stay as she hatched Chris's plan of escape.

Her stained and damp pantsuit felt too hot to wear on a bright June day. She changed into her skirt and peasant blouse, rinsed her underwear in the creek, and hung them in the sun to dry. "Welcome home, Celeste."

Someone called, "Talking to yourself?"

Startled, she sprung straight up, hitting her head on a low branch. She gripped a stick, holding it like a sword. Her pulse ricocheted.

Matt pushed his way through a thicket of coyote brush. "Hungry?"

"Jesus, you scared me," she said with irritation and surprise, but mostly relief.

Matt squatted on the ground. "Sorry, Celeste. I should've identified myself." He opened a bag, offering her a peanut butter and jelly sandwich and a package of cookies. "You smell like cheap soap and shampoo."

"How'd you find me?" She ripped open the cookies, stuffing wafers into her mouth. She offered him one but hoped he'd decline. It would take all the willpower she had to ration this dessert until Sunday, when Chris promised he'd bring food.

Wiping crumbs from her chin with the pad of his thumb, he smiled. "I've spent a couple years exploring these woods. This meadow is between the place where I dropped you off and one of the only trails to Basscombe that doesn't go through poison oak brambles. I figured you're a smart explorer." He opened his backpack, removing a few Stony Brooks and more sandwiches.

She tore the sandwich in half and bit into the center, swilled a beer, and thanked him for the food.

"Use the empty bottles to gather drinking water from the creek." He kissed her, his mouth parting hers, his tongue circling.

He tasted like weed and toothpaste rather than weed and molasses, or weed and fried eggs, or weed and her. They stopped kissing long enough for her to sip more beer, eat another cookie and sandwich. She could go on like this all day. Booze. Sugar. Lips. Tongue. Peanut butter.

Reaching into the front pocket of his backpack, he removed a box of condoms. "I went to the store and bought you a present."

When they'd had intercourse twice in the garden and once in the cabin, she hadn't thought about protection. "We were careless, weren't we? I can't have a baby."

"I doubt you're pregnant after one time."

She held up three fingers.

He slipped his hand from her knee to her thigh, saying "I like you," as he shook a condom from the box into her palm.

She'd never seen a rubber before and wondered how something that fit inside a square smaller than a cookie could slide over a penis. She almost asked him to put the condom on to see how it worked but didn't want to jump into intercourse. Enjoying her beer and eating another sandwich were her priorities.

His hand inched farther up her thigh. "No panties is an open invitation."

Pointing to the patch of sun where her underwear hung across a branch, she shrugged. "Laundry day. I didn't know I'd have company."

"I was thinking you needed something else to wear other than a miniskirt and an ugly pantsuit." He pulled a red halter dress from his backpack. "I'll buy you other clothes. Anything you need. Obviously, panties is on your list." He handed her a small grocery sack.

"There's more?" Inside the bag was a carton of sanitary napkins and a sanitary belt. Blushing, she stammered, "Umm…"

"It's only a matter of time before you need those. I know women."

When she'd packed the duffel and run away, she hadn't thought about getting her period, and felt embarrassed he had. "I appreciate everything."

Matt said, "Follow me. I have something to show you." He grabbed his backpack and led her through the meadow, holding branches aside as she passed through. He stopped near a tree and pointed. "A hidden shelter." Willow branches crossed, forming an inverted nest.

"Wow," she said. "It's beautiful."

Matt crawled through the small opening. Using a flat stone, he swept the area clean of forest debris, then took a pad, sheet, and blanket from his pack and made a bed. "This is for you. Come in."

"You're a gallant knight, Matt."

"I doubt you're a damsel in distress." Wrapping her in his arms, he said, "I don't know what I'd have done if I hadn't met you when I did. I was starting to hate people."

"Condom?" She wanted sex, not sentiment. Wanted strength, not confession. Wanted temporary pleasure, not displays of need.

Ripping the package open with his teeth, he unfurled the condom over his erection.

She touched the sheath. "That's how it's done?"

"You've never seen a rubber before?"

"No." She fingered the extra sheath at the tip. "It doesn't fit."

"That's where the semen pools."

She wondered if Chris and Luc used rubbers. No, probably not. They wouldn't need to, would they?

As he laid over her, the latex sheath slid in and out. He rubbed her breasts, licked and sucked her nipples, pumped a few more times, climaxed. Yanking the condom off, he held it in front to her. "Proof this works."

"How does anyone get pregnant with such a teensy bit?"

Matt laid the rubber on the ground near his head and rolled over to face her. "Are you being sarcastic or are you plain stupid?"

"I'm plain stupid."

"That's not true," he said, and laughed. "You're one of the smartest girls I've ever met. Certainly the ballsiest."

Staring upwards at the inverted nest, she wondered how to ask him to satisfy her. She didn't know the word cunnilingus. Considered cunt and pussy derogatory labels. Labia and vulva and clitoris sounded too old fashioned and doctorly. The sun, high in the sky, lit the branches. The forest sounded alive with chirping and wind rustling the leaves. "Will you do to me what you did in the garden?"

"Eat you out?" He wiggled downward and nuzzled his face against her, his tongue finding the spot. He paused to ask, "Did you find the boy at Basscombe?"

"In a shower stall with his boyfriend." She brushed her fingers though Matt's hair. Thick and long, soft.

"Were they fucking or sucking each other off?"

"I'll leave the details to you." She tried to push away images of their bodies blending in light and shadows, Luc holding onto Chris.

"Say you like me to eat you out." Glancing up at her from between her legs, he grinned. "Say it."

She playfully tugged his hair. "Eat. Me. Out."

He gripped her waist, flipped her onto her stomach, yanked her hips in the air, pressed his body against her, and stroked his penis until it hardened again. "Were they doing it like this?"

Leaning on her elbows, she stared where the willow branches had been forced into earth. Splintered and ragged, tied and woven with string, if she pulled one end, the entire dome could snap, collapsing.

"Too late for a rubber, Little Cutie," he said, and came.

Untangling herself, she climbed from the nest, went to the creek, scrubbed her genitals, hoping to wash away his semen. Next time he came to the meadow, she'd insist he put on protection and insist he pleasure her.

Cowering behind the manzanita hedge outside the school on Sunday, Celeste watched as Chris walked to the edge of the garden, then ducked as he ran toward her.

Chris flew into her arms, his grip tight.

A moment later, Luc did the same. "Bonjour, mademoiselle."

"You're here, too? Bonjour." By daylight, she admired this boulder of a man. This exotic man. This tall, muscular man. This man who represented everything Bernadette hated. Black. Foreign. Queer.

Luc pulled a leaf from her hair. "Buckeye."

"You're coming with us?" She'd wanted Chris to herself. She wanted to discuss the plan for their future.

Luc said, "If this is fine with you."

Chris slipped his arm through Luc's. "She's happy you're joining us. Aren't you, Celeste? You're happy." Standing beside Luc, Chris looked as delicate as an eggshell.

"At least this time I am clothed," Luc said with a smile.

Blushing came easy as she pictured Luc in the bathhouse, bent over Chris. She turned and led them to the hidden redwood circle. The sky barely visible above the statuesque trees. Sunlight streaked in magical spears. "Our secret fairy ring."

Chris said, "A fairy ring for fairies," and he handed her a paper plate, contenting, "Your Sunday supper as promised."

She folded back the aluminum foil, releasing the aromas of meatloaf, mashed potatoes, green beans, and apple pie. "How do you say the word delicious in French?"

"Magnifique," Luc said.

"Magnifique," she repeated. The illusion of the meal superseded the actual taste. Celeste didn't care. She was hungry.

Chris put his hand over hers. "Don't be mad." Before she had the chance to respond, he said, "I called my parents to tell them I heard from you. Bernadette's been phoning them."

"What? Bernadette knows where I am?" Her heart felt as if it would explode through her chest.

He shook his head and quickly spoke, "I told them I heard from you. I didn't say I saw you. I said you're somewhere in Alaska."

Huddled against the trunk of a redwood, she uttered, "Somewhere in Alaska?"

"It seemed like a place you'd go to get lost, doesn't it? Bernadette and George need to know you're not dead in a ditch. You owe them that much."

"I doubt they've even bothered to walk down the street and look for me." She wiped her mouth on her sleeve. "If I had parents like yours, I wouldn't have deserted them. I'm an incidental in Bernadette and George's lives. I don't owe them anything."

Chris looked at Luc and said, "A dramatic interpretation of a high school girl's suburban life as retold by Celeste."

He knew nothing about her last day at home, the drunken rant, the terrible words Bernadette called them both. He wasn't present to witness George's pathetic response. Chris hadn't felt the fury she did when she threw the frying pan at the bourbon decanter. Celeste said, "They'll be better off without me." Scooping gravy, she slathered it over the meatloaf and stuffed it in her mouth.

Luc said, "Appelez-les au téléphone. Let them hear your voice to know you are safe." While he spoke, he stroked the curve of Chris's neck and squeezed his shoulder.

"I'm not going to call them." She balled up the aluminum foil and dropped it on the empty plate. "Even the idea makes me queasy."

Luc said, "If they believe you're doing well, they'll be pleased for you."

Celeste wadded the napkin in her fist. "You don't know Bernadette and George. George is only pleased when Bernadette is happy. She's only pleased if she's got a Limestone in her clutch."

Luc said, "Any parent would be relieved to hear from their runaway child. C'est la vérité?"

"Stop talking about Bernadette and George. They're my past," she said with annoyance at Luc's interference. "Chris and Walden are my future."

"Luc, too, " Chris said.

"Then, I'm inviting Matt," she said. "Maybe."

Luc put his finger to his lips. "Shhh. If we're loud, we call attention to ourselves. If I'm caught outside the school's boundary with you, I'll lose my job. I'll be sent back to France."

"That's not why you'd lose your job," Celeste said, tilting her head toward Chris.

"You make an excellent point, mademoiselle. My crime is loving Chris," Luc said.

Celeste groaned louder than she'd intended.

"Celeste's not her usual bubbly self." Chris kissed Luc. "She's turned into a skeptical pessimist who doesn't believe in romance."

She said, "I'm a realist."

"Believe in romance, Celeste," Luc said, "or you'll break my heart."

"The girl has a terminal case of lingering melancholy. Seeing others in love irritates her," Chris said.

"No, it doesn't," she said, shaking her head and frowning.

Chris and Luc exchanged a glance. Chris said, "What do you call it then?"

"Compared to you two, everyone's melancholic." Celeste pictured the inverted nest, Matt between her legs, but he stopped, turned her around, and rammed into her, asking if that's what Chris and Luc had done when she found them. Her, unsatisfied and sore. Him, coming when she answered yes.

Luc placed his hand against her forehead. "Is your illness contagious? This realism you speak of? Should I be afraid of becoming sad, too?"

"No, don't become sad," Chris said.

Celeste understood how Luc's beautiful accent would seduce a gay schoolboy who loved everything French. She said, "My heart split in half the day Chris's parents made the worst decision of their lives."

Luc said, "For me, this is the opposite. This is the best choice his parents could have made. I don't mean to diminish your grief, Celeste. Chris and I sont chanceux en amour."

She tried to recall some French she'd picked up from watching a film Mr. B showed in the library's audiovisual room. The movie was for students studying at the junior college, but Celeste had snuck in. "Vivre sa Vie. Vivre sa Vie. Breaks easily. Same old story makes the world go around."

"You know this film?" Luc asked. "A naughty cinema, Celeste."

"Which is why I sat through it even though I had no idea what they were talking about," she said. "The character's suffering was mixed with joy and sex."

"Every love story has its ups and downs," Luc said. "This is the surprise, don't you think? Soon you will fall in love and you will be up."

Celeste said, "You two are the ones who'll soon be up."

They burst out laughing. Shoulders rose and fell, heads tossed back, mouths open, eyes watering.

The levity helped Celeste build trust with Luc. Of course Luc fell in love with Chris, she thought; who wouldn't? "I can't wait for you to see my willow nest shelter." She didn't mention Matt coming to the meadow to feed and clothe and screw her. Too difficult to explain how she wanted but didn't want him. How his intensity frightened and thrilled her. She'd save that conversation for another time.

Luc said, "Your nest I would like to see someday, mon petite oiseau."

"Luc specializes in earthy elemental design," Chris said. "I fell madly in love with Professor Laurent the moment he handed me the syllabus for his art elective."

"Sexy syllabus," she said.

"I read it so many times I memorized every single word of it." Chris stood up, brushed off his pants, and recited, "Intro to Natural Design. We will construct a tile mosaic with the depiction of a bird sailing through the sky toward a jungle. On each branch, fruit hanging like miniature suns. A smaller bird, primed and ruffled, resting on a nest in the Rousseau foliage, a dainty head turning, gazing at a field of poppies growing along the entire base of the mural. Your task will be to recreate the essence of this image. See me for details."

"He did come see me for details." Luc grinned.

Chris laughed. "I sure did."

"Celeste," Luc asked, "do you believe in love at first sight?"

She recalled her dread about Chris being alone for the rest of his life while she was forced to marry and have a dozen children. "I don't know," she said. "It's never happened to me."

"Luc and my many rendezvous in the bathhouse are full of visionary magic," Chris said.

Celeste said, "The shower stall isn't exactly a Quixotic windmill."

"Au contraire," Luc said.

She needed a new plan. Chris wouldn't live in the forest without Luc. The nest was barely big enough for two people. She'd have to find a more accommodating *Walden.* Maybe Paris was the answer.

Yellow from head to toe in waterproof clothing, Matt stomped past the oaks and into the meadow. "I brought you an umbrella and rain jacket." He held the items in the air. "A big summer storm's coming. You need to move. This campsite will turn into a slough."

Sitting next to the willow shelter, Celeste looked up at the blue sky. "What are you talking about?"

"It's already cloudy at the cabin." He set the rain gear down, then yanked a bud from his beard, crushed the weed between his fingers, took a pipe from his pocket. Cupping his hand around the match, he puffed until he'd emptied the bowl.

"I doubt it's going to rain."

He ripped apart another bud. "Look up."

As if Matt orchestrated the change in weather, white clouds paraded through the blue sky, stacking one on top of the other. Soon, they were rimmed with gray. He handed her the pipe and lit a match.

"I'll take my chances." She didn't want to journey in the opposite direction of Basscombe. Chris promised to meet her the following Sunday in the redwood circle. She needed to be close.

"Unwise decision, Cutie. Good luck when this place turns into a swamp. The ground gets as spongy as quicksand," he said. A breeze blew. He had to relight the pipe. "Your shelter will flood."

The temperature dropped a few degrees. She tucked her legs beneath her, hugging them to her chest. "It's not going to rain."

"I've lived here for years. You've been in Wilder a week. Who do you think knows what they're talking about?" Holding a lit match to the bowl, he urged her to take a quick puff.

"What if my photo's all over town, and I'm spotted riding in your truck? We'll both be in trouble," she said, exhaling smoke.

Matt ducked through the doorway of the nest, gathered her belongings, and stuffed them into her duffel. He poked his head out to say, "We're not going to town today but even if we did the people in Wilder don't give a shit about who you are, what you do, or who you do it with. The locals only care about supporting their meager, pathetic businesses now that logging's no longer viable. This place was about to blow off the map until hippies and resisters showed up, bought supplies to build houses and crap to put inside them. Everyone wins if everyone looks the other way."

"What if there's a reward for me?" There would be a reward, wouldn't there? she thought.

"If you're worried, you can dye your hair. Cut it. Wear hats. Change your clothes. Become a ghost of your past. Like me. I'm not real." He tossed the packed duffel at her feet and climbed out of the nest, scooped the rain gear in his arms. "I've been hiding awhile, and not one person has paid any attention."

She said, "You told me the draft begins in December. You have six months before they'll come looking for you."

"Little Cutie, Vietnam War resisters make all sorts of mischief. Don't you watch the news?" He raised his fist in the air, then flashed her the peace sign.

"Handmade bombs?"

"Do I look like a violent man? Not bombs. Sit-ins. Marches. Riots. Broken windows. Molotov cocktails."

"Molotov cocktail?" She clasped the narrow pipe stem between her lips. Holding smoke inside her lungs. Exhaling, she said, "I need to be close to the school. Chris won't know where to find me."

"This rain will keep everyone inside for a few days. He won't be looking for you until this shit storm passes."

Her shoulders drooped. She shrugged, hoping to shake off the heaviness.

"Once I have you cornered, you'll be greatly rewarded." Laughing, he took the pipe from her, shook ashes onto the ground. "Let me show you." He pushed her dress above her waist and knelt before her.

A squirrel zoomed past. Big and boisterous.

Luc, sensual and dark and romantic, came into her mind. She imagined him watching them, then asking to experiment with her. "Eat me out," she uttered as she came.

"You like that? You like what I do to you." Taking her hand, Matt pulled her off the ground. "Time to get out of here. Rain's about to begin." He slung her duffel over his shoulder.

Droplets clung onto the leaves and branches, falling over and around them. She slipped into the rain jacket and followed him up the trail to his truck.

On the seat was a new magazine. The cover showed a large-breasted woman. The subheading: "Come to me, Daddy." The tip of her tongue poked between pink lips. Celeste said, "Why do you read stuff like this?"

"Free love, Little Girl. Free pussy. Free cock. Free fucks." Rain pounded the windshield.

"Stop calling me 'Little Girl.' I already told you that."

"That's what you are, isn't it? A little girl running away from her big, bad mama and papa."

Celeste rolled down the window and tossed the magazine into the woods. "I'm not a runaway anymore. I'm an outlaw citizen of Wilder."

"Jealous of my big-boobed woman?" he said in a singsong voice. Putting the truck in reverse, he backed down the dirt road until he found a spot to turn around. He sped past madrone trees and through an oak canopy, stopped, jumped out, opening a gate that didn't need to be there. Barbed-wire fence broken on one side, nonexistence on the other. Clouds thickened. Rain pelted. Matt continued driving along a rutted road, over a hill back toward the river, then straight ahead until his truck almost slammed into the doors of a dilapidated barn.

'Where are we?" She felt an inkling of fear. "This isn't your cabin."

"Ranchers used to bring sheep to this old barn for shearing. The ground's stomped to shit from all the livestock. Not good for crops or much of anything else." He gestured wide. "The barn's yours for as long as you want. We're standing on the southern corner of my forty acres."

"I can live here? Seems too good to be true." Was he corralling her until Bernadette and George showed up, and he could collect his reward?

"You'll need to fix it up," he said.

"Chris can live here, too?"

He picked up a stone and tossed it at the wooden siding. "Yours to do what you want. As long as you keep my secret."

"I told you I'd keep your secret if you keep mine." She glanced around. On one side of the barn, a cobbled creek ran through a thicket of oak and madrone. On the other sat a tireless, rusty flatbed truck. "How do I get to Basscombe? Is it far?"

"Trail runs along the creek to the river. Takes about an hour." He reached into his pocket and pulled out a web of thread, eyed the wad, tossed it on the ground. She'd noticed this habit of his before, pulling items from his pocket, studying the contents, throwing whatever away.

Pointing to a bright star burning through the drizzle, she said, "Mars."

"The Greek god of men," he said. "Love is a kind of warfare."

Impressed he quoted Ovid—one of Mr. B's favorite authors—she kissed him, long and deep and heartfelt. She'd never initiated a kiss before. "You're generous and kind to me. Thank you."

"You're all the thanks I need, Little—"he paused, eyed her up and down—"Cutie."

Above, black clouds swirled. Little Cutie seemed almost as bad as Little Girl, but for now, she'd stay quiet. Matt gave her a place to live, the foundation for Walden. She'd acquiesce to his diminutive name-calling and his demand for sex. If that's what it took to live in the barn, she'd be compatible. She liked Matt fine, but she loved the chance to build a future with Chris.

Matt kicked open one side of the double door. Straw-strewn floor. Horse stalls with broken gates and intact walls. The smell of manure and mold wafted from the wood. "We'll clean this place up. It'll be almost as good as new," Matt said, and climbed a ladder to a hayloft. He leaned over the banister. "Your bedroom. Come see."

A mouse darted past her foot, disappearing through a hole in the wall. "I need a cat," she said, hurrying up the ladder. Hay bales lined the perimeter of the loft. Through an open window, wind blew, cleaning away the manure scent.

With the side of his arm, Matt swept loose straw into a pile, fluffing and shaping the hay into a pseudo bed. He pulled her down beside him. Straw poked her backside. The eerie sound of a churning storm rustled through cracks in the siding and roof. "I can't stay long today," he said, untying the cord of his pants. "Visitors coming to my cabin."

"Visitors?" she said, surprised at the pang of jealousy stabbing her gut.

"Business associates. I'd take you with me, but I'm not ready for them to meet you. They'd want me to share. I want you all to myself."

"I'm not yours to decide what to do with." His fingers inside her proved this may not be entirely true. She shifted her weight, leaned on her elbows. "What's your business?"

"Grass and snow."

"Grass and snow?"

"Pot and cocaine."

"Cocaine?" She didn't want to be having sex with a drug dealer. "Is that another reason you're hiding?"

"Don't worry about everything. It's no big deal. A little extra cash flow, a little extra fun to keep me revved." Taking a condom from his pocket, he ripped the package open. "Put this on my cock."

As she unfurled the rubber, rain pounded the roof. Through the window, a cool drizzle. The ceiling had a spiral pattern of knot holes. Celeste moaned, "Fly me to the moon, Matt."

"I'll fuck you to Mars," he said. Running his hand through her hair, he lifted the strands, brushed her breasts with the ends. "You're the best thing to come into my life in a long time."

Any reservations she'd had about Matt disappeared. He gave her a barn. Her home. Chris's home. Freedom. Release from earth's gravity. Floating off into the wild frontier of space and the woods of California. Her *Walden*. The comfort of having someone else to care about.

The rumble of Matt's truck was a welcome relief to a night and day spent alone. "Did you find a cat to catch the mice? They were active last night," she asked.

"Not a cat. I do have presents, though." Lifting a tarp, he named each item as he loaded it into a wheelbarrow. Bottle of bleach, wire brush, broom and mop, insulation, tarpaper, tacks, plywood, saws, and hammers.

"The Fuller Brush man arrives on my doorstep," she said, then told him about George's profession.

Matt joked what a corny job that would be to ring doorbells, forcing a hard sell on women who'd rather be doing anything other than cleaning up after their husbands and kids. "Your old man probably got a few bored housewives throwing themselves at him."

She'd never considered George capable of an affair. He doted on Bernadette, but maybe she was wrong. Maybe he just endured his wife.

An overhead cloud released a barrage of rain. Laughing, Matt hurried with the wheelbarrow to the barn. "It's cool you call your parents by their first names. Antiestablishment."

"I'd call them Mommy and Daddy if they acted like that."

He pulled her damp peasant shirt over her head but didn't grope her. Instead, he draped the blouse over the edge of a horse stall to dry. He threw his down jacket around her shoulders. "I need to buy you some warm clothes."

She slipped her arms through the sleeves and zipped. Putting her hands in the pocket, she found a receipt. He'd spent close to seventy-five dollars.

Matt placed a mousetrap near the front doorway. When Celeste asked if he could put it out of view, he snickered. "You need to get used to seeing dead animals if you live in the woods."

"No, I don't." She laid straw over the metal trap. "You can't make me."

They laughed together. "I can't make you? Wanna bet?" Matt stroked the nape of her neck. He bent close and kissed her. A pleasant kiss. A gentle kiss.

"How was your meeting with your business partners?" she asked.

"Know what happens when you drop your guard and people you thought were trustworthy shit all over you?"

"Sounds awful." A pipe, bud, and match were in the pocket of his jacket. She crumbled the bud, stuffing it in the bowl. Struck the match, inhaled.

Matt grabbed the pipe from her, grumbling how she'd packed it too loose. "They screwed me. Literally and figuratively."

"What do you mean?" She felt a tinge of trepidation about hearing the answer.

"While my business partner gave me head, his girlfriend stole cash behind my back. When I fucked her, he packed the car with snow." Matt spoke loudly, beating out the barrage of rain on the roof. He emptied the bowl, dropping ashes onto the barn floor.

"Your business partner robbed you?" The rest of what he said confused her. What did he mean by 'gave me head'? She wanted to know but didn't want to ask.

"Living in the wild means you gotta stay alert, Little Cutie. Never let the other person know all your plans, and don't steal from those who provide for you." He picked up a hammer.

His sentence seemed like a warning. "I'll never take anything from you, Matt. I hope you know that."

"You took a bud without asking." He used the claw of the hammer to pull nails from the top of a horse stall.

Celeste unzipped the jacket to give back to him. "I won't steal from you. I won't lie. I shouldn't have taken the bud."

"It starts with the little things," he said. "Keep the jacket on. It's chilly."

Stroke his ego, she thought. Stroke his id. Stroke whatever would prove her trustworthy. "Wearing your coat, I felt like your girlfriend. Is that stupid?"

"Why would that be stupid?"

"Do you want a girlfriend?"

The creaking of long nails pulled from wood echoed in the empty room. "You're my little pussy cat."

"I need a real pussy cat to catch the real mice," she said, taking the broom and sweeping straw and dust.

Over the following few hours, they shoveled horse and sheep manure into the wheelbarrow, took it outside, emptying it in the spot Matt said would be a good place for a garden. They scrubbed stalls with bleach, mopped the floor until the pine glistened. Outside, Celeste held plywood over large holes in the siding while Matt hammered it into place. Light sparkled in rain puddles. The air had the tangy, lemony scent of pennyroyal.

Nails held between Matt's teeth gave him the appearance of a madhouse carnival clown. When Celeste told him this, he forced a comical snarl. "Want me to eat you out?" The nails wiggled up and down as he spoke.

"Not at the moment," she said, and giggled.

"I've got my eye on you, Celeste. I'm vigilant about people in my life," he said. "Here's some advice. Plan ahead. Always be two steps ahead of everyone else." Rolling tarpaper on the floor, he used box cutters to slice thick strips, then took it outside, climbed on the roof, securing the rows in place with wide squat tacks.

Celeste barely listened as she went up and down the ladder, heavy tarpaper slung across her shoulders, carrying rolls the weight of a small child. The heaviness strained her neck. She stopped to rub her muscles. "Can I take a break for a minute?"

Matt snapped his fingers. "You're a mountain girl now. If you want to survive, you're going to have to toughen up."

She didn't argue. She knew he was right.

After they'd hammered the last of the tarpaper, Celeste stood on the waterproof roof, looking around at the sweeping view of the meadow, the oak and madrone forest, rusty truck, dirt driveway, creek. "I love it up here."

As he climbed down the ladder, he said, "I've got to take care of a few things in town. I'll bring more supplies when I come back."

Shielding her eyes from the sun, she peered at him. "Tonight?"

"Wait and see," he said. Within moments, his truck zoomed away.

She gathered the tools, putting them in the corner of the barn. Crickets sang. Bats swooped close, diving after mosquitoes.

At the creek, as she was undressing to bathe, the box cutter she'd stashed in the pocket of Matt's jacket dropped to the ground. Using her thumb, she pushed the blade from the shield, stared at the metal, the slanted edge. Sharp. Dangerous. She grabbed a strand of hair, slicing through. It fell to the ground, long and wavy. The color of California hills at the beginning of summer. Light brown and sun-streaked. She sliced another. Sliced more. A breeze tickled as if she wore a hat made from wind. Wisps of hair clung to her temples and the nape of her neck and the top and sides of her scalp. Wisps like fairies. She felt light. She felt free. She felt brave. She scooped her old hair, tossing it in the water, then submerged her body, rinsed her scalp, watched locks swirl and float away. If a Missing poster hung in the town square, no one would recognize her. Celeste, the changeling. Girl to woman.

She lay on the bank, listening to birds. Later, in the near dark, she woke shivering.

Matt's truck was parked in the driveway. Walking through the door, she called, "Don't be alarmed."

He turned toward her. "Holy shit. Kissing you will be like kissing a Basscombe boy." Brushing his hand across the top of her head, he smiled. "Could be nice."

"I hope not," she said, but maybe Chris would like her better this way? Maybe he'd find her boyishly attractive?

Matt unzipped the jacket and reached inside, cupping her breasts. "Nope, still a girl." He gestured to crates of kitchenware and food. "While you were butchering yourself, I went to town and got a few supplies."

"You're buying me all of this?" More debt. More to owe him.

"Who's going to stop me from doing what I want to do?" Putting utensils in a jar and glasses on a shelf, Matt looked at her, his eyes narrow. "The night we were in the garden at my cabin, I told you something. Do you remember?"

"You said quite a few things."

"Free love is what we do around here. No barriers and boundaries. Democracy is the cause America claims it's fighting for. Bullshit propaganda. Fucking each other until our hearts bleed red, white, and blue is true power."

Celeste said, "I don't understand what you're saying."

"Stupid girl, I'm saying I want to fuck you like you've never been fucked before."

Bare and covered in goosebumps, her legs felt weak as if standing in gelatin. "You're the only one I've ever had sex with."

"I've got a surprise for my girlfriend. In the hayloft." With one swoop, he flung her over his shoulder, carrying her up the ladder.

The straw mattress was covered with a cotton pad, sheets, blankets, pillows, and a flowered bedspread. Indian tapestries hung from the ceiling, creating the illusion of walls. A kerosene lantern sat on a wooden platform. Lined along a makeshift shelf sat a dozen books.

"Books?" She scooted over to take a peek. Austen. Brontë. Fitzgerald. Steinbeck. "Are these yours?"

"Bookmobile. I'll take you when it's time to return them."

Matt cared for her. Cared for her happiness. Cared for her mind as well as her body. As long as he wanted to provide for her, she'd let him. As long as Chris could live there, and Luc, too if it came to that. She kissed Matt. "I love this hayloft, Matt."

They tussled like puppies, then like beasts. On the floor below, she heard the snap of a mousetrap.

The hike from the barn to Basscombe took close to an hour. "You must live in the present, launch yourself on every wave, find your eternity in each moment," Thoreau whispered in her soul as she walked along the trail, hoping not to get lost.

Luc was the easiest person to spot in the sea of white faces. Chris, she assumed, would be somewhere close by. She'd decided not to wait until Sunday to see Chris. Even if she didn't get the chance to speak to him, a glimpse was all she needed. If lucky, and he spotted her and could get away, she'd tell him about the land she'd named Walden Creek.

From the perch behind the manzanita hedge, she watched as Luc dipped a trowel into a metal bucket, scooped a gray mess, smearing it across the wall. Swab. Cross swab. Wiggled in a tile. Boys gathered around the project, watching him. At his signal, they bent over buckets, scooped and smeared as he'd demonstrated, then began placing mosaic pieces in patches of gradated color. One of the boys—it had to be Chris—brushed Luc's rear end with a trowel. A sparrow on the branch above her chirped. Chris twirled his trowel in the air like a cowboy with a pistol. The bird flew off. Another flew in.

The bell rang. A voice over the loudspeaker announced, "Sloppy Joes. Onion rings. Peach cobbler. Basscombe Boys, time for lunch."

The mural students rinsed tools with the hose, put lids on the grout buckets, and sprinted away, disappearing into what she assumed was the cafeteria.

Chris and Luc hung back, picking up bits of scattered tile. They were close enough to kiss. She prayed they wouldn't. Luc pointed to the building. Chris saluted and left his post like a well-trained military school student. Before the cafeteria door closed, he turned toward Luc, thrusting his hips forward and backward, and blowing Luc a kiss.

She ducked behind the manzanita, sneaking to the garden. Butterflies and bees zoomed. A hummingbird's wings whooshed. Celeste whistled, trying to sound like a bird.

Eventually, she and Luc made eye contact. Hurrying to her, he pulled Celeste down behind the deer fence. "What are you doing here? Merde." He brushed her scalp, tugging the tufts. "Where is your hair?"

She'd scraped her knee against a garden stake and wiped the beads of blood with a leaf. "Probably in the Pacific by now."

"You did this with what? A handsaw?"

"Box cutter," she said.

"I will bring scissors and help you with this. You'll be a French pixie," Luc said.

She shrugged. "I don't want to be a French pixie. I want to be an outlaw. A Wild West outlaw in disguise."

Luc blew streams of air through his lips. His accent sounded stronger, as if frustration confused the letters. "We arranged for your visit on Sunday. You can't come here anytime. It is not a safe option."

"I wanted to tell Chris that I moved," she whispered. "I live in a barn now."

"You found a barn?"

"I'm fixing it up. There's even a rusty old flatbed Matt said I could have. The motor doesn't run, but he'll teach me car mechanics." Her scuffed knee continued to bleed. She pressed another leaf over it.

Luc reached into his pocket and pulled out a terrycloth rag. Finding a corner not spotted with mortar, he dabbed her cut. "You live there with this man?"

Shaking her head, she said, "He lives in his cabin. The barn's on the edge of his land. A trail connects the two. Matt's helping me make the barn habitable. I can stay as long as I want. It's mine. Tell Chris to follow the stacked stone markers along the river."

"Is this place hidden? Is it safe?" Luc peeked past her, eyeing the main school building.

"Completely secret. I'm in hiding. Matt's in hiding. Chris will be in hiding." She paused, then added, "You can be in hiding if you need to."

"Celeste," Luc said. "Do you really have a secret barn?"

"I do. Matt won't give me away. He's a wanted man. He's got a lot to lose, so he understands my whereabouts have to be a secret." She inspected her knee. "When you see Chris, tell him I called my parents. They think I'm fishing… in Juno. They told me to be wary of grizzly bears."

"Très bon," Luc said, stabbing a twig through a dandelion leaf, weaving flowers and leaves.

"They're happy to be rid of me. They don't care that I dropped out of school."

"Somehow this is hard to believe," he said. "Either you are not telling the truth, or your parents are monsters."

She sighed. "I will call them one of these days. Once I get to a phone. Tell Chris that I did, okay? I don't want him to keep worrying about it."

Luc picked up a pliant twig, looped the ends, tied them together, and set it top of her head. "I crown you a forest fairy."

Reaching up, she touched the leaves, stems, blossoms. "It's sweet."

Cradling her cheeks between his palms, he kissed one, then the other. Before he opened the garden gate to leave, he said, "Chris will meet you in the redwood circle on Sunday. You can tell him about the barn."

Celeste's fairy crown stayed on her head as she dashed to the hedge, watching Luc examining the mural. Voices and announcements; bluejay squawks and sparrow chirps. Cafeteria doors opened. Chris went in the direction of the cabins. A few moments later, Luc followed him. She hoped they'd be careful.

A Beginning

Standing at the town's only payphone, Celeste deposited a dime in the coin slot. She was about to ask the operator to place a collect call, but then she heard a rumble and stopped. A truck bounding down the road crossed the bridge and parked beside the plaza. Painted on the side: BOOKMOBILE.

"Saved by books." She hung up, happily spared from listening to Bernadette's accusations, spared from suffering through George's stutter, and spared from concocting a false narrative about her new life in Alaska with snowdrifts and canoes and whaling ships. She jiggled the handle to get her dime back. She'd only decided to call them because Chris would keep bugging her until she did. She didn't want to lie to him.

The truck door opened with a pneumatic hiss. "Good afternoon." The librarian, an older man with a long beard and short hair, came around from behind the wheel, extending a hand to welcome her inside. "Let me know if you need assistance."

The entire hour the bookmobile was parked at the plaza, Celeste spent reading. A stack of books grew around her. Her fortress of literature.

When the time came for the truck to move to the next town, the librarian said, "Wilder isn't very literate." Not one other patron had come by.

The Dewey Decimal System makes shelving easy, Celeste

146

thought as she began putting books back.

The librarian said, "What infuriates me is when no one bothers to check anything out."

She shrugged. "I don't have a card."

"I'll set you up with one."

"Maybe next time." What if he recognized her from a missing-persons poster, turned her in, and collected a reward? She moved toward the door.

His mouth twitched as if a bee was trapped inside. "Take this gal's card." He pulled one from a file box. "Haven't seen this lady in a good ten years. Or you can have your choice of any of these." A dozen cards littered the counter. "Check out a couple of those books you were skimming through."

"I can have a card? Are you sure?"

"If you're a local and bring the books back, go ahead."

Celeste said, "I'm a fast reader. I'll return them on time."

He stamped the due date on the index cards and slipped those into the pocket sleeves of *Pride and Prejudice* and *Invisible Man*. "Before you skedaddle, let me do my official duty of recommending a book I think a young person like you will particularly enjoy." He removed a book from the shelf. "Mesmerizing read."

She stared at the title: *The Book on the Taboo Against Knowing Who You Are*, by Alan Watts. Opening it, she read, "Other people teach us who we are. Their attitudes to us are the mirror in which we learn to see ourselves, but the mirror is distorted."

"What do you think?" the librarian said. "Suit your fancy?"

Celeste read it over again more slowly. "I think I have an idea what it means. We see ourselves by how others see us?"

"You're my kind of girl. Willing and adventurous and mischievous. That's how I see you." He smiled, taking two more Jane Austen books from the shelf. "You were looking at these. They need to be read."

Feeling nostalgic by the thud and clink of the date stamp, she named him Mr. BM, which stood for Mr. Bookmobile.

"I'll be back in two weeks and will have more for you to choose from." He put the selections in a cardboard box.

Celeste hoisted her box on her hip and struggled down the steps. "I probably shouldn't take this many books. I hiked here."

Mr. BM called, "Do you need a ride? I'm heading up the ridge."

"That would be nice," she said.

The engine revved. The belly of the truck rumbled. All those library books, secured in place by tilted shelves and centrifugal force, shook and rattled but didn't fall. Celeste stood by the checkout counter, talking to the librarian. He gripped the wide knob of the stick shift, shifting gears as they moved up the hill, slowing when they turned corners. The bookmobile chugged along the windy road.

"Quite the gearshift, isn't it? They only hire librarians who know how to handle a stick this far from the shaft. I told them I have plenty of practice." Mr. BM turned toward Celeste and smiled.

She worried maybe he was trying to figure out where she lived, and he'd inform the authorities and collect a reward. She asked him to pull over at a random dirt road. "I hope you didn't go out of your way to drive me home."

"I'd drive to Timbuktu for someone who loves the library the way you seem to," he said. When she got out, he honked the horn twice and drove off.

Waiting until the bookmobile vanished around a bend, she balanced the box on her hip and started walking. She recognized the rusty, broken gate at the entrance of Matt's driveway. Since his cabin was closer than the barn, and the books heavy and cumbersome, she headed in his direction.

His truck wasn't there. Chickens zipped around her feet. After sipping water from the hose, she settled in an outdoor rocking chair. Taking *The Book* from the stack, she read through the index and flipped to a chapter entitled, "How to be a Genuine Fake." Wind rustled the trees, a soft beckoning to birds. She skimmed through the chapter and paused when she read, "Sex is no longer a serious taboo. Teenagers sometimes know more about it than adults." Inside the cabin, she stripped off her clothes and sprawled on Matt's bed, eager to prove Alan Watts right.

Eventually, Matt stumbled in. Drunk. Falling on top of her, he put his mouth against her, then laughed. "I forgot you don't have a cock. You look like a boy now."

"I'm not a boy. I've got boobs," she said.

"And a pussy." He passed out with his face between her legs.

She freed herself from his clasp and dressed. She stashed the box in the cab of his truck, grabbed *Pride and Prejudice* from the pile, and walked the trail to the barn. She didn't want to be in his bed when he woke up in the morning, hungover and grouchy.

Sunday, Luc, not Chris, met her in the redwood circle. "Where's Chris?" she asked. "Is he on his way?"

Luc handed her a plate of food. "He's not coming."

"He's sick?" The plate felt warm in her palms.

"KP duty." Luc smelled of cigarette smoke and grout, but beneath those scents, she recognized bathhouse soap. "KP duty means a boy's in trouble."

"What happened? What did he do?" Her stomach hurt.

"During a random locker search, they found a graphic cartoon he'd drawn of a person giving another one a blowjob."

"A blowjob?" Her voice rose in pitch. "They know about him?"

"Not that he's queer, no. He made up a story that he'd been fantasizing about his girlfriend giving him head."

"Giving head means blowjob?" Celeste folded her arms across her chest to hold in her rage.

Luc nodded as he removed the foil from the plate, encouraging her to eat. Biscuits. Gravy. Slices of turkey thin enough to be transparent.

Celeste scooped a spoonful of potatoes. "He needs to be more careful."

"It's been almost two months of our relationship. We can't keep our hands off one another. Being near him without touching, I'm miserable. He's miserable." Luc said.

Speaking with a mouthful of turkey, she said, "It's called self-control for a reason."

"The situation gets worse, Celeste." Luc paused a moment. "His new roommate saw me sneaking into Chris's bunk. Heard us. The boy swore he wouldn't tell anyone, but rumors have already started."

Celeste shook her head, disapprovingly. "Chris should runaway and come live with me."

"He wants to graduate high school."

"Graduate? I'll talk sense into him." She'd never graduate high school, but she didn't care.

Luc scratched his forehead. "Chris and I came up with an idea. Want to hear it?"

"I guess. Yeah, sure."

"I told the headmaster my lady is pregnant. I need to move off campus to be with her." He plucked a green bean from Celeste's plate, popped it in his mouth, chewed, and swallowed before he continued, "A plausible scenario, you agree?"

The turkey tasted salty. "I don't know."

"The headmaster told me if I leave Basscombe, I lose my position as a foreign exchange teacher. No work visa. Goodbye to US and hello to France," he said. "Gladly, I give all this opportunity up. I cannot live without Chris. He cannot live without me. We are desperately in love and wanting to make love without fear of getting caught."

Celeste felt like Chris was about to jump from behind the hedge and say they were joking. He didn't. She studied Luc's expression. "Let me get this straight. You got your fake girlfriend pregnant, and you're quitting your job? The job that pays you? The job that provides room and board?"

"They're patrolling the bathhouse and cabins at night. We have no place to meet. If he's caught, Chris will be sent to a harsher school for delinquents. If I'm caught, I'll be arrested for having sex with a student." Luc exhaled air through clenched lips. "Chris thinks I should live in the barn with you."

Celeste wanted Chris in the barn. "You move in with me?" She pressed her palms into her eyes and rubbed.

"You offered before. That day we met."

"I'll need to talk to Matt." How would he react if she brought Luc home?

"Isn't it your barn? Yours to do with as you please?"

"True, but Matt's paranoid about people," she said.

"We tell him I am also an outlaw in hiding. Also, a hard worker."

"Umm," she said, closing her eyes to envision what Chris had to say about this. If Luc lived with her, someday he would, too. Basscombe graduation was a year earlier than their old school, because it went year-round. Only ten more months. Celeste had nothing to lose and everything to gain. Luc would fix the barn, the truck, put in a garden, teach her French. Matt would appreciate the help. A revised version of *Giovanni's Room* in Walden Creek.

A week later, Luc prepared a horse stall to use as a bedroom. He flung sheets and blankets across a camping pad set atop hay bales. He didn't have much to unpack. A few clothes, toothpaste, almond oil, and a Polaroid of Chris. He pushed a thumbtack through the top of the photo, positioning it on the wall near his pillow.

Celeste hadn't yet told Matt about this arrangement. She decided meeting Luc in person was best, because Matt would fall under the lure of the dashing Parisian, as she had.

Leaning against the horse stall, she said, "Matt hasn't been here in a few days. He never goes longer than three or four. He doesn't trust many people. When I say he's paranoid, I mean really, really paranoid."

"I'll tell him his secrets are safe. Soon, you will see, he grows to like me." He winked. "If he lets me live here, I do whatever he needs. Help anyway I can."

"Be careful how you phrase that offer. His business is illegal. Sells pot and cocaine." She noticed a pair of scissors in Luc's suitcase. "Will you fix my hair?"

Luc smiled wide. "It will be my honor."

"Save me from this mess I've made," she said. Her hair, Matt teased, stuck up like a pinecone.

Luc tossed a towel around her shoulders. He snipped and measured and snipped some more. "French Outlaw Pixie."

Without a mirror to see, she figured anything had to be better than a box-cutter hairdo. "Merci," she said, rubbing her hands over her scalp.

In the late afternoon, Matt's truck rumbled down the driveway.

Celeste said, "Luc, give me time alone with him to break the news about you." She ran outside to greet Matt.

His truck came to a stop beside where she stood. Leaning through the driver's window, Matt said, "Hello, Little Cutie. Glad to see me?" He handed her grocery bags and asked her to help him unload a cushiony purple loveseat. "Look what I brought you."

"Nice," she said. She grabbed hold of one end and helped guide it to the ground. "I have something to tell you, but please don't be angry."

"Not a good way to begin a conversation."

"I'd never do anything to jeopardize either of us," she said. "Especially you."

"What the fuck did you do, Celeste?" The way his pupils narrowed made her anxious.

Clasping his cord belt, she untied the hemp and knelt on the ground. He'd asked her to do this countless times, but she'd refused.

If there ever was a time to make him happy and get what she wanted, this was the moment. She closed her eyes and kissed the tip. Mossy.

Matt held onto her head, controlling the rhythm. Slow. Steady. Slow.

She prayed Luc couldn't see them. How embarrassed she felt with Matt's penis between her lips.

Slow. Steady. Slow. Increased speed. Without warning, he thrust hard enough she almost choked. He moaned, "Little Cutie Cocksucker."

Her mouth filled with semen, salty and rancid. She hated everything about this. Hated the hardened dirt under her knees. Hated Luc for putting her in this compromised position. Hated Matt's insatiability. Did his business partner do this to him? Is that what Matt meant when he said the guy gave him head? He let a man do this, too? But he liked her. She didn't understand anything. Spitting onto the ground, she held back tears.

Matt grinned and tied the cord on his pants. "Takes getting used to." With the heel of his hand, he wiped his crotch. "Practice makes perfect, Little Cutie."

Standing, she brushed the pebbles pressing into her legs. "I need a glass of water."

Matt shoved Celeste aside, knocking her off balance. "Who the hell is he?"

Why didn't Luc wait inside the barn like he said he would? Furious, her cheeks flushed with anger. "He's Luc, Chris's lover. The Frenchman. The teacher. He's who I wanted to talk with you about."

Luc walked toward them. "Bonjour, Matt."

"He's got secrets like we do," she whispered. She pulled a bud from Matt's braid, broke it apart, stuffed it in the pipe he kept in his pocket. Lit the weed. Inhaled. "He could get arrested."

Luc offered his hand for Matt to shake. "Merci for allowing me to be a guest on your land."

Matt glanced from Luc to Celeste. He took hold of Luc's hand and didn't let go, then jerked Luc forward. "I didn't."

The taste of ejaculate coated her tongue. Puffing on the stem of the pipe, she longed for oblivion. Smoke swirled toward her nostrils. "We all have things we're hiding," she said.

Luc put his hands on his hips, fingers twitching like a sheriff preparing for a gunfight. "Matt, I know how to keep privacy."

Matt's fists clenched as if he, too, were a gunslinger.

Worried Matt would slug Luc, she stuck the pipe in his mouth. "Take a hit."

The stem wobbled between Matt's lips when he said, "You're the teacher banging the Basscombe boys?"

Luc frowned. "Merde. No. I am in love with one boy."

"Luc can help with the garden," Celeste said, her voice rising in pitch. "Work on the barn. He's got skills."

Matt snickered. "I bet he's got skills."

"If my being here is going to be a problem, I'll leave," Luc said. He backed away from them. Walked toward the barn.

Frowning, Matt grabbed Celeste's arm and tugged her toward the creek. "You didn't ask my permission, Celeste."

"You promised this is my barn. Why should I have to ask?" Water rippled over stones.

He cupped her shoulders, spun her around, forcing her on all fours. "I'm the one who takes care of you." One hand gripped her torso, the other yanked her skirt up, her underwear down.

"You are. You do."

"I told you not to tell anyone about me. It's the one goddamn thing I asked." He slid his finger inside her. "You're on the rag?" He wiped menstrual blood across her thigh.

A twig, poking through the dirt, sliced her palm. Her period had started? She wasn't prepared. "I thought you'd be glad for the help. He's strong."

"You blew him like you blew me? The faggot taught you?" He held onto her waist and pushed himself into her, the slap of his hips stinging. "He has a big cock?"

She stared at the lace of fungus growing along the trunk of a black oak. Orange, white. Ribbon candy. "Luc is Chris's boyfriend. You're my boyfriend," she said. Where was Luc? In the barn, packing? Coming to the creek to check on her? Watching Matt take her from behind like a caveman fucking a cavewoman in heat?

Matt kissed the nape of her neck, whispered into her ear, "Don't screw him before I do, hear me? Don't. I'm the only man you'll fuck. Say it."

Confused by what he said, she turned, trying to look at him. "You're the only man—" She said, "Matt, you're my boyfriend." Boyfriend, whatever that meant.

He pushed, pumped and pumped, then stopped before he came, letting his erection slide from inside her. He collapsed on the ground, squeezing her tightly against his chest. "You take advantage of me, Celeste."

"I don't mean to," she said. What an idiotic mess.

He brushed his fingers along the curve of her waist and hip. He said, "You fuck up a lot."

"I promise Luc will keep quiet. He has more to risk than either of us. Plus, he'll work around the barn. He's gay like Chris. You're not jealous, are you? Don't be jealous." She unbuttoned her shirt, bending over, guiding her breasts to his lips, hoping that would shut him up. "I'll do to you what I did by the truck if you let him stay."

"I don't need you to blow me to get something you want. I want you to blow me because you can't keep your mouth off my cock." He flicked her nipples with his tongue. "If he ever touches these, he's gone."

"I'm pretty sure he doesn't like boobs," she said.

Matt forced his penis into her mouth. Instead of earth, it tasted of iron. Blood. Her blood. She winced and pulled away, but he held on to her head. "If I can eat a girl out when she's on the rag, you can suck a cock that's been inside a bloody cunt."

She pushed him off. "But you didn't eat me out."

He laughed. "If you let him fuck you," he said, and pointed a stick at his head, "bang." He left her lying there. After a few minutes, she heard his truck drive off.

When the meadow grew silent, she waded into the creek. Cum and blood fanning around her like the tail of an exotic bird. She dunked beneath the water, rubbing dirt from her elbows, knees, face. Cold seeped into her bones. She stayed immersed until her shivering rattled her core.

In the kitchen, a corner of the barn, Luc emptied the grocery bags. "Matt brought these inside and said the food's only for you. Your man? Il n'est pas élégant. Too rough."

She walked past him toward the ladder. "You shouldn't have come from the barn when you did."

Shelving the canned goods, he paused. "I hope you didn't do anything out of the ordinary because of me."

From the hayloft, she called, "Like giving Matt a blowjob? Don't worry, everything I do is for Chris." She secured a clean pad in the sanitary garter, wrapping the ends around and around to secure it, then put on old underwear. "Don't forget to drag the loveseat into the barn. If it sits outside all night, animals will destroy it. Understand, Luc? If you're going to stay here, you've got to work."

Luc said, "La bonne nuit et merci."

Taking *Invisible Man* from her pile of books, she curled into a tight ball to read. "Live with your head in the lion's mouth. I want you to overcome 'em with yeses, undermine 'em with grins, agree 'em to death and destruction, let 'em swoller you till they vomit or bust wide open."

Celeste thought of Bernadette's fury and felt grateful for it, because her mother trained her to withstand anything. No one, not even Matt, could unhinge her.

PART THREE

Matt's latest gifts were a treadle sewing machine, a bolt of cobalt blue fabric, shears, needles, and thread. "You said you love to sew." He designated the stall opposite Luc's as the sewing room.

She felt absolutely certain she'd never told him such a stupid thing. "All I've made is my miniskirt and a gym bag." Bernadette's the one who likes to sew, she thought. All those ugly, old-fashioned dresses I had to wear, but how pretty Juliet of Province's outfits were.

"This cobalt color reminds me of you, Little Cutie," Matt said with a smile. "As fresh as a cool ocean breeze."

Preparing for the inevitability of what always came after he gave her a present—even one she didn't want—she glanced around for a soft place to land.

Matt did not push her to the floor. He fished a matchbook and a sliver of a roach from his pocket and sat on the sewing stool. "Put your feet on the treadle and rock like this." As his foot moved, the hand wheel turned and the needle bobbed, the machine clicked and clacked, sounding like a toy train. "Where's Luc? I have a proposition for the grand homme."

Over the month that Luc had lived here, Matt had begun complimenting him on the amount of work he accomplished in the garden, around the barn, and on the rusty flatbed. Luc took the flattery in stride, but Celeste felt triumphant. Matt trusted Luc. Someday, he'd trust Chris, too.

Matt pinched the twisted end of the joint and struck a match. It was too small to clasp, so he tossed the roach, smoky and lit, on the floor, grinding it with the toe of his moccasin. Lifting his chin toward Luc's disheveled bed, he said, "I could use a strong back to help with the new weed crop. Frenchie's an ox. A big, black, beautiful man." He scooted past her, flopped on Luc's bed, and pointed to the photo of Chris. "The boy you're both in love with sure is a dainty kid."

"Luc's boyfriend. My conceptional twin."

"Luc's boy-fuck."

"Matt, shut up. Don't talk like that."

"Sew yourself something nice."

A row of safety pins secured the ripped seams on her skirt. Grass stains streaked across the paisley fabric like renegade comets. "This is fine."

"Make something I'd like."

The supplies were plentiful. Bobbins. Pins. Pincushion. Elastic. Rickrack. Buttons. If she could master the treadle, she'd design something demure and prudish. Floor-length. Shapeless.

Pulling down his pants, Matt said, "Cock's lonely."

Celeste frowned and picked up a pair of scissors. "I want to sew."

"I'll ask the faggot to suck me off."

"Don't say stuff like that." She cut a few yards of fabric, and held it around her waist.

"Where is he?"

"At Basscombe, taking care of paperwork."

Hs hand gripped the base of his penis, and he tilted it toward Celeste. "I promise, Little Cutie, I'll let Luc stay forever if you give me head. Wasn't that your idea?"

Celeste put the scissors and the material on the sewing machine. Closing her eyes, she bent over Matt. He moved her hands to his testicles, encouraging her to stroke and squeeze. She did, disgusted at the way his balls rolled around inside their sack. He asked her to stick her finger up his ass, but she refused. How would she survive his never-ending perversions? Was Matt depraved or adventurous? Was she the problem? Was she a staunch Catholic, judgmental, goody-goody prude? Was sticking a finger up there something everyone did? Feeling him shudder, she pulled back. To keep this semen from soiling Luc's blanket, she wiped it with her hand and wiped her hand on her safety-pinned skirt.

Matt kissed her. "You're getting better. I love you, Celeste. I really do. You like it now, don't you?"

Her heart felt like a nugget of charcoal.

"Come to the cabin for a meal and a shower," Matt said. "You do want a shower, don't you?"

"I can bathe in the creek," she said, but a warm meal and a warm shower did sound good.

"I started cooking this morning. I think you'll be surprised. Go get in the truck."

She hated when he ordered her around. "I've got work to do in the garden." She walked outside and stood next to the wheelbar-row and shovel. Autumn leaves fell. Live oak. Black oak. Buckeye. Clouds floated overhead, puffs of mirth. The patch of sheep-grazed, hardened ground that Luc loosened with the pickaxe needed forest loam and mulch.

"Eat. Shower. Get in the truck," Matt said, coming toward her. He put his arm around her waist, guiding her, opening the door, pushing her in. "You'll be glad you made this decision."

"Okay, Matt," she said, "but you have to promise you'll help me put in the garden."

"I'll do whatever you want." On the drive, he spoke endlessly about his love for cooking. "Everything I know I learned from my mom. Her kitchen is stacked floor to ceiling with cookbooks."

Celeste recalled Bernadette's stained and splattered Redbook cookbook.

In the cabin, Matt laughed at the messy counter. "Homemade chutney. Do you know what that is? It's like a spicy jam." He began to chop vegetables and tofu. Threw them in a pan, sautéed, added spices. "What are you doing standing there? Shower while I finish cooking." Matt handed her a clean towel and tee shirt.

She shampooed her short hair and scrubbed her feet, genitals, underarms, breasts, and neck. Judging by the dirty runoff, pooling near the drain, she had needed a shower.

The table was set with a bottle of wine, curried tofu, white rice, and chutney. Matt had cleaned up, too. His hair, loosened from braids and brushed, draped across his shoulders like golden holiday ribbons. His eyes gleamed in the candlelight. His trimmed beard couldn't disguise his rosy, full lips. He pulled the bench out for her. "You look beautiful. My shirt suits you well," he said.

He's a good guy, she told herself. Unreliable, but good. Rough at times, but generous. Crude, but also sweet. "I've never had curried tofu or spicy jam. I have had white rice," she said with a smile.

He poured the wine and clinked his glass to hers. "What kind of cook is your mom?"

"Bernadette's predictable: Sunday, chicken; Monday, spaghetti; Tuesday, beef something; Wednesday, pork chops; Thursday, lamb chops; Friday, fish; Saturday, leftovers or Chinese takeout."

"No wonder you'd rather have my cock in your mouth."

She hated the way he messed with her emotions, bringing her to a pleasing high, then smashing her down without warning. Disappointed and angry, she jumped from the bench and hurried to the door. "I'm not hungry."

The path from the cabin to the barn was well-worn and easy to navigate, even in the dark. No pants. No shoes. Her anger kept her warm. Self-doubt snuck into her mind. Why had she gotten upset? If she was willing to blow him, why did it bother her when he said it?

Luc wasn't at the barn. She worried the paperwork he'd been summoned to sign was a ruse for sending him back to France. That wouldn't be so bad. She'd console Chris. He'd move in with her. She'd keep him content.

From her hayloft, she heard the door open, heard footsteps across the floor, heard Matt calling, "Little Cutie. Little fucker." He climbed up the ladder. "You're forgiven for ruining my dinner."

"You're not forgiven for saying stupid shit to me." In one hand, she held a box of matches; in her other, a match. She struck the red tip against the black strip, then held the flame to a hay bale. A spark ignited, tiny but fierce.

"You're nuts." He beat the flame with his hand, crushed embers between his fingers. "Your craziness is what I like most about you. It makes me horny, Little Girl." The scent of smoke lingered. He straddled her, pinning the back of her head against the blackened straw.

"Get off me," she tried to say. At that moment, she realized she'd enlisted in a war she couldn't get out of.

In the safety of the redwood circle, Celeste opened the paper bag Chris had brought for her. "There's something sweetly normal about a brown lunch sack and sitting next to my best friend." She started to cry.

"I didn't expect this reaction." Chris offered her a handkerchief. Monogramed on one corner was the fancy letter B.

Celeste dabbed her eyes. "B for Basscombe?"

"B for best friend."

"I miss our old life." She bit into the slice of apple pie, savoring the tastes of Macintosh, sugar, and lemon zest. She pictured the Armstrong's backyard. Their doughboy pool. The abundant citrus. Mrs. Armstrong calling her sweetheart and asking her to stay for dinner.

Chris shrugged. "What I don't miss about our old life is the desperation of believing no one in the world would ever fall in love with me."

"No, not that part, and definitely not my pathetic need to lose my virginity." She slid the tongs of the fork across her plate, spearing crust. "Do you feel sad Luc couldn't come with me today?"

"Sure, but if he has to help Matt with the crop to stay with you, that's what he has to do," Chris said. "I am sad we haven't had sex in almost a week."

"How would you react if you didn't want it and Luc insisted?"

"Impossible," he said with a smile.

"But what if that happened?"

Chris poked the stems of wild daisies through each other. "Is this about your boyfriend?"

"He's not my boyfriend. He thinks he is, and I tell him he is, but he's not."

"Your lover then."

"Lover implies love," Celeste said.

"The guy you screw around with?"

She put the empty plate and fork back in the brown bag. "Matt's a problem."

"I don't like that his business is illegal. I keep warning Luc to be extra careful." Chris placed the necklace of flowers over her head. "At least Matt's letting him stay."

She wanted to inform Chris that she had to blow Matt to make it possible and hated doing it. Did he do that to Luc, or did Luc do that to him? She supposed they did it to each other. "The lemon zest in that pie reminds me of the day we read Baldwin under your tree and decided to find a man to share."

"The day you decided to find a man to share. I was only interested in having a man," he said.

She lifted the daisy blossom necklace and sniffed. No fragrance. "Matt's a lunatic."

He laughed. "As are you, my celestial friend. Aren't you the girl who wanted to spend her life in a spaceship taking care of chimpanzees?"

"He's a lunatic in a different way. Unpredictable."

Chris pulled his shoulders back. "Do you feel safe with him? If you don't, you should move. We'll find somewhere else."

"He wouldn't hurt me. He's not violent." She paused a moment before adding, "Walden Creek is ideal. There's no place better to build our family. I have Matt under control. Don't worry."

Clanging bells in the background signaled the end of Chris's free time. The sun filtered through the redwoods in streaks of white. "Give Luc a huge kiss for me. Tell him I miss his gorgeous—" He laughed before he added, "soul." He hugged her and dashed to the manzanita hedge.

"Until we meet again, garçon beau." She watched Chris crawl on his belly to the garden. When he stood, he twirled a marigold in the air.

By the time she arrived at Walden Creek, almost four hours later, Matt had set up a gravity feed line that brought water from a nearby spring to a platform at the backend of the barn. He'd built an outdoor shower from a funnel, spigot, brackets, elbow joints, PVC pipe, and plumbing glue. The shower head as big as a sunflower hung from the top.

"No more creek baths, Celeste," Matt said, standing on the platform. "Take the maiden voyage."

"Don't we need walls for privacy?" she said.

In the garden, Luc split apart overgrazed earth. He sunk the end of the pickaxe in the dirt and waved at her, calling, "You've arrived. Have a good hike?"

"Chris sends his love."

Luc grinned as he approached. "How was our boy today?"

She brushed the front of the new shift she'd sewn. "He brought me apple pie, as you can tell by the cinnamon sugar glaze."

Matt said, "Wash it before the stain's permanent."

Celeste said, "Chris feels optimistic about the future."

Matt said, "Enough about Chris. More about the shower." He twisted the faucet. Water sputtered before flowing in a wide circle. "Want to take one, Luc? I offered the honor to Celeste. She's suddenly prudish."

"I have not bathed in too many days," Luc said, undressing.

Celeste had only seen three penises before that moment, and none of them looked like Luc's. Torpedo-shaped.

"She's curious about your prick," Matt said, and he winked.

Luc glanced down. "Because I'm uncircumcised?"

"What do you mean?" Celeste asked.

"The doctor didn't cut off the tip when I was born," Luc said.

"Why in the world would a doctor cut the tip of baby's penis?" Celeste said.

"Americans are a barbaric nation full of castrating warmongers," Matt said.

Luc dropped his clothes and climbed in the shower. He immediately jumped away from the spray. "L'eau gèle."

Pointing to the coils of black hose connected to the pipe, Matt said, "Give it a few seconds for the solar to heat the water."

Celeste stared at Luc, trying to understand how cutting off the tip of a penis entirely transformed its appearance. No knobby top. No pink head. A slim point, like a rocket ship. "If I ever have a son, I'm not letting a doctor cut him. Why would anyone do that to a baby?"

Matt said, "Religious reasons, cleanliness, fathers wanting their son's little dicks to look like their own little dicks."

Luc said, "Tradition."

Tugging a bud from his beard, Matt crushed weed between his fingers and stuffed a pipe. "I've heard the foreskin's extra sensitive. The uncircumcised man's pleasure is heightened. My parents robbed me of that. Assholes." He lit a match, held the flame over the bowl. Weed sizzled in the air like a sparkler. He moved closer to Luc and offered him a hit. Luc leaned from the spray of water, clenched the pipe between his lips.

Celeste's cobalt blue dress was in the shape of a rice sack, hiding everything womanly about her, but beneath it, her body sizzled when she looked at Luc.

"The best shower," Luc said, drying off. "If you want, all yours, mon petite oiseau."

"I guess I'm ready to shower," she said.

Matt showed her where to hang her clothing. "Hooks here, away from the spray." He opened a metal box. "A bar of soap and shampoo."

Matt and Luc walked to the barn together, punching and jostling like kids.

Under the water, Celeste closed her eyes, imagining Luc beside her, his erotic penis rising and elongating. She wanted to discover if the foreskin was more sensitive. Sometimes, she felt like she'd grown up too fast. Other times, she felt grateful not to be a dumb, bored eleventh-grade girl living at home with disinterested parents. Maybe my independence started the year Kennedy died and I spent three days drunk and on my own, she thought, or maybe it started in Michael Paul's bed when I decided I didn't have to get married to have sex.

She shuddered and opened her eyes. "Matt, not now."

Matt pinned her body, fucking her against the wooden stake. Rough hewn. Brackets holding the pipe in place. The sun went down and the water ran cold. Eventually, he groaned, turned off the faucet, and reached for a towel, wrapping her as tightly as a cocoon. "You have small cuts on your back. You should have told me I was hurting you."

Luc came around the corner, whistling. Dressed in a heather turtleneck and jean bellbottoms, he said, "Almost ready, Matt?"

Matt gestured to himself. "Do you want me to go like this? It would be titillating for all those Basscombe boys if a naked man showed up at the party."

Celeste frowned. "What party? Where are you going?"

Luc said, "Matt's driving me to Basscombe for a celebration."

"You don't work there anymore, but they're letting you come to a party?" she asked.

Luc said, "Americans are generous people."

She eyed Matt. "Why are you going? Who will you say you are?"

"His pregnant wife's brother," Matt said. "Or cousin. Or uncle. Who cares?"

"There will be a talent show," Luc said with a smile. "Chris and some guys are dressing in drag and doing a mock ballet."

Matt said, "I'll be back in a minute. Dressed and ready to go."

Her gut clenched. When Chris brought her the apple pie, he hadn't mentioned anything about a talent show. No arabesque. No fouette. Nothing. "I'll come with you. You can introduce me as your wife."

"Too late for you to be my alibi," Luc said. "You would be showing a belly by now."

"I'll stuff a pillow under my shift."

Luc stooped to look her in the eye. "I'm sorry to tell you this, and please don't be offended, but you don't look like a Basscombe faculty wife."

"What does that mean?"

"Your appearance isn't apropos to the clean-cut image the school puts forth."

"Being a fag is apropos?"

"Celeste," he said. "Don't be cruel."

"You're embarrassed by me, but you're not embarrassed by Matt? He's a hippie."

"Mon petite oiseau, the headmaster would never believe I'm married to—" He paused, rubbing his chin, before continuing, "a crazy girl with short, unruly hair. He sees me as a straight, conservative Frenchman."

"I'll wear my red halter dress. I'll look respectable."

"You're a teenager, Celeste. You can't possibly be my wife."

"Chris is a teenager, too. Someone you were supposed to be educating."

Luc said, "That's unkind."

Matt interrupted them. He'd pulled his hair into a low bun and trimmed his beard. He wore one of Luc's button-down shirts and a pair of dress trousers. He looked decent.

"Matt doesn't know Chris," she said. "I do."

Matt took a joint from his back pocket and handed it to Celeste. "Get stoned."

"I'm sorry your feelings are hurt, Celeste. I wish you could come with us," Luc said, then lowering his voice, he continued, "One more thing. Please don't use the word fag again."

She wondered if Chris told him about the fight they'd had when she called him the same thing and he didn't speak to her for weeks. "James Baldwin uses it."

Luc said, "Because he is one. We can say it. Not you."

Matt said, "Smoke this joint, Little Cutie. Have a pot of chamomile tea. Relax."

Walking away, Luc looked over his shoulder. "When we come back, I'll tell you all about the talent show."

The tires kicked gravel as the truck sped away.

Her life felt ridiculous, irrational, impulsive. She'd made bad choice after bad choice. She should be at home in her childhood bedroom with her books and her stash of Heavenly Hill. Not by herself in the center of nowhere, fucking Matt in a goddamn pipe shower. She sprinted from the barn to the garden to the creek to the meadow, her body hurling through space.

Pulling the pickaxe from the dirt where she'd wedged it the day before, she started splintering the ground, earth crumbling around her feet. Redwood needles spun in the air. Poison oak, with its vibrant red and shiny and alluring leaves, grew thick throughout the woods. When Matt had picked her up hitchhiking, he'd warned her of the plant's danger. Its beauty caught her by surprise.

Hearing her name called, she turned. Dressed in his school uniform, jacket unbuttoned and tossed over his shoulder, his tie loosened and trousers dotted with foxtails, Chris waved to her. Had she manifested an illusion, or was this happening? She propped the axe against a fence post. "Are you a mirage?" she asked, moving toward him. "It's not Sunday. How'd you get away?"

"Guest speaker panel. It'll last for hours. I faked a stomach-ache and got sent to my cabin. They'll probably check on me before dinner. Is Luc around?"

"Working on the crop," she said.

Taking her hand in his, he said, "I'm excited to see Walden Creek."

She led him to the barn doors and slid both of them open to allow sun to light the interior.

His smile grew wider. "Genuinely impressive."

Pointing to Luc's stall, she said, "Your future bedroom."

Chris sat on the hay bale bed, running his palm over Luc's blanket. When he noticed the photograph of himself, he said, "I look like such a little kid, don't I?"

"A lot can change once you start having sex with a man," she said.

In unison, they both said, "But I'm a man, I cried! A man!"

"Why didn't you invite me to the talent show?" she asked. "I had to stay here by myself when everyone was off having a blast."

"As the only girl on campus, you'd be scrutinized. Don't be angry with me. Please. You'd be caught and sent away."

"I was really disappointed," she said, "and sad, but I get it. Thanks for looking out for me."

"Matt's a lunatic, isn't he?"

She pulled back to look him in the eye. "Did he do something to embarrass himself?"

Chris shrugged. "He was a complete gentleman during the party. It was afterwards. We'll talk about it another time. Not now. Show me your hayloft." Chris followed her up the ladder and sat on her bed. "You have quite a few books for a small space."

What Chris said about Matt acting like a lunatic didn't surprise her. Honestly, she didn't want to know what embarrassing thing he did. It would make it even harder to tolerate him.

She handed Chris her tattered copy of *Walden*. "The librarian, Mr. BM—that stands for Mr. Bookmobile—lets me keep these as long as I want. I'm his favorite client."

"You must respect him if you named him after Mr. B."

"Mr. BM's recommendations are interesting. He treats me like an adult."

"Someone has a crush," he said, wiggling his eyebrows.

"He's ancient and smells like mothballs." Immediately, she felt bad for saying something mean about Mr. BM. "Smart, too. Literate."

Curling in the hay beside her, Chris fiddled with the clasps on her overalls, unhitching and hitching them, the sound of metal against metal making a tune. "Me, you, and Luc living here, it'll be our semi-platonic ménage à trois."

"A what?"

"You know what a ménage à trois is, don't you?" Before she had the chance to answer, he said, "Three people together. Usually having sex."

"That's definitely not you, Luc, and me."

He giggled. "Why I said semi-platonic."

She clutched a handful of dried straw. Ash from a stick of incense fluttered. "This is how our life will be after you graduate. Luc and Matt working on the crop. You and me lounging around reading and talking. You and Luc having sex in his stall. Matt and me in the hayloft." She traced Chris's freckles, connecting the dots as if she could create a new constellation all their own.

"The last time my parents phoned, they said your parents are miserable. Freaked out you're missing."

"Good." She wanted Bernadette and George to worry.

"I reassured my parents I heard from you and you're safe," he said.

"When your parents shipped you off to Basscombe, I was so angry with them."

"You know when you can tell someone regrets a decision? I'm pretty sure they're almost at that point." He shrugged. "Mad at themselves for not trying to fix me at home."

She nodded, chewed on the end of a piece of straw, and took it out, pointing it at him. "Your yearbook prank turned out to be a good thing. You and Luc in love. Me in Walden. And as a bonus, your beautiful marijuana artwork adorning the entire yearbook. I bet you liberated a lot of kids. Showed them the establishment is fucked up and can be challenged."

"All I showed any of them was how to get sent to military school." He frowned. "Speaking of Basscombe, I should go."

Hours after he left, it started to rain. Slanting sideways, water found holes in Walden Creek's siding and roof. Drips ricocheted in buckets, dotting the floor. Pings resounded in the room like a decrepitude symphony. Worms wiggled as if they'd been sent from the underworld to be eaten by birds.

Luc didn't come back until the following day. He and Matt had been caught on the mountain when the storm blew in. They had to dig trenches and fortify the deer fence around the crop. She didn't mention Chris's visit.

Matt hammered a hook into the barn's wooden siding and looped a wire over it. He hung a framed photo showing Celeste in the garden staring straight into the lens. Her hair, grown to the base of her neck, an umbrae of sun blonde and fertile earth.

"Where did you have this developed?" she asked, terrified someone would recognize her.

"Don't worry. Pot seals secrets." Matt tugged a bud from his braid, rolled a joint and struck the match. "I like this picture of you. The way your dress falls off your shoulder and your tits poke the fabric. Makes me want to fuck you."

She took a hit of weed, then moved away from the nauseating stench. Her stomach twisted. "Next time, ask my permission to take a picture." Sitting at the table, slumped over, resting her head on her arms, she felt weary. Weary from Matt.

Matt clasped the belt on her robe.

She swatted his hand away. "Stop."

"Tonight, we'll bang so hard Luc will peek into the hayloft to see what he's missing. He wants to fuck you, you know."

"Stop it, Matt."

Matt said, "Luc, come here. Tell Celeste what you said to me the other day."

Celeste's heart bounced in her chest. "Matt, you're ridiculous."

"Give me a chance to wake up." Luc peeked over the edge of his horse stall. "Coffee, please?"

Matt lit the propane stove and set the kettle over the flame. "I like this photograph of you because you look goddamn innocent, but I know differently."

"I am goddamn innocent," she said.

The kettle whistled. He poured water, plunged the French press. "Coffee's ready, dawling."

Luc came around the corner, dressed only in briefs. He pulled his shirt over his head, took the mug from Matt, sipped, glanced at the photo, walked over, and tilted the edge of the frame, straightening it.

"Celeste's our nymphet." Matt tapped the end of the joint into the sink, ashes raining down.

"I wash vegetables in there," she said.

"After what I did to you last night, I'd think you'd be in a better mood," Matt said.

He had been exceptionally attentive when he'd climbed over her, his muscles straining, body writhing, ribs protruding, pelvis lifting, grin like the sliver of moon outside the window.

Matt smiled at Luc. "I went down on her like she was the last woman alive."

Celeste said, "Shut up, Matt. Please."

Luc pulled on his pants and socks, then rummaged through the pile of shoes near the door. Lacing his work boots, he said, "She doesn't like to be teased." He put on his rain jacket, gathered his tools, and left.

"Don't worry about this picture giving you away," Matt said. "The guy who developed it thought I'd found an old negative. He assumed you were a starving dust bowl urchin."

"No more pictures of me. My hair's growing out. I've gained weight. I'm starting to look like my old self."

When Matt kissed her goodbye, his tongue thrashed in her mouth like a crow in a cage. "I love my urchin."

"If you love me, be kind. Don't talk about having sex with me in front of Luc."

Matt said, "Luc likes it. He's horny for more eclectic adventures than just your golden boy."

She felt a complicated flush and turned away before Matt noticed her pink cheeks. Thinking about Luc in a sexual way betrayed Chris.

Matt slipped into his raincoat and rain boots. "I like to imagine you and Luc getting it on."

"He's gay."

Matt laughed, saying, "He is. He sure the fuck is," and closed the door behind him.

"He's in love with Chris," she said, but Matt was already in the truck.

She opened the ice chest and combed around for leftover oatmeal. Not finding it, she slammed the lid and grabbed a cookie. Rancid taste, but she ate it anyway. Her plan for the day was to plant the tray of seedlings lining the window ledge. On her way to the hayloft to change into work clothes, she paused near Luc's stall. Seeing his unmade bed, she fell onto the pillow, searching for the scent of almonds. Wrapping herself in his blanket, she fell into a sleep she hadn't expected.

Lately, she'd been staying up too late and waking too early. Her mind ruminated on everything that could go wrong in the world. The possibility of an atomic bomb destroying Walden Creek. The never-ending Vietnam War. The December start date of the draft. How the Armstrongs were doing without Chris. Was Bernadette drinking more or less now that she was out of the house? How did George handle his wife? When would Chris come live in the barn?

Matt shook her awake. "Want to have a little fun?" he whispered in her ear.

Celeste pinched her nose. "You stink."

"Luc got to the shower first." His hands slid along her ribcage to her hips, kneading her lower back.

Celeste told Matt she wanted to eat, not have sex. "I slept all day. Sleeping worked up an appetite."

He knelt beside her. "I want to have fun with you and Luc. What do you say?"

Was Matt testing her loyalty to him? She kissed the top of his head, brushed her hands through his hair, twisting the ends around her fingers like she used to do with her parents' telephone cord.

Luc came in from the shower and looked through his suitcase. He grinned at Celeste. His chest and back glistened with oil.

Matt untied her robe. "Doesn't she have glorious tits, Luc?"

Luc said, "White like sweet milk."

"Kiss her," Matt said.

"Kiss me?" Celeste said.

Luc perched on the end of the hay bale. Reaching for her hand, he squeezed, then brought it to his chest, placing it over his heart. His beat slow. Hers, rapid. Luc's towel came undone, exposing one thigh. He licked his lips, slid the towel from beneath himself, hanging it over the stall. "You want me to kiss you, Celeste?"

"I don't know," she said, but thought, yes.

He leaned over, cupped the back of her head, his lips parting, his tongue circling hers.

She saw his penis. Saw Matt's hand caressing it. She reciprocated the kiss, convincing herself she had not lost her moral compass. She'd decided to go along with them, because she needed to feel loved by the man who loved her favorite person in the world. Kissing Luc brought her closer to Chris.

"Little Cutie." Matt reached between her thighs and stroked. "Far out."

Luc's foreskin contracted, blending with the shaft as the tip grew.

"You like this, Little Cutie? You like Luc's French cock?"

Whether her body reacted to the pleasure of Matt's touch or Luc's erection, she couldn't say.

Matt stretched beside her. "Luc, get it on with Celeste. Fuck her."

"Oui, ma petite fille?"

Through the window, clouds floated by. Leaves fluttered in the breeze. When Luc eased himself into Celeste, she thought of a spaceship coming home to dock.

Luc whispered, "Merci, ma belle femme."

She held onto him, his skin sleek, back muscular. Held tight as he rocked, his voice and words melodic. Held on as he slid in and out, then in again, his erection stroking and exciting her.

Matt said, "You two turn me on."

Celeste felt a sensational rise of lust, felt her body moving in rhythm with Luc, felt Matt's tongue on her breasts. She came, startled by the intensity. She'd want Luc again. She already did.

When Luc orgasmed, he didn't slip out. He stayed inside her until his penis softened.

Matt pushed him aside and climbed over her, wiggled and grunted. "Luc and my girl getting it on. Pretty tits. Handsome prick. Look what Chris is missing out on." He groaned and ejaculated.

Oh, god. This is wrong. I shouldn't have done it, Celeste thought as she rose from the bed and rushed up the ladder, needing to be away from them.

"That felt good," Matt called. "We're made for loving."

"Shit, shit, shit," she shouted, angry with Luc and Matt. They hadn't held her down and forced her, though. Despite her fear of admitting this realization, she knew the truth: She'd wanted Luc. She'd enjoyed it.

The following morning, they were gone. She planted the seedlings—bush beans, acorn squash, carrots—and worked on securing the deer fence. Dunked in the cold creek. Jumped in the hot shower. Dunked in the creek again. Wondered if she should hike to Basscombe and admit her sins to Chris no matter what? She felt terrified of hurting him.

Matt and Luc didn't come back to the barn until three days later. Despite how much she regretted what happened, how guilty and awful she felt and how many times she'd told herself she wouldn't participate, when they asked her to sleep with them, she rushed to bed. Luc's penis slid from the shaft and slid into her. The weight of his body heavy. Matt performed cunnilingus on her afterwards, saying he wanted to savor the taste of Luc's cum. She'd told him not to talk like that, but she didn't stop him from pleasing her. In the middle of their bodies, in the middle of the sensations, she felt lost. A day later, they did it again. Matt giving Luc a blowjob, then screwing her while Luc laid beside them, sucking her breasts. Celeste coaxing another erection from Luc. She felt like an addict. Wanting to stop. Unable to stop. Making excuses for not stopping. For the entire week, either morning or night, and sometimes both, they climbed in the hayloft and fucked.

Sunday was a natural break. Matt and Luc went to the cabin. She walked to Basscombe, each step hesitant.

Chris brought her a lunch of meatloaf and baked potato and green beans. "Is everything okay?" he asked. "You seem spaced out."

"Nothing's wrong. Everything's fine," she said, shoveling meatloaf into her mouth to avoid blurting her sin.

"Luc showed up the other night and surprised me. I'm a lucky guy."

"What did you talk about?" Her mind, a pinwheel spinning, please not about me, please not about me, please not about me.

He made kissing sounds and laughed. "Talk? We didn't talk." He gave no indication he'd heard what she, Matt, and Luc had been doing in the barn.

Someday she'd be honest. Someday. After she got stronger, gained willpower, and stopped having sex with Luc, she'd tell Chris of her enormous mistake. Someday, she'd confess. Or maybe she wouldn't. She couldn't risk losing Chris's love. When the bell rang and their time was up, she walked back to Walden Creek, feeling miserable and lonely and ashamed for keeping this enormous secret from him.

The sun, low in the sky, disoriented her. Sunrise or sunset? Owls or mourning doves? The scent of pot and burnt onions wafted through the blackened hayloft. Slipping into her sweater, she took one rickety rung at a time, hoping she wouldn't fall. Downstairs, she tiptoed. The floor creaked.

Lit by the glow of the kerosene lamp, Matt grasped Luc's erection in one hand, holding onto his pelvis with the other, pummeling and grinding into him. Celeste stepped backwards and bumped against the sewing machine. It rattled. Matt glanced over his shoulder and smiled, half grimace, half joy. "You like my cock the best. Better than your boy."

Luc, facing away from her, uttered,"Oui. Ahh. Merci." His fingers gripped the bedspread, the material creasing like smocking on Juliet's pinafore.

Matt grabbed Luc's afro, pulled his head back. "You goddamn peacock."

Luc said, "Bonjour, mon grand homme."

"Bon-fucking-jour."

Hurrying outside, she dropped her face into her palms. She hadn't suspected Matt and Luc had sex without her. Hadn't suspected that at all. Their threesomes were nothing more than fools having fun, weren't they? Those two together seemed intimate. Did Chris know? Wrapping her sweater tighter, she slid into the cab of Matt's truck, and curled into a ball. If regret compounded into a brick, she'd be dead from a wallop upside the head for every stupid decision she'd made involving intercourse and passion and selfish desire. Overcome with dread, she whispered, "I betrayed Chris. I betrayed him. Luc's betraying him. Chris doesn't deserve to be hurt." Her breath on a cold night made her words appear ghostly, each phrase fading as another appeared.

The thunderous knocking against the truck's window startled her. Before she had a chance to respond, Matt opened the door, climbed in behind the steering wheel. He pushed in the cigarette lighter. "Either we're all goddamn cheaters or we're all into sensual freedom." He lit the end of a joint and inhaled.

"I didn't mean for it to go this far." The sentence of a guilty woman. I. Didn't. Do. It. On. Purpose.

"You and Luc banged. I call that going far."

Fogged, the window hid the stars. She couldn't locate Mars or Venus. "I didn't mean to sleep with him."

"You didn't mean to sleep with him over and over and over? You didn't mean to encourage him to penetrate your pussy? You didn't mean to like it when he watched me eating you out? You're such a fucking liar." On the steamy glass, Matt drew the side view of a man with an exaggerated erection. He licked the image away. "I'm absolument certain Luc's balled all of us multiple times. You least of all."

Overhead, the moon tinted the stars blue. "Luc's not like that. He's not like you." She wanted to believe the truth of this statement.

"How little you know," he said.

"I know Chris and Luc love each other."

"Sure, he loves his schoolboy, but Chris isn't around much, is he? Luc needs his cock sucked by a man. He needs to be fucked by a man. I'm that man."

"I hate you."

"He and I need to fuck a girl together. You're that fortunate girl."

Panic was a stranglehold. Panic was death. She said, "I need to move away from this place."

"Little Girl, I don't know what you're going to decide to do, but I'm going to my cabin to get away from your soap opera." He leaned across her and lifted the passenger door handle. Briefly, his arm held her against the seat. His face came close to hers when he said, "You could have told Luc no." He pushed her out the door. As he drove away, the truck's exhaust pipe sputtered.

Hurrying through the barn, she tried to sneak past Luc's bed, but the scent of pomade and weed made her head spin. She stopped to let the dizziness pass.

"Mon petite oiseau," Luc whispered. He lifted his covers. "Come to me."

Stooping beside his mattress, she crossed her arms to avoid slapping him. "Chris will be crushed when he finds out what we've done. What you did with Matt."

"Not a simple situation," Luc said, gesturing for her to lie down beside him. "You're shivering. I'll keep you warm."

"Chris loves you."

"I love him, too. I love him with all my heart. What Matt and you and I do isn't about love."

"It's called making love for a reason," she said, understating how stupid she sounded.

"Is what you and Matt do in bed about love?" Throwing the coverlet around her shoulders and pulling her down beside him, he sighed. "Chris and I make love. That hasn't changed."

"Chris wouldn't ever look at someone else. He's the most loyal person I know."

Luc shifted his weight, tucking her under his arm. "You worship your boy. Your savior."

"Matt's going to dig his claws into you and hold on." She felt the vein on her wrist throb. Her pulse irregular. This is how it feels to be dying, she thought.

"Oui, Matt's a beast who takes what he wants for his own pleasure. Et il ne sera pas durent."

"Speak so I can understand," she said, sounding more like Bernadette than she wanted.

"This won't be the last time Matt and I do it, is what I said. Won't be your last time with him, either. It doesn't have to be our last time."

She pushed herself up. "I'm going to find Chris and let him know what's going on in this insane asylum," she said.

"Mon petite oiseau? He's been with us."

"I don't know what you're talking about."

"Matt, Chris, and me."

If an atomic bomb fell from the sky and hit her on the head, she wouldn't have felt the shock she did in that moment. "No, he hasn't."

"The night of the talent show," he said.

This made no sense. "Chris never said anything."

"I suppose you did?" Luc said. "You told him about the three of us?"

"We've betrayed him."

"If the sex is for enjoyment, it's not betrayal. If I fell in love with Matt, or I fell in love with you, that would be a betrayal."

She dashed from the barn.

Barefoot, bare legged, she didn't have the energy to hike to Basscombe. She tried but got no farther than the junction where a madrone, as tilted as a carnival ride, marked the trailhead. She sat down near a cluster of pennyroyal, hoping the medicinal fragrance would cleanse her mind. Shivering, she hugged her knees to her chest.

"I went to the woods because I wished to live deliberately." Keeping Thoreau's words in mind, every interaction, from this moment on, mattered. She couldn't blame anyone else for the way her life evolved.

Shame kept her from hiking to the Basscombe redwood circle the following Sunday. Shame and fear. Shame for what she'd done with Luc. Fear that Chris already heard and was waiting to ambush her. Innocent Chris. How impossible to believe Luc about what happened the night of the talent show. Chris wouldn't sleep with Matt. Two people couldn't be more incompatible. Truthfully, she probably would have denied Chris's involvement even if she walked in on the three of them doing whatever it is three men do together. Chris was loyal. Unlike her.

Luc and Matt stayed away from Walden Creek, as if they understood she didn't want them around. For this one small act of kindness, she felt grateful. She also hated them for starting this chaotic life.

Then, a few weeks later, she walked from the barn to the cabin. She had no food left. No money to buy food. Hunger lured her onward.

Matt opened the door and pulled her in for a hug. "I've missed my girlfriend."

Luc sat at the kitchen table, smoking a cigarette. "Chris grew frantic something happened to you when you didn't show at Basscombe the last couple of Sundays. I told him you haven't been feeling well."

"Does he know about us?"

"He won't care." Matt asked if she wanted to get high as he lit a joint. "The first weed of our harvest." The cabin had the heady smell of chloroform and damp wool blankets.

"No pot. I'm starving," she said. She'd become the human equivalent to a cat. Feed. House. Pet.

Matt made her a couple of honey and peanut butter sandwiches and opened a beer. While she ate and drank, he sliced potatoes into strips, doused them with oil, and put them in the oven to bake. "I've needed you, Celeste. Luc's great, but he's not you." He winked at Luc.

"No one's like Celeste," Luc said. On his lap, a sketchbook showed a design for a new mosaic. An oak tree, red-capped mushrooms, fairies dancing. "Wouldn't this be lovely to create on the outside of the barn? Our next project for when I come home."

"Isn't this your home? You haven't been to the barn in weeks," she said.

Luc said, "The cabin is vacation. The barn, home." Filtered light shone through the open window. Pale hairs on her arms shimmered. Luc knelt beside her, his fingers barely moving across her, yet the places he touched—wrist, forearm, bicep—sizzled with longing. He kissed her on both cheeks in a greeting.

Matt said, "Our delicate Little Cutie. Our sweet, sweet girl." He twisted his hair into a bun, the ends poking through, carefree. "Are you back for more fun with us?"

"I came for food," she said, biting the last of her sandwich.

"Mon petite oiseau." Luc smiled as he lifted her shirt over her head and helped her from her pants. His tongue moved slowly, full of promise.

Pushing her legs apart, Matt nuzzled. "Sweet girl."

Luc said, "Le bonbon aiment le sucre." He held her head, guiding her mouth toward his erection.

"Give him head," Matt said, his sentence interrupted by licks. "Do it."

Celeste slid her tongue along the shaft of Luc's penis. Unlike the soil taste of Matt, Luc tasted lemon. She convinced herself intimacy with Luc was important for the utopian life she'd created. Important for Chris. Important for her. Important for the stability of Walden Creek.

How eager the men were to please her. How little she had to do.

Matt uttered the words pussy and cock and all their equivalents. Luc rambled in French. Celeste's mind wandered, aware how far she'd come from that girl in Michael Paul's bed. Far, but not really. Hadn't she begged Michael Paul like her body now begged Luc and Matt? Where did Chris fit in all this? At Basscombe, studying like a responsible guy. Trying to graduate. Loving Luc. If she allowed herself to spend too much time in her head, she'd scream at her betrayal.

They moved from the table to the mattress. A jumble of bodies. What fun they had. What fun the men had. What fun she had. What misery, too. The disconnect between pleasure and pain, between self-deception and longing, felt palpable. They kissed her and whispered words of love. They kissed one another. She concentrated on love, brushed away how confusing a term it was.

Saturated and spent, Luc pulled away. Slipped a button through a buttonhole.

Matt said, "Something smells like they're finished baking."

Celeste sat on the table, a blanket wrapped around her. After she ate the potatoes, she walked to Basscombe.

The best time to signal Chris for an unplanned visit was before mealtime, when everyone headed into the cafeteria. If Chris heard a strange bird's chirp, he'd try to sneak away to meet her. If he couldn't, he'd flash her the peace sign. She waited until the dinner bell ceased ringing, then whistled. Two low, one high. Two low, one high.

Chris stopped to speak to a teacher, then pretended to head to his cabin. Out of view of the cafeteria, he ducked low and crawled to the garden. From there, he sprinted to the manzanita hedge, then to the redwood circle. "I haven't seen you in forever. Are you feeling better?"

He smelled like soap and shampoo. Those scents transported her to the shower stall and what she'd seen that night. Back then, she'd never have imagined her own intimacy with Luc. She wondered if the fragrance of the ménage à trois lingered on her skin. Was she brave enough to tell him the truth? "I need to talk to you."

He circled her wrist. "Come with me." They crawled deeper into the forest, stopping at the base of a redwood. He pointed to a small stone shrine. "Look at the fabulous temple I built in honor of the Goddess of Love. My array of offerings to woo her." He indicated a vessel of water and a jar of wildflower honey.

She squinted. "I don't understand."

"I'm performing goddess of love worship," he said, and paused to smile at Celeste. "I'm perfectly serious in a cult sort of way."

"Jewtherans have goddess rituals?"

He poured water over a river slick and explained, "This is called a lingam. A Hindu phallus." The shape and smoothness resembled an uncircumcised penis. He'd propped the lingam in a clay ring. "I sculpted this part in pottery class. Told the teacher it was an ashtray for my dad. It's actually a yoni. A yoni is a representation of a vagina."

"This is how a girl's private parts look to you? Like an ashtray?" she said, inspecting the clay ring.

Chris spread a thin layer of honey onto the tip of the lingam, then placed a daisy into the droplet. "I've been reading about rites to honor various goddesses. This was my favorite, unless you'd rather slaughter a goat."

"You made the right choice," she said, laughing. "Why are you worshiping a goddess? Is it for an assignment?"

"I have the feeling you need protection." He knelt down, pressing his forehead to the earth. "Kowtow," he ordered, patting the ground.

"Chris?" she whispered, her body huddled like a sleeping baby. "I have to tell you something."

"I know, Celeste," Chris said. "I know about it."

When she sat up, a bindi of dirt decorated her third eye. "What do you know?"

"Luc told me everything," he said, stretching on the ground.

"I'm a terrible person. I'm fucked up."

"You're not."

"I'm so stupid, Chris," she said, shame like the universe exploding with her in the center. "I don't understand why I'm doing it. Am I a nymphomaniac? I am, aren't I? Is there something wrong with me?"

"You're always worried about being a nymph. Your Catholic punishment for liking sex."

"I suppose."

Chris wrapped his arms around his knees, drawing them against his chest. "Did you hear what Matt, Luc, and I did after the talent show? I wanted to tell you when I came to the barn, but wasn't ready to talk." He whispered, "Luc asked me to have sex with Matt. I was really hurt."

"Luc asked you to do it? He told me about it, but I didn't believe him." Her eyes filled with tears, but she didn't want to cry. "I feel trapped. I feel like I can't get out. Do you feel trapped?"

"Luc convinced me I'd like it. He convinced me that Matt would be a good experience. Especially since I'd only been with Luc."

"Same with me. Matt encouraged us. I liked it more than I should have. Liked the feelings."

"I hated it so much," Chris said. "In a weird way, your sleeping with them is doing me a favor. You replaced me."

"I'm doing you a favor?" Relief washed over her. "Do you mean that? Am I really doing you a favor?"

"As long as Luc loves me." His smile grew faint. If she'd blinked, she would have missed seeing it.

Was this absolution? Chris absolved her? It couldn't be that simple, could it?

She said, "When you move to the barn, it'll stop. Luc will have you. He'll tell Matt no. Matt will have me. I'll tell Matt yes. Luc will never sleep with Matt or me again."

Chris sighed. "How do you deal with Matt? His aggression?"

"I've gotten used to it."

"Do you want to sleep with both of them?" he asked, breaking twigs into a small pile.

"It helps pass the time," she said, hesitant about saying exactly how much she needed the intimacy. "The part I hate is worrying about hurting you."

"Matt's the one who hurt me."

"He'll leave you alone. I'll make him. I won't sleep with him if he bothers you again."

Chris brushed aside the sticks he'd broken. "Are you protecting yourself? You're sixteen. You can't have a baby."

"They wear rubbers. Mostly. Sometimes it's hard to convince them to put one on. Especially Matt." She'd make a fertility calendar, highlighting her ovulation window with condoms and the rest of the days with shooting stars.

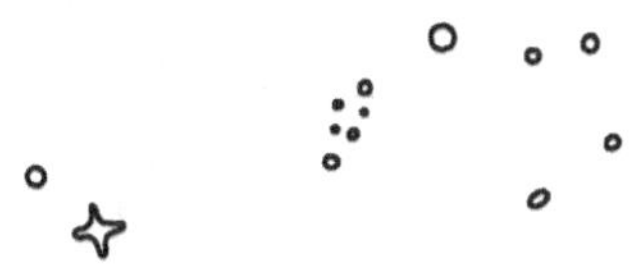

Chris handed her a paper plate, a napkin, and a fork, then made an elaborate display of rolling back the aluminum to reveal a rectangle of lasagna and soggy salad.

Her stomach twisted. The scent of marinara sauce sickened her. Basil, Italian seasoning. She covered her nose with her sweater.

Chris said, "Can you breathe in there?"

"That smell is making me sick."

He pushed the plate aside, touched her forehead. "You're not hot."

"Why does everyone always think you have to have a fever to be sick?" She sprawled on her belly. Redwood needles poked her cheek, but she didn't move. "Talk about something else."

"These last few months, since the draft's been implemented, it's all anyone at school discusses. We're dreading the day our numbers are called."

"Shit." Celeste ran to a cluster of ferns and vomited. After hiding it with dirt, she went back to Chris and rinsed her mouth from the thermos of water. "You can't go to war."

"If I'm living with you at Walden Creek or if we're living in Paris, I'll be a draft dodger."

"I'm really sick."

Taking the piece of plain white bread from the plate, he handed it to her. "The draft and war make me sick too."

No, no, no, she thought, no to coffins carrying young men, some of them not much older than Chris. No, no, no to warmongering President Johnson. "You can't be shipped to Vietnam the day you turn eighteen."

"Kids killing kids while the big generals look on," Chris said.

"Kids." Then, as if entering a stage on cue, the minuscule solar system inside her womb, stirred and burst into a universe of cells. Her words, barely a whisper: "Am I pregnant?"

"What?" Chris stared at her.

She stared at him. "Can I be pregnant?"

"I don't know."

How idiotic she was for not making the ovulation calendar as she'd intended. "A baby? I can't have a baby."

They sat still for a moment, then filled the silence with shits and goddamns.

"You're probably not pregnant, but if you are, a baby isn't a bad thing." Chris spoke of the time he wrote an alphabetical list of names for his future child—Abel and Bentley all the way through the alphabet to Xander and Zion. When he realized he was gay, he grieved for Dudley and Elmer and all the other babies he believed would never be born. She'd been a witness to his disappointment. "It could be a good thing."

"I'm sixteen," she said.

"You'll be seventeen when it's born," he said, as if that made it any easier. "It'll be okay, Celeste. You'll be okay."

"If I am pregnant, what'll I do? Should Matt take me to Tijuana to make it go away?" Her face a panic mask, the veins on her neck throbbing. "Matt won't take me. He won't risk getting caught."

"Imagine you as a mother," Chris said. "You'd be a good one."

"Why aren't you freaking out?" she whispered. "I can't have a baby."

"We can," he said. "We can do this. If you want, that is. If you don't want to, I'll find a way to get you to Mexico."

"We can do this?" Was this a way out? Maybe Matt would leave her alone.

"You and me and Luc," he said, clutching her hand, "and Matt, I guess."

Shaking her head, she said, "I've never been nurturing."

"You nurtured me through the worst part of my life," he said.

A child at Walden Creek would make her endless days seem bearable. Someone to love and someone who'd love her. "I'm barely able to take care of myself."

"I'll take care of you." Leaning close to her womb, he cooed, "Baby, it's me, Papa Chris. I'm going to be one of your daddies."

She swore she could feel the yolk inside her wave hello. "I feel like Queen for a Day showing the TV host my dilapidated barn, lusty men, scorched loft, unstable life, and my prize is a baby. Really? A baby?"

Chris said, "Hippie communes have children, don't they? I've seen photographs. Dirty, happy kids running around in the woods."

Placing her hands over her belly, she said, "If you are in there, I'll be your hostess for the next nine months."

Chris said, "I think it'll be a boy. Either that or a girl."

"It's a boy, and his name is Thoreau." She clenched her abdomen as nausea roared through in waves. Hurrying off and huddling next to a redwood, she retched. "Morning sickness?"

Chris dabbed her mouth with his handkerchief. "This monogrammed B isn't for Basscombe. B is for Baby."

"B is for baby," she said. Nothing about this moment seemed real.

"How about the name Sunny? For a boy or a girl?"

"Boy. Thoreau. I know this as surely as I know who his father is." The second she spoke those words, fear crept through her. How could she be certain of the baby's father?

Chris squeezed her arm. "Whether it's Matt or Luc's, it'll still be your baby. Mine too. I'll love him or her, no matter whose sperm penetrated your cute egg." Gesturing toward Basscombe, he added, "I feel worthless being stuck in school. I need to be with you."

"I don't want Matt to be his father," she said.

"Matt likes you, Celeste. He'll take care of you and the baby." Chris rubbed her belly.

Stellar jays and squirrels sounded lively. The occasional humph of deer. Animals celebrating. Mother Nature welcoming her Thoreau to earth.

Chris reassured her he'd be the one to break the news to Luc. "Do you want Luc to tell Matt, or do you want to?"

She folded her hands in front of her heart, bowed her head, conjuring Saint Christopher. "You gave life, I pray no act of mine may take away or mar the gift of thine." Miraculously, relief soothed her fearful soul as if Saint Christopher heard her prayer and painted a rainbow across the sky, ensuring she and Thoreau and Chris and Luc and Matt were protected by the beauty.

"Enceinte?" Luc said. "If your intention was to create life, you did your job well, vagin magnifique. You too, pénis magnificant. Mine or Matt's. Either way, magnificant."

"We were supposed to protect ourselves from this happening." She pulled a strip of rubbers from between the hay bales. "Look at all these still in the package."

Luc pressed his lips to her abdomen. "Hello, mon bébé doux, mon petit amour doux."

"Are you glad or sad this happened? Tell me the truth."

For a moment, Luc didn't respond. "I am not unhappy about it. I am concerned, yes. Concerned I will be accused of taking advantage of you."

"It may not be your baby. If it is, we won't tell anyone you're the father."

"I'm black, Celeste," Luc said. "The only black man in these woods."

She sprinted from the barn, vomited in the forest, covered it, rinsed her face, brushed her teeth, and returned to Luc's bed. "My breasts are bigger, aren't they? They're sore."

"Beautiful." He rattled off a list of girl's names. "Suzanne, Camille, Ailene."

After listening patiently—like the mama she hoped to be—she repeated what she'd told Chris. "Boy. Thoreau."

"Thoreau? The American writer of your *Walden*?" He reached for his jacket. "I love this name. If a boy."

She closed her eyes and yawned. "He's a boy. I feel it."

"I'm going to pick mint and make you tea. Climb under the covers and relax." Luc helped her slide beneath the blanket. He tucked her in.

It had been almost ten months since she left home, and she rarely thought about Bernadette and George anymore, yet the baby inside stirred a familial warmth. What kind of grandparents would they be? Would the love of their grandchild overpower their prejudices against gay and black and foreign? Hippie and draft dodger and pot grower? Dr. and Mrs. Armstrong were kind people. Would they accept Chris as one of the papas, since the baby would look nothing like him? What about Luc's parents, the Laurents? He didn't speak much about them except they worked in a produce market in Paris and raised him to treat women well. Would they accept Thoreau? Matt's mom would cook up a feast in celebration. She'd probably be thrilled to have a baby to love. Celeste mused her future and faded into sleep.

That evening in the hayloft, Matt pulled her sweater over her head. "You're one bon motherfucker. Your tits are huge." His erection bobbed about in the air like a blimp.

You're the motherfucker, she thought as she eased herself onto the mattress. Already, her belly curved as slight as a new moon.

As he moved over her body, his braids draped across her thighs. He used the ends to tickle her. "You're getting fat."

She blurted, "I'm pregnant."

Looking up at her, he said, "What did you say?"

"I'm not fat. I've got a baby in here." She pointed right below her belly button to the spot where fallopian tubes intersected and a womb expanded while atoms divided.

"How do you know?" He stretched beside her and cupped her face in his hands.

"I've missed a few periods. I've got morning sickness."

"I'm going to be a father?"

She nodded, then shook her head. "I'm not sure if he's yours."

"You're a princess locked in a castle. What other cocks are you around except Luc's and mine? Is it one of those Basscombe boys? Luc says they're horny as hell."

Hay scratched her back. She leaned forward to loosen the sharpest one. "Yours or Luc's."

"You're balling the brilliant bookmobile librarian you're always rambling on about? You trade sex for all these free books?"

"Mr. BM? You're joking, right?" She stared him in the eye. "Don't be dumb. He's old."

"What other cocks have you been letting in here?" Matt stuck his finger inside her. "This is my pussy. Mine and Luc's." This was not an unexpected reaction. Matt trusted no one.

"I don't belong to you," she said, wiggling away. "You don't own me."

"Who. Else. Have. You. Fucked?"

She didn't want to fight. Wrapping her hand around his penis, she leaned over. Blowing him was the last thing she wanted to be doing, and she resented it. He could have been kinder. Could have been nurturing. If she'd caught him in a good mood, she wouldn't have to do this. He'd be satisfying her.

Matt held her in place and wouldn't let her pull away. She gagged from the scent of his testicles, sweaty and unwashed, and the sour taste of him, the spill of semen. Finally, he went limp. "Luc and I wear rubbers."

She drank water until she'd emptied the container. "No, you don't. Hardly ever." The forest grew quiet as if snow started falling. Jays weren't squawking or squirrels chattering.

He slipped on his pants. Tied the cord. "Did you ever think I might have wanted to try and have a baby with you someday? Our baby? Not Luc's."

"You've never told me that."

"Because you're sixteen years old. You're not old enough to have a kid."

"I'll be seventeen when he's born." She paused, inhaling through nausea. "You're probably the father. You and I mess around a lot more than Luc and I do." She slipped into a tee shirt and climbed down the ladder. In the kitchen, she put on the teakettle.

Matt followed her, jumping a few rungs at a time. "If it's black, it's Luc's? White, mine? That's how it goes?" He paced the length of the barn, forging a path through the dust. "We need to tell Luc together."

"Luc knows."

"You told him before you told me?"

"Chris told him."

"Chris knows?" Matt dropped teabags in their cups. "So, everyone except for me, the fucker who feeds and houses you, found out before I did?"

The view from the kitchen window framed a thicket of madrones. Paper-thin bark peeled from their twisted, orange trunks. She'd once imagined Henry David using it as writing paper, scribbling his thoughts with a charcoaled tip of a twig. "It's just the way it worked out. Chris guessed. Don't be angry. You're my boyfriend." She stood close to him, kissing his cheek.

Matt turned off the teakettle, poured water into their cups. "You're a runaway. You're a minor. You can't go to a hospital. How are you going to see a doctor? You can't put my name on the birth certificate. Did you think about any of that?"

"Did any of us think about any of that when we were in bed together?" Her heart pounded against her ribcage.

"No one forced you to fuck me. You can't say I made you do anything you didn't want to do."

"Before meeting you, I never even had sex," she said. Her voice rose in pitch until it seemed to fill the entire room. She sipped her tea, willing herself to calm down.

Matt interlaced his fingers through hers, leading her across the floor to the ladder. "Climb," he said, and pushed her upward.

When Matt was angry, he fucked hard as if wanting to make her feel pain. During those times, she'd let her mind float away, imagining herself with someone kinder. Anyone who wasn't him. Luc. Michael Paul. The Persian cat boy. Foxy David. Any of the Basscombe students or teachers. Even Mr. BM would be easier to tolerate than a pissed-off Matt.

He said, "Get in bed."

She crossed her legs, needing a moment to regroup and prepare herself for a night of bombardment. Matt's bark. Matt's bite.

He fluffed the mattress, smoothed the covers, and tucked her in, saying, "Sleep, Little Mommy," and then he backed down the ladder.

"Sleep?" She heard his footsteps tromping. Heard the barn door slide open and slam shut. Surrendering to his mercurial whims was an everyday part of her life at Walden Creek. She didn't want her child to experience it, yet what other choice did she have? She prayed Matt wasn't the father.

Heartburn replaced morning sickness. Forgiveness and patience, traits she cultivated with rigor, replaced dread. Once she began showing, Luc and Matt stopped the threesomes, as if that erotic intimacy suddenly seemed wrong.

On the morning of her seventeenth birthday, Matt dropped off a bag of maternity clothes and a bundle of cloth diapers and stayed for spearmint tea. Leaves clung to the side of his mug. He plucked one, making an elaborate display of licking it. He winked at her and begged for the taste of chatte—his feeble attempt at speaking French no Frenchman would tolerate, even from an American.

Celeste didn't tell him no. Orgasms relieved pressure. She liked his tongue fondling, his hands gripping her thighs when she came, how he wouldn't let go until every last drip of pleasure emptied from her body. This was her life now. Luc and Chris in love. Luc and Chris lovers. Luc and Matt lovers. Her and Chris in love. Her and Matt lovers.

"Come to the cabin tonight for a French meal," Matt said, kissing her. "I'm trying new recipes."

If Matt made birthday dessert, she'd save Chris a piece.

After Matt left for work, she fell asleep.

Naps were difficult to wake from, but a growling, empty stomach forced her eyes open. Showered and dressed in her newest handmade shift, a replica of her boxy one but roomier, she trudged the worn path from barn to cabin.

Matt opened the door before she knocked. "Bonjour."

Her stomach rumbled.

Matt said, "At the bookmobile a couple weeks ago, I checked out books on cuisine française. I've had plenty of time to plan this birthday menu."

Sitting at the table, Luc studied a cookbook, his chin cupped in his hands, looking like a schoolboy might. Looking like their child could. "Matt wouldn't let me in the kitchen to help. I had to sit here and watch. How is our baby? How is his mama?"

"Thoreau's fine." She patted her belly. "Getting bigger."

"You, mon petite oiseau, are quite pretty," Luc said. He reached around her waist, pulling her into his lap. "Bon anniversaire."

She rested her head on his shoulder, inhaled almond.

Matt put down his book and came over. He slipped his hands beneath her shift, stroking her belly. "Bon anniversaire to you turning seventeen and bon anniversaire to us on the day we began this love affair."

"In the garden beneath the Milky Way," she said.

Matt said, "When I picked you up hitchhiking, I knew we'd fuck."

"You did?" She jerked her head from Luc's shoulder, frowning at Matt.

"Why do you think I drove you here instead of Basscombe?"

"Wasn't Basscombe too far? That's what you told me."

"Gullible," he said, and plated the food.

They ate Soufflé au Fromage—despite falling, it was still tasty, the eggy surface like thick, cold soup. Pommes aux Epinards made with Maidenblush apples picked from a neighbor's orchard. Profiteroles au Chocolat, with a flaky pastry shell and melted dark chocolate dribbled over whipped cream.

"Tell me my profiterole is the best you've ever had," Matt said, holding the pastry to Luc's lips. "Bite."

"Délicieux. Almost French."

"Almost?" Matt said.

Luc bit into the dessert. "You have the technique, but for perfection, you would need Parisian water, flour, sugar, and butter. You need to be in France."

Matt scooted the kitchen bench back, scraping the legs on the wooden floor. "I don't want to be in France. I wanted to bring France to you." He crossed to the countertop and slammed the cookbooks into a cardboard box, set them on the table in front of Celeste. "Return these to the bookmobile when it comes tomorrow."

"I'm teasing you, Matt," Luc said. "C'est extraordinaire."

"I won't turn the cookbooks in. I'll renew them," Celeste said. She hoped to lighten Matt's mood. "I can eat like this all day."

"Then you'll grow to be as huge as a whale," Matt said. "Luc isn't impressed. He wants to go back to Paris and stuff himself with real French food and real French cock."

Taking another profiterole, Luc said, "I have enough on my hands with my American cocks."

"You French prick." Matt grabbed Luc by his collar, pulling him from his chair.

Celeste looked from one to the other. "Matt, stop it. Leave him alone."

"Your profiterole is the best I've ever had, grande homme," Luc said, his hands sliding down to Matt's crotch. "Sincerely."

"You're a shit liar, Luc. You're an asshole," Matt said. He pushed him through the door and slammed it in his face.

Standing at the open window, Celeste searched for Luc, but he'd disappeared into the woods. He'll come back, she thought. Luc won't leave me alone with Matt in his maniacal mood, especially on my birthday. "Go after him and apologize, Matt. He didn't deserve that."

"How do you know?" Matt said. "Luc's been egging me on all day. Bragging about fucking his sweet seventeen-year-old birthday boy. Sucking off his sweet seventeen-year-old birthday boy. I finally had enough."

Her cheeks flushed. Luc would never talk like that about Chris. Another example of Matt's perverted vernacular. "Luc loved your cooking," she said.

"He tolerated it, just like he tolerates me." Matt folded back his coverlet, climbed in bed, patting a place beside him. "Stay overnight." A demand.

Silhouettes of dirty dishes lined the table. The sink stacked with pots and pans. Normally, Matt never waited until morning to clean up. Kitchen messes guaranteed mice. She rolled up her sweater sleeves. "I'll wash."

"I asked you to come here," Matt said.

Her body tensed as if preparing to sprint away. Where did Luc go? Why had he left her there? In that moment, she hated him. Hated them both.

Matt crossed the floor, guiding Celeste to the bed. He slid her sweater and shift over her head.

"I'm going to the barn," she said, grabbing her clothing, trying to dress. She didn't want Matt. She didn't want Luc. Sad and disappointed they'd spoiled her birthday, she wanted her body to be left alone. She wanted the hayloft and sleep.

He snatched the clothes from her, tossed them across the room. "You're not walking home tonight."

She didn't want to fight. Didn't want adrenaline throttling her womb and startling Thoreau. The fragrances of eggs and milk and sugar saturated the air. She closed her eyes. Profiterole. Chocolate and cream.

Matt said, "Fuck me, Little Girl." He pushed into her.

Celeste said, "If you call me Little Girl one more time, I'll never speak to you again."

"That's the biggest threat you can come up with? You don't have to speak to me, Little Cutie, but you do have to fuck me." He bucked and bolted as if he'd forgotten how to have sex without being angry.

Celeste apologized to the baby for her willingness to put up with Matt's insanity. Apologized to herself for her lack of imagination on how to stop him from behaving this way. She braced herself for a long night.

In the morning, Matt solved his messy kitchen problem by throwing all his dishes and pans outside. The chickens scrambled, then flocked back, pecking at the dried food. "Screw everything French," he shouted into the woods. "I hope you get deported, you stupid French peacock."

Celeste went to the bathroom to wash away the stickiness of Matt and the scents of French sauces and whipped cream. In the bright early June sunlight, a dusting of white powder blurred a small mirror. She'd never seen cocaine, yet knew that's what it had to be. Was this the reason Matt picked a ridiculous fight with Luc, then balled her like a madman?

Matt remained silent when he drove her and the box of cookbooks to the plaza, dropping them an hour before the bookmobile was due to arrive. "You have to find your own way back to the barn." He shifted gears and sped away.

"Fine," she said, carrying the box to a bench in the plaza. He didn't have any excuse to be angry with her. She'd praised his food. She'd spread her legs.

She stared at the payphone. A reminder of her connection to home. She still hadn't called Bernadette and George. She relied on Chris dropping hints to his parents, who'd tell her parents how well she faired in Alaska making a fortune fishing salmon or cod or whatever fucking fish swam in the frigid ocean.

While she waited in the plaza, she skimmed Matt's cookbooks. The recipes he'd dogeared were complicated. She almost felt sorry for him. He'd wanted to please Luc.

The bookmobile came bounding down the road and crossed the bridge. After it parked, the door swished open. Mr. BM helped her carry the box up the steps. "You're looking more pregnant each time I see you," he said. "You're shapely. You always had quite the figure."

"The baby's safely tucked away," she said.

"How you feeling?" he asked.

"Fine, except I need the father not to get deported."

"Marry him," Mr. BM said. "He'll get a green card."

"What's that?"

He searched the card catalogue. Repeating a decimal number out loud, he led her to a shelf and tapped the spine of a book on immigration. "Make him a taxpaying citizen. In the long run, money's all that counts with the government."

She threw her arms around his neck and kissed his cheek. "You have no idea how happy I am right now." Whether or not Luc was the dad, he had to stick around for Thoreau. For Chris. For her. For Matt.

Mr. BM ran his hand along her backside. "Glad to make you happy."

She scooted away, wondering if he mistook her hug of gratitude for a hug of provocation. More likely, he touched her by mistake.

He pulled a second book from the shelf. "How long do you have before the baby's due?"

"Four or five months," she said.

"Better start reading this book on pregnancy now." He smiled as he stamped the card.

Celeste sat on the cushioned bench in the back of the truck. Flipping through the book's pages, she grew increasingly startled by the chapters entitled, "Mastitis" and "Episiotomies." The baby fluttered, and she wanted to cry.

When the time came for Mr. BM to drive to the next town, he gave her a lift like he often did. She stood by the counter, talking with him and watching the forest slide past the truck's enormous window.

"You're a real honey. You're going to make that green card touting man a fine wife, and that baby a fine mom." Pulling over, he put on the emergency brake, opened the pneumatic door, and helped her down the steps. "See you in two weeks."

When the bookmobile was gone from sight, she continued along the road, glad for cool weather. Off in the distance, she spotted someone. She squinted for a better view. As she got closer, she saw a hitchhiker sitting on the ground, leaning against a backpack.

"Need help carrying that?" the hitchhiker asked. "Looks like a heavy load."

Matt didn't like strangers coming to the barn, but she felt tired and didn't care. She had no idea if Luc was home or already back at Matt's cabin, begging for a pardon and a good time. She handed the box to the stranger.

The hitchhiker's name was Freedom. He traveled the United States, collecting donations with the intention to go to Vietnam and offer condolences on behalf of Peaceniks. Celeste and Freedom's sex was casual. He never asked about her pregnancy or where or who the father was. His grip on her enormous boobs loosened her grip of obligation to Matt. Freedom gave her freedom. He spent hours working in the garden, planting tomatoes and lettuce, and peeking under leaves for sowbug colonies. He built a pillbug circus with a flying trapeze made from rubber bands and a matchbox, a tightrope from twine, a trampoline from a piece of cloth, a flaming hoop crafted from a gasket seal dipped in kerosene. By the time Freedom left, a few days later, she wasn't sad to see him go. He ate with his mouth slightly ajar, masticating loud enough for Thoreau to stir. Worse, he always said the same thing when he climaxed: "I'm coming. I came. I've come."

Celeste barely had time to remake the bed before Luc burst through the barn doors, calling, "Mon petite oiseau." The soiled sheets lay in a heap on the floor.

Luc's breath sounded labored, as if he'd been running. "I shouldn't have stormed out of Matt's and left you alone with him when he's high on coke and in a bad mood."

Celeste frowned and told him she agreed. "You shouldn't do cocaine."

"Très bon. I don't. He does. We have long days with the crop. Sunrise to sunset. He says it gives him energy to get the work done."

Celeste scooped the laundry and carried it to the creek, dropping the sheets in the water.

Squatting beside her, Luc took the bar of soap from her hands. "Doing laundry is my job. It would be easier if I took this to Matt's."

"No," she said.

"Sit under the oak and rest while I wash."

For the past three days, she'd relaxed against that very tree, reading literature on citizenship while Freedom worked in the garden and played with his bug circus.

Dipping her hand in the creek, she watched water drip from her fingers. "While you were with Matt, I had a lover."

"How lovely," Luc said. He rolled the bar of soap over the sheet.

"You don't believe me, do you?" She wanted him to see her as a complicated person. As someone more than the third corner of their love affair or Chris's best friend or Matt's girlfriend. She wanted the possible father of her baby to see her as an independent woman.

"Where is this figment of your romantique imagination?"

"Vanished." Maybe better if Freedom remained elusive.

"Poof," he said. "Gone into the atmosphere."

"Like Chris this past week," she said. Chris hadn't shown up at the redwood circle on Sunday, which meant he'd probably been caught for some indiscretion and had KP duty. "What do you think he did this time? Another naughty cartoon?"

Luc shrugged when he said, "Who knows? A lot of Basscombe's menial labor gets done by putting boys on KP duty."

Luc's passive response bothered her, but she'd been passive, too, hadn't she? Playing around with Freedom for three uninterrupted days without worrying about Chris. "Doesn't seem fair," she said.

"What's fair at military school?" He pushed his fingers into his afro, fanning it around his head.

"On my eighteenth birthday, you and I should get married. That's how you can stay in this country. Mr. BM told me about it. He gave me a book on immigration. I've been studying the law."

"I have heard of his idea before." Luc dipped the sheets in and out of the water. "I had a friend who came to America, married his sweetheart, and never went back to France."

"To freedom and screwing the INS."

Luc wrung the sheets and hung them on a branch to dry. "Don't forget, et à l'idylle et à l'amour. Ma belle jeune femme." He stroked the thin brown pregnancy line, running from her public bone to her navel.

"Mr. BM also gave me a book about prenatal stuff. We can look up why I suddenly have this weird streak on my stomach."

"You need medical help from a doctor. Not a book."

Celeste placed her hands protectively over her belly. Thoreau's transition from bean to baby had caused her skirts to fall below her belly and her shirts to rise above. Her navel stuck out like a control knob on a spaceship.

In August, Matt found Jasmine, Midwife to the Outlaws. Draft dodgers and pot growers paid her what they could afford or bartered for her expertise.

Jasmine arrived at the barn, carrying a large, worn leather satchel. "You're having a baby, and you haven't been to any kind of doctor since you got pregnant?"

"Not yet," Celeste said.

"Which one of you is the father?"

"I am," Luc said, resting his hand over his heart.

"My super sperm did the dastardly deed." Matt nudged Luc with his hip.

"I don't know," Celeste said.

"One thing is for certain," Jasmine said, glancing from Luc to Matt. "When the baby's born, we'll have a pretty good idea which man it belongs to." She took out her stethoscope and laid the pad against Celeste's abdomen, moving around, then stopping in a spot below her breast. "Want to listen, Mommy?"

The speedy beat of the baby's heart made Celeste freeze. "I've got a human in here."

"You sure do," Jasmine said.

Luc asked to listen. He closed his eyes. "Strong heart. Sounds excited to meet us."

Matt said, "Beating too fast?"

Jasmine shook her head. "Exactly in the range it should be."

"This homebirth method is not dangerous?" Luc asked. "Why don't you midwife in a hospital like we do in France?"

Matt handed the stethoscope back to Jasmine. "Want to get us all thrown in jail?"

"I want Celeste and the baby to be safe," Luc said.

Jasmine reassured them she'd delivered hundreds of babies in the safety of the home, all perfectly healthy. "No maternal or infant deaths."

At the mention of death, Celeste gasped and covered her mouth. Thoreau jumped.

Jasmine added, "Don't worry. I have privileges at the hospital in case you or this little one are in distress. I promise, rarely does anything go wrong." Then she admonished Celeste for having waited until she was six months pregnant to make an appointment. "The first trimester is critical for the health of the baby and the mother."

"I take good care of myself," Celeste said. "Eat well. Walk in the forest. Sit by the creek. Send him good thoughts. No alcohol or weed."

Matt said, "Celeste's stubborn. You can't make her do anything she doesn't want to do."

"A baby will change that," Jasmine said. She asked Matt and Luc to wait outside during the checkup. "I'm sure you've both seen her cunt before," she said with a smile, "but let's give this girl some privacy." Jasmine went to the kitchen sink, washing her hands, and drying them on a dishtowel she took from her satchel.

Matt said, "I need a smoke anyway."

"Merci beaucoup, Jasmine, for being here to help with our baby and his mama," Luc said.

After the barn door slid closed, Celeste laid on Luc's bed and pulled down her underwear. "I wish Chris was here." She pointed to the photo pinned above the bed. "He'd want to meet you."

"Another potential father?" Jasmine inserted two lubed fingers into Celeste's vagina and moved them around. Her free palm pressed Celeste's abdomen.

"The spiritual father."

"I'd like to meet the spiritual father."

"He's in school at Basscombe. If you come on a Sunday, I'll arrange him to be here."

"May I ask your age?" Jasmine said.

"I turned seventeen in June. Chris and I have the same birthday."

"Seventeen? No wonder the men are worried about you." Jasmine sighed. "I'll try to come on a Sunday. If not this week, next. I want to meet every member of the birth team." Jasmine prodded inside Celeste. "Your gestation estimation is close. We're looking at an early November birth." She removed her fingers, washed her hands, gave Celeste a package of vitamins and a list of what and what not to do during pregnancy. Included on the to-do list was the word Sex.

"Sex?" Celeste said when she came to that directive.

"With three men in your life, that shouldn't be difficult. Orgasms help prepare the uterus for contractions. Penises keep the vagina exercised and flexible. My advice? Choose the man with the biggest wanker and screw to your heart's delight." She told Celeste she'd return in two weeks.

"What if the one with the biggest penis is the one I least desire?"

"Then find someone else to satisfy you. Your cunt, your life." On her way out the barn door, Jasmine said to Luc and Matt, "The pregnancy's official."

Luc sprinted across the barn floor and knelt, resting his head on her belly. "J'aime mon bébé."

Matt read the list of instructions. "She's advising you to fuck?"

If Celeste heeded Jasmine's wanker advice, she'd shoo Luc away and pull Matt's pants off and demand he get started. However, if she were going to have sex with either of them, she wanted Luc's sensual, uncircumcised penis rather than Matt's thrashing ogre. "Jasmine told me it helps with the delivery."

"I'll accept my fatherly duties and bone you," Matt said. "Luc, we've been granted access. Given the green light."

Luc rested his elbow on the top of the horse stall. He laughed when he said, "I'm here to do what I can."

Matt had rough, eager hands that slid under Celeste's shift to squeeze her breasts. He unzipped his pants and pulled her to the edge of the mattress, lifting her hips.

"You must be gentle with her in this condition," Luc said.

Matt said, "The baby's floating around in the little sack of water. It's not being bothered."

Up until Jasmine's affirmation, Celeste hadn't given much thought to birthing. Now, the potential of what could go wrong terrified her. She needed Chris. Needed to be around the man who'd understand how to soothe and comfort her.

When Matt came, he shifted his weight on the hay bale. "It's a groovy happening here in Walden Creek. Celeste's our queen. We're the kings. We're helping our Little Celeste." He nudged Luc with his elbow. "Fuck her."

"Doesn't she need a chance to rest?" Luc asked Matt, as if he were the one in charge of her.

Celeste did need a rest, but it had been too long since she'd slept with Luc, and she missed him. He'd been cautious with her since she began showing. "Luc, come here."

Luc's erection slid in. "Sex for an easier birth. For you, ma petite."

"For an easier birth," she said. For my pleasure, she thought.

A few nights a week, Matt slept alone with Celeste, pumping like a piston. Finished, he'd collapse, rest for a second, then move down her body. "Now, I'm going to eat you out, Little Mommy. Doctor's orders."

Other times, she'd wake and find Luc in the hayloft, his arms wrapped around her like protective armor. "I want the little bean to know, as he sprouts arms and legs and fingers and toes, his papa is here, wishing him well on the evolutionary journey." He'd stroke her until the uterine walls expanded and contracted.

Every few nights, they'd all climb into Matt's bed. A tangle of men's erections and mouths and asses, her vagina and breasts and constant need for the assurance her baby would be healthy.

On her next appointment, Celeste told Jasmine, "The guys are extremely attentive."

"I see this all the time. You've known you're pregnant for months. The men finally realize a baby's the cause of your round belly and round tits, and they're the reason for the change."

"I can't wait for you to meet Chris," Celeste said, lying on her back and lifting her shift. "He's the most excited of any of us."

Jasmine said, "Pregnancy and childbirth are monumental events to go through."

Panic roared through Celeste. "What if I can't get the baby out? What am I doing? What did I do?"

"Crying's good. Let those tears flow. You don't want to keep fear inside." Jasmine patted Celeste's arm, handed her a tissue, then put the speculum in her vagina. She peered with a flashlight, reassuring Celeste the birth canal looked pink and resplendent. "Everything about you is young and healthy and strong. Your body's in prime condition."

"How am I going to push a baby through there?" Celeste wiped her runny nose with the tissue, her eyes with her sleeve. "How am I going to be a mother? I don't know anything."

Jasmine unclamped the device, rinsed the metal in the kitchen sink, wrapped the speculum in a cloth. "Right now, the best you can do is to follow my big wanker advice, and make those men give you orgasms. No need to worry." She closed her medical bag. "Matt likes fucking, that's for sure. Everyone around the ridge has been with him. He's renowned."

"Renowned?"

"Doesn't have any children, though. Not that I've heard of, anyway. Makes me suspicious about his sperm count."

Celeste put her underwear back on. "What about his sperm?"

"Probably low, or there'd be a dozen kids that look like him running around these woods." Jasmine continued, "Who do you think will step up to the task of fatherhood? I'm not talking about who the biological dad is, because it's most likely Luc. I mean sticking around and helping you raise the kid."

"Papa Chris. He's the most loving." Celeste smiled as she rubbed vitamin E on her skin, where tiny pink stretch marks surfaced like striate across a rock face.

Chris's graduation was the first Friday of autumn, and it killed Celeste she couldn't be at the ceremony.

"Too many people will be in attendance," Luc said. He secured his tie in place with a silver clip. "Including his parents."

"I can hide behind the manzanita and watch the commencement. No one will see me." Her heart cracked open as she pictured Chris receiving his diploma. Later, showing Dr. and Mrs. Armstrong his emancipation papers and introducing Luc as the man he planned to live in a barn with for the rest of his life. She imagined two potential outcomes for this day: either the Armstrongs would hug Chris, congratulate Luc, and offer them an envelope of cash to start their new life, or the Armstrongs would declare the emancipation papers illegal, grab Chris by the arm, throw him in the backseat of their station wagon, and zoom away like they'd done fifteen months ago—except in the opposite direction.

"Celeste, mon petite oiseau," Luc said, stooping to look her in the eye.

She took his hand, placing it where the baby squirmed. "Do you love Thoreau?"

Luc frowned when he said, "You need to ask?"

She did. Over the past few weeks, he'd been absent from the barn, staying with Matt in the cabin. The couple of times he'd slept with her, he wasn't affectionate. If they had sex, Luc was mechanical as if performing a duty, not a privilege. Had she done something wrong? Was Luc disgusted by her enormous body?

When Matt walked through the barn door, she gasped. He'd shaved his beard and cut his hair. Wispy bangs swirled across his forehead. Sideburns swooped in front of his ears. His lips looked rosier and fuller. Brown eyes, the color of driftwood. Scrubbed clean, he looked younger, suave, charming, and flirty.

Celeste said, "Where will you stash your weed?"

Matt patted his jacket pocket.

Luc said, "L'homme est beau. Matt is my date for my boyfriend's big day."

Celeste said, "I should be the one to go."

"Say here and rest up. We'll bring Chris home tonight and have a celebration," Matt said.

"In such a big crowd, someone will recognize you, Matt. You'll get busted," she said, trying not to yell for the sake of the baby.

"I doubt anyone's looking for a clean-cut, war-resisting, militant, draft dodger at a military school. Do I look like someone who's spent years in the mountains hiding?" Matt handed Luc a tie. "Help me with this."

Luc stepped closer, threw the striped gray silk around Matt's neck, looped, knotted, tightened, and straightened it. "You wear ties well."

Matt said, "Merci. I appreciate you lending it to me." He gave Luc a lingering kiss. "Feels like I'm stepping back into my old life of debutante balls."

"You were a debutante guy?" Celeste asked. "Aren't they restrained and refined?"

"I was in high demand. Does it surprise you that girls wanted me to escort them to dances?"

"Looking like this, no," she said.

Luc stroked Matt's chin. "I will miss the tickle of your beard and braids on my back."

The baby flipped over, stuck his fist up Celeste's throat, causing her heartburn to sizzle and flame. She hurried to Luc's stall, collapsing on the bed.

Matt followed. He placed his hand on her forehead. "What's wrong, Little Mommy?"

She hated being privy to Matt and Luc's intimacy. The goddamn kisses. The tying of a tie. The image of Matt's hair brushing and tickling Luc. How would Chris fit in? She'd assumed the couples would be Luc and Chris. Matt and Celeste. The occasional dalliance between Luc, Matt, and her. Not Luc and Matt's romantic coupling.

"Is it the baby?" Luc brought over a glass of water and helped her to sit up and drink.

"I need to see Chris graduate," she said. "I need to see his mom and dad. I need to feel normal."

Luc shook his head. "We'll bring Chris here tonight. Late. After his parents go back to their inn."

Matt said, "Don't be stupid, Celeste. You can't see his parents. They'll take one look at you and send you home."

She said, "Chris and I were supposed to graduate together."

"Poor Little Mommy." Matt sighed, brushing his fingers through her hair, combing the tangles free. "Celeste's been depressed lately, Luc. Not good for the baby." He scooped her in his arms, helping her stand. "I'll drop you at the school's entrance."

"Non, idée terrible."

"If she's hiding behind the manzanita, no one will see her. They'll be looking at their sons on the stage," Matt said. He turned to Celeste, adding, "Dress in dark colors. Stay in the shadows."

Luc repeated, "Non, idée terrible."

"Either I go with you two or I walk." Celeste hurried to the sewing machine stall and slipped into a long-sleeved, navy shift dress she'd recently finished. She pinched her cheeks.

Matt said, "You and your pregnant belly slay me. I concede to your demands. Your will is my will." He cupped her face in his hands, kissing her.

Luc removed his tie clip, using the clasp to secure her hair. "A new barrette. Chic."

Matt said, "Do we have time for a quick fuck?"

"Her or me?" Luc asked.

"Celeste," he said, slipping his hand up her dress. "She's easier to access." Matt eased her onto the hay bale, lifted her hem, and unzipped his fancy pants. Even without his bud-adorned beard and long hair, without his outlaw grooming, while fucking he remained the same madman.

After he finished, Celeste went to the kitchen sink, wet a washcloth, and wiped herself clean. "I'm ready to go."

Luc said, "I don't have a good feeling about this. Celeste should stay here."

"A promise is a promise." Matt took the cloth from Celeste and handed it to Luc. "Wash my cock."

"Imbecile," Luc said, but he lifted Matt's softening dick and stroked it.

Matt unbuttoned Luc's trousers. "Blow him, Celeste."

"We need to get to the graduation," she said, and left. Matt and Luc didn't follow, and she knew what they were doing. She climbed in the truck and honked the horn. Matt shouldn't be blowing Luc on Chris's graduation day.

When Matt came out, he called toward the barn, "If you want a ride, hurry up, Luc."

"We can't be late," she said.

Luc slammed the passenger door and shook his head. "You are making trouble for Chris."

She said, "I won't be a problem." The truck bounced along the road. The men, flanking her body, kept her in the seat. She stroked both their legs, a gesture of thanks for bringing her along.

Basscombe maintained its natural architecture by not covering the grounds with balloons and banners like her high school did for its graduations. Arches with trailing vines and orange chrysanthemums adorned the stage. The podium faced the manzanita hedge, which meant the audience couldn't see her peeking, but the faculty and graduates would if they looked beyond the rows of relatives. She doubted the dean would point at her and shout, "Intruder," or jump from the stage to chase away a peeping, pregnant girl.

When she saw the Armstrongs walk across the grassy meadow to find their seats, she almost sprinted over to give them a hug. She had to bear down in her spot, willing herself to stay put, squeeze her mouth tight, take a deep breath, and not call their names. The Armstrongs, her pseudo family, the people she'd loved, then disliked for what they'd done to Chris. Now, she forgave them. Their decision to send him away had set her and her baby's trajectory.

Perched in the back row, Matt stretched his arm on the empty chair beside him. His fingers drummed the wood. He shifted in his seat. She wished Matt had taken his time and pleasured her earlier, instead of only himself. An orgasm would have settled her nerves.

The forest seemed strangely calm, as if the Basscombe faculty had bribed the stellar jays and the gray squirrels to take a break from squawking and chattering, allowing the speeches to resonate.

"Pomp and Circumstance" played, and the sea of families stood. The faculty entered and walked up the steps to the stage. Among them was Luc, wearing the same silk gown as the other professors. Why had they included him? Soon, everyone would be startled watching Professor Laurent leave the ceremony hand-in-hand with one of his former students. Was the reason Luc had grown distant a prelude to this event? His unconscious way of prepping her for a gain at the expense of a loss?

The boys shuffled in, and the audience clapped. Alphabetical order; Chris came first. Seeing him in his cap and gown, she winced. He'd messed up their chance to graduate together. She'd messed up her chance to graduate at all.

"Mr. Christopher Armstrong," the dean said into the microphone.

Dr. Armstrong lifted his camera. Mrs. Armstrong clapped. She loved their simple kindness. Wanted to sit beside them, whispering how much she admired their parenting skills. She stood, held the manzanita hedge aside, almost slipping through. If Chris hadn't started speaking, she would have.

Chris gazed at the faculty, pausing a moment at Luc, then searched the crowd, waving at his parents. He cleared his throat and began, "Ladies and gentlemen, Mom and Dad, distinguished professors, and fellow students, I came to Basscombe a mischievous boy. I leave a responsible young man. To quote my favorite author, Mr. James Baldwin, 'Love does not begin and end the way we seem to think it does. Love is a battle, love is a war; love is a growing up.'" He adjusted the microphone, leaning closer, his exhale audi-ble."In conclusion, I'd like to add that when I become a father, I hope to emulate my own. Furthermore, I'd like to acknowledge my parents. If they hadn't sent me to Basscombe, I'd never have found my true love."

She covered her mouth. Had he just said that?

The audience murmured and coughed. The dean's expression contorted into confusion. The graduates giggled. The faculty fidgeted. Among them, Luc remained stony faced. All she could see of Dr. and Mrs. Armstrong were the backs of their heads.

The audience sat perfectly still until someone clapped and others politely joined in. The dean, taking the podium, requested everyone wait until the end of all the speeches to applaud.

Chris smiled at Luc before he took his seat. Luc inclined his head slightly.

Redwood needles and cones twirled in the autumn sky. Confetti. Ticker tape. She wanted to run onto the meadow and ask Dr. and

Mrs. Armstrong what they thought of Chris's speech, if they realized he was gay. Pride, fear, and longing intertwined around her heart like a helix.

The ceremony ended. People milled throughout the meadow, engaging in conversation. She envied the mingling of boys and mothers, boys and fathers, teachers and parents, flowers and food, hugs and kisses.

Standing, she smoothed her dress, patted her hair, dusted the dirt from her knees, and walked through the open gates.

Chris, flanked by his parents, shook his head at her, mouthing, "No." Quickly, he led them toward the main building and away from her.

She kept walking.

At the punch bowl, Luc dropped the ladle. He held his hand like the crosswalk-guard Jesus.

Matt, still seated in the back row, waved her over to sit with him.

She ignored Matt and continued forward. The daisies, lining the driveway, reminded her of the buttons Bernadette had sewed on one of her favorite dresses. She plucked a flower and stuck the stem behind her ear. The softness of a petal brushed her cheek. Seeing the Armstrongs, she felt like a child again, cared for and safe in their presence.

Chris led his parents in the direction of the mural. Their backs turned away from her.

Before she stepped off the driveway and onto the grass, Luc sprinted, blocking her. "Merde, Celeste. What the hell are you doing? C'est erroné."

She said, "I want Thoreau to meet his grandparents."

"He will someday. After he's born." His voice rose with each word. "Please don't expose your whereabouts. If you don't care about that, please don't incriminate us and ruin everything for Chris."

Celeste said, "Didn't you hear his speech? He told them about you."

"He implied he'd found love. He wasn't specific." Luc took her arm, guiding her back up the driveway. "Don't be a foolish, impetuous girl."

She watched as Chris ushered his parents to the porch of the main building. Away from the meadow. Away from her. "I want them to know about the baby," she said, her voice rising.

Luc gestured for Matt to come help. "Please believe it is best for everyone if you wait."

Matt dashed over, slipping his fingers between hers. "I'll take this wild filly home," he said.

Sweat beaded on Luc's forehead. "Everyone is wondering who you are. They'll think I got someone else pregnant."

"You did get me pregnant," she said, and frowned. "I want Dr. and Mrs. Armstrong to see me."

Matt said to Luc, "If anyone asks, say she's my wife, and we're friends of yours."

Luc tucked a flop of hair behind her ear. "Celeste, be reasonable. His parents won't see this as Chris's baby. Not yet. We must handle the news in the correct way. Not ambushing them in a public place."

"He's more Chris's baby than he is either of yours," she said.

"What a ridiculous illusion to maintain," Luc said, irritation coating his words.

Matt pulled her against his side, his hand rubbing her back. "Calm the fuck down before we're busted. You want Luc and me charged with rape? That's what will happen."

Luc exhaled, a burst of air through pinched lips. His breath a blend of cherry punch and tobacco. "If you genuinely love Chris, leave."

"You can't question my love for him. He's my conceptual twin. My only real friend."

Matt gripped her wrist and led her up the driveway away from the party. "Whoa, Little Girl. You're a mess."

She said, "I'll hide behind the manzanita and watch the reception. I won't cause any more of a scene."

"This craziness is what I get for persuading Luc to let you come?" Matt opened the truck's door, offering a hand to help her climb in. When she didn't take hold, he pushed her inside. "I'll make you a good meal, tuck you in bed, and do whatever you want me to do."

As he went around to the driver's side, she jumped from the seat and ran. She couldn't have made more of a scene if she'd parachuted from outer space. Everyone outside turned to look as she sprinted across the lawn, her hard, round belly pressing against her dress as if any moment the seams could split and a baby would tumble out, her enormous boobs bouncing, her hair as mussed as Juliet's ballerina bun before Chris buried the rat, Luc's shiny silver tie clip trying to hold her bangs in place. A girl lost. A girl needing to be found.

From a distance, she watched Mrs. Armstrong standing on the porch, shielding her eyes from the sun. Dr. Armstrong pinching the bridge of his nose, squinting in her direction. Chris swung open the door to the faculty lounge, coaxing his parents inside.

Celeste stopped in the center of the crowd. She stood next to a table of cakes and apple pies, her eyes darting from where Chris had disappeared with his parents; to the Basscombe boys and their families; to the professors; to Matt, who had chased her; to Luc, who kept his distance.

Matt handed her a piece of cake, wrapped his arm around her shoulders, pulling her in for a lingering kiss as if she were his wife and her jarring behavior the normal consequence of pregnancy hormones. "Are you trying to ruin everything for us? Because if you are, you're doing a fucking fantastic job."

"I'm coming clean," she said. "Being honest."

"You're the maddest motherfucker I've ever met. Get your goddamn shit together," he whispered. If anyone heard him, they didn't intrude. They were too polite to insert themselves in a perceived domestic squabble.

Embarrassed, her cheeks flushed as proof. "I'm sad, Matt."

Matt took her plate of cake and set it on the table. He gripped her elbow, escorting her back to the truck. On the way, he said loud enough for everyone to hear, "I love you, sweetheart. You're exhausted. Let's get you home."

Luc stood near the bird mural with a group of boys and their parents. He glared at Celeste when she passed by.

Matt drove to his cabin, ignoring her protests to go to the barn so she could sleep in her own bed. "I can't leave you by yourself. You've gone completely bonkers, Little Girl. You and your childish tantrum."

"When Chris brings his mom and dad to show them the barn, I want to be there to greet them," she said. "They're practically my in-laws. I want to let them know I forgive them."

Matt twisted the faucet, filling a glass with water. "Your make-believe in-laws would ship you off to a home for insane, delusional, teenage, unwed mothers."

Collapsing in a chair, she covered her face with her hands. "I spent more time at his house than mine. They didn't even recognize me."

Matt's voice softened. "You were a football field away, mixed in with a crowd. You're pregnant. You're the last person they'd expect to see at Basscombe." He opened his stash box, ripped a bud into pieces, and stuffed them in his pipe, inhaling, holding his breath, exhaling. "For being book smart, you're an idiot."

"But forcing Chris to have sex with you and Luc makes you brilliant? You're perverted."

Matt looked her in the eyes and laughed. "I'm the perverse one?"

Shoulders slumped, she whispered, "Chris will do a better job of raising a kid. I'll only ruin his life." She'd never felt this terrible. Not when Bernadette was drunk and dismissive. Not when she discovered Matt and Luc were lovers. Not when Chris was sent away.

Matt set the empty pipe in an ashtray and crossed the room, balancing on the armrest of the chair where she sat huddled. Slipping his hand under her hair, he rubbed her neck, pressing his thumbs into knots the size of acorns. "You're Queen of Homosexual Land. You're bringing forth our Little Prince. Or princess. What would we do without you?"

Dropping her forehead into her hands, she said, "Be normal. Be sane."

He filled the kettle to make her a pot of tea. "Relax, Little Mommy. You've got nowhere to go and nothing to do. This herbal will help. I'll cook a pot of soup and make cornbread."

Celeste laid her head against the back of the chair. When he brewed the tea and offered her a cup, she sipped. Woodsy in flavor. Fresh leaves swirled on the surface before settling at the bottom. "What is this?"

"An herb Jasmine recommended to help keep you calm."

On her second cup, it tasted stronger, as if she were lying in the forest, mulch her pillow, loom her blanket.

Matt hummed as he diced and sautéed onions and garlic. Boiled water. Chopped vegetables. Measured barley. Smoked pot. Smoked cigarettes. Drank beer. Snorted coke. Poured her a third cup of tea.

Shadows shifted. The bright day turned to dusk. She wondered if Chris told his parents about his lover, and if he took them to the barn to show them where he and Luc would live. She hoped they'd notice the photograph Matt took of her in the garden and demand an explanation. Sleep came over her like a black cloak.

The sun, barely peeking over the horizon, lit the kitchen in streaks of yellow. Matt stood in front of the stove, all fires flaming. A mess spread across the counter, mixing bowls, wooden spoons, grocery sacks, spice jars, and a milk bottle. He scooped pancake batter from the bowl, licked the thick paste off his finger, and smacked his lips.

The aromas of cinnamon and nutmeg lulled her upward. She thought she'd fallen asleep in the chair with her clothes on, but she was in Matt's bed, naked. "Wasn't I dressed?"

Matt smiled. "And then you weren't."

She went to his bathroom to shower. It felt sticky between her legs. She called out, "Did we have sex last night?"

Matt called back, "What a question."

While soaping and scrubbing herself, the scene came into focus. Luc and Matt at the table, drinking and smoking. Luc had glanced at her and said, "Chris is free, mon petite oiseau. He's emancipated. He's mine. He's yours. He's ours. Our golden boy will be with us soon enough." Then Luc bent over a mirror and sniffed, and soon afterwards, bent over her, whispering how much in love he was.

Celeste stayed in the shower until the water ran cold. She knew Matt liked the zing and buzz of cocaine, a kickstart to the head and heart, but Luc told her he never tried it. Slipping into Matt's robe, she breathed in the musty fragrances of pot and soil, pomade and almond oil. The combined scents of Matt and Luc. Their shared robe. If she possessed magic, she'd make those two vanish and make Chris appear. The previous Sunday in the redwood circle, his final one as a Basscombe student, Chris had fallen asleep with his ear to her belly.

Next to the bathroom sink, Matt kept a toothbrush for her, although she rarely slept over. She squirted paste on her brush, ran the bristles across her teeth. The details of the night were fuzzy. She rinsed her mouth and rinsed her face.

Matt said, "Pancakes." Slivers of butter and maple syrup dribbled down the sides. He sipped coffee, added more cream, and grinned. He sprinkled powdered sugar over his stack. "Chris's parents weren't thrilled about the emancipation, but he had the paperwork done on time, so what could they do? The kid's smart."

She rubbed her eyes with her fists. "Did they ask about me?"

"I doubt they even thought of you. They're spending today helping Chris move out of Basscombe."

"To the barn?" If they saw evidence of her, would they demand answers? Come looking for her? Take her home to Bernadette and George? Have Luc and Matt arrested?

"Of course to the barn," Matt said. "Where else is he going to live?"

The kitchen felt hot. She loosened the robe. "Did they meet Luc?"

"The esteemed Armstrongs haven't met their queer son's lover. Not yet. They haven't accepted their son is queer. They think his speech was about a girl."

"When they find out about the baby, that'll cheer them up."

Matt speared a bite of pancake, holding a taste to her lips, urging her to eat. "Arrangements have been made. You're living with me now."

Pushing the fork away, she said, "No, I'm not."

"Little Mama, last night in the middle of us fucking each other until our brains exploded, you agreed to live with me and let Chris and Luc have the barn." He folded his pancake in half and stuffed the entire disc into his mouth at once.

"I'm not staying here. I'm going home."

"This is home. You've been traded. Swapped."

Celeste shoved the chair from the table, slipped into her shoes and dress. When he tried to stop her, she slugged his arm hard enough that her knuckles throbbed.

Gripping her shoulders, Matt pulled her down to look in her eyes. "Idiot girl, you can't give birth to the kid in a barn."

"Fuck you, Matt, for telling me what I can and can't do."

"Chris and Luc agree. It's safer here."

Until that moment, she hadn't considered the difficulty of climbing the ladder to the hayloft with a baby in her arms. She'd have to trudge to the outhouse. The barn had no electricity. "I need to talk to Chris about it. I'll talk to Jasmine," she said.

Matt unfastened Luc's tie clip from her tangle of hair. "Our wild child."

"The tea you give me last night? What was it?" She'd been so tired she could barely lift a hand. Barely open her eyes.

"Valerian leaves. You were out of your mind at Chris's graduation. Jasmine mentioned if you had trouble sleeping, the valerian in the forest would help you relax. You asked for a second cup. A third." Matt sat back at the table and ate his pancakes, sipped his cup of coffee. "I'll take good care of you and our baby. I love you. I love mon Grande Homme. And it's only a matter of time before Chris and I fuck. We'll be one big groovy free love happening." He waved his arms, and the fork slipped through his fingers and skidded across the floor near her feet.

"Chris doesn't want to have sex with you." She couldn't see where his fork landed. She could barely see her toes. Thoreau stirred. "All misfortune is but a stepping stone to fortune." Henry David told her to buckle down, weather the storm, grind though.

It took a couple of days for the valerian to wear off. Thoreau seemed quieter, too. Celeste stayed in Matt's bed, hidden by covers, exhaustion overwhelming her. Matt brought her meals, placing a tray on the mattress. He rubbed her lower back, used his tongue to coax orgasms, loosened the birth canal with his wanker, did her laundry, washed her hair, scrubbed her body, tucked her in bed. A decent person would feel grateful for his attention. She did not feel decent.

"Have the Armstrongs gone home?" she asked.

"They left, yes."

"Drive me to the barn. I'm too tired to walk."

Matt stood at the kitchen counter, washing dishes. "Not yet."

"I need to see Chris. I've been patient. I've been more than patient. You owe me this."

"I owe you?" he said, shooing her away with a flick of his wrist.

Kneeling, she untied the cord on his pants, eased his penis into her mouth, and sucked until he hardened.

Matt tugged, pinched, and squeezed her neck. "You're a cunt, Celeste. You get what you deserve."

She pulled away from him, looking upward. "Why did you say that?"

"Have you ever told me you love me? I've said it to you a thousand times. You think a blowjob will get you what you want?" He stuffed himself back in his shorts.

She didn't love him. Blowjobs did get her what she wanted, usually. Standing, she leaned against the kitchen counter. "There are lots of things I love about you. You protect me. You're protesting the war and resisting the draft. You're an amazing cook. A great lover. The best."

"You love all that about me, do you?" He finished cleaning the kitchen and made the bed. "Get dressed. I'll drive you to see him, Little Mommy."

Scattered across the barn floor were Luc's dark suit and briefs, Chris's gray trousers, white shirt, cap and tassel, boxers, socks, and spit-shinned shoes.

Matt lit a cigarette, crushing the burning match between his finger and thumb. "Three days later and they're still in the hayloft."

It saddened her that Chris hadn't been dying to see her like she'd been dying to see him. The price for her indulgences with Luc? She sprawled on Luc's bed and covered her nose with the blanket. Cigarette smoke sickened her.

The ladder shook and wobbled. Chris jumped the last few rungs. Stumbling to the horse stall, he grinned wide, sat cross-legged at the end of the bed, hugging Celeste. "I can't believe how happy I am."

She held him as if any moment he'd float into the heavens, rapture-like, and leave her stuck on earth. "I wondered when I'd get to see you," she said.

"At my graduation, you really scared me. You went batshit." As he spoke, he held her at arm's length, frowning.

"I wanted to say hello to your parents." Her heart grew heavy with guilt—a brick of uranium, atomic weight—for disrupting his celebration, then for being in bed while Luc and Matt went at each other, then at her, with a crazed, cocaine intensity. She had no defense for any of it. "Your graduation was a bad day and a worse night for me."

Matt said, "She's a crackpot."

"I'm here now, Celeste. In the barn. Luc's in the barn. You're in the barn. Basscombe's a distant memory."

Matt said, "I'm in the barn, too." He climbed to the hayloft, poked his head through the opening. "Luc, we've got a shitload of work to do. Vacation's over."

Luc said, "Coffee."

Celeste told Chris, "You and Luc move into my hayloft. I'll take his horse stall."

Chris said, "The plan is for you to live with Matt at his cabin."

"No, I'm staying here."

"Better for the baby. Better for you. At least for now, okay?" Chris patted her belly. "Hello, my sweet dumpling. You've gotten bigger."

Thoreau shifted. What if the baby was Matt's? What if it came out blond and brown-eyed? Mean and needy? What would she do? Love him, of course, but she'd keep Matt at a safe distance from corrupting him. Kissing Chris's cheek, she squeezed her eyes shut as if her desire and want could manifest paternity.

"My parents hate the idea of me living in a barn. It completely freaked them out," Chris said.

"What did they say about your emancipation?" she asked.

"Shock and sadness. They think I'm punishing them."

"Have you told them about Luc?"

"When that day comes, I want them to love Luc, not think of him as the one who turned me gay. They're living in the dark ages. I'm still their straight little boy."

Meeting Chris's baby, his spiritual baby, will make everything better, she thought. She imagined their smiles when she introduced them to their grandson.

PART FOUR

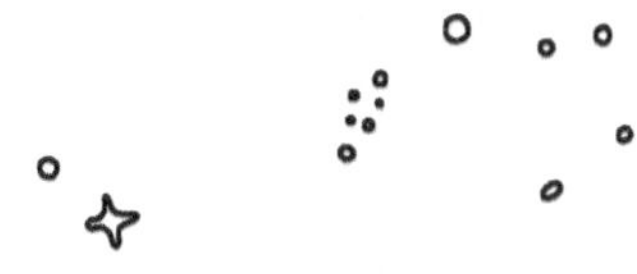

Shaking herself awake, Celeste struggled toward the bathroom as a gush of water ran down her legs and puddled on the floor. She thought she'd peed, but the liquid looked clear and had no urine smell. She called, "Guys, my bag of water's flooding the hallway."

"Ce qui?" Luc said, rushing to her side. "Matt, get up."

Luc and Chris had moved to the cabin a few days prior. Without phones, information would've been too difficult to share.

Chris whispered, "Celeste, are you in labor? Is this finally the time?"

Before he finished his question, Celeste felt the answer twisting her womb. She said, "Contraction." She wanted her baby out. He was almost two weeks post-due date.

Luc reached for a towel and dabbed her inner thighs, following the trail of amniotic fluid. "Belle, Mamam."

When Chris pulled Celeste into his arms, his foot swirled a rag through the puddle. "We've done this."

"I haven't done anything yet," she said. The familiar flash of anxiety zapped her chest. If the baby was Matt's, they'd all be trapped forever.

Chris spun her around, singing, "We're going to have a baby. We're going to have a baby."

"Don't make me dizzy, or Thoreau won't know which end to come out of." She collapsed on the couch, her teeth chattering from cold and fear.

Matt rolled over, facing her. "The baby's coming?" He brought her a wool blanket, tucking the corners across her chest. In mid-November, frost iced the windows. "I'll build a fire. Get you warmed up." After laying kindling and wood in the stove and striking the match, he smiled at Chris. "You certainly look cute in your school pajamas, Basscombe Boy."

Chris said, "Shouldn't you call Jasmine and let her know what's happening?" Jasmine had lent Matt a ham radio. Matt wouldn't let anyone else use it.

"Good idea, smart boy," Matt said. He stood before the contraption, twisting the knob until he heard a buzzing and clicking.

Frowning, Celeste placed her hands on her abdomen. "They've stopped. False alarm. I woke us up for nothing. I'm never going to have a baby. All I'll ever have is a bowling ball on steroids."

"Mon amour, the womb water doesn't break in false contractions." Luc stroked her forehead with the back of his hand.

Matt spoke into the receiver and gave his call signal, "Midwife Flower. Cabin Girl's ready." He'd been instructed never to use their real names in case the government listened in.

"Tell her I'm no good at this." Celeste threw the blanket off and heaved herself to standing.

"You're good at everything," Chris said, clasping her hand. "You're Celeste, the chimp vet in space. Brave. Fearless. You can achieve the impossible. You built Walden Creek. You survived pregnancy."

Luc guided her back to the couch. "Oui, tell Jasmine we need her."

Celeste felt as if she'd gulped a quart of Heavenly Hill and hopped on a merry-go-round, resulting in a gamut of dizziness and emotions and sensations and nausea. "Let her know I'm scared and don't know what to do."

Matt nodded at Celeste and listened to Jasmine. When he hung up the mouthpiece, he said, "Jasmine reassured me at the beginning stage of labor, contractions are sporadic. We're supposed to call her back when they're three minutes apart."

"Three minutes?" Chris gasped, almost choking on those two words. "She'll miss the birth, and we'll have to deliver the baby ourselves."

"My water broke," Celeste said. "Did you tell her?"

"Do you think it matters?" Matt opened his drawer and dug around for clothes. Dressing, he said, "By lunchtime, you'll be holding my baby."

"Your baby? You mean Celeste's baby." Luc went to the kitchen to make peppermint and licorice tea. Jasmine had told them the combination aided labor. "We'll soon meet him or her and your pain will be finished, Celeste."

Matt reached across Luc for a tin of coffee. He lowered his voice as if whispering a secret for everyone to overhear. "I've banged Celeste hundreds of times. The baby's mine. How many times did you?"

"You were there. You should know," Luc said.

Chris stepped between them, his finger to his lips. "He'll be the baby of Walden Creek."

"He'll have three daddies." Luc kissed Chris, bending him backwards like a sailor with a gal.

Matt added more wood to the fire and waved a magazine, igniting flames.

The spicy, sweet scent of the peppermint-licorice tea sickened her, but she sipped anyway. If it sped the birth, she'd gulp a pot of it. As she watched Matt fan the fire, images of a light-skinned, screaming infant filled her mind's eye. Matt had been exceptionally attentive since she moved to the cabin. Cooking and cleaning. Following Jasmine's instructions. He'd also left Luc and Chris alone, which meant the most to her.

Chris checked the pile of items they'd need for the home birth: hot water bottle, towels, bowls, sterilized receiving blankets, extra pads, sheets, the camera. He prepared Matt's bed, laying down a shower curtain to protect the mattress and sheets from bloodstains, then remade the bed with an old sheet they'd throw away afterwards. Jasmine had warned them how much bodily fluid can be spilled during a birth.

Luc pressed a teeny dressing gown over her abdomen. "Fits perfectly. Through maybe a little alteration here." He tickled her below her breasts, where her stomach curved like a vision of the horizon through a drunken sailor's periscope.

She whispered, "I need him to look like you, Luc. I need him to be yours."

"Ce sera," Luc said. "Matt's rather handsome. You can't go wrong having a baby with Matt's genes."

This baby had co-opted her body for almost ten months. She resigned herself to a life with her outlaw boyfriend, her platonic best friend, and Luc as their shared lover. Maybe someday, she and Luc could give Thoreau a brother or a sister. Luc had the stamina. She had the desire.

"Mon petite oiseau," Luc said.

The clock barely moved. The world conspired to come to a halt. Celeste picked up a book and sat by the kerosene lamp. The print strained her eyes, blurring into a mishmash of unintelligible words. "What if something bad happens? What if he gets stuck? What if my body won't cooperate?"

"Women have been having babies forever," Matt said.

Chris said, "I love you, Celeste. Even if I don't say it enough. I really love you."

Luc smiled. "We all love Celeste."

"We've all loved Celeste, if you know what I mean," Matt said. "Except you, Chris. You keep your little boy dick in your pants."

Chris narrowed his eyes. "I am about to become a father, so shut up."

Luc said, "You two are pesky gnats."

Matt said, "Little Boy is jealous of all the fun you and I had while he was locked away with all those other Little Boys."

Luc put his hand over Matt's mouth. "Shhh. Stop bothering him."

Hobbling outside, she stood beneath the dome of stars, arms outstretched to the heavens and the planets. "Protect my baby," she said. The stars blinked. The frigid night took her breath away.

Her next contraction felt like someone threw a massive tantrum inside her. She went back to the house. "I don't have the patience to raise a willful child."

Chris laughed. "I guessed right? We're having a little Celeste?"

Luc held her hand. "A girl like you? How sweet this will be."

If her child was a girl, Celeste wouldn't degrade or reprimand her. She'd teach her daughter to be as strong as any man. She'd tell her to have sex with whomever she wanted, and never let a man touch her unless she asked him to. She'd give her daughter the confidence not to put up with anyone's aggression. She'd encourage her to settle down with one guy, not three, and live happily ever after. Or become a nun and not have sex at all. Or have multiple partners, but on her own terms.

By sunrise, her labor pains became regular. Matt turned on the ham radio and let Jasmine know the time had come. "Midwife Flower, Cabin Girl's ready. Three minutes apart."

"What if she doesn't make it?" Chris whispered to Luc and Matt. "What if Jasmine's late?"

"Shhh!" Luc said. "Celeste will hear you."

"What if I don't make it?" Death in childbirth seemed a possible scenario. Celeste had read plenty of Victorian novels in which the outcome wasn't pretty. Pain shot through her as if strangling from the inside.

Jasmine came through the front door, carrying a large black duffel bag of midwifery accessories: Doppler, fetoscope, birthing stool, and portable oxygen tank. After placing the objects on the bed, she excused herself to wash her hands, unwrapping a new bar of soap.

Celeste stood close by and watched Jasmine through the open bathroom door, scrubbing up and down her arms, in between her fingers.

"I'm going to take a peek." Jasmine told Celeste to lie back. She spread her labia, guiding her fingers inside. "The baby's in the perfect position. Excellent. You're about six centimeters dilated."

Matt and Luc sat at the table, staring at each other, not her, as if they'd never seen a vagina up close before and didn't want to start now. Chris, who had never seen any kind of vagina, knelt beside Jasmine and peered in. He uttered, "I think the hole's too small for a baby to come through."

Matt said, "She'll stretch wider."

Celeste dropped her head. "I hoped I'd be almost ten centimeters by now."

"For how long you've been in labor, six is excellent. Because the water broke, we need to urge the baby into the birth canal. Why don't you go outside and take a walk? The fresh air and sunshine will feel wonderful. Revitalize you." Looking at Matt, she scolded, "The next time you go through this, if there is a next time, be sure to mention to the midwife the bag of waters broke. You left out a really important detail, Matt. You put her and the baby at risk of infection."

"No harm done. Everything's okay." Matt scratched his cheek.

Jasmine flung the stethoscope around her neck. "The more information you can feed me, the better. Celeste, take your walk. Guys, keep her company. I'll boil water."

Celeste said, "It's morning already?" She hadn't noticed when the house lights went off and the sunlight came in.

Chris took her hand as he opened the door. "Let's jiggle this baby downward."

Luc grinned at Chris. "We're going to be daddies soon."

On the walkway, leaves fell, twirling from the madrones and redwoods like an autumn rain.

"When you first told me you were pregnant, I tried be calm, but inside I was freaking out," Matt said. "What a fucking lot of responsibility a kid is. Especially for an outlaw."

Luc said, "When Celeste and I get married, she and I won't be outlaws. Chris isn't. You're the only one, Matt."

Matt shrugged. "Since the day I met Celeste, I knew she'd be trouble."

"But you took her home anyway," Chris said.

Luc kissed Celeste on her cheek. "We've gotten ourselves entangled with trouble."

Celeste was uninterested in their rambling conversation. Her only interest lie in birthing a baby.

"Merci, Celeste, for everything you have done for us. I'm in love, love, love," Chris said. The birds and squirrels and wind in the trees sounded happy and gay.

Celeste squatted, breathing through a contraction. "The lingam at your goddess of love shrine came through in a big way."

Chris said, "The lingam always comes through in a big way."

Luc said, "You should know."

Their laughter sped up the contractions.

Matt sprinted back to the cabin to see if Jasmine needed any help.

"I'm glad he's gone," Celeste said.

Luc said, "Matt's not a bad guy. He's taken good care of you."

"He's taken good care of you, too," Chris said to Luc.

"He'll take care of you if you'd let him."

"That's absolutely the last thing I want," Chris said. "The absolute worst experience of my life. Ugh, Luc."

"Shh." Celeste glanced from Chris to Luc and back to Chris. She squatted again, pushing into another contraction. "Shh."

Luc said, "I'm also going to check in with Jasmine." He kissed Celeste, squeezed Chris's bicep, and left.

"Luc and my little spat didn't take your mind off the pain?"

"You can't take my mind off the pain," Celeste said. "You can exasperate it, though."

Chris looped his arm through hers, guiding her along the trail.

In the cabin, she slumped in the chair, wrapping her arms across her chest. "Jasmine, is this normal for labor to go on for so long? Something's wrong. Tell me the truth."

Jasmine assured Celeste she was exactly where she was supposed to be.

This news did not comfort Celeste. "Come on, Thoreau. Hurry up." She wanted to be finished with pregnancy. She wanted her baby, not this somersaulting alien.

Half an hour later, she dilated to nine. In that moment, centimeters seemed bigger than God.

Matt roasted potatoes. The cabin filled with the scent of rosemary and olive oil. "You need nourishment," he said to Celeste.

Jasmine encouraged Celeste to be active. "It'll help your pain and let the baby know it's time to be born."

Celeste moved around the room, holding onto the edge of the kitchen table and lowering herself to the floor, bending at the waist, lying on the rug, and pulling her legs up. She soaked in Matt's bathtub and thought she might give birth there, but the water became cold. Chris remedied the problem by turning the hot faucet on. The water, bouncing against her sides, irritated her. She stood, dried off, stumbled to the bed.

Chris, Luc, and Matt acted like bumbling stooges. They wandered about, falling over each other.

Matt said, "So much easier when all I had to do was bring on Celeste's orgasms."

Chris said, "Don't talk about that now."

Luc slid his arm around Chris's waist. "You're such a prude, and I love you for it."

Jasmine pulled more objects from her bag and set them on a towel. Celeste couldn't see what they were but imagined a tray of scalpels and sutures. By this point, she didn't care how Jasmine got the baby out. She wanted the birthing to be over. Her vision blurred with pain.

Jasmine took Celeste's hand, guiding her fingers towards her parted thighs. "Celeste, feel down here."

Celeste touched her vulva, swollen and tender. "Puffy like a cloud."

Jasmine held a mirror for Celeste to see. Celeste was surprised how much it looked like a shrine flower, rosebud-pink and multi-petaled, as if a goddess manifested where a vagina had been. "Beautiful."

"Cunts are magic," Jasmine said. "Transforming into an exquisite pillow for your child to be comfortable as he or she slips into this world. Your cunt, Celeste. Yours. Don't ever let anyone think differently."

Matt said, "Her pussy is something wonderful."

Jasmine told Matt, "Check the water. Make sure it's still simmering."

Luc whispered in Matt's ear. Matt responded by laughing.

Jasmine said, "You two, stop mucking about and help."

Chris nodded in agreement.

The contractions intensified. Jasmine guided Celeste to kneel on all fours.

Celeste leaned onto her heels, coming forward again, bearing down, her back rising.

Jasmine said with a smile, "Your baby's on his way."

Luc, Chris, and Matt bent at the foot of the bed and stared, their eyes and mouths as wide open as Celeste.

"I can see the top of the little head." Luc's voice rose in pitch. "Dark, curly hair."

"Oh God, oh God. We're practically parents," Chris said.

"Time for you to push, Celeste," Jasmine said.

"Push," the guys repeated.

Celeste gripped the mattress. Every cell of her body bore down. She whimpered, "Come on, sweetheart." For what seemed like an eternity, she pushed with all the strength she had. "Come meet your mama."

The baby slipped forth from his watery nest into Jasmine's hands.

Luc gushed, "Our baby. Our Thoreau."

Matt said with resignation in his tone, "He's yours, Luc. The kid's not mine."

Celeste sat up, clasping the baby in her arms.

Thoreau's tiny fist raised as if waving goodbye to the womb. His hair stuck up in a messy tangle of seaweed drenched in the fading liquid of his first home.

"Thoreau, Thoreau." Celeste couldn't stop saying his name.

Chris whispered, "He's grinning."

Celeste said, "He gets his smile from you, Chris."

"Mon bébé," Luc said.

Matt said, "Your baby, Luc. Obviously yours. Chris, you had nothing to do with it."

Celeste frowned at Matt. "He has everything to do with Thoreau being here. He built the goddess of love shrine. I believe in his magic spells."

Luc and Chris cut the umbilical cord, holding the surgical scissors hand over hand like dignitaries. Matt stood to the side and watched, eyes narrowed.

When Thoreau's head rested against her heart, droplets of colostrum dripped from her nipples. His tiny mouth opened and closed like a baby bird's.

Matt brought her a warm washcloth, wiping her forehead. "I'll never look at a cunt the same way again. No more for me."

"Stop saying macho shit like that," Jasmine said. "Soon, you'll be begging her for a fuck."

"I'll have to erase this day from my memory."

Celeste ignored Matt and brought the baby to the breast, guiding the nipple between his lips.

Jasmine leaned close, scrutinizing. "You're doing well with breastfeeding. Usually babies don't take to it right away."

"She's got perfect tits," Matt said. He put his mouth on the free nipple and sucked. "Luc, with the triumphant sperm, have a sip. See what all the fuss is about."

Despite being annoyed with him, Celeste felt the relief from Matt's mouth.

Jasmine said, "Her milk will let down in a couple of days. There'll be a hormone overload. Celeste will be sensitive and emotional. Dote on her and do what she asks."

Celeste leaned back, closing her eyes. Her suckling babe. A hush. A lullaby. "We're parents, you guys."

Chris said, "I'm a daddy. You're a mommy. How'd we get here?"

Jasmine said, "Birds and bees, and horny men."

When the time came for Celeste to birth the placenta, Luc and Chris took the baby and stood in the kitchen, passing him back and forth. Matt removed the potatoes from the oven. He opened the refrigerator and took a Stony Brook, popped the lid, and swilled.

Placing her hand on Celeste's abdomen, Jasmine said, "When you feel a contraction, push hard."

"Feels like I'm having another baby. What if I have twins?" Before that moment, Celeste had never thought about the placenta, and her lack of knowledge, her naiveté and ignorance, frightened her. "What am I doing, Jasmine? I'm not ready for this responsibility."

"No one's ready," Jasmine said. She pulled on the cord.

Celeste bore down, grunting and straining and delivering the placenta.

Jasmine dropped it into a bowl. "Want to see what this looks like? What's been nourishing your baby these past nine months?" She picked up the crimson, gelatinous blob and stretched it wide, showing Celeste the delicate web of arteries running through. "Lovely to see something your body made for your child."

"Panes in a church window." Celeste called the guys over to see. They shook their heads and said they'd rather stare at Thoreau than a clot of blood.

"This tore from your uterus and left an open wound the size of a dinner plate. Be careful with your body for a few weeks." Jasmine scooted Celeste over to the chair, then yanked the stained sheet and shower curtain from beneath her. Underneath was a freshly made bed. "I'll put a towel down for the bleeding. You'll need to wear a monstrous menstrual pad for awhile." She put a package of heavy-duty sanitary napkins beside Celeste.

"I'm going to keep bleeding?" Celeste asked.

"Here's a list of instructions for self-care," Jasmine said, handing her a sheet of paper. "Soaking in a tub of warm, salty water. Putting a cabbage leaf on engorged breasts. Nursing through painful mastitis. Refraining from sex for at least four weeks."

Celeste said, "No sex for four weeks?" She hated thinking of the effort it would take to keep Matt away.

Jasmine snapped her fingers to get the men's attention. "Are you young bucks listening to these instructions? Celeste shouldn't fuck until her body's healed. When the time is right, it will be for her to decide. Plan for more about a month. You can go down on her if she wants."

Matt said, "Tongue on pussy. No cock in pussy. Got it."

Chris cradled Thoreau against his chest. "Quiet. Don't talk like that around him."

"Don't say pussy around him or you? Sissy man. Pansy man." He nodded at Chris. "My cock in your mouth or in your ass? Is that better?"

"You've proved your he-man status in this family, Matt. Be quiet for once." Jasmine packed up her objects and turned to Celeste. "If getting the baby to nurse ever seems difficult, have a bottle of beer and relax. Remember, your nipples are made to fit in his mouth. Your breasts are made for making milk." Jasmine said goodbye, leaving them alone with their baby.

Matt said, "Congratulations, Luc. I mean it. The best sperm won the egg." He kissed Celeste on the lips, kissed Thoreau on the cheek, stood taller, shoulders back. "Celeste and I will try to make our own kid someday. We'll be one big happy family."

Celeste said, "Give me a chance to take care of the one I have now." Her breasts swelled and dripped, soaking the robe. She handed Thoreau to Chris and hobbled into the bathroom, strapped on a sanitary belt, tied the ends of the pad through the metal clips on the garter. Waddling back to bed, she said, "I feel like a duck."

Luc sang, "Fais do do, Thoreau mon petit amour. Fais do do, t'auras du lo."

"This is the best day of my life," Chris said, laying Thoreau in the cradle of her arms.

Thoreau gave a comical tremor of his head as his lips puckered and searched for her nipple. When he latched on, Celeste felt connected to every mother who'd ever lived. Not just every nursing mother, every mother who grew a baby, birthed a baby, fed a baby, loved a baby. Even Bernadette. She'd once cradled Celeste against her chest, changed diapers, wiped dribbles from her baby's chin. Even Bernadette.

Being a mama with three papas was a breeze. The men cooked, cleaned, gardened. They held, swaddled, and rocked Thoreau. They giggled at the sounds the baby made slurping milk as loud and lustily as a pub full of Irish Catholics.

When Celeste conceived, she didn't have a notion of the fierceness she'd feel; a baby seemed abstract, like a Jackson Pollock painting she'd seen in a book. Yet, here he was in her arms, as real as could be. She pulled the baby close, whispering his name to the gods, Thoreau, Thoreau, Thoreau. Her incantation for protection.

One day, Luc brought home a parcel, shipped from France and delivered to their shared post office box. He made an elaborate display of opening the package, saving the decorative French stamps from tear. "Someday, Thoreau may collect these," he said. He smiled at the package contents: a navy-and-white striped sweater, red knit pants, and a tiny jacket with an embroidered rabbit on the front. He translated the card from his parents: "We are very happy about Thoreau. We also like the name. An American writer? Your Basscombe contract will soon be up. Where will you live? Paris is a wonderful place to raise your children. We would like to meet your lovely wife and our grandson."

Celeste interrupted, "I'm glad you told them about Thoreau, but their letter makes it sound like they don't know you quit your job at Basscombe." The baby startled. Her nipple slipped from his mouth, spraying his face with a milk galaxy. Using the edge of her sleeve to wipe the droplets from his cheeks, she continued, "And it sounds like they don't know you're gay."

"It's easier having them believe I'm an employed straight man, than telling them all the ways I am not who they expect me to be," Luc said. He poked the logs in the wood stove with the tongs. A burst of air scattered ashes onto the hearth.

Celeste switched Thoreau to her other breast. The baby nestled in with a quiet murmur of satisfaction. "Tell them you're in love with the other father of your son."

"This is serious business, this coming out, this confession, especially to people of old-world values. It's one of the reasons I'm on a different continent," Luc said.

Chris folded the diapers. "Don't be judgmental, Celeste. Your parents didn't know you were pregnant. They don't know they're a grandma and grandpa."

"Bernadette and George would flip if they saw me right now. Saw us. Saw this life," Celeste said. She'd considered emancipation when Chris went through the process but decided it would be too risky to get the paperwork started. "Bernadette and George would love him if they met him. How could they not?" She wanted to believe this but doubted it would ever be true. The second they saw his coloring, they'd turn him away. She dropped her head, resting her chin on top of Thoreau's head, breathing in the scent of her child.

"You're saying your parents would be upset if they saw you living and thriving in the midst of Sodom and Gomorrah Land?" Matt kissed her, his mouth parting her lips, his tongue swiping hers. "If I could get in touch with my mom, if that ever becomes a possibility, I'll tell her exactly what's going on in my life. Tell her about Luc. Tell her about Thoreau. I'll tell her about you, Celeste. How I love and hate you equally."

"Jesus, Matt. What did I ever do to you?" She turned away from him and brushed a piece of lint from Thoreau's curls. How normal it had become to ignore Matt's cruelty. Easier than getting angry about something she couldn't change.

Chris said, "I can't wait to break the news to my parents."

"Patience." Luc added more wood to the fire and stated the obvious: "Celeste's still underage. Matt and I are not."

Chris waved a diaper in the air. "When she reaches the age of consent."

"She's old enough to decide who she wants to fuck, so I don't see a problem." Matt offered them each a bottle of beer. He'd redrawn the label, adding two more men, a woman, and a child. "They'll insist you're not his real father, Chris. He doesn't look like you."

Chris said, "After they meet Luc, they'll accept I'm Papa Chris. He's Papa Luc. She's Mama Celeste."

"I'm not included in your suburban scenario?" Matt said.

Chris sipped his beer, eyeing Matt as if deciding the best response. "It's up to you. Are you Papa Matt?"

"I may not be related to Thoreau, but I'm banging his mama and papa. I'd do it to you again, Little Boy Cutie, if you weren't such a goddamn prude about it."

"But you're not having sex with Luc anymore," Chris said, "and you're sure not having sex with me."

To keep this from escalating into an argument, Celeste said, "Matt, of course you're included in parenthood."

Matt plopped down beside Chris. "Your parents don't believe you're a fag? Look at you, Dainty Boy."

Luc said, "Détendez. Calm down."

Matt stroked Chris's cheek with the back of his hand. Before Chris could protest or pull away, Matt held Chris's head and kissed him. "Yummy boy. Yummy. You're a good kisser."

Chris's face turned pink, then red. He shoved Matt off the bench onto the floor. Stood above him. "You had your fun; now leave me alone."

Luc said to Matt, "Stop pestering my boyfriend." He looked at Chris, adding, "Matt's trying to rile you. Ignore him."

"You're not my type, Matt. Not in the slightest." Chris wiped his eyes.

"Big wankers aren't your type?"

"Cruel men aren't my type," Chris said, forehead scrunched, arms folded.

Celeste put her nose into Thoreau's curls, breathing in his beautiful scent. "Stop fighting, please."

"Chris and Celeste are a blast to tease," Matt said, laughing. "Gets them flustered. Shows how young they are." Matt lifted Celeste's peasant blouse. He flicked her free nipple with his tongue. "Yummy girl. Yummy. You're one lucky baby, Thoreau."

"Matt, you're an ass," Chris said.

Matt said, "That's what Luc likes about me. How different I am from you, Little Boy. He can't dominate me like he can you."

Celeste swatted Matt and said, "Leave Chris alone." Her breasts felt engorged, painful. Switching Thoreau to the other side, she winced when he latched on.

"Does it hurt? Can I get you anything?" Matt asked.

"I feel like a concrete monument to boobs."

Matt went to the bathroom and came back with a warm wash-cloth compress, pressing it against her. "Relieved? Soon your tits will be back to normal. Your milk won't be squirting everywhere."

Celeste glanced at Matt. "These breasts are doing their job well." She didn't want to admit it to him—Matt's ego didn't need inflation—but when he sucked, it brought tremendous relief.

Chris said, "I have a present for you, Celeste." From outside, he brought in a smooth stone. On its surface, in Indian ink, he'd written a quote by Henry David Thoreau: "We linger in manhood to tell the dreams of our childhood."

Matt said to Luc, "Those two bore me."

Luc said, "They don't bore me."

Celeste wrapped Thoreau in a swaddling blanket. "Better to bore you than excite you, Matt."

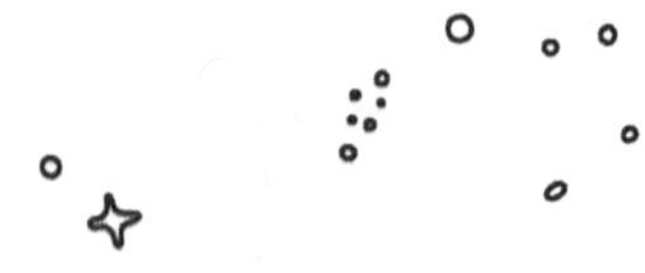

Thoreau evolved from a gurgling newborn into a double-chinned, drooling baby. The hue of his skin remained similar to the day he was born, except what once seemed translucent turned opaque like a desert sunset. Everything he did they clapped at, commented on, treated as though he were the cutest baby in the entire world. Which, of course, he was.

Celeste wondered how anyone got anything accomplished when they had an infant; she never wanted him out of her sight. When he wasn't nursing, she'd share him with the papas, feeling exceptionally generous for letting them hold him.

Jasmine came to the cabin for the eight-week post-birth checkup. She shooed the men out, demanding time alone with Celeste. Without the three men around, arguing and tripping over each other, the atmosphere settled into calm. Jasmine prodded Celeste, her fingers gentle. "Your vulva and vagina feel healthy and healed. How long did Matt leave your cunt alone?"

"He tried to have sex with me at three weeks. I pointed to the calendar. He tried at three and a half. I pointed to the calendar. At five weeks, we had sex. My milk leaked everywhere. He was annoyed at the mess."

"He's got enough people around these hills to fuck. He doesn't need to interfere with your sensitive cunt and your sensitive tits. Those belong to you. Next time, tell him to piss off."

Celeste laughed. "Easy to say, hard to do."

"He's insistent, that's for sure."

"He and Chris don't get along," Celeste said. "They can barely be in the same room. Chris refuses to have sex with him."

"Matt doesn't like it when people tell him no." Jasmine checked Celeste's breasts and explained what to do if she got mastitis. "Inevitable side effect of breastfeeding. The only cure is to nurse through it. Painful, but trudge on."

Celeste said, "Matt's really mean to Chris."

"Matt doesn't like people he can't fuck or blow." She lifted Thoreau, undressed him, inspected his body, his reflexes. "I'm not a pediatrician, but this kid seems strong and healthy. Nice big, round nursing cheeks."

Celeste said, "He's perfect."

"You're pretty perfect yourself. Your body's adapting to motherhood. Seems like your temperament is too."

"I'm tired of sex."

Jasmine nodded. "You'll want it again someday, but until you do, be brave, say no."

Celeste said, "If I don't sleep with Matt, he'll keep bothering Chris. It's a kind of trade. Sex with Matt for Chris's happiness."

"Your cunt, your choice what to do with it." Jasmine packed up, wished Celeste well, and left.

Celeste lay on the bed, cradling the baby. Hours went by and all she'd accomplished was staring at him. Long eyelashes, tight curls, perfect fingernails, folds in his elbows, dimpled knees.

That night, Matt said, "I want to have a kid. I think we should make one of our own. My jizz. Your egg." He stroked her belly. The pregnancy curve, a memory. "You're the sweetest mother of them all."

She glanced at Thoreau, asleep in the bassinet. "Another baby?"

Matt shifted his weight, climbed over her, guiding his erection in. No condom. "Imagine Thoreau with a sister."

Outside the window, the silhouette of forested hills against the darkening sky. Inside, Matt above her. His brow knit in concentration, hips lifting, smile like the sliver of moon.

Celeste debated whether or not to mention the likelihood of Matt being sterile. She decided against it. "I don't want to go through months of morning sickness." Not the most romantic segue into orgasm.

"Celeste," he said, and put his finger to her lips.

"Stretch marks," she said.

"Anyone can have young, unmarked flesh. I love the way your body's a map of your experience." When he touched her breasts, her milk let down, sprouting like a fireboat. He wiped her chest with the edge of the sheet and pulled her close. "I love you."

"You love parts of me," she said. "Not me."

"Are you kidding? I love everything about you." Gripping her lower back, he ground himself into her.

"Matt," she said, "can you be gentler?"

"I can. I won't. Let's fuck until your legs are wobbly and your pussy's full of my cum. You're going to have my baby."

"No baby. Not yet," she said, shaking her head. "Just sex, Matt."

"Just sex, Matt?" He rolled off her and slouched on the edge of the bed. "Goddamn it, Celeste. Why don't you want to have a kid with me? I'm not good enough for you? I'm not Luc, the French fag? I'm not beautiful, precious Chris, the American idiot? I'm merely the wage earner, supporter of all of us, owner of the barn, the cabin, the guy with the biggest cock, but that's not good enough for you to have my baby?"

"It's more than good enough. You're more than good enough." She went to the bathroom for a washcloth, pressing it against her swollen breasts, soaking up the flow of milk. "Calm down." A tantrum would disturb the baby. It had taken hours to get Thoreau to fall sleep.

"You're telling me to calm down. Fuck you."

If she ever got pregnant again, it wouldn't be with Matt. A baby deserved stable genes to develop a healthy brain. Not a rattled, paranoid, cruel one. "My uterus needs time to recover before another fetus moves in."

"How long does your precious fragile body need? Six months? A year? Two? Ten?" He stuffed his erection into his jeans. "Thoreau's a replica of Luc. If he wasn't attached to your tits all the time, no one would think he's your kid." Matt jumped from the bed and slammed the door behind him.

Thoreau let out a panicked screech.

"Sweetie," she whispered, picking him up, and sitting in the chair to nurse him back to sleep. "Matt's loud, isn't he? I'll keep you safe."

If Matt's current mood continued spinning into a downward spiral, her body would be the collateral. Their unfinished conversation screamed as loud as a colicky babe in church.

The morning light streaked through grimy cabin windows.

"Matt?" she said, stretching. "Do you want me to make tea?"

No answer. A seething Matt was worse than a screaming Matt. Silence bred hostility. She slipped into his robe, wrapped Thoreau in a sling, and went outside. She'd apologize for hurting his feelings. She'd do what she needed to do.

A hint of fog left the ground spongy. The orange bark of the madrone glassy and wet, its leaves slick and dripping water pearls. She liked this time of day when the jays hadn't begun their frantic calls.

Thoreau grinned up at her.

Spotting Matt near the stack of firewood, she called, "Come home. We can talk about having a baby. You're nurturing. You've taken good care of me. You provide for Thoreau. You and I will have a beautiful baby." It's good he's probably sterile, she thought. He can't replicate himself.

Matt stopped and turned around, kicking dirt with the toe of his boot. "I like Thoreau, but he's not my kid, is he? You guys make it perfectly clear every time you huddle around him oohing about what a miracle you've created." A jay landed on a branch, opened its beak but kept quiet.

"Pregnancy's exhausting. That's all I was trying to say. My body needs time to recoup."

"I know how hard hatching a kid is. Who was with you the entire nine months? Me. It wasn't easy," Matt said, his voice rising.

Thoreau's eyes widened. He reached a hand toward Celeste's face. She rocked side to side. She'd make a secret appointment at the clinic where Jasmine worked and have an IUD inserted. An insurance policy in case Matt had one active sperm.

Flipping her off, he said, "Your pussy's not made of gold."

"It's not?"

"Those nine months you were an emotional shit," he said. "A first-class bitch."

She felt like an inept woman sent to diffuse a bomb. "If I was so terrible to be around, why do you want me to get pregnant again?"

He pulled a pipe from his pocket, ripped a bud apart, lit a match, blowing smoke toward her. "Who am I to you, Celeste? You treat me like I'm some disgusting prick, not the man who tells you he loves you even if he never hears it back."

Celeste covered Thoreau's ears with her palms. "It's hard to love someone who's constantly calling me names."

Stepping forward, he raised his hand.

"If you hurt us, I'll turn you in," she said. "I don't care if I'm sent home."

"Conniving cunt." He dropped his arm and disappeared into the woods.

Exhausted, she sat at the base of an oak and opened the robe to nurse Thoreau. He wiggled and fussed, latched on, gurgling. She stayed under the tree until her baby fell asleep and her pulse slowed.

When she got back to the cabin, Matt greeted her, smiling. He strutted around the room, singing, "Love shack," and performed a slow striptease. He draped each item of clothing over a different piece of furniture. Placing his hands on her shoulders, he said, "You're beautiful." He lifted sleeping Thoreau from her arms, put him in the bassinet, pushed Celeste onto the floor. Rough-hewn. Uncarpeted. Splinters. "I'm not an unlovable asshole, Little Girl. Luc loves me, Boy Scout's honor." He held up two fingers in a pledge, then slid them into her.

"Thoreau's diaper is wet. He needs to be changed," she said, trying to squirm away.

"I packed us a picnic. We're going to find a romantic place in the forest to fuck until I've planted enough seed in you that you'll be sprouting a dozen of my kids."

Trapped beneath him, she opened her mouth and bit his shoulder.

"Want to play rough?" He thrust himself into her.

She'd flee from the cabin, the barn, the land, and never come back.

Thrust, pump. Thrust, pump. Thrust, pump. "I need you, Celeste. I love you, Little Girl."

She'd ask Mr. BM which book he'd recommend for understanding psychopaths. She imagined he'd suggest Raymond Chandler's *The Simple Art of Murder,* because he'd once mentioned it as an interesting read. The next time she went to the bookmobile, she'd check it out and study the text word for word.

Thrust. Pump, pump, pump.

Matt told her he loved her when he came. He told her he loved her when he dressed. He told her he loved her when he stood over Thoreau, singing, "Blackbird." Take these broken wings and learn to fly... The baby cooed. The baby smiled. Matt grabbed Thoreau and tucked him into his shirt, then took his backpack and ran out the door.

She bolted after him. "Where are you going? I'll carry Thoreau." The robe blew behind her. Semen dribbled down her thighs. "Come back. You need to come back."

Matt ran up a deer trail into a thicket. "We're having a picnic," he said. An enormous downed redwood spanned the length of a landslide. Matt climbed onto one end. He looked small on that ancient tree, but he wasn't small. Thoreau was.

"Give me Thoreau." Her heart beat fast. Blood rushed through veins, draining from her head. She felt dizzy but remained standing, arms outstretched. He'd never put Thoreau in danger. Only her. He'd never been mean to her baby. Only her. Her and Chris. "Please give him to me." She forced herself to sound calm. "I'll do anything. Anything you want." The baby was so tiny against the backdrop of that redwood.

"You have to come and get us," he said, balancing along the tree's entire length, hundreds of feet long. If the redwood had been erect, its top would pierce the sky.

As she climbed, the shaggy bark scraped her bare chest, her belly, and her legs. Splinters hurt, she thought, relieved for the physical distraction. "Let's go home and make a baby," she called.

Matt started singing again. "Blackbird fly, blackbird fly. Into the light of a dark black night…"

"Matt, wait for me," she said. "Please."

He pretended to stumble, and laughed when she screamed.

On the ground below the log, a gully of ferns. Soft. Soft. Cushion. Soft landing. She stared at the earth, then up, keeping her eye on the bulge under Matt's shirt. Her baby.

"Look at your mommy, Thoreau. She's shaking because she loves you, not me," he called, jumping off the other end.

Celeste screamed again. Her voice startled the birds and insects into silence. Death had come. Running to the spot where they'd disappeared, she covered her eyes. "No, no, no."

"We're fine." Matt stood at the base of the tree, his face turned upward, smiling at her.

Celeste slid into a mossy indentation left by the shallow ball of roots and sprinted toward them. "Give him to me," she demanded, ripping Matt's shirt open.

"Don't be dramatic," he said, handing Thoreau to her.

Cupping the baby with her hands, she pulled him close to her chest. If she didn't have Thoreau in her arms, didn't feel his skin against hers, she'd have slugged Matt to the other side of the universe.

Squatting, he raked redwood needles into a nest. "Sit down," he said, tugging her beside him. "You've got to get it together, Celeste. Your paranoia isn't good for your son."

Am I the insane one? she wondered. Imagining danger where there isn't any? Vilifying Matt instead of myself? I'm the lunatic, aren't I? She had an urge to get away. She'd wait for the perfect moment and run.

Matt opened his backpack and took out a paper sack, unwrapping slices of bread. Dribbling honey across the top, he stuck a nasturtium blossom into each center, handing one to her. "For you, Little Girl."

Where would she run? Through coyote brush? Through poison oak? Through ferns and nettles? If she removed Matt's robe, she'd be naked, camouflaged. Harder to spot. Where would she go? To the barn? No, that's the first place he'd look. Where would she take Thoreau?

The baby gazed at her and grinned the dopey grin of someone too innocent to understand insanity.

"Put him here. Where the ground's soft," Matt said.

"I'm going to hold him." She'd wait until her legs were steady. She tried to picture the best place in the forest to hide and wondered how to keep Thoreau quiet.

Taking the baby from her arms, Matt set Thoreau in the nest he'd prepared. "Stare up at the wonders of nature, Little Man. See the bright sky? The fluffy clouds?" He kept one hand on Thoreau's chest, the other on Celeste's knee, squeezing. His fingers pinching her flesh.

She prayed, "Keep the devil away, keep the devil away," as if she could conjure Chris's bowl of rose petals and blades of grass.

Thoreau lay in the forest, kicking and punching the air, seemingly content under the patch of blue.

Matt pinned her hips with his hips, her thighs with his thighs, her chest with his chest. "For fuck's sake, Celeste. When are you going to learn you're mine as long as I want you to be?"

How did a girl who grew up planning to orbit the galaxy become bound to earth?

The forest was saturated with the fragrance of tangy sorrel and sweet rhododendron. Needles and leaves twirled in the air. Overhead, a gregarious woodpecker hid acorns in the trunk of a tree.

A curtain of paper butterflies, hung at the entrance of a horse stall, created a cacophony of multicolored wings.

Matt lifted a strand, examining the handiwork. "Apropos I've brought you this damaged Queen Monarch."

Celeste's eyes darted from Chris to Luc. She started to speak but felt unable to form a sentence. They'll sense how much I hate Matt, she thought. They'll feel my seething in their bones. They'll rescue Thoreau. They'll rescue me.

"Our Queen and Little Prince." Luc kissed Celeste's cheek as he reached for Thoreau.

Celeste clung on, and she wouldn't give the baby to him. She'd clung to the baby as Matt pulled her across the downed redwood through the woods to the cabin. Clung to the baby when she changed from her filthy, earth-stained robe into a shift. Clung to the baby when Matt yelled he'd take her to live in the barn like the animal she was. Clung to the baby when Matt screamed her cunt wasn't worth the goddamn trouble. Clung to the baby when he smirked and said she was no different than any other bitch he'd been with.

Thoreau squirmed, stretching his little arms.

Taking him from Celeste, Luc said, "Thoreau's soaking wet. He needs to be changed."

Celeste flushed in shame. Her baby was drenched. He'd get a rash.

Luc asked Celeste, "What's wrong?"

"She's on the rag," Matt said.

"I'm not."

Chris frowned at Matt. Clasping Celeste's elbow, he guided her away from him. "Are you okay? Can I get you anything? What can I do to help?"

"She's got her period, Chris. She's not dying," Matt said.

Celeste stood frozen, only her eyes able to move, watching Thoreau.

Luc laid the baby on the hay bale bed, opened the bottom drawer where they kept diapers. Folding the cotton into a triangle, he raised Thoreau's legs, slipped the diaper under him, ran the safety pin through his hair before sliding it between the thick folds. He tossed the wet diaper into a bucket. "Voilá."

Chris said, "Papa Luc, you're an expert diaper changer. You're good at everything you do." He pushed past Matt and kissed Luc on the lips.

Matt dropped Celeste's duffel bag on the floor. "Celeste's moving into the barn with Chris. She's worn her welcome with me."

Chris said, "I'd love you to move here."

"Little Girl doesn't want to be fucked anymore, so Little Boy, you're the perfect impotent for the job."

"What an asshole," Chris said.

Luc said, "Stop it, Matt. Chris, shhh. Don't get caught up. He's trying to rile you."

Matt smiled. "You'll live with me, Luc."

Luc shook his head. "Idée stupide," he said. He cooed as he dressed the baby in overalls, topping his head with a knitted cap.

Celeste's muscles tensed. If she needed to, she'd take Thoreau in her arms and run across the universe, skipping star to star, planet to planet, constellation to constellation, stopping on Gemini, Chris and Thoreau by her side.

"A sensible idea, not stupid," Matt said. "You and I have tons of work to do. The crop's going to be massive this season. Once it's sold, we'll be flying high with cash. We can add an addition onto the cabin. Live together under one roof. One big happy communal fag fuck. How's that sound to you, Chris? One big happy orgy."

Chris said, "Sure, Matt. Sure. One big fag fuck."

Luc said, "I don't need to move into the cabin to get the work done."

"We'll do more than just work." Matt cupped Luc's groin and winked at Chris. "A fair trade, don't you think? Two for one, or are you worried I got the better end of the bargain?" He wrapped his arm around Chris's shoulders. "Sweet Little Boy."

Shrugging him off, Chris said, "We're not trading Celeste and Luc and Thoreau like they're cattle."

Matt laughed. "Fine. We'll trade them like they're racehorses. I get the stud. You get the filly and colt."

Celeste eyed Chris. She eyed Luc. Avoided Matt. While they argued, she picked up the baby and took him to the garden. Near a patch of lavender, she collapsed. Lavender usually helped calm her nerves. Nursing him, she whispered words of love.

The gate squeaked open. She looked around for a forgotten tool. She'd use it to smash Matt's skull.

Chris approached her. "Matt's stuck on a rage fueled merry-go-round and can't get off."

Unable to voice how terrified she'd been when Matt ran off with Thoreau, how fearful thinking her baby was gone forever, she abbreviated the horrendous scene. "Matt wants to have a kid with me." Honeybees buzzed. Ladybugs strutted toward aphids.

Chris tucked a sprig of lavender behind her ear. "That's it? He wants a baby?"

"I love Thoreau's little mouth," Celeste said, focusing on her beautiful boy instead of what happened in the woods. "It's shaped like a heart."

"When he's sleeping, he looks like you." Chris said.

"Matt, a renegade comet, hurling through space, causing havoc. A wounded man is a dangerous man."

Chris brushed his hands through her hair. He twirled the ends between his fingers. "The guy's intense."

What if it wasn't as bad as she thought? What if Matt just wanted the assurance he was a good father? What if all he'd wanted was to romance her with a picnic in the redwoods?

"He doesn't hurt you or Thoreau, does he?" Chris asked, his question spoken softly.

She shook her head vigorously. Wanted it to be true. Needed it to be true. "He'd never hurt the baby."

Chris laid back in the grass. "Luc's been acting different."

Celeste hadn't paid enough attention to notice. Luc was attentive to the baby. Kind to Chris. Not exactly like the early days, but a lot had changed since then. "What's he doing different?"

"He keeps bugging me to sleep with him and Matt again. Says it will be good for us to be more adventurous."

"Tell him no. Tell him to fuck off."

"I tell Luc I'm adventurous enough by ignoring the fact that the man I love is sleeping with someone else. I pretend I don't care. I pretend I'm not jealous." Chris cradled Thoreau's foot in his hand. "I'm not like they are. I love Luc. One man. He used to appreciate that about me."

"Stay how you are, Chris. Don't become someone else for him," she said. "The night of the talent show? Did any part of you want to be with Matt?"

"I was enamored with Luc. I'd do anything he asked. Even humiliate myself by letting Matt screw me while Luc jerked off."

Chris picked a blade of grass and tossed it aside. "They went after me like beasts, and I was their kill. I hated it."

Celeste said, "Oh, god, Chris."

Chris winced. "Luc saw how upset I was. He promised he'd never let Matt touch me again. Now, he bugs me all the time. 'Let's fuck Matt together.'"

"Because I've dropped out," she said. She felt a stab of guilt in her heart.

"This has nothing to do with you."

"It's my fault. I can barely tolerate Matt touching me."

"Luc promises this threesome thing is about fun. I tell him I don't want to be with Matt. I tell him I don't like Matt. I remind him that Matt hurt me. You know what Luc says?" Before she answered, he continued, "'If Celeste can handle Matt's cock, you should be able to.'"

"Luc said that? He wouldn't say something like that about me." She switched Thoreau to the other breast.

"That's why I said he's different," Chris said. "He never used to be vulgar."

She brushed her thumb across a thistle flower and was tossed into a memory of George bringing her home a nail brush. "Luc will get back to his regular self. He loves you."

"Will you come with me to the barn? I have a surprise for Thoreau." Chris offered his hand and helped her off the ground.

Cradling the baby, she followed him and scanned the room for Matt. Nowhere in sight. She wanted to live with Chris. Wanted this peace and quiet.

"Look what we made," Chris said. On the wall in the back of the barn was a mural of a tiger, reclining against a bodhi tree, a butterfly perched on its paw. Propped in one corner of a crib sat a ballerina doll. A dancing bunny, not a rat. "Babette de Paris." Chris tickled Thoreau's cheek with its whiskers.

"She's like Juliet of Province." Celeste held the doll, admiring the craftsmanship. The ballerina bun. Green eyes. Freckles. This time, the muslin had been soaked in coffee, turning it a shade of brown. "Thoreau will love her."

From the hayloft came the sound of footsteps. Matt climbed down the ladder. "Tonight your boy's sleeping in his very own room." A smear of white powder lined his nostrils.

"He's too little to sleep alone." She tucked Thoreau's body between Babette de Paris and her chest.

"The kid's tougher than you think." Matt reached into his backpack, took out a bottle of sparkling wine. "My plan was to enjoy this with Celeste on our picnic, but the mood wasn't right." Holding his palm over the top, he slowly twisted the wire.

She hated the way he stifled the cork, not letting it soar.

Luc peered over the railing. "Do I hear the sound of Champagne?"

"Get down here, Luc. Instead of toasting to making my baby, I propose a toast to having a bumper crop." He poured himself a glass of wine and held it in the air. "To all the motherfuckers I love to fuck."

"Glad I'm not one of them anymore," she said.

Luc took the bottle, filled three more glasses. "Les personnes de marques d'amour font des choses folles. We will not be fools today." Dilated pupils. Flared nostrils. "We will love one another."

Chris slipped his arm around Luc's waist. "We will always love one another."

Matt set the bottle on the dresser. "I'll leave this for you kids to enjoy, Little Girl and Little Boy. Take good care of Little Man, your precious Thoreau Laurent Armstrong." He turned to Chris. "Convince Celeste the baby needs a sister or a brother. One that looks like me."

"Sure, Matt. Whatever you say." Chris kissed Luc, and said, "Stay here, Luc. Please."

"Whatever I say?" Matt reached over and grabbed Chris's crotch. "You hard for me?"

Chris hit Matt's hand away. He grabbed Luc's sleeve, shaking him hard. "Tell Matt to leave me alone."

Luc lost his balance and fell against the siding. "Chris," he scolded. He straightened up, then tossed a few clothes into his suitcase. "Think about joining us in the cabin. Think about all the craziness the three of us will create." Luc held Chris in his arms, tilted him back, groped his body from head to toe. "Rest up. I'll see you in a few days, mon amour." He left. He left with Matt.

Chris yelled, "Fuck you."

Celeste stood at the window. The truck zoomed away, sputtering pebbles and leaving dust in its wake. Luc was going along with this plan, but why? Blame it on Chris's need for monogamy. Blame it on Celeste dropping out of the ménage à trois.

"I'll sleep with Matt. I'll do it for Luc," Chris said.

"No, you won't. You can't do that." Gazing into the sky, Celeste counted the stars as they slowly appeared. Mars pulsed. Venus, stationary. Never again would she let a man ridicule her. She wouldn't let it happen to Chris, either.

The bookmobile rumbled down the road, pulling into a parking place at the plaza. She hadn't been in months and needed a new stash of books. Chris stood at the payphone, making his weekly call to his parents.

Mr. BM cranked the door open. "Welcome, Celeste. I haven't see you in a long time."

"Look what I've got," she said, pulling the wrap aside to show him Thoreau.

Mr. BM said, "How'd you get a colored baby?"

"What did you say?" she said.

"He's colored." The librarian peered closer.

"He's my baby. I'm his mother." She backed out of the bookmobile and rushed across the plaza.

Chris looked up from the phone booth. He held his hand over the mouthpiece, calling, "What happened?"

Celeste collapsed on a bench. Unwrapping Thoreau from his sling, she lifted her shirt, settling him against her breast. This was how interactions would be for the rest of her life, wasn't it? People questioning her maternal connection to her own baby? While pregnant, she'd read Baldwin's book, *Another Country*. Baldwin wrote about interracial sex, bisexuality, fear, and black rage. She'd read as a curious white woman. As someone who loved a homosexual. As someone who was having sex with a black man. As someone who tolerated a bisexual. Baldwin described himself as a "bastard of the West." Thoreau was born out of wedlock. Did society consider him a bastard? Would this be Thoreau's fate? Growing up in a country that refused to evolve? Living at Walden Creek, her baby had been protected from the prejudice of others. Mr. BM broke that spell.

Mr. BM poked his head from the bookmobile and waved her back. "Check out some books, Celeste."

She looked away.

He hopped down the steps, coming toward her. "I've got a few waiting for you."

Celeste said, "Leave me alone."

Chris hung up the phone and sprinted across the road, sitting on the bench beside her. "She doesn't want any of your recommendations today." He wrapped his arm around Celeste, pulling her close.

"I didn't mean to hurt your feelings," Mr. BM said. "I was surprised, is all."

Thoreau's mouth opened, and her nipple slipped out. The baby cooed and smiled.

"Leave me alone," she repeated.

Bending closer to Celeste, Mr. BM grinned. "The book you should read next is *Lolita*. 'She was beautiful and apple sweet.' Sounds like Nabokov wrote this passage with you in mind."

Chris said, "Get away from her."

"Celeste's not shy," Mr. BM said. He chewed a piece of chapped skin from his lip. "She likes my recommendations. Don't you, Celeste?"

The books he'd suggested over the past year and a half, from citizenship and prenatal care to the strange Alan Watts, from *Confessions of Felix Krull* to *Lady Chatterley's Lover* to *Fanny Hill*, she had enjoyed. She'd looked forward to their talks about protagonists and antagonists, plots, settings, and points of view. Whenever their conversation turned to sexuality and courtship in the classics, she'd felt mature. College-bound.

Celeste squinted at him. "Is everyone nuts around here?"

"My little cup brims with tiddles," he said, and chuckled. "Mr. Nabokov's brilliant sentence, not mine."

Chris stood and held his fists in the air, a flimsy attempt at imitating a boxer.

"You've got yourself a fine-looking baby," Mr. BM said. As he walked back to the bookmobile, he added, "And you've got yourself tiddles worthy of a great writer. Apple sweet."

More sad than angry, she said, "I liked you."

Before climbing in the bookmobile, he said, "I liked you, too. You knew exactly what you were doing to me."

She had enjoyed the power she wielded as Mr. BM shifted from behind the steering wheel to come around the checkout counter. Had she been aware how often he brushed against her as he shelved books? Aware of the bulge in his trousers as he retrieved literature he insisted she'd enjoy? His impressive knowledge overtook the perpetual stench of cheap aftershave and the pallor of a man who never spent a day in the sun. Celeste cringed recalling how once, after discussing Rodolphe Boulanger's easy conquest of Emma Bovary, she'd allowed Mr. BM to ogle the soft crest of her breasts as if her body were corseted and restrained, not clothed in a red halter dress.

The pneumatic doors closed. As the truck drove away, dozens of library cards—her alias's?—flew like paper arrows splintering the sky. A book skidded along the road, flipping over until coming to a halt, upended like a stinkbug.

Chris said, "I've got to see what cryptic message he's leaving you."

"Whatever it is, let it get run over," she said.

Chris crossed to retrieve it. "Goethe. We read this in tenth grade, didn't we?" He showed her the title. *The Sorrows of Young Werther.*

"Great. Mr. BM's planning to shoot himself in the head." She grabbed the book from Chris, flung it across the plaza. Pages and spine catapulted, landing in the dry fountain.

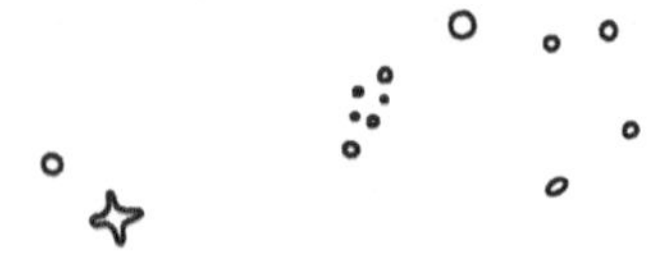

Goodbye, Walden Creek

The barn leaked when it rained. Droplets plinked in buckets. Despite the discomforts and nuisance of a wet floor, Celeste had the domestic life she'd envisioned. She and Chris, almost a married couple. Parenting, cooking, gardening, sewing, sleeping together. Platonically.

Chris laid Thoreau on the hay bale bed and reached for a clean diaper. Around them, the barn looked like a fleet of sailboats in a harbor. White cotton hung from rafters and stalls, fluttering in the draft. "I love our wee babe."

"Rub almond oil onto his scalp, please," she said.

They hadn't seen Luc and Matt in a couple of weeks, and it had started to worry her. Luc usually came to the barn every few days to see the baby and spend time with Chris in the hayloft. She'd never forgive Matt for the horrific picnic in the woods, and she reiterated their sexual relationship was over. He made lewd comments, but instead of begging or belittling her, he complained about the difficulty of finding sellers in a backwoods market where everyone grew weed and sold cocaine.

Chris finished oiling Thoreau's hair. "Sleek baby," he cooed.

She slid the diaper pin through the cloth. It poked her thumb. A prick of blood sat on the tip of the skin like a crimson crystal ball. "There's a break in the weather. Let's go for a walk. Maybe we can stop by the cabin. Thoreau needs to see Papa Luc."

"Matt doesn't like to be disturbed when he's busy with the business," Chris said. "Remember that day when I went to the cabin to drop off the cartoon I'd drawn for Luc? Matt ripped the paper apart, shoved us though the door, yelling how we were nothing more than a prize rooster and a laying hen."

"Matt's ridiculously childish."

"I miss Luc." Chris had been saying a version of this sentence everyday for the past two weeks. "Let's take a chance and visit them. The worst that could happen is we'll get tossed on our asses. The best, we'll be invited in for lunch." He wrapped Thoreau in the cloth sling. The baby squirmed, thrusting his arms and legs, wanting nothing to do with being held captive.

Fresh green shoots emerged on the redwood needles. White and yellow trillium and wild purple orchids bloomed. The blue sky looked bluer. The white clouds, whiter. A buck standing on the trail eyed them before darting off. A breeze rustled Celeste's hair when he fled.

When they arrived at Matt's driveway, chickens flocked around them, pecking the ground at their feet. Matt's truck wasn't there. Celeste called, "Luc? Matt?"

No answer.

"We're here for a visit. We've missed you. Is it okay if we come in?" Chris waited a moment, then pushed the door open.

The cabin stood empty. Everything gone. Table and benches. Chair. Bed. Bedding. Clothes. Weed. Pots and pans. Food. Them.

Celeste shook her head. "What's going on? Where are they?"

In the sling, Thoreau began to wail. Chris placed his hand on top of the baby's scalp and kissed his forehead. "Luc probably packed a picnic, found a beautiful spot, stuffed himself, fell asleep, and lost track of time. He'll be as shocked as we are Matt took off." He stared at Celeste, frowning.

Celeste slid Thoreau from the sling and sat on the floor to soothe and nurse him. "Matt's old business partners did this same thing. Robbed him. Stole the crop and the money."

"I know Luc's favorite place to be alone. That's probably where he is. Should I go find him? I'll go find him." He left in a hurry.

Cradling Thoreau against her chest, Celeste said, "Shh, baby, you'll see Papa Luc soon." She searched through cupboards for some indication or explanation. Looked through dusty corners and cobwebbed doorways. Near the wood stove, a baseboard stood ajar, one end upward like a teeter-totter. She pried it open and pulled out a velvet bag. Inside, she found a slip of paper. In Matt's print, the words, "Fare thee well, motherfuckers. Fuck you both. Fuck each other. I won."

"What does that mean? What's he saying?" She raked through every detail from their last evening together. Thoreau in the crib, sleeping. They'd sat around the kitchen table, playing pinochle. Luc didn't seem unhappy. He'd whispered to Chris, "Mon beau garçon d'amour." He'd kissed Celeste, his tongue swooping against her lips. "Belle mère." Cooed to Thoreau, "Mon beau bébé." Luc couldn't have fallen out of love with three people at once.

Celeste jumped when Chris opened the cabin door. Thoreau, sitting in the middle of the floor, whimpered at the sudden noise.

Sweaty and panting, Chris rushed to Thoreau and apologized for scaring him. "I can't find him. I can't find Luc."

She handed him the note. "I don't understand. Do you understand?"

"Luc's my boyfriend," he said. His arms fell limp at his sides, dropping the paper. It caught a draft, fluttered. Grabbing the note from the ground, he reread it. "You should go to the barn. I'll stay here in case Luc shows up."

"He's gone."

Chris's brow furrowed, eyes darkened. "Someone turned Matt in for drugs. Luc went into hiding. He'll be back when it's safe. Luc loves us. Luc loves Thoreau. Luc loves you. Luc loves me."

"He did love us," she said. "He doesn't."

Settling Thoreau into the sling, Celeste took the long way to the barn, wandering along the ridge and into the neighboring woods. The daffodils and narcissus that Luc had planted in the fall poked their cheery yellow heads through the soil. Sword ferns and tiny orchids colored the pathway along the river. Heartache festered into anger. Anger felt easier than sadness.

When Chris showed up hours later, she saw he'd been crying. Eyes swollen, cheeks flushed. "I have to file a missing-person report. I know you think Luc left us. I know he wouldn't do that," Chris said.

"Don't get the law involved."

Heading from the room, he called over his shoulder, "They'll help me find him."

"They won't care if a grown man's missing." She hurried toward him, reaching her hand to stop him from leaving.

"I care. You don't?"

Hesitating, she inhaled, studying his determination. "If you're going, I'm coming with you."

"You can't go to the sheriff's office. You'll be caught."

She said, "I'll take my chances. I'm almost eighteen. There's not a lot they can do to me."

They hitchhiked to town in the back of a pickup truck. Along the way, they discussed what to say, agreeing to keep their stories simple: Chris and she are friends. Chris is emancipated. She'd be eighteen in three weeks. They needed to find Luc Laurent, a man who'd been living in a cabin with a man named Matt. If asked about Thoreau's father, she'd say he was a wandering peacenik she'd met, but he was long gone. They wouldn't mention their sexual involvement with Luc and Matt.

A photograph on the sheriff's desk showed him holding a kitten toward the camera. The sheriff's fingers pulled the feline's mouth into a wide grin, mirroring his own. "That kitty is now the office cat," the sheriff said. He indicated the animal who'd settled comfortably on Celeste's lap, purring in rhythm to his typing.

The office felt damp. She was glad to have the cat for warmth.

"Cold?" The sheriff switched on the thermostat. The heater clicked a few times before bursting with the sound of contained flames. Although accommodating and friendly, he eyed them both, his glare suspicious.

Chris's voice cracked, tears withheld, when he said, "Luc Laurent taught art at Basscombe. He's disappeared, and we don't know why. It's been two weeks."

Celeste said, "Leaving without telling us his plans isn't something he'd normally do."

"Identification? Driver's license?" The sheriff held his hands in front of them.

Chris, being the only legal person at Walden Creek, always carried his Basscombe student ID in case of emergency. "I graduated last fall and moved in with her. I'm emancipated."

The sheriff phoned Basscombe and gave Chris's name. The conversation was brief. After hanging up, he motioned to Celeste. "Identification?"

"I left my license at home." Celeste squirmed. The cat hopped off her lap. She reached for Thoreau. He'd been fiddling with Chris's leather bracelet. A present from Luc.

"How old are you?" The sheriff sifted through reports.

She mumbled, "Eighteen. Almost eighteen."

"Where are your parents?"

"Southern California," she said.

"Name?"

"Celeste."

He scrutinized her face, then searched through a cabinet, pulled out a manila file, and held a photograph, eyeing it, eyeing her. "You're the runaway we heard about two summers ago," he said. "Mary Celeste Roderick."

Her tenth-grade picture showed a much younger girl. Long, wavy hair; gray-green eyes; a dab of Fuller Brush fuchsia lipstick on her lips and cheeks. "That girl doesn't look anything like me." She felt the truth of this. She'd morphed into someone completely different.

The sheriff unclipped his handcuffs from his belt, slipped them around Chris's wrists. "Afraid I'm going to have to arrest you for harboring a runaway."

Chris shook his head, shook his cuffed hands. "She and I are best friends. We're the same age. We have the same birthday. June 1, 1953. Almost eighteen. I'm not harboring anyone."

"You're emancipated, Mr. Armstrong, which makes you liable for her welfare."

Celeste tried to block Chris from the sheriff. "The guy who harbored me is Matt Briggs. We were living in a barn on his land. Chris and I've been friends since third grade," Celeste said. "You can't arrest him."

"I'm the baby's papa."

"Is that so?" the sheriff said. "You and the child don't share the same coloring."

"Thoreau needs me. Celeste needs me," Chris said as the sheriff led him down the jailhouse hallway. The metal clink of a door opening. Slam. Lock.

Celeste yelled. "I wasn't living with Chris. He didn't harbor me. Matt did. You have to let Chris go. This isn't fair. This is stupid. Stupid. Stupid."

When the sheriff came back into the room, he said, "Coincidence your name happens to be Celeste?"

"Celeste. Not Mary Celeste," she said. Thoreau worked up a howl, his brow knit. She pivoted in the chair and lifted her shirt, settling Thoreau against her chest.

"Mr. Armstrong mentioned you share the same birthday. That date also happens to be Mary Celeste Roderick's birthday."

"Lots of people were born that day."

The sheriff said, "I'm about to make someone's parents very happy." The cat jumped onto his lap.

"My parents won't be happy." A cloud of resignation descended over her. Luc left his son. Left his boyfriend. Left the mother of his child. "They're glad I ran away."

"You're admitting you're Mary Celeste Roderick? Left home on your sixteenth birthday?" The sheriff scratched behind the cat's ears. "How'd you live out there?"

"Matt Briggs gave me his barn. When Chris moved into the barn, I lived with Matt in his cabin. Matt harbored me, not Chris." She'd repeat this until the sheriff unlocked the jail cell and let Chris go.

The sheriff dialed, spoke, dialed, spoke.

Celeste knew she'd be sent home. Her heart burned like a fuselage. Blame this predicament on Matt. Blame it on Luc for not being satisfied with a boy as beautiful as Chris, a baby as delightful as Thoreau, a girl as willing as her.

The last of his conversation: "Mr. and Mrs. Roderick, come get your lost girl. She looks healthy. No, I'm sorry, you can't speak to her. She's indisposed at the moment." He briefly mentioned Chris but said nothing about the baby.

"My mom and dad are coming for me? Today?" She switched Thoreau to the other breast.

The sheriff nodded, and the accruements on his belt rattled. "They thought you were in Alaska. They sounded relieved. Tremendously relieved."

"Relieved?" In a peculiar way, she wanted to go home. Wanted to introduce Thoreau. Wanted a bed where she'd be left alone.

The sheriff searched through more files. "Basscombe says they hired Mr. Luc Laurent, but he left to be with his girlfriend and their baby. Is that you?"

Celeste didn't respond.

"He's Afro-Franco descent," he said, looking at Thoreau. "Seems about right."

"Luc lived in a cabin with Matt," she said. "They've disappeared."

The sheriff flipped through paperwork. Made more phone calls. "We can't find any evidence a man named Matt Briggs exists. Are you sure you've got his name correct?"

She rocked Thoreau, trying to soothe his crankiness. "The draft board probably has a record of him. Last year he was in the initial lot of birthdays called. That December draft." She'd prove Chris's innocence. He'd be released, and they'd go home together. Matt should be punished for betraying her. The law should punish him. "You can release Chris, since he's innocent. My parents can take him home."

Over the next hour, the papers and files on the sheriff's desk grew taller, teetering when the cat nestled against the pages. "Apparently, the place where you've been living belongs to a land trust. There's no Briggs on the paperwork. Looks like you're squatters." He showed her a topographic map.

"Matt told us the land belonged to his family," she said.

The sheriff opened a small refrigerator. He offered her a cold soda. "Men lie."

She gulped, thirsty. "Matt talked about his mother. His sisters. He even cried a few times because he missed them."

"That could all be true. Everything except his name and owning the land. If he is a draft dodger, it would make sense he'd have a false identification."

"Who is he then? Whose land is it?" she asked, as if the sheriff were psychic and this mystery would be quickly solved.

"Did you and any of the men have an adult relationship? Was this a communal kind of arrangement?"

She ignored his question, ashamed and disgusted with herself for believing Matt cared about her and Thoreau. "Will you help us find Luc?"

"Is Luc Laurent the baby's father?"

Thoreau squirmed and babbled and smiled. She said with conviction, "Papa Luc loves Thoreau." Because he once did, and he would again.

"Were you involved in illegal activities? The marijuana trade up here is getting out of control. Cocaine. Heroin. Psychedelics."

Thoreau gnawed on her knuckle. She said, "Chris and I hate drugs."

The sheriff cleared his throat. "When we find Luc Laurent, he'll be arrested for statutory rape." He bent over his typewriter, filing out another form.

Covering Thoreau's ears, she said, "Luc didn't rape me."

"Are you aware of his age?" He didn't wait for her to respond. "According to the Basscombe papers the secretary read to me, he's thirty-three."

"He's around twenty-four. Close to Matt's age." She wiped her eyes with her sleeve.

"Which would still be an adult, if true. He was born in nineteen thirty-eight. You were born in fifty-three, correct?" The sheriff put the cat on the ground. Opened a can of food, shook it into a bowl. "Mr. Laurent has a degree from a university in France."

Celeste buried her face in Thoreau's curls. "He's twenty-four. He's not thirty-three. He loved us once."

"Do you know he's divorced?"

"He was married?"

"Apparently." Pulling his jacket from the coatrack, the sheriff spread the cloth on the floor. "Your baby needs to stretch."

Thoreau wobbled, straightened himself, waved his arms in the air as if he could fly away. Celeste drew her legs to her chest and rested her cheek on her knees. Luc had been married before? He'd been with a woman? He'd pretended to be inexperienced with a female's anatomy. Acted timid around her vagina. Why? To gain her trust? To make her fall further into the illusion? "I think you have the wrong Luc Laurent. Our Luc is gay."

The sheriff squeezed his lips together, shook his head. "If either of those men had sex with a minor, they'll be arrested for statutory rape. You may be close to eighteen now; however, when you conceived the baby, you were not at the age of consent."

"No one raped me," she repeated with less conviction.

"I'll tell you what I think, if you care to listen," the sheriff said. He handed her a box of tissues. "Luc and Matt got mixed up in a messy business. Dealing drugs to the wrong people will land you in a whole lot of cow manure. They were probably in over their heads."

Celeste called, "Are you listening to what he's saying, Chris?"

"He can't hear us talking," the sheriff said.

She turned back to the sheriff. "Do you think they left town because they're in trouble?" If true, it meant Luc didn't stop loving them. Didn't stop loving Thoreau.

"A possibility. Where there's a lot of money being made there's a lot of shifty people." The sheriff set a cheese sandwich and a bag of chips on his desk in front of her. Clearly his own lunch. Tossing her a quarter, he said, "Get the baby a treat from the vending machine. He's a cute kid. Has your greenish eyes."

She dropped the coin in the slot and pushed a number. A lever slowly shifted, and a package of wafers fell, startling Thoreau. She unwrapped the package. Until that moment, Thoreau only nursed and ate mashed banana. When he bit into the cookie, he squealed, clapping his hands. "My boy's entire life is about to change. I'm not ready."

"I think for the better," the sheriff said.

Sneaking away from the office wouldn't have been difficult. The door and windows were left wide open. The sheriff busy with paperwork, phone calls, and tending to Chris. She'd stayed put because she didn't have anywhere to go.

When Bernadette and George walked through the doorway, Celeste gasped, surprised by her complicated emotions. Bernadette's entire face was shinning from tears. A fresh coat of coral lipstick framed her frown. She said, "I made your birthday quiche, Mary Celeste. I put the whole thing in the freezer the day you left. We can have some when we get home." Bernadette kissed the top of Celeste's head but didn't comment on her scrappy clothing or ask what the lump was beneath the blanket.

George said, "You scared the Devil out of us, Mary Celeste." He held onto his wife's elbow as they stood at the counter, speaking with the sheriff and signing papers. George had on his best Fuller Brush suit, although the trousers looked wrinkled from the drive. The robin's-egg blue handkerchief, poking from his jacket pocket, was elaborately folded. Celeste had forgotten how much she loved watching George pleat those squares, touching corner to opposite corner, pressing the diagonal fold with the pad of his index finger, folding again to create a fan.

"I didn't leave the house for months," Bernadette said, turning toward Celeste. "I stayed by the phone, waiting to hear from you. We were crushed."

As a mother now, Celeste understood how terrifying her disappearance must have been for her parents. She'd be respectful and kind to them; her apology.

The blanket slipped off. The baby stirred, his voice a murmur of need.

Bernadette hurried over, bent low, and peered into the sling. "Whose baby? You have a baby? It's not yours, is it?"

Celeste held him in her lap. Thoreau reached up and patted her chest, grinning. "He's mine. Meet your grandson, Thoreau."

George's eyes watered. "You have a son?"

"He's black, Mary Celeste." Bernadette's lips pinched. "A black baby?"

"My baby."

"You don't need to disclose any of the details," she said, her words slightly slurred. She began to sway, as if she'd topple over any moment. "What happened to you?"

"I got pregnant and had a baby."

"Where's his father?" Bernadette pulled a hankie from her purse and wiped her nose.

Celeste said, "I don't know where Luc is."

"Well, of course you don't," Bernadette said. "He had his fun, and now you have a black baby."

Celeste put Thoreau on her chest, burping him. "You're the reason I didn't come home. Those kind of comments."

George said, "Girls, we just got back together. Be civil."

The sheriff said, "You can take your daughter home. We'll keep Chris Armstrong here."

George's mouth twitched. He wanted to speak, but his stutter kept the words trapped.

Bernadette said, "Christopher told his parents you were in Alaska."

"I made him say that," she said. "He begged me to phone you. I lied and told him I did."

"Why didn't you call?" Bernadette said, her voice quavering and low. "Why put us through this heartbreak?" Her hair was swept into a low, unadorned bun. No foundation or powder. Ballerina flats. Drab housedress. To anyone else, she probably looked fine. To Celeste, Bernadette looked like a goddamn mess.

George said, "We'll talk about what's been going on with you once we get in the car."

"Can the baby and I say goodbye to Chris?" she asked the sheriff.

"Better to leave with your parents," he said.

"Chris, I love you. You'll be out of jail soon," Celeste called.

At the sedan, George opened the door for Celeste.

Bernadette climbed in the front seat. "I'll research and find a Catholic charity that finds homes for babies. There's probably the perfect Negro family dying to adopt a light-skinned child. Your unfortunate circumstances can stay between you and the Blessed Virgin."

"You sound as ignorant as always." Celeste tried to open the car door to escape, but George sped out of the parking lot and wouldn't stop when she asked him to. "I'm not giving my baby away."

"Mary Celeste, you're in our safe keeping," George said. His stutter elongated the sentence. "We won't let you go again. With or without the child."

"We have an important discussion ahead of us," Bernadette said. "For the time being, lay down on the backseat and get some sleep. You look like you haven't slept since the day you turned sixteen. George, stop at the store so I can buy formula and bottles."

"No bottles. No formula." Celeste lifted her shirt to nurse Thoreau. "I'm breastfeeding." If they tried to snatch him, she'd hold on tight and run.

"Oh, Mary Celeste," Bernadette said. "Diapers then, and Gerber's carrots and peas or apples and pears."

Celeste thought her parents would've been exhausted after six hours driving to the sheriff's station and facing another six hours until they got home, but Bernadette and George were wide awake and talkative. Bernadette rambled on about the Virgin answering her prayers.

Celeste felt terrible she'd left Chris behind to rot in jail. How lonely and frightened he must feel, especially without Thoreau. "Turn around. Please, bail Chris out," she begged.

Bernadette said, "His own parents can deal with that nonsense."

"Your mother went to mass every morning, Mary Celeste. She lit votives for your safe return." George turned toward Bernadette. "We got two in the bargain, Bernie."

Bernadette sighed again. This time louder. "The Blessed Virgin obviously looked the other way for a brief interlude. I forgive her neglect. I'm sure this baby will be a welcome gift to a sterile, married couple."

Celeste stared straight ahead, refusing to speak. Her silence overpowered three hundred miles of highway, sirens, car horns, gas stations, drug stores, eating food from a drive-up diner, George's reminiscences of traveling this route as a Fuller Brush man. It didn't matter what their plans were for her. She'd be eighteen in June. Three weeks away. Chris would get out of jail, because the bastard Matt would be caught and sentenced for being the asshole who harbored a runaway and kidnapped an innocent French professor, then she and Luc would get married, Chris would move in with them, and they'd all be happy.

The white picket fence surrounding the yard highlighted a row of magenta dahlias bent from the wind. The flowers leaned against the fence like a brigade of drunken soldiers. As George pulled into the driveway, Celeste whispered to Thoreau, "This is your grandparents' house. This is where I grew up."

The rolling bar stood in the center of the room, decanters and bottles amber and gold, glasses sparkling, polished silver ice bucket glistening. The hallmark of home. Her parents had a new television console. Technicolor vertical stripes hummed and buzzed. That, and the pile of dishes in the kitchen, were the evidence they'd rushed to come get her. Bacon and eggs. The stench of a greasy breakfast reminded her of Sundays and church. The coffee table had the waxy gleam of Fuller Brush polish.

Bernadette opened a box of saltine crackers and handed one to Thoreau. "You need more to chomp on than Mary Celeste."

Celeste didn't protest. Offering him something to eat was the closest Bernadette came to accepting Thoreau needed tending.

George walked from the kitchen, tossing the ice cube tray from one hand to another, saying, "Brr." He twisted the aluminum handle and shook cubes into the bucket. "We've been through a lot, but we have our daughter," he said, clinking his glass to Bernadette's.

"She's home. She's finally here," Bernadette said, sipping.

"We should get some rest. It's been a long day." George squeezed Celeste's arm, pinched Thoreau's nose, grabbed Bernadette's hand, and led her upstairs, the ice in both their tumblers rattling.

Celeste considered rushing to the Armstrongs' to beg them to save Chris. If exhaustion hadn't overtaken her, she'd be out the door.

Her room looked the same as it did on her sixteenth birthday. Fragrances of detergent overwhelmed her. She hadn't slept on clean, crisp linen since leaving. Matt's were usually rumpled and stunk like sweat and semen. Her hayloft bedding had pinpricks from the straw. Luc's creek-fresh sheets had the lingering scent of algae, dappled sun, and almond oil. She settled Thoreau beside her. "You're my baby boy. My Thoreau."

In the morning, Bernadette knocked on her bedroom door. "I've brought you breakfast," she said, setting the tray on the side table. Thawed and reheated Quiche Lorraine. "I cooked instant mashed potatoes for the baby. Easy to digest. He won't choke."

As Celeste bent over the plate of eggy pie, her breast loosened from her shirt, brushed against the baby's cheek. He gurgled and latched on, oohing and stroking her chest with his fingertips. Celeste glanced at Bernadette, wanting her mother to see she was Mommy to Thoreau. She'd conceived him, birthed him, and fed him from her own body. He was her baby.

Bernadette said, "After you eat the quiche, you need to wash up, Mary Celeste. The priest's coming over to say hello. I'll watch Thoreau while you bathe."

"He stays with me," Celeste said.

Bernadette scooped some potatoes onto a spoon, saying, "Yum, yum." Thoreau stopped nursing, turned his head, and licked the potatoes. "He's about six months? Time to wean."

Celeste carried Thoreau down the hallway to the bathroom and sat him on a folded towel, locking the door behind her. Under the water, dirt ran down her arms, pooling around the drain like a muddy river after a typhoon. She slumped against the shower tile. "Fuck you for leaving us, Luc," she repeated over and over.

Bernadette knocked on the bathroom door. "He's here," she called.

"Luc?"

"Father Murphy."

Thoreau squealed when he heard Bernadette's voice. He clapped.

She didn't want to see Father Murphy but needed to save her arguments for more important issues. Bringing the baby into the shower with her, she lathered his body and shampooed his hair. He reached for the spray of water, bouncing off her chest. "I won't let anything happen to you. I promise. Mama will never let you go. I'll never leave you."

On her way downstairs, Celeste heard Bernadette tell the priest, "The sheriff hinted what poor Mary Celeste had to deal with. You understand me, Father? She was taken advantage by a grown man and forced to give birth in a barn." Bernadette crossed herself, dabbed her eyes.

"Bringing forth a blessed life in a stable like someone else we know," Father Murphy said. He gave a nod to the gilded portrait of Mary and Jesus, hanging on the wall opposite the couch.

Bernadette said, "The sheriff is looking for the man."

"That's not what happened," Celeste said. "I lived in a cabin when the baby was born. We had a midwife. The happiest day of my life." She twisted one of Thoreau's tight curls around her knuckle.

Bernadette's face drained of color. "A midwife, Mary Celeste? Like an improvised pregnant woman in the olden days?"

"Like someone who didn't want to get caught."

Bernadette frowned, turned to the priest. "Father, do you hear her?"

The baby wore a disposable diaper but nothing else, because she wouldn't put his dirty clothes back on after bathing him, and she'd left all his clothing behind in the barn. With his round belly and chubby arms and legs, he resembled the fat baby Jesus in the picture.

"He's a lovely looking boy," Father Murphy said. He was a large man obviously content with parishioners' cakes and Sunday potlucks; his abdomen hung over his belt.

Celeste turned to Bernadette. "I need to speak with Father Murphy alone."

"Mrs. Roderick, give Mary Celeste and me a moment to chat," Father Murphy said. He reached in his pocket for a handkerchief and blew his nose. "Pardon me."

"I'll leave you to your confession." Bernadette disappeared through the kitchen door.

"I'm not putting Thoreau up for adoption no matter what my mother insists I do," Celeste said. The baby sat on her knees, playing with the buttons on her shirt.

After a long pause, Father Murphy said, "Thoreau needs to be baptized."

"He isn't Catholic."

"How can you make this decision for him?" Father Murphy asked. Again, he blew his nose, the honk loud enough to startle Thoreau.

"How can you?"

"I can't, but God can."

"I'm his mama. I'm raising him JewtheranCatholicNothing."

Father Murphy ran his index finger around the rim of his collar, as if to emphasize she was in the presence of a priest. "I see you have proclivities to religion. A righteous start."

"Your assumption's wrong. I have no faith."

Bernadette entered the room. "Gingersnaps and two cups of milky coffee. Enjoy," she said, backing out.

Father Murphy dipped his cookie into his cup, biting off the soggy end. "You don't have to raise him Catholic, but please get him baptized. Think of the ritual as an insurance policy for your baby's soul in case one thousand, nine hundred and seventy-one years of history turn out to be true." He smiled.

Celeste watched the way the priest chewed, his lips pressed tight as if he couldn't fathom the thought of one crumb escaping. "I'll let Thoreau be baptized on one condition."

The priest wiped his mouth with his napkin. "A condition?"

"My mom and dad will never speak about adoption again."

"A fair compromise," he said. He called Bernadette in for a council.

George must have been in the kitchen, too, because he walked into the living room, clasping Bernadette's hand. He settled on the couch next to the priest. Bernadette sat in the chair, crossed her ankles, sipped her morning Limestone.

Father Murphy said, "Mary Celeste is clearly the boy's mother. He's well loved." He explained the terms of Celeste's demand. "Arrangements for a baptism must be made soon."

"He'll be baptized?" Bernadette swished the ice cubes around her tumbler.

Celeste nodded. "He's my baby. I'm his mother."

"Oh, Mary Celeste, you always were a stubborn girl," Bernadette said.

Father Murphy said, "She loves her child. Can't you see that?"

"Because she's been through a traumatic situation. She's not clear in the head," Bernadette said.

"Judge not lest thee be judged," Father Murphy said. "It's a little early for a cocktail, don't you agree?"

Bernadette set her glass on the coffee table next to their coffees. "It's been a difficult two years. I missed my daughter, and now I have a grandson."

If anyone in her life prepared Celeste for the hugeness of this victory over Bernadette, it was Thoreau. No matter how much she didn't want to be in her parents' living room with a priest, agreeing to a baptism, she had the most important person in the world nestled in her arms, and he was saved.

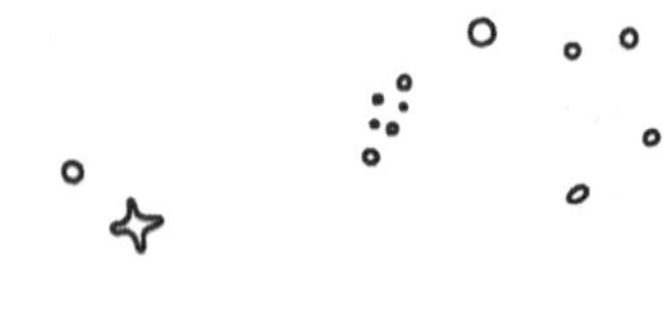

The dogwood tree in the center of the Armstrongs' lawn had lost most of its leaves, and there weren't any blossoms. Tulips and pansies once lined the walkway, but the flowerbeds sat empty. The house looked as cold and gloomy as if an enemy had dropped an A-bomb on the roof, destroying human existence.

Celeste stood beneath the flickering porch light with Thoreau cradled in the crook of her arm, facing outward. The first thing they'd see when they answered the door were his sweet, chubby cheeks. They'd invite her in, offer her a cup of tea, and accept Thoreau as their grandson. Celeste knocked.

Mrs. Armstrong pulled the curtain aside and peeked out. A second later, the door swung open. "Celeste? Is it you?" She gestured Celeste into the foyer. The buttons on her cardigan were misaligned. "You're back from Alaska? Do your parents know?"

"I'm staying with them." Celeste had requested Bernadette let her break the news to the Armstrongs about Chris's arrest. The phone receiver had been clutched in Bernadette's hand, but she hung up before dialing, admitting she wasn't sure what to say.

"That's lovely," Mrs. Armstrong said.

Celeste's throat constricted. Dressed from clothes in her closet, a blouse with a Peter Pan collar and checkered pedal pushers, Celeste felt like she did in her school days, stopping by to study with Chris.

Thoreau whimpered.

Mrs. Armstrong glanced down. "Babysitting?"

"This is Thoreau. He's mine."

"Yours? You have a baby?"

"Yes. He's Chris's, too."

"Well, that can't be true." She escorted Celeste down the hallway and into the living room. "He doesn't really resemble Chris."

"I need some legal advice."

"Have a seat and tell me about your situation," she said. "Your baby looks healthy. Born in Alaska, I assume?"

The last time Celeste sat there, she'd been a witness to the consequence of Chris's yearbook prank. It alarmed Celeste how, in the intervening two years, their home appeared in decay and they seemed not to notice or care. Stitching on their pristine couch was loose. Dr. Armstrong's chair stained from spills. Shag carpet flattened in a straight line from the kitchen to the coffee table to the bathroom. She'd been angry at them for sending Chris away, but obviously they'd suffered. Chris was happy at Basscombe, making love with Luc in the shower stall and then in the barn, while the Armstrongs lived brokenhearted and full of regret.

Dr. Armstrong came into the room, puffing on a cigarette. "You've got yourself a baby? A very cute baby."

"Thoreau Laurent Armstrong." She ringed Thoreau's wrist with her fingers, lifting his hand to wave hello.

Dr. Armstrong stubbed his cigarette out. "Did I hear that correctly?"

"Armstrong?" Mrs. Armstrong cocked her head. "You gave him our last name?"

"He's Chris's," she said.

"How is Chris involved?" Dr. Armstrong asked.

"Thoreau and I have been living with him."

"After you left Alaska, you've been staying in that raggedy, dilapidated barn?" Mrs. Armstrong said.

Dr. Armstrong flicked his lighter, held the flame to another cigarette. "A terrible habit. I need to quit."

Mrs. Armstrong brushed a wisp of hair from her face. "Is Chris still living there?" Her gaze shifted away from Celeste and toward Dr. Armstrong. "He hasn't phoned in a few weeks."

"He couldn't get to the payphone," she said.

"What happened in Alaska?" Mrs. Armstrong asked. "What legal advice do you need?"

Her story, altered but mostly factual, didn't take long to tell. Running away, but not to Alaska. Living in the woods. Sneaking to Basscombe. Finding Chris. Living in the barn. Living in the cabin. What she couldn't explain, without disclosing the secret of Chris's homosexuality, was his relationship with Luc.

Mrs. Armstrong urged, "I don't mean to be rude, but I'm trying to understand the dynamics."

Celeste breathed in the scent of Thoreau. Not almond oil. Fuller Brush shampoo. "A guy named Luc is a mutual friend of ours. Luc and I had a relationship. Throughout my pregnancy, Chris talked to my belly, saying, 'I'm Papa Chris. I love you, my little baby.' He was at the birth."

"That doesn't make him a father," Mrs. Armstrong said.

Celeste closed her eyes, taking a moment to find the correct words. "Thoreau has two papas. One biological, Luc. One spiritual, Chris. Chris is his papa."

Mrs. Armstrong patted Celeste's knee. "For as long as we've known you, for as long as you've been Chris's friend, we've seen the special bond you two share. You honored that by giving the baby his last name?"

Celeste settled back on the couch, resting her head against the cushion. "You both have been kind to me over the years. Growing up, your home was my favorite place to be. Better than my house."

Dr. Armstrong held his arms open. "Mind if I hold this little guy?"

"Thoreau, meet Grandpa Armstrong. Can he call you that?" She sat the baby in Dr. Armstrong's lap.

"Grandpa Armstrong suits me fine, I suppose," he said.

Thoreau's eyes widened. He stuck his fist into his mouth, then extended his chubby fingers to the ceiling. He babbled and blew spit bubbles.

Mrs. Armstrong said, "I don't understand how talking to a pregnant woman or being at the birth makes Chris a father. Did he adopt him? Are you two a couple?"

Dr. Armstrong put his ear to the baby's chest and closed his eyes. "His heart's robust."

Celeste said, "Chris was the first person I told I was pregnant. Also, the happiest and most accepting. He's been with me through everything."

Mrs. Armstrong's brow crunched. "Is this what his speech at graduation was about? Loving Thoreau?"

Celeste said, "Mostly."

Thoreau's hand wrapped around Dr. Armstrong's finger. "Strong grip you've got there, tyke."

Mrs. Armstrong wiped her eyes with her handkerchief, leaving a wisp of black on her temple. "I have a feeling there's more to this story. Why isn't Chris here with you? Where is he?"

Celeste took a deep breath. She started at the end, telling them Chris was in jail and she hoped Mrs. Armstrong could find a way to get him released.

"Harboring a runaway his own age?" Dr. Armstrong said. He set Thoreau on the carpet.

"He's an emancipated minor, which makes him culpable." Mrs. Armstrong stood up. Smoothing her skirt, she added, "I forget to offer you tea."

Dr. Armstrong asked, "The baby's real father? Who and where is he?"

Celeste swallowed, hesitating before confessing, "Luc Laurent.

The art instructor from Basscombe. We don't know where he is."

Dr. Armstrong looked at Thoreau. "The artist from France? The teacher?"

Mrs. Armstrong heaved such a heavy sigh, the curtains fluttered. "He's a man twice your age. He took advantage of you, Celeste. What he did is against the law, even if you're unaware of that fact."

"Everyone keeps telling me this, but what they don't understand is I was willing. He and I had a loving relationship," Celeste said.

"In California, the age of consent is eighteen. Even if you were willing, what he did is still against the law. Considering the length of gestation, plus Thoreau's age, I can reason you were barely sixteen when it started. That's immoral."

Chris was also sixteen when he and Luc had sex, Celeste wanted to confess. She remained quiet.

"I'll phone Basscombe," Dr. Armstrong said, standing up, Thoreau on his hip. "I need to let them know what's going on right under their noses. They should be more selective about what kind of people they're hiring. Where's the address book?"

Mrs. Armstrong said, "After you do that, I'll call the sheriff's office about our son."

"Luc and I are engaged," Celeste said. "We're getting married when I turn eighteen. He'll get his green card, and the four of us will live together. Two fathers, one mother, one baby. Don't report Luc. He didn't take advantage of me. Maybe I took advantage of him."

Mrs. Armstrong said, "Celeste, I sincerely doubt that you, a beautiful teenage girl, took advantage of a full-grown man."

Dr. Armstrong rummaged through a shelf, mumbling about finding the Yellow Pages. "This entire fiasco sounds fishy. Luc Laurent needs to be held accountable for his actions."

Mrs. Armstrong said, "We've got to get Chris out of this mess."

Celeste put her face in her hands. "Being one of Thoreau's papas is not being in a mess."

"I'm talking about jail," Mrs. Armstrong said, patting Celeste's knee. "Not you. Not the baby."

"My parents wanted me to put Thoreau up for adoption." Celeste accepted the tissue Dr. Armstrong handed her. "I'm having him baptized. That's our compromise."

"They're in shock. As are we," Mrs. Armstrong said. "They're concerned. As are we."

"My mother called him a mulatto."

"Unfortunate choice of word." Dr. Armstrong lit another cigarette, puffed, exhaled.

"Intentional choice of word," Celeste said. "She may be in shock, but I'm her daughter. She should be decent. She should be nicer. She should not be telling me to give my baby away."

Dr. Armstrong found the phone book and ran his index finger along a list. "We sent Chris to learn a lesson about staying out of trouble. Basscombe hires people who teach the opposite? People who get youngsters in trouble? Unacceptable." He dialed the phone and asked to speak with the headmaster.

Celeste pleaded for him to hang up. "Please give Luc a chance. He'll make it right."

Dr. Armstrong said into the mouthpiece, "Give the headmaster my number and have him call me back. This is a delicate matter. I won't leave a message."

Celeste said, "I'm worried my parents will wait until I'm not looking and snatch Thoreau. Can I stay with you? They don't want him to be my baby."

Mrs. Armstrong bit her lip. "You can temporarily move into Chris's room. Dr. Armstrong and I will sort it out with your parents. We'd love your company. We need life around this place." She excused herself and went to the kitchen. "I'll phone Bernadette to discuss the possibility."

Thoreau squirmed and let out a cry. He pounded his knees with his fists.

"He's hungry," Celeste said, reaching for him. She threw an afghan blanket over her shoulder, covering herself before nursing him.

"No need for modesty around me. I'm a doctor. Poor tyke must be stuffy under the polyester crotchet," Dr. Armstrong said. "Breastfeeding is the healthy option that's unfortunately gone out of style. Glad to see you chose it."

Celeste shoved the blanket aside. Thoreau smiled. Milk dribbled down his chin. She whispered, "Your Grandma and Grandpa Armstrong love you."

Half an hour later, Mrs. Armstrong sat beside Celeste. "All settled. You're staying with us for the time being. Your mother will come by in the morning."

Celeste loved the idea of living in Chris's room, but wondered why Bernadette and George didn't put up a fight to keep her and Thoreau at their house. She admitted this to Mrs. Armstrong. "I'd do anything for my child."

Mrs. Armstrong rested her hand on Celeste's shoulder, squeezing. "Try and understand her point of view. You devastated them when you ran away; then you show up with a baby. They never saw you pregnant. They need time to adjust."

Thoreau stopped nursing. Giggling, he reached up and pinched her nipple. "Ouch," she said, and buttoned her shirt.

"Your parents suffered while you were gone," Mrs. Armstrong said.

Celeste wanted to mention that Bernadette's drunken rant and name-calling drove her away but decided not to betray her mother's failings. Everyone has flaws. Traits they aren't proud of. Disappearing suddenly from someone's life, for example. She'd done that to Bernadette and George. Luc had done that to her and Chris and Thoreau.

"And suddenly discovering they are a grandfather and a grand-mother," Dr. Armstrong said.

"Your mother's also furious with the art professor, as am I," Mrs. Armstrong said. "If caught, he will be charged on several counts."

"No," Celeste said. "That won't help anyone."

Dr. Armstrong stood. "Enough legal talk for now. Let's show this girl her room."

They led Celeste upstairs. Nothing had changed since the day she stood in the doorway, wondering where Chris had disappeared to. "Perfect," she said.

Dr. Armstrong slid a drawer from the dresser, laid it on the ground as an impromptu cradle. "I slept in one of these until I outgrew the length. This will do until we buy a crib."

Mrs. Armstrong stripped the blue sheets from Chris's bed, remaking it with a flowered set. "Not glamorous, but comfortable."

If they'd known she'd been sleeping on a straw mattress in a hayloft, or sharing a bed with a maniac, they wouldn't be apologizing for anything.

Mrs. Armstrong hugged Celeste and stroked Thoreau's cheek. "If you need anything, we're downstairs. I'm going to phone the sheriff. I'll let you know when I have more information."

After they closed the door, Celeste climbed under the covers, tucking Thoreau beside her. She swore the pillowcase smelled like Chris's dime-store cologne.

Bernadette showed up the following morning with a plastic-wrapped, sugar-glazed coffee cake, a few baby outfits, and a grocery sack of clothes for Celeste.

Mrs. Armstrong set the breakfast pastry on the coffee table next to the tea tray, then went to the kitchen for plates and forks.

On a blanket, Thoreau clutched a wooden spoon. When he struck a cake pan, he jumped at the ting. He hit the metal again and again.

Bernadette peered at him. "Is his father a musician as well as an artist?"

Celeste could contrive Luc to be anyone she wanted him to be. Thoreau deserved the myth of a talented, generous papa. Without Matt and money and coke and lies, Luc was a fine man. He'd loved Chris. He'd cared for her and the baby.

Mrs. Armstrong poured cups of tea and said, "We hardly heard a peep out of Thoreau all night. When Chris was little, he wailed and hollered."

Bernadette reached into her cigarette compact and pulled one out. "My daughter is an unwed mother."

Celeste said, "Do not call Thoreau a bastard."

"Some would say he is," Bernadette said, then softened her voice, adding, "Not me, Mary Celeste. He's your baby."

Mrs. Armstrong gave a polite nod.

Bernadette clenched the end of her cigarette between her teeth. "I'm concerned for both of your welfare, Mary Celeste, and yes, I'm concerned for your reputation, as well."

"You've always been worried about my reputation," she said. "Even when I was as pure as the Virgin." Thoreau struck the tin and giggled.

Walking through the living room, Dr. Armstrong stopped and ruffled Thoreau's curls. "Off to work. I'll see you when I get home, Slugger."

Mrs. Armstrong sliced the coffee cake.

"My daughter's too skinny. We need to fatten her up," Bernadette said. "Clearly you've been through an ordeal. I'm not sure what you did out there in the wilderness, and I don't want to know the specifics, but something's changed in you."

"I've had a baby," Celeste said. "Pregnancy. Birth. Other things."

"I want to be sure you're—"Bernadette paused before continuing—"how can I say this without hurting your feelings?"

"Say whatever you want to say," Celeste said. "I'm sure I've heard worse."

Mrs. Armstrong cleared her throat.

Bernadette sipped her tea, peering at Celeste over the rim. "Mentally healthy."

Celeste had no intention of crying, but in that moment, she was unable to hold back tears. Thoreau glanced at her, his bottom lip quivering.

Bernadette glanced from Celeste to the baby and back again. Stubbing her cigarette in the ashtray, she wiped her hands together as if getting rid of a chill. "May I hold Thoreau while you freshen up? Please allow his Grandma Bernie to soothe him."

Celeste shook her head.

"Your mother, his Grandma Bernie, is offering a peace branch," Mrs. Armstrong said. She placed her hand over Celeste's. "This shows good faith."

Celeste hesitated, then picked the baby up and set him in Bernadette's lap. She wanted this to work. She wanted Bernadette to love him.

Thoreau stopped crying. He patted Bernadette's cheeks with his palms, gurgling and squealing and babbling.

In the bathroom, washing her face, blowing her nose, Celeste thought about Bernadette questioning her mental health. Did that include gullibility? The day she ran away from home and climbed in Matt's truck, she'd been enamored with his antiwar beliefs, wildness, and sensuality. Matt shook her confidence to the marrow. He'd inflicted cruelty. How had she responded? Blowjobs and three-somes and fucking? Bernadette had every reason to worry about her mental stability.

Every few days, Bernadette came by the Armstrongs' with various breakfast pastries, baby shampoo and sweet-scented oil, onesies in yellow and green and blue, a canopy crib, dresser, changing table with a musical mobile of twirling ladybugs. Items overflowed from Chris's bedroom into the hallway, turning the house into a baby-product showroom.

One morning, Bernadette frowned, saying, "Obviously, you can't go back to high school. How will you finish your education? You're a smart girl."

"I'm not thinking about school right now."

Mrs. Armstrong said, "When you're ready, you can work on obtaining your GED. I'll facilitate the process if that's the route you decide to go."

Thoreau banged a cooking spoon against the floor.

"The only thing on my mind is helping Chris get out of jail," Celeste said, "and finding Luc to sort this out."

Bernadette said, "The French don't consider paternity important? Is everything over there laissez faire?"

"Luc cared about us." Celeste closed her eyes, picturing how supportive he'd been about the pregnancy. He'd lied about his age, though. Lied about his divorce. If he loved them, why had he lied?

"Any updates on Chris's case?" Bernadette asked as she sliced into a lemon crumble cake and handed the largest piece to Celeste.

"The paperwork requires perseverance," Mrs. Armstrong explained. "I'm scouring through all the possibilities to prove he's innocent of harboring Celeste. Once we get him out of jail, we'll bring him home."

Celeste took a bite. The taste of lemon zest conjured sunbathing in the backyard beneath the citrus, drinking lemonade, and reading James Baldwin and Henry David Thoreau.

Bernadette said, "You've got a child to support. Luc should take responsibility and help pay for him."

Mrs. Armstrong said, "Apparently, the third party mentioned in the sheriff's report used a false identity. Makes it infinitely harder to track him down." She added, "The crumble cake smells delicious, Bernadette."

"Homemade," Bernadette said. "Back to my Betty Crocker cookbook."

Mrs. Armstrong said, "Celeste, what else can you tell us that will help identify this man? Anything you haven't told us already?"

The only part she hadn't shared, and couldn't, was having sex with Matt, and Matt having sex with Luc, and Luc having sex with Chris, and Luc having sex with her and Matt, and how many times Matt wanted sex when she didn't, but he fucked her anyway and fucked her hard, his entire body angry.

Mrs. Armstrong said, "The man known as Matt Briggs told the kids the barn was his, the cabin was his, the land belonged to his family, none of which is true."

Bernadette clasped an unlit cigarette between her fingertips. "I don't know the law or how this works, but is it possible for Mary Celeste to sign an affidavit stating the man who told her his name was Matt Briggs is the person she was living with?"

Mrs. Armstrong opened her briefcase, took out Chris's case file. "If Matt Briggs is a draft dodger and a war resister, his fingerprints are in the system. He can't leave the country. Unless, of course, he snuck across the border to Canada. Perhaps Quebec? Luc would fit in with the language." She tapped the pen against her lips.

Heart palpitations and stomach somersaults overpowered Celeste as she imagined Matt and Luc together in Quebec. Who else would they find to seduce? Another girl? Another boy?

Mrs. Armstrong said, "Let's give Bernadette's idea a try. I will write a statement for you to sign and have the paperwork notarized. Celeste, is there any chance Matt Briggs is Thoreau's father?"

Bernadette excused herself. "I need to use the powder room. This crumble cake's falling apart in my lap."

Celeste waited until her mother left. "Matt's not Thoreau's father. Matt's white. We were intimate, though. For almost two years."

"If you admit you and Matt lived together and were intimately involved, there's a chance the case against Chris will be dismissed,"

Mrs. Armstrong said. "You were in the cabin with Matt. Chris was in the barn. Matt harbored you. Chris did not. Do I have these facts correct?"

"I screwed things up, didn't I?"

"We'll unscrew them," Mrs. Armstrong said.

When Bernadette returned, she spoke quietly. "You're going to learn, Mary Celeste, how the decisions and choices you make will affect your entire life. You also need to forgive yourself for mistakes you've made; otherwise, you'll never want to get out of bed. I found this out the hard way. I was rough on you. When you left home, and I thought I'd never see you again, I had to come to terms it was probably my fault." She handed Celeste a package. "By the way, you never got to open this gift."

Smiling, Celeste unwrapped the present. In the bathroom, she changed into the dress Bernadette had sewed for her sixteenth birthday. The bodice felt tight across her breastfeeding boobs and the hem too long to be fashionable, but the dress meant love. It meant home. It meant Bernadette wanted to make her happy.

The day of the baptism, Thoreau wore Celeste's christening gown. Covered with elaborate lace, the ivory frock trailed past his booties. The sleeves puffed like profiteroles. The neckline reached to his double chin. Thin white ribbons, woven in and out of every seam, were tied in bows.

As Father Murphy poured the stream of holy water over Thoreau's head and prayed, Celeste felt confident this simple act ensured Bernadette's acceptance of him. The priest drew the oily sign of the cross on Thoreau's forehead, and the baby squealed in delight.

Usually at baptisms, the pews were full of family and parishioners. Not Thoreau's. Gathered around the baptismal urn, the only people present were Thoreau, Celeste, Father Murphy, and both sets of grandparents. In her purse, Celeste had a picture of Chris taken the year they met in elementary school, beautiful curls framing his freckled face, Juliet's tail sticking from his pocket. Celeste had no photos of Luc. Not one. She had nothing to prove he even existed. Except, Thoreau.

Celeste wished she could be swept away by the sacredness of the moment—a transcendence into bliss—yet all she managed to summon was a yearning to get away from the judgmental eyes of the Pious Virgin statue. Thoreau giggled and yanked on the gown's ribbons, putting them in his mouth, mashing and gnashing silk.

George, the Protestant, didn't cross himself, but he did close his eyes in prayer. Dr. Armstrong stared at the painting of Jesus as if inspecting the wounds for the best way to bandage them. Mrs. Armstrong grinned at her grandson. Bernadette, the triumphant Catholic, beamed with pride and devotion as her coral-stained lips moved in silent repetition with the litany. Her coiffed hairdo and carefully chosen ensemble—a flared navy dress, cinched at the waistline with a narrow belt; cleavage adorned with pearls; hands covered in silk gloves—placed her in the spotlight.

A reception followed in Bernadette and George's living room. Bernadette set a spread consisting of mushroom canapés, deviled eggs, and tea biscuits. After they ate, she and Mrs. Armstrong went to the kitchen to make a pot of coffee.

The grandpas and Father Murphy smoked cigars and spoke about work and the Vietnam War.

Celeste lay on the carpet next to Thoreau. Angling away from the men, she unbuttoned her dress to nurse.

George said, "Mary Celeste, wouldn't you rather be upstairs?" He walked to the rolling bar.

Dr. Armstrong said, "Good that she's breastfeeding. Better for the baby."

George said, "Gentlemen, may I get you a drink?"

"Whiskey sour will do fine." Father Murphy tapped the cigar ash into the ashtray. "I find baptisms quite comforting."

"Nice ceremony," Dr. Armstrong said. "Whiskey neat, thank you, George."

"Important for the soul's salvation," Father Murphy said.

Celeste stared at the pink of Thoreau's lips and the dimples on his cheeks. "His salvation comes from being loved."

George said, "That's true for all of us."

The grandmas walked into the living room, talking and laughing. Bernadette glanced at Celeste, waved an empty coffee cup in her direction. "Don't lay around on the rug like a wayward dog."

Celeste cradled Thoreau in her arms and carried him upstairs to her room. She put him in the playpen Bernadette had bought for the rare occasions Celeste spent the night. On her own bed, she stared at the ceiling and spoke to the baby: "When Papa Chris comes home, we'll rescue Papa Luc from Villain Matt and have a huge wedding in the park. Someday, you'll have oodles of brothers and sisters to play with." Her words halfhearted. The further away she was from Walden Creek, the harder to convince herself Luc had ever been sincere.

She awoke to Thoreau's whimper. The luminosity of the streetlight outside her window filtered through the curtains. The room glowed yellow. As a child, she'd pretended the lamp was a planet and she an astronaut buckled in a spaceship soaring toward it, hoping to discover an alternate universe.

Days later, as they gathered around a strawberry layer cake, Bernadette lit birthday candles and dimmed the lights. "Do you want us to sing?"

"As loud as you can," Celeste said with a smile. "I've waited a long time to turn eighteen."

The dramatically off-pitch birthday song got interrupted by an exuberant knock on the front door. Poised to blow the flames, she saw the apparition of Chris appear in the kitchen. The candles melted into colorful wax puddles on top of the cake.

Mrs. Armstrong clapped. "I kept his homecoming a secret. Are you surprised?"

Dr. Armstrong grabbed Chris in his arms. "Welcome home, son. Happy birthday, my boy."

"It's not often Mary Celeste's speechless," George said. Everyone laughed.

Spotting the baby in George's arms, Chris reached for him. "Papa Chris is here. I'll never leave you again." He nestled his face into Thoreau's neck, his words lost to kisses. Chris's hair had grown into a wild mess. He tucked curls behind his ears, but they sprung free, as they had when he was a boy.

Thoreau's mouth pinched before he smiled. He wrapped his fist around Chris's finger.

George slid open the buffet where he kept miscellaneous items and rummaged around for his Kodak Pony. Finding the contraption, he lifted it to his eye, pointed at the group. "Say Fuller Brush."

As if the flashbulb awakened her from a stupor, Celeste bolted forward and looped her arms through Chris's. "My wish came true."

Chris said, "Mine too." If a smile could replace birthday candlelight, his did. He was a bit thinner than three weeks ago; his cheekbones protruded, and his eyes looked larger. Celeste thought he resembled a Renaissance beauty.

Bernadette picked melted wax from the cake and dropped the pieces into an ashtray, then smoothed the frosting with a butter knife.

"My legal statement worked?" Celeste asked Mrs. Armstrong.

"Legal statement?" George asked. "News to me."

Mrs. Armstrong briefly explained how the court dismissed the case after she mailed them the signed affidavit confirming Celeste's cohabitation was with a man going by the name of Matt Briggs, not Christopher Armstrong.

Bernadette said, "Can this discussion wait until after we've had birthday cake?" She scored the top into eight pieces. "We'll discuss it when we get home, George."

Hearing her relationship with Matt summarized this succinctly was exactly what Celeste needed. Without acknowledging the bribes, threats, pot, cocaine, and endless fucking, her life sounded almost wholesome. She'd lived with a man in a cabin in the woods. Period.

Dr. Armstrong's arm stayed wrapped around Chris's shoulders, as if he were afraid his son would drift away like a dandelion puff caught in a breeze or a hot air balloon in a storm or a reckless teenage boy.

If anyone would have predicted she'd be celebrating with Chris in Bernadette's kitchen on their eighteenth birthday, she'd have called them delusional. If miracles superseded magic, this was a time to believe in God.

After the celebration and hours of conversation, Chris held Thoreau as they walked through the neighborhood toward his parents' house. They detoured past their elementary school, stopping to show Thoreau the place where his mama and papa spent years discussing their dreams and fears. Under the magnolia tree, Chris sat on the sandbox railing. "Did someone spike our parents' drinking water with a love potion?"

"Thoreau's the love potion," Celeste said.

"We had some important discussions in this sandbox, didn't we?"

"Between ballerina rats and diffusing atomic bombs, we saved the world." Celeste leaned into his side.

"This is where you tried to make me like you instead of liking boys," Chris said. He nuzzled close to the baby, saying, "Thoreau, your shameless mama made me feel her boob. It didn't work."

Celeste laughed. "You can't say boob in front of him." She dribbled sand through her fingers. "Thoreau's been baptized."

"Baptized as in Catholic?"

"Bernadette wanted me to put him up for adoption," Celeste said with a long sigh. "Baptism was the compromise Father Murphy and I worked it out with her."

"She seems to like him now." Chris kissed the top of Thoreau's head.

"Not the same as your parents, but Bernadette's coming around. He's hard to resist." She settled the baby in for his late-night snack.

"We have to find Papa Luc." Chris stretched in the sandbox, arms and legs flung wide. "I've got to see him and find out what happened. He needs to see Thoreau."

"He lied," she said. "He abandoned us. That's what happened."

"I bet there's a ton of shit we're unaware of. Like Matt threatening to harm us if Luc didn't leave with him. Luc's being heroic." Chris rolled over, leaning on his elbow to face her. "I guarantee he was forced to flee. I know him better than anyone."

Celeste switched Thoreau to the other breast. "Did you know he's thirty-three?"

Chris said, "I didn't ask him how old he was. It doesn't matter to me."

"Did you know he was married before?"

"Not uncommon for a closeted queer." Chris sighed.

"Those secrets don't bother you?" She raised her voice in frustration but lowered it when Thoreau whimpered. "It should bother you. He's old. He's been married, which means he had sex with a woman. He acted like it was a grand, treacherous adventure to have sex with me. What a liar."

"He would have told me everything eventually," Chris said. "Luc wouldn't have left me for Matt. You'll see. This is a terrible misunderstanding. One of these days, he'll come walking back into our lives and we'll live happily ever after."

"Be realistic."

"You want me to be like you? I'm an optimist, not a pessimist," he said, stroking her cheek.

They moved closer and kissed. A shared relief of loneliness. A release of sorrow.

"I spent a lot of time in jail thinking about going to Paris to find Luc. I'm sure that's where he fled to get away from Matt and his fear of being arrested for impregnating you. We'll need passports," Chris said as he folded laundry.

"We're not going to Paris in search of Luc like two amateur detectives. We're staying here and forgetting about that asshole."

He flicked his wrist dismissively. "Do you have Thoreau's birth certificate proving you're his mother, or did we leave it in the barn?"

"Jasmine filed the official one in the Wilder Courthouse." Celeste asked Chris to pass her a clean diaper. "Your mom helped me send for a copy."

"Paying for plane tickets won't be a problem. We'll become couriers and fly for free. A boy I met at school flew all over the world as a courier until he was caught and sent to Basscombe. All we need to do is transport a package from Point A to Point B."

"Do you hear how stupid that sounds?" Celeste took her eyes off changing Thoreau. He giggled and crawled away.

"It's a real thing," he said.

"I'm suspicious. What kind of package?"

"Businessmen needing important business stuff delivered in person." He insisted the scheme was legit. "We'll look for an ad in the paper with France as the final destination. Once we're in Paris, we'll search for Luc."

"We don't have money." Celeste swooped Thoreau in her arms, laid him on the ground to finish changing him. "Food. Rent. Transportation."

"I've got this all figured out, Celeste. I had three weeks in jail to plan everything," Chris said. "The day they dropped me off at Basscombe, my parents promised they'd give me my accumulated allowance when I came home."

"You're talking about leaving home." She wadded the dirty diaper.

"I came home first." Putting the clean laundry clothes in the drawers, he started counting. "I get twenty-five a month. That's more than five hundred bucks. According to Luc, the franc's cheap compared to the dollar."

"According to Luc? He lies."

Chris patted her arm. "Fine, according to my research, the franc's cheap."

"Your parents will be sad. They're grateful to have you home. They love Thoreau. They'll miss him," she said. "Forget about idiotic Luc." She rattled off reasons his idea was unreasonable. Behind each one, she emphasized not wanting to see Luc ever again.

"We need his signature so I can officially adopt Thoreau." Originally, back when everyone got along, they agreed Chris would adopt Thoreau and become a second father. Thoreau Laurent Armstrong, a lad with two dads, as Chris had teased.

"You don't have to officially adopt him to be Papa Chris," she said.

Chris carried the basket of dirty diapers and clothes into the laundry room and dumped them into the washer, turning the knob to hot. "I'm going to Paris to find Luc. I want you and Thoreau to come with me." He shook detergent over the pile and poured bleach.

She pressed her back against the washing machine, wanting the filtered heat and the chug chug chug of a motor, proof of the domesticity of her simple life with Chris. "We don't even know if he's in France."

"His family's there."

She shrugged, pausing a moment before asking, "When will you tell your parents about you and Luc?"

Chris lowered his voice. "Tell them my professor and I had sex at school before he got you pregnant?"

"If we go to France, find Luc, and bring him home, what's next? The four of us living in your bedroom?" Celeste switched Thoreau from one arm to the other. He patted her cheeks, squealing.

"We'll get jobs. Pay for our own place," Chris said. "You two will get hitched; he'll be a straight citizen by day. He and I will be lovers by night."

"That arrangement sounds better for you than it does for me."

Their discussion spanned the wash and rinse cycle, drying and folding and putting diapers away, and continued into the night,

Thoreau nestled between them. Celeste realized that until Chris confronted Luc, he'd never accept the betrayal. He'd stumble through life wearing rose-colored blinders, waiting for Luc's return. Luc represented the past and bad choices. She and Thoreau represented the present and the future.

At Bernadette and George's house, Chris waited until banana cream pie and cocktails were served before he explained the Paris idea to their parents. If the spaceship Mercury had bounced across the carpet, the hatch had opened, and Martians had danced around singing show tunes, there wouldn't have been as much commotion.

Bernadette slid her cigarette back in the silver case, snapping the lid closed. "Fly to Paris?"

"To find a jackass?" George said, his stutter elongating the final word.

Mrs. Armstrong said, "Well put, George."

Chris sat up taller, pulling his shoulders back. "I need to be Thoreau's official father. Luc's name is on the birth certificate."

Celeste went to the rolling bar and mixed another Limestone for Bernadette, a whiskey on the rocks for everyone else. Her old familiar fallback for diffusing volatile situations. "We need Luc's signature on the adoption form. Otherwise, Chris is left out of everything legal."

Mrs. Armstrong said, "You don't need Luc's signature if he abandoned the baby."

Celeste tucked Thoreau against her chest, lifted her shirt to nurse him. "Really? Is that true?"

Dr. Armstrong said, "Let the man be. He's not worth your time."

Chris said, "Thoreau and Celeste need to see him."

Celeste wondered if Chris would confess his love for Luc. When Chris pinched his mouth shut and stayed silent, she said, "I have unanswered questions."

Bernadette said, "Luc isn't moral. He should be arrested, not rewarded with a conjugal visit."

"Bernie!" George said.

Dr. Armstrong set down his tumbler. "The man squandered an amazing opportunity and betrayed the trust Basscombe put in him. A grown man should have behaved better."

"I knew what I was doing," Celeste said.

"At sixteen?" George said, squinting at her. "You did not know what you were doing. You obviously still don't."

Chris said, "When I adopt Thoreau, I'll be responsible for his welfare. Not Luc. Thoreau will be better off."

They argued for nearly two hours, but it felt like two days. If their parents intended to wear them down, it almost worked. Finally, Celeste said, "We're eighteen. We don't need your permission, but it would feel better if we had it."

Thoreau stood at the coffee table, pounding the surface with his fist. He reached for the reclining figurine of St. Bernadette. Sticking the saint's head in his mouth, he gnawed on her halo.

Bernadette pried the figurine from the baby's grasp and dried the saint's head with her sleeve before moving it to a shelf. She set a teething ring on the table in exchange. "Will seeing Luc bring either of you relief?"

Chris said, "Do you understand what it feels like when someone you cherish is suddenly missing from your life? When you can't fathom they're gone? That's how it is for Celeste." Meaning: That's how it is for me.

They finished their cocktails in polite negotiations. Cautiously, the grandparents agreed to pool money together for the trip on the condition Celeste and Chris return home before Thoreau's first birthday.

Bernadette lit her cigarette and opened the window, letting the warm summer evening carry her smoke away. "To keep our children close to home, we need to send them half a world away."

"Well stated," George said, stuttering the w's, s's, and t's.

If Celeste had been in their position, and Thoreau wanted to fly off in search of his no-good, lying, cheating boyfriend, she'd have bought every last ticket to Paris to keep him from leaving.

Être amoureux à Paris

They wandered the streets, looking for a youth hostel. Piles of dog excrement made walking along the sidewalk tricky and unpleasant. Doorways smelled like urine. She'd imagined Paris a world of motor scooters and scarves, cafés and coffee, not cigarette butts, crumbled newspapers, lecherous men reaching out to finger the hem of her skirt. Not stifling summer heat.

Celeste shifted Thoreau to her other hip. "Did we take the wrong bus from the airport? Are we in a different town? I don't see the Eiffel Tower." Thoreau fussed and clapped his hands against her cheeks. The flight had been long for the baby. If they hadn't had a long layover on the East Coast before crossing the Atlantic, she'd probably have demanded the pilot turn the plane around, drop them at home, and forget this nonsense of finding Luc.

"We're following the map," Chris said, running his fingers across it. "We're not lost."

"We have to find a place soon. Thoreau and I need to get some sleep." She drew the baby close to her chest. Thoreau's little hands lifted her blouse, and he dove straight in, latching on to nurse. Celeste adjusted her clothing to cover herself, yet as exhausted as she felt, if anyone had said a word to her about indecency, she'd have raised her shirt higher to spite them.

After meandering in circles, they stood in front of a green, splintered door with a brass plaque reading, "Travelers's Hostel."

"This looks affordable." Chris rang the buzzer.

A man wearing a bowler hat unlatched the lock. "Vous voulez la pièce?"

Thoreau grinned and clapped and almost jumped out of her arms to grab the man's face.

"My baby's half French. His father's Parisian," Celeste said. She teared up, surprised at the sudden hit of emotion. "He recognizes your language."

"Your brother?" the manager asked, pointing to Chris.

"Je suis ami," Chris said. "Her best friend."

She wanted to say Chris was the Parisian's lover and the baby's other father. Instead, she yawned. "We need to sleep."

The manager gave them a book to register their information—home address, passport numbers, names—then gestured for them to follow him. He carried Celeste's duffel bag up five flights of rickety, narrow stairs; Chris carried his own suitcase and Thoreau's diaper bag; Celeste carried Thoreau.

The room looked bare. Two twin beds. One table. One lamp. No dresser or closet, since hostel rules required them to take their belongs during the day. The communal bathroom was located down the hallway.

Chris and Thoreau stood at the window. Off in the distance, the top of the Eiffel Tower poked through the skyline. "Papa Luc's somewhere out there," Chris said. "All we have to do is find a fruit market with owners named Laurent." He asked the manager if he knew of such a place. The manager did not.

Celeste tried to hide her shock at how rundown and ancient the place appeared. Worn wooden floor. Dinged plaster walls. One grimy window. The scent of hundreds of people.

The manager cranked the window's silver handle, letting a breeze swoop in. "Oui, bonne vue," he said, and gestured to Thoreau. "J'apporte une bassinet de bébé. A crib?"

"Oui, merci," Celeste said.

"I get for you." When he left, he closed the door behind him.

Thoreau crawled, grabbing at dust motes and trying to put crumbs as hard as stones into his mouth. Using the side of her hand, Celeste swept the mess into a mound and tossed the bits in the bin. She looked for other potential hazards. Thankfully, the sockets were window height, so the electrical cords in the room were beyond his reach. Exhausted from nearly twenty-four hours of travel, she sat on the side of the bed, her sigh plaintive. "Chris, what the fuck are we doing?"

Chris spread open the map of Parisian streets and jabbed his finger on the location of their hostel. "From here, we go in search of our man." The only information they had about Luc Laurent was that he grew up near a park, studied art at a university, his parents immigrated from the Ivory Coast, his father owned a produce market. "A fine start."

Someone knocked. For a brief moment, she hoped Luc followed their thought waves and landed on their doorstep. Despite everything they'd been through with him, she believed in happy outcomes. She flung the door open, saying, "Bienvenue."

The manager smiled and offered a bassinet and a broom. He indicated, using gestures and a blend of French and English, that since Thoreau had Parisian heritage, he'd allow them to keep their items in the room during the day instead of packing everything to haul around until nightfall. He returned a moment later with wooden crates to use as a dresser, three sets of towels, and a tin pail for the diapers. "Pour laver les couches-culottes du bébé."

"Merci beaucoup, Monsieur." Celeste hugged him. He responded by kissing one cheek then the other. After he left, she looked at Chris and lowered her voice to ask, "Will he want me to have sex with him in exchange for letting us keep everything here?"

Chris's eyes narrowed, and he frowned. "Celeste, he's being kind."

"Matt was too, at first."

"It's not the same at all. This is his business," Chris said. "But if sex with you turns out to be this guy's motive, we'll leave. We're not trapped."

She wondered if she'd ever trust men again, especially generous men.

They paid for one week of lodging, hoping it gave them enough time to locate Luc. They had no idea where they'd go if, after seven days, they hadn't discovered him. Or worse, found him shacked up with Matt.

Celeste admired the ornate buildings studded with black iron planters and red geraniums that lined the lazy Seine; the boulangeries, cafés, and marchés decorating city blocks; the scents of pastries, espresso, fruit, and cheese wafting through the air. Soon, even their own scrappy neighborhood gained a charmed appeal. She stopped noticing dog messes and started seeing the beauty of peeling paint and laundry lines, old men smoking and lounging on chairs, women speaking French too quickly for her to make out a single word. In the boulangerie near their hostel, the baker always gave Thoreau a cookie and sold them a baguette for half price.

Borrowing the hostel's phone book, Chris looked up all the Laurents and dialed. No one he spoke with knew Luc. Defeated, he said to Celeste, "Maybe Luc's parents heard Basscombe authorities are looking for him. Maybe they're hiding him. We'll find him."

"People who don't want to be found, generally aren't."

"He wants to be found. He wants us to find him."

"Sure," she said.

On their fourth day, they rode on a river barge. From its vantage point, Chris said he'd be able to spot Luc on a rue or crossing one of the picturesque bridges.

"Sure," she said.

Another day, they climbed the Eiffel Tower, taking turns carrying Thoreau. From the second platform, the entire world opened. Paris, infinitely more vast than either of them had suspected. The people below looked like ants; impossible to distinguish from each other. Anyone of them could be Luc. Or not.

Celeste said, "When we got here, I thought it would be easier to see him. Black faces are few and far between."

"Narrows the search," Chris said. "Luc will stand out."

"We have to accept the fact that we may not find him," she said.

Chris swatted her arm. "We will. There's no other way this can end. I'm positive."

"It can end with us not finding him." She felt the sooner Chris accepted that truth, the sooner his heart could heal.

At the small Eiffel Tower café, Chris bought an espresso for them to share. "A sip of coffee will give us energy to keep up the search." He sat at a table to drink it. In his lap, Thoreau banged the tiny spoon against the tiny cup.

"You have more faith in Luc than I do." She'd seen Luc and Matt in bed together, acting like the last two men alive. Luc didn't seem to miss Chris. Celeste kept this observation to herself.

During their daily Parisian wanderings, they'd stop in every produce market they passed. Chris would ask, "Connaissez-vous un marché par un famille africain?"

The answer always a shake of the head and a speedy reply, "Africain? No."

"Laurent?"

"Laurent? No."

Once, Celeste put her hand on Chris's shoulder, pulling him back from entering yet another shop. "Are you sure his parents own a market? Maybe that's a made-up story, too." Her pulse quickened. She didn't want to feel angry.

"Why would he lie about his parents owning a market? That doesn't make any sense." He jerked away from her.

Arguments weren't uncommon for them; they'd tussled since childhood. How futile, though, to try and convince Chris they'd never find the Laurent produce market in a town where every other corner had a produce market. "I surrender. Go on in and ask."

At the Sorbonne, they marveled at its glaring, white-marbled beauty while hoping Professor Luc would appear. Thoreau's squeals rattled the hallowed and silent passages as he dipped his fingers in the fountain.

Their American dollars stretched their francs into the future. They paid for a second week in the hostel.

Locked in their dingy room at night, twin beds pushed together, Chris and Celeste held each other close. Thoreau usually fell asleep while nursing; then she'd transfer him to the bassinet. His body curled like a c for cute. Their bodies curled like c's for Celeste and Chris.

They spent days in Jardin des Tuileries feasting on loaves of bread, rounds of cheese, and summer produce. Thoreau crawled on the grass, chasing bees and butterflies and the occasional stray cat. Beyond the row of trees, the Louvre towered; barracks of a medieval garrison. Chris pretended it was the only barrier between him and Luc, as if somewhere in the hallways of antiquities and art, Luc was held captive. "I'll rescue him, and we'll make love in front of a painting of a battle scene. Victory will be ours."

"Victory isn't easy, but it is possible," she said.

They paid for a third week at the hostel. Then a fourth and a fifth. They settled into a daily routine of walks and parks and spectacular scenery, ignoring the truth that their plan to find Luc was falling apart.

The faint scents of ammonia and bleach wafted from the hemp line in their room, where diapers and laundry hung to dry. Chris drew faces on the clothespins, making them look like a parade of naked, bald people, each with a silly expression. "Funny little Parisians, aren't they Thoreau?" Chris held the baby for a closer view. Thoreau swatted the clothes pins. The laundry danced.

Celeste cut paper dolls out of old newspapers and strung them corner to corner. "Friends for the clothespin people," she said.

One day, standing across the street from Les Deux Magots— the restaurant Baldwin mentioned in his writings—they watched fancy waiters shuffling from table to table, trays balanced in one hand, the others tucked behind their backs, pressing into their spines as if this simple act kept them from tumbling over.

Chris said, "If Baldwin came to Paris, nearly broke, and found what he was looking for, we can find Luc."

"Did Baldwin find Luc?"

"He found a place to write great books," Chris said. "He found a place to be gay and black."

She repeated her question, "Did Baldwin find Luc?" Realizing her harshness and sarcasm hurt Chris's feelings, she kissed his cheek. "You're right. Let's keep the faith."

Weekly, from the phone on the manager's desk, they made collect calls to their parents. The conversations joyous and brief. "How's our baby?" one or another of the grandparents would ask. "We're holding our breaths until you return." No one inquired about Luc. Perhaps Chris and Celeste's tone of voice indicated they hadn't found him yet.

A few times, spotting a black figure from the distance, Celeste's heart leapt. Her excitement lasted only until the stranger lifted his hand, or turned his chin, or made any movement that wasn't a gesture of Luc's.

"If he's walking the streets of Paris, we'll see him," Chris said. He began to approach anyone with dark skin, asking in French if they were familiar with Luc or the Laurents. No one who took the time to answer knew anything.

Celeste suspected Luc wasn't even from Paris but kept those doubts to herself. She understood Chris needed hope.

The crowded boulevards had a daily noisy, celebratory feel. Instead of overbearing American friendliness, everyone brushed past them. No one paid particular attention to her and Thoreau. No double takes. No questioning glances. No one asked whose child he was. It felt as if the entire population of France was given a tutorial on how to be polite and stay out of other people's personal lives.

Exhaustion replaced eagerness. When neither Chris nor Celeste were in the mood to dodge scooters, or leap over buskers' open violin cases, landing ankle deep in a pile of gutter trash, or their feet were too sore to walk along cobblestone streets, one of them would stay at the park with Thoreau while the other continued the search. Thoreau seemed content with not being carried for hours at a time. He acted giddy, crawling after children, birds, and dogs.

In August, the heat trapped them. Their room on the top floor baked. Without air-conditioning, unable to sleep, they'd sit in the little neighborhood park until it began to cool down.

Celeste pointed across the boulevard. "Men here always lean into doorways to pee."

Chris said, "Luc used go against the barn door like it was his birthright to piss wherever he wanted."

Celeste shook her head, sighing. "When I was pregnant, I asked him not to do that. The smell made me nauseous."

Chris said, "Whenever I asked him to go farther away, he'd scoot closer to the doorway."

"He listened to me. He wanted this baby so much, he was willing to walk to an oak tree to pee." Her smile changed to tears. "Why would he abandon us?"

Chris wrapped his arm around her shoulders. "I'm feeling his presence less and less. It's like his existence is being erased."

Celeste said, "We don't need him."

"I need him," Chris said.

They paid for another month. Their final thirty days before their return ticket home.

When Chris read *Giovanni's Room* and discussed living in Paris, the bohemian scene her mind concocted had resembled what they'd manifested. A cityscape of antiquity. Fashionable men. Suave women. Lovely, spoiled dogs. Picnicking on a blanket in the park. Baguette, wedge of cheese, and one pink macaroon to share between them. She hadn't imagined a church; Notre Dame surprised her. Sunlight streamed through stained glass windows in fluid arcs of red and blue, purple and yellow. Tourists wandered the perimeter, gazing at the altars and shrines. The Gothic ceiling formed the symmetry of two hands meeting, fingertip to fingertip. Jesus hung as a martyr should, suffering but strangely serene.

Day after day, she left the hostel, strolled along the Seine, and crossed the bridge to stand beside the enormous cathedral, marveling how the structure survived multitudes of ambushes and bombings throughout its long history. A testimony to beauty. Even someone like her, a non-Catholic Catholic, basked in its purity.

"When you're in the church, do you confess how you used the Sacred Heart of Jesus statue to hide notes to your gay boyfriend?" Chris asked her.

Celeste blinked. "I don't confess. I listen."

In the silence, she'd slip into an awareness of the present moment. The hard wooden bench pressing into her thighs. People whispering. Feet shuffling on the marble floor. Cameras clicking. Drops of water from the baptismal urn. Prayers. Mostly prayers.

As a girl, she'd hated the confines of being forced to sit still, listening to litanies and hymns. She'd close her eyes and envision piloting her own rocket ship, flying high, mending sick chimps in space. A jet-age St. Francis. In Notre Dame, when the bells rang, she felt her soul leap from the pew, soar through constellations, devour ether, bringing heaven and earth together inside herself.

Nearing their final week, they climbed into bed, the fading Parisian light filtering through the curtain. The faraway silhouette of the Eiffel Tower taunted their failed venture.

Clutching her around the waist, Chris whispered, "Luc doesn't want to be found."

Celeste remained quiet for a moment, pausing to consider this truth. "He was an illusion. A mirage."

"Thoreau, our immaculate conception," Chris said. He nestled his face in her neck.

She removed her camisole, wiped his tears, then drew him close. "Two sixteen-year-old fools believing the men who were fucking them loved them."

"It's good to believe we were loved," he said.

Celeste shrugged. "We showed up in Luc and Matt's lives as stupid kids eager to please them. Open for anything they asked. Why did we do that? Because they were handsome? Charming? Sexy? They desired us?"

"They cared for us." Chris drew a heart over her own. Colored it in with a kiss.

"Do you feel like you loved someone who can't possibly live up to what your mind created?"

"My perfect man," Chris said. "Except for the leaving part and begging me to have sex with Matt part."

"Are Luc and Matt nothing more than figments of our imagination?"

"They did love us," Chris said, pulling away to look her in the eye. "That seemed real."

"Then why didn't it last?"

Chris said, "'Love him and let him love you. Do you think anything else under Heaven really matters?' Baldwin, the wise queer."

She stroked Chris's back and his chest. How different he felt from Luc or Matt. Bony, not muscular. Slim hips. Slight stature. A narrow trail of blond hair from his belly button to his pubic bone.

Chris whispered, "Luc fell out of love with me."

"The day you fall out of love with him, you'll be free." She brushed her hands through Chris's hair, his curls like those on the statue of Saint-Michel. Angel-winged and beautiful. Sword in hand.

Wrestling with the devil. Saint-Michel, triumphant. Chris would be, too.

"Falling out of love had been happening bit by bit, as if I'm discarding scraps of my memories of Luc. It's painful."

"Oh, Chris," she said. "I'm sorry he's gone. I'm sorry he did that to you."

Chris said, "If I saw Luc right now, if he walked through that door, I wouldn't take him back. I'd be tempted. We'd make love, then I'd kick him out."

The heat, the anticipation of leaving Paris, the failure to find Luc, and the revelry on the street below the hostel kept them awake late into the night, talking about their future without Luc. Thoreau slept in his bassinet, ignorant of their despair. Tristesse.

"If my baby could have only one papa, I'm glad he's you," she said. Taking Chris's face in her hands, she kissed him. He kissed her. Tenderness transformed into a quiet lust.

"Je t'aime belle femme, Celeste."

She pulled him into an embrace, their eyes meeting, their lips parting. "Je t'aime."

"You and I?" he said, his smile shy.

"You can pretend I'm Luc if you want," she whispered.

Chris shook his head. "I don't want him here with us, Celeste. Do you?"

"I don't want him here."

This was not the jackhammer fuck of Matt's eager cock, nor the gentle slide of Luc's receding foreskin, nor the jolt of two cocaine-frenzied pricks jousting for attention.

Celeste and Chris, restless pilgrims yearning for home.

Declarations of love and friendship and devotion floated from the hostel window. Their words carried by the late summer breeze across Paris.

"The god and goddess of love," she whispered.

"Lingam and yoni."

Luc and Matt extinguished stars. Gaseous explosions of bygones. Once important and vital. Now, unnecessary.

Celeste whispered, "Veux-tu m'épouser?" Because in her heart, marriage to Chris seemed inevitable.

He said, "Oui, mon amour."

They fell asleep holding hands.

The following morning, they asked the hostel manager if he knew someone who could perform a wedding.

The manager said, "Your French amoureux d'homme is found?"

"Disparu." The correct word to indicate Luc had vanished?

"L'homme better for you. I see the love of you two together," the manager said. He picked up the phone and made a few calls on their behalf. The pastor in the neighborhood chapel would fit them in for a quick, symbolic ceremony. "C'est bon."

Small church. Gray stone. Narrow, with two windows on either side of the carved wood door. On top of the altar, a candle flickered. The minister, dressed in a black suit and tie, flung a silk purple scarf around his shoulders and welcomed them in. "Vous êtes Luthern?"

"We are a Jewtheran-Catholic family," Chris said.

"Très bien," the pastor said. He didn't appear to understand but gave a polite response.

Perched on his papa's shoulders, Thoreau giggled and clapped. Celeste and Chris locked arms.

The pastor said, "Le prêtre, Christopher Armstrong, voulez-vous prendre, Mary Celeste Roderick comme épouse? Et promettez-vous de lui rester fidèle. Dans le bonheur ou dans les épreuves. Dans la santé et dans la maladie, pour l'aimer tous les jours de votre vie?" He paused, then pointed at them. "Oui?"

The bride and groom nodded and said in unison, "Oui, we do," and slipped imaginary rings on each other's fingers.

Thoreau patted the top of Chris's head.

"Vous êtes mariée," the pastor said.

Celeste and Chris kissed as if love, not oxygen, sustained them.

Afterwards, they stepped out of the chapel and onto the sidewalk. Beside them, a flower stand burst with vibrant color. Chris bought Celeste a bouquet of peonies.

When they'd arrived in Paris, the dark clouds blended with the buildings, obscuring their long-range view. Now, the sun shimmered against glass, the Seine, puddles of water, brass thresholds.

Celeste wore a wreath of roses in her hair, Chris wore a rose bouton-nière, and the baby held a rainbow pinwheel for their civil ceremony at the California courthouse. Legal. Brief. Binding. A seal on their commitment to coparent Thoreau.

Compared to the serene Parisian chapel, this atmosphere felt sterile. The room had a beige carpeted floor, two rows of blue plastic chairs, and a stern judge who sat behind a desk, frowning as brides and grooms waited for their appointed matrimonial times.

When it was their turn, he muttered at Celeste and Chris as he glanced over the paperwork on his desk.

Bernadette, standing behind Celeste, snapped her fingers. "Sir, speak clearly, for God's sake. We can't understand a word of what you're saying."

The judge glanced up from his desk, presumably to reprimand Bernadette's rudeness. "Pardon?"

Bernadette said, "This union may not mean much to you. It's important to us."

The judge cleared his throat and repeated the question. "Young man, do you take this woman to be your lawful wedded wife?"

Celeste whispered to Chris, "He mumbles so much, I thought he said, 'Your awful wife.'"

Chris said, "I do," then lowered his voice, adding, "I do take this awful wife to love and honor and obey and cherish."

"Young lady, do you take this man to be your lawful wedded husband?"

Celeste said, "I do. We'll stay true friends forever and ever."

"You may kiss the bride."

Their kiss was friendly and sweet. Arms intertwined, Thoreau clutched between them.

"Where are the wedding bands?" Bernadette asked. She glanced around, her gaze landing on Thoreau crawling near their feet. "He's the ring bearer, isn't he? Where's the little pillow I made for him to hold?"

"We aren't wearing rings," Celeste said. "We don't need to mark each other as property owned."

"Oh, Mary Celeste," Bernadette said. She coiffed her sprayed hair.

Dr. Armstrong puffed on a cigar. Smoke swirled up to the dappled courtroom ceiling. "Our kids march to their own music, don't they?"

The judge shooed them from the room. "Rings or no rings, it's time to move along." This time he spoke clearly, no mumble.

Chris wrapped his arm around Celeste's waist and pulled her to the side. "We're married. Loosely interpreted."

She laughed when she whispered, "And we won't let anyone into our lives who likes both men and women. No chasing Baldwin's Paris. No *Giovanni's Room.*"

"No ménage à trois. Nope."

"Probably not a two à trois either," she said, and smiled. At their wedding in Paris, they'd made a pact promising to remain friends forever. Lovers again? Probably not.

The Armstrongs and Bernadette and George stood in the parking lot, waiting by their cars.

"Ready to go celebrate?" Bernadette called to them.

Celeste said, "We're walking home."

Dr. Armstrong said, "Take your time, kids. Enjoy yourselves," and he opened the passenger door for Mrs. Armstrong.

"May we take Thoreau with us?" Bernadette asked.

"He'd like that," Celeste said.

Bernadette lifted him from Chris's embrace and climbed in the sedan, the fat baby bouncing in her lap.

George said, "Taking a love stroll, you two? Going to stop in the park and neck?"

Bernadette said, "The kids these days call it 'making out,' George. Necking is from our heyday."

After their parents drove away, Celeste reached for Chris's hand. "They'll never understand that sex isn't why we're hitched."

"But you're my wife! My wife!" Chris said with a grin.

"You're my wife."

"Someday, I'll tell my parents I'm gay."

"Thoreau's going to grow up believing it's perfectly normal for a man to love a man," Celeste said.

"A man who loves a man who loves a woman who loves a different man," Chris said, interlacing his fingers through hers.

The Armstrongs held the wedding reception at their home. Vanilla cake adorned with pink frosting roses. Chris and Celeste held onto the knife and sliced. George snapped a photo.

Dr. Armstrong put on Peggy Lee's "I've Got You Under My Skin," then grabbed Mrs. Armstrong, holding her against his chest.

George bowed before Bernadette. "May I have this dance?"

Chris and Celeste ate cake and sat on the couch, watching their parents fling themselves across the room, then back into each other's embrace. Thoreau pressed into the edge of the coffee table and bobbed his little legs, his hands raised in the air as if praising Jesus.

When the party ended, George insisted he and Bernadette babysit Thoreau for the night. "You lovebirds need a honeymoon."

"We won't take no for an answer," Bernadette said. She gathered Thoreau, his diaper bag, and a plate of plastic-wrapped cake. "Say night-night to Mama and Papa, and Grandma and Grandpa Armstrong."

Celeste said, "I've never been away from him before."

"Then this is perfect timing," Mrs. Armstrong said. "Your honeymoon will be special."

"He'll be fine spending the night with your parents. Good for his development," Dr. Armstrong said.

The grandparents and Thoreau tossed flower petals as the newlyweds ascended the staircase to Chris's room. The theatricality of the moment seemed silly to Celeste, but an undisturbed night sounded divine.

Bernadette lifted the baby's wrist, encouraging him to wave.

Thoreau said, "Bye. Bye. Bye."

Celeste whispered to Chris, "This is good for Bernadette's development, too."

They walked down the hallway to his bedroom, now crowded with a full-sized bed, crib, baby buntings, musical mobile, and a diaper pail.

Chris said, "Sexy atmosphere."

Changing into their pajamas, they stood before each other, smiling. Chris laid his hand over the curve of her abdomen. "I love this part of your body. Our baby's first home."

She climbed into bed, lifting the sheet for Chris. "We need a first home of our own," she said.

Chris nestled, his arm cradling her neck. "I'm glad we made love in Paris. I'm glad it happened."

"We made love. We. Made. Love," she said. Not fucked. Not screwed. Not forced. Not coerced. "Love. Love. Love."

They kissed and hugged, falling into uninterrupted sleep.

A few weeks after their wedding, Celeste and Chris rented a two-bedroom apartment in a bustling low-income housing complex, close enough to both sets of grandparents to keep them happy. Chris started a job cleaning office buildings. George, thrilled to have a janitor in the family, supplied him with Fuller Brush products.

When Bernadette came to visit and help Celeste set up the apartment, cigarette smoke trailed after her as she inspected the rooms. She gushed about the quaintness of the place. "We really need to get you a coffeepot."

"I'd rather have a rolling bar," Celeste said. "I'm joking. A coffeepot would get more use."

Bernadette pointed at Thoreau. "The baby's teetering around this place as if he's the family drunk."

Celeste enjoyed Bernadette like this, tipsy enough to be entertaining but still in control.

"You brought this little Eiffel Tower knickknack all the way from France?" Bernadette said.

"We did." A tribute to Luc, the man who changed everything. Someday, if Thoreau asked about his birth father, they'd explain how Papa Luc helped make him.

"I'm glad you have Chris for a husband. I'm glad I was wrong about him. He obviously makes you happy, and he's a loving dad. My votives worked."

Celeste said, "As Homer wrote, 'Two souls inspired.'"

Bernadette said, "Funny how much I love someone I've known for only half his life," she said with a smile. "My grandson." She played with the baby while Celeste arranged the secondhand furniture. Donations from the Roderick and Armstrong households, flea markets, charity shops.

Later that evening, Chris came home from work and scooped Thoreau in his arms, kissing him before he helped Celeste unpack the final few boxes.

"How was your day?" Celeste asked, kissing his cheek.

"I'm grateful for the job that pays our rent, but I don't want to clean buildings for the rest of my life."

"I'll start looking for part-time work," Celeste said. "Bernadette offered to watch Thoreau a few days a week."

Chris said, "My dream career is to become a cartoonist."

Celeste carried a roll of shelf paper to the kitchen and paused, turning to look at him. "Like the funny papers?"

"Political cartoons," he said.

She measured and sliced pieces of contact paper. "All those caricatures on your Sacred Heart of Jesus notes used to crack me up. Your sabotage of the yearbook? Genius. Cartoons suit you. It's a really good idea." The paper stuck to the shelf unevenly, creasing. She used her arm to squeeze away air bubbles. "Is there a trade school for learning how to do comics? Art classes, maybe? Illustration?"

"If there is, sign me up." Chris took the largest cardboard box, cut windows and a door, and used a marker to draw a castle. Pretending to be a dragon, he gnawed on Celeste's leg and roared at Thoreau. The baby squealed as he toddled across the living room.

"Scoundrel, dragon," Celeste said, laughing.

Thoreau crawled through the castle door, stuck his face and hands out the window. "Mama. Yum." His newest phrase for breastfeeding.

"Someone ordered yum? I won't fit in your castle." She lifted her shirt, gesturing for him to come to her. She said to Chris, "Your cartoons and drawings made a huge impact on your own life. Now, you'll make an impact on the world. I can feel it."

Printed in the *Free Press*, Chris's debut cartoon: A commentary on the law stating homosexuals aren't allowed in the military. The image depicted a messy recruitment office, crammed with football trophies and ornate family photos. Center page, a sneering, bulky sergeant held a paper showing a birth date, June 1, 1953, and a draft number. The sergeant's speech bubble said, "Prove you're a queer, Faggot." Standing in front of the sergeant was a civilian wearing a tee shirt with a peace symbol on the front. The civilian's pants were dropped around his ankles. He had an enormous erection with the identical draft number imprinted in bold font across it: 015. The civilian's speech bubble read, "Admiring the proof, Sergeant?" The caption, sprawled along the banner at the top, read, "Get out of the draft! Plead Fag!"

"Brilliant," Celeste said, examining it. "If they drafted women, would I have the same number as you?" He'd used their birthday date for the cartoon, and seeing it in print made the situation more alarming to her.

Chris opened a drawer and handed her a letter. "Here's the military notice. My call to arms. It came when we were in France."

She had to stop herself from ripping the note apart and eating the draft notice, making the words travel through her stomach, intestines, colon, ass. "Fuck this goddamn war."

"I can't shoot anyone," he said. "I won't leave you and Thoreau." He stuffed the notice back into the envelope. "At Walden Creek, I hardly worried about what would happen when I turned eighteen and my notice came. I thought we'd be in hiding in the woods with the other draft dodgers."

Celeste felt her chest clench. "Plead fag. You won't be allowed to serve."

"I need a doctor to write me a homo diagnosis."

"What are you talking about? A doctor's note to say you're gay?"

"The draft board requires proof of queerness. That's what my comic makes fun of," Chris said. "The proof needs to be from a physician."

"Holy hell. Has the government lost its mind?" She went to check if Thoreau was still napping or if her outburst had disturbed him.

Chris whispered, "They consider being queer a medical condition."

She covered Thoreau with a blanket and stepped from the room, leaving the door slightly ajar. "We'll ask one of your father's friends."

"I have to let my dad know," Chris said. "He should hear it from me, not someone else."

"You can't be drafted, Chris. Tell your dad you don't want to go to war and the only way out is pretending to be a homosexual."

"I'm tired of pretending," Chris said. "Every time I'm around Bernadette, the way she scrutinizes me, I'm afraid she's going to yank me out of the closet."

"Bernadette believes her years of lighting altar candles worked. We're married. You're cured."

Chris said, "I'm afraid to disappoint my parents again."

"They don't want you fighting in Vietnam and getting killed." She tried to sound more upbeat than she felt. "We can tell your parents together if you want."

"Can you imagine how humiliating it will be for my dad to ask a colleague, 'Write a diagnosis for my son saying he's a homo'? Use a prescription pad to let the army know it's official.'"

"Homo, and I don't mean sapiens," Celeste said, hugging him to her chest. "We've been through worse."

Soon afterwards, they sat in the Armstrongs' living room. Thoreau toddled around, keeping his grandparents entertained. Chris leaned forward, elbows on knees, hands clasped. "I have something serious I need to talk to you about."

Dr. Armstrong said, "Were you denied the adoption?"

Chris shook his head. "That's still in process." He gazed at his mom, then his dad.

"What, son?" Dr. Armstrong said. "What's wrong?"

"Oh, God," Mrs. Armstrong said. "Are you sick?"

Chris said, "No, I'm not dying. I'm a homosexual," as straightforward as he could.

"You're a what?" Dr. Armstrong said.

"A homosexual. I'm gay."

"I know what a homosexual is, son." Dr. Armstrong turned to his wife. "He's gay?"

His parents seemed as puzzled as if he'd confessed he was a four star general, and they hadn't noticed until that moment.

"But you're married to Celeste," Mrs. Armstrong said. She fiddled with an ashtray, moving it from one end of the side table to the other. Her eyes darted from Chris to Celeste to Dr. Armstrong.

"We are married, I love Celeste, and I'm gay. Luc and I were in love, too. All of these things are equally true." Chris picked up Thoreau and twirled him in the air.

"Thoreau's father? That Luc?" Mrs. Armstrong said. "I'm not following."

"Luc's gay," Chris said.

Dr. Armstrong said, "This is Professor Laurent's doing, isn't it? He turned you into one." Dr. Armstrong fished a cigarette out of his pack. Unlit, it dangled from his mouth, wobbling. "Pervert. Criminal."

"If Luc's a pervert, so am I," Chris said.

The baby struggled from Chris's arms and toddled after a toy. "Ball. Ball," he repeated.

Celeste forced herself to stay quiet. Chris had wanted her to be with him for emotional support but requested she let him do the talking. Putting her hand over her mouth, she corralled words. Otherwise, she'd have told them Chris was the least perverted person she knew.

Chris said, "I was gay long before I went to Basscombe."

"Why didn't you tell us?" Mrs. Armstrong squeezed Chris's arm. "Are we the kind of parents you can't talk to?"

"Luc Laurent is twice your age," Dr. Armstrong said. "That's why I called him a pervert. A grown man, a teacher going after a student. That's what's perverted."

Chris stuck a match, holding the fire to the end of his father's cigarette. "Luc and I were madly in love. Our relationship fell apart because of Matt."

Dr. Armstrong said. "I don't understand."

Mrs. Armstrong said, "Matt's gay, too?"

"Matt won. I lost." Chris sighed. He didn't want to explain Matt's sexuality to his mother. "You and dad are parents I can talk to. I just wasn't ready before. I'm telling you now."

Dr. Armstrong said, "Professor Laurent took advantage of your naïveté. What a playground that school must have been for him. All those innocent boys."

"It wasn't like that," Chris said. "Luc loved me. I loved him. It was pure."

"How can you love a man?" Dr. Armstrong said.

"How can you love a woman?" Chris asked.

"Will someone explain what's going on?" Mrs. Armstrong stared at Celeste. "Is Luc Thoreau's father? He sleeps with everyone? Matt Briggs sleeps with everyone?"

Celeste said, "Sometimes. Please don't keep prying into that. It's personal."

Mrs. Armstrong stood. "I'm making a pot of tea, then we can discuss this like civilized human beings." Before opening the door, she turned to Chris. "None of this is logical. One of these days I'll figure out what type of marriage you and Celeste have."

"A loving marriage," Chris answered. "A marriage of friendship and parenthood."

Celeste followed Mrs. Armstrong. The kitchen door swung shut behind them. She waited until Mrs. Armstrong finished filling the kettle. When the faucet turned off, she said, "Chris has always been gay, and we've always been in love."

Mrs. Armstrong fumbled with the tea canister, measuring four rounded teaspoons of dark, narrow leaves. When the kettle screeched, she poured hot water into the pot. "What happened with Luc and Matt? I need answers. Luc is Thoreau's father. Where does Matt fit in? How is any of this possible?"

"Chris is gay. Luc is gay. Matt likes both women and men. Matt started liking Luc more than he liked me. Luc and I? It happened between us, but I'm not going to talk about that." When Mrs. Armstrong didn't respond, Celeste added, "All you need to understand is that Luc betrayed Chris. Hurt his heart. Hurt his confidence. Luc was not the person Chris believed him to be."

Mrs. Armstrong said, "I'm completely turned around. My head feels like a ball of yarn in the hands of an orangutan."

Celeste poured herself tea and blew the steam rising from her cup. She dropped a sugar cube in. Grains dissolved. "What's consistent is Chris and I love each other. We're friends. Best friends. We love Thoreau. We're his parents."

Mrs. Armstrong stacked saucers and teacups, creamer and sugar bowl, spoons, and teapot on a silver tray. "What about marital relations? You're content to live like this? With a man who's a homosexual?"

Celeste said, "If either of us ever have a relationship with someone else, we'll remain committed to one another. We're eternal. The more people to love Thoreau, the better."

"You two baffle me." Mrs. Armstrong took the tray. "Open the door, please?"

Dr. Armstrong sat on the carpet, playing with Thoreau.

Chris said, "If you fall in love with a boy, you fall in love with a boy."

Dr. Armstrong took a deep inhale. "That may be, but you fell in love with a man twice your age. Not a boy."

Mrs. Armstrong set the tray on the coffee table, then put her hand on Dr. Armstrong's knee. "We don't need to keep reminding Chris of this."

Celeste spoke softly, "Love is a kind of warfare." If they heard her, no one responded in protest. How could they? The ancient Greek sentiment was conclusive.

One afternoon, Chris came home from turning in his deferent papers at the induction center. "Where's the baby? I need the baby."

He lifted Thoreau in his arms, raised him above his head. "Flying Tiger. Flying Tiger."

Thoreau laughed and patted his papa on the top of the head. "Vroom. Boom," he shouted in his baby babble. "Roar."

"How was your appointment? How'd the interview go?" Celeste asked.

"You should have seen the sergeant's haircut. High and tight, like the military loves," Chris said. He spun Thoreau a few more times before setting the baby on his hip. "The guy had three rows of ribbons and black epaulettes with gold stripes over his pocket. Intimidating." Kissing Thoreau's cheek, he added, "The sergeant called me a fairy."

"Can he say that?" Celeste shook her head, frowning.

Chris saluted, demonstrating his response. "Yes, sir. A fairy, sir."

Thoreau's hands stretched into the air. He shouted, "Vroom. Boom. Papa."

Celeste reached for the baby, because she needed the room to be quiet to listen to Chris. She sat on the couch, cradling him.

Thoreau lifted her camisole. "Mama. Yum." He latched on, gazing at her, and playing with her hair. Cuddling him helped soothe her. She needed to be calm for Chris.

"The officer shook his finger in my face." Chris lowered his voice and continued, "He told me, 'Mr. Armstrong, I wish we could send you off to Vietnam quicker than your cock-sucking dirty little mouth can holler for your bitch of a mama.'"

Celeste couldn't speak. Words jammed inside her throat. A stranglehold.

"When the sergeant came from behind his desk, he stood so close, my nose was practically against the razor-sharp crease in his trousers." Chris paused for a moment, looking around as if he were gathering his thoughts and putting them into sentences. "I wanted to say, 'Looks like you've got a piddly little prick, sir.'

Instead, I started giggling. He pulled me up by the collar, shouting, 'I bet your father's ashamed of your sorry ass.' I said, 'No, sir. My dad loves me, sir.'"

"Your dad does love you," Celeste said. She leaned into him and could feel his heart slamming against his chest.

"I'm hated for being myself, Celeste. Despised because I'm queer," Chris said. "The whole thing makes me sad, but at the same time, I'm relieved not to go to Vietnam. I'm relieved to be out of the closet."

Celeste reached across the baby to stroke Chris's cheek. "Out and in the open, and your parents didn't disown you."

"The sergeant was right about one thing. My dad is ashamed of me."

Celeste said, "That's not true. Your father got you the doctor's note. He's trying to understand. He's old-fashioned. He's not ashamed."

Thoreau stopped nursing long enough to say, "Papa?"

"Flying Tiger," Chris said, "Papa's okay."

"Draw more of your draft-resistance cartoons. We'll send them to all the underground newspapers and publications in the country. Think of the guys, gay and straight, you'll keep out of Vietnam." What else could she do except squelch injustice and support the man she adored?

Eventually, through a rebel, queer press, Chris published a comic book series based on his "Plead Fag!" editorial cartoon. The protagonist was a homosexual infantryman forced to hide his relationship with the guy he loved but had to leave behind to go to war. The story followed the blond, curly-haired infantryman as he fought in Vietnam, lonely and afraid, sustained only by memories of his boyfriend, a boulder of muscle and beauty. After a few tours, the infantryman returned home to his lover. Together, they protested homophobia and the military's unjust law. Walked streets, knocking on doors, urging citizens to take a stand for equality.

Confronted a villainous pastor who preached against the sins of homosexuality. Protested against a politician who'd suggested rounding all the queers and locking them in barracks in the desert. To defy the pastor, politician, and people like them, the former infantryman and his lover flaunted their relationship. They threw parades, danced in gay nightclubs, fucked in bathhouses, and through all their wild escapades, they stayed devoted to one another. These comic books gained a cult following.

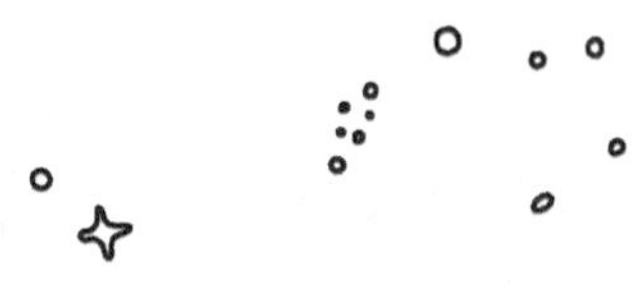

A Point in Space

Their apartment looked festive, decorated with cardboard cutout campfires and cardboard silhouettes of bucking broncos. Celeste's stomach was tied in knots as she waited for their parents to come over for Thoreau's cowboy-themed birthday party. She and Chris hadn't seen Dr. and Mrs. Armstrong since he broke his news. His parents had called but Chris wouldn't answer the phone.

Chris finished icing the cupcakes. "Can you imagine the conversation our moms will have about me being a homo? Especially Bernadette after drinking a few cocktails."

Celeste pantomimed holding a cigarette in one hand and a tumbler in the other. In her best impression of Bernadette, she slurred, "I had my suspicions the boy was a genuine fruitcake."

Chris licked frosting from the butter knife. "Haven't heard the term fruitcake in awhile."

"But I'm a man!" Celeste said with dramatic flair, flinging her arms wide open.

"A fruitcake who's in love with a girl. A fruitcake who slept with that girl." Putting the cupcakes on a platter, he turned to Celeste, grinning when he said, "We wrote our own version of a Baldwin story, called 'Parisian Hostel.'"

Celeste removed the cornbread from the oven, rested the pan on a wire rack to cool. "We needed one another, plain and simple. No regrets."

339

"No regrets," Chris said. "I love Celeste. I love men. I'm inclusive, not divisive."

On Thoreau's plate, Celeste cut an apple butter sandwich into the shape of a star. Thoreau liked to open sandwiches and lick the inside, then squish the bread between his fingers. "I can't believe he's one year old already."

"I can't believe Luc's missing his son's birthday." Sticking tiny plastic cowboys in the centers of the cupcakes, Chris frowned. "Next time I meet someone, I'm going to hire a private detective and do a deep investigation into the guy's background."

"Isn't that against the nature of falling in love?" she asked.

"I suppose, but now we have Thoreau's welfare to consider," he said. "No loonies. No druggies. No liars."

"We're not sixteen. We're not idiotic. We're older and wiser." Celeste lifted the lid on the pot of chili, stirred and tasted. "I call this dish 'Roundup Stew.' All the cowboys eat it." The fragrance of cumin turned her stomach. She rushed to the bathroom.

"We're off to a good start," Chris said.

Splashing her face and brushing her teeth, she prayed everything would go well between Chris and his mom and dad. Prayed if Bernadette heard the news of Chris's coming out, she'd be on her best behavior. Prayed George wouldn't stutter trying to say the words homosexual and queer.

"They're here," Chris called. "My nerves feel like a pile of Parisian dogshit on a hot city street."

Celeste woke Thoreau from his nap. "Howdy, cowboy. Ready for your birthday party?" She dressed him in fringed regalia, a wide-brimmed hat, sheriff badge, bandana, and cowboy boots.

Bernadette had hired a local woman who brought a dappled pony that whinnied on command. On that cold autumn day, it rained hard. Dr. Armstrong ran alongside the Shetland, holding an umbrella over his grandson. George and the grandmothers dodged mud kicked from the pony's hooves. Chris and Celeste held hands, their smiles like sunshine. When the dappled gray trotted off into the horizon, Thoreau cried. Bernadette promised to bring it back on a clear day.

Despite the storm, the lamp above the kitchen table lit the room in cheery yellow streaks. Everyone gathered, passing bowls of chili. Celeste handed Bernadette a slice of cornbread. "For you, Mom." Saying the word mom felt strange, but right. Mom.

Bernadette said, "Your hair looks shiny beneath that overhead light. All those pretty waves."

Celeste said, "Pre-runaway hairdo. Pre-boxcutter haircut." Her parents would never know the depths of self-depravation she'd suffered. How she'd allowed Matt to treat her like shit. His never-ending verbal assaults. His physical aggressions. She shivered, picturing him standing on that downed redwood, Thoreau barely held in place by Matt's flimsy shirt. Matt's smirk. Growing her hair seemed a ritual of renewal and rebirth. Birth.

Dr. Armstrong patted the cigarette package in his jacket pocket. He didn't take one out. "You cooked up a feast worthy of a cowboy and his posse."

Celeste said, "Chris made the cornbread."

"Nicely done," George said.

After dinner and cupcakes and a marathon of cowboy songs, Thoreau fell asleep. Dr. Armstrong offered to carry him to his crib. Celeste followed, wanting to tuck her birthday boy in. Unclasping the sheriff's badge from Thoreau's vest, Dr. Armstrong said, "What a successful party." He set the star on Thoreau's dresser.

Celeste whispered, "Chris is afraid he's disappointed you."

"I'm not disappointed," Dr. Armstrong said. "I'm glad that as Chris was growing up, navigating all those emotions and suspicions about himself, he had you for a friend. I'm relieved he wasn't lonesome."

She pressed herself into Dr. Armstrong's chest, comforted and content. He had the scent of men's cologne, spicy and strong and chemical. Her stomach churned. Covering her nose and mouth with her fist, she had a realization. "Can someone conceive after being intimate only once?"

"If a woman is ovulating at the time of ejaculation, conception is entirely possible." Dr. Armstrong placed his fingers on her pulse and closed his eyes, concentrating. "Your heart's racing."

"Even if she's breastfeeding?" Celeste asked.

"Breastfeeding is not a guaranteed method of birth control."

"If I am pregnant, it's Chris's," she said.

Dr. Armstrong stood silent for a moment. He reached for her hand, squeezing it when he said, "Then we'll have two grandchildren to love."

"Will you keep this confidential? Chris doesn't know, yet. He'll never believe it. Never believe we made a baby." She could barely believe it herself, but the symptoms felt the same. Nausea. Tender breasts. Enhanced fragrances.

Dr. Armstrong said, "If you are pregnant, this is unexpected and utterly good news."

Celeste placed her palms over her abdomen. "Welcome."

Did reproductive magic awaken the day Chris read Baldwin's words, "I'm sort of queer for girls, myself?" This baby, a constel-lation of molecules expanding, sorting into brain cells, heart, lungs, legs, arms, eventually genitals.

George and the grandmas stood at the kitchen sink, washing and drying dishes, talking and laughing about Thoreau's fascination with everything western.

Picking up Thoreau's scattering of toys, Chris laughed. "Our boy sure loves cowboys."

Dr. Armstrong patted Chris on the back and started singing, "Home, home on the range."

Swirling a dishtowel across a plate, George sang, "Where the deer and the buffalo play."

"And seldom is heard, a discouraging word, la la la." Although Bernadette's hands were plunged in a sink of bubbles, she spun around, soap splattering everywhere.

Mrs. Armstrong sang, "And the skies are not cloudy all day," as she stacked dishes in the cupboard.

Celeste said, "Giddyup, wanglers. Giddyup, cowhands." Giddyup to this precious being growing inside her womb.

The room gleamed spick and span, as George was fond of saying. The grandparents gathered their belongings.

"The four of us are continuing this party at our house," Bernadette said. "Nightcaps."

Dr. Armstrong hugged Chris. "You're doing well, son," he said, releasing his grip momentarily before pulling him in again. "Quite well. What a charming papa you are."

Chris said, "I learned from the best."

When the door closed, Celeste opened the living room window, inhaling the fragrances of grass and soil after rain.

"Successful party," Chris said. "My parents were fine, weren't they? No weird looks or awkward silences. They didn't out me to yours. A huge weight lifted."

Celeste smiled. "Chris? I'm pretty sure we came home from France with a Parisian hitchhiker."

"What?" He glanced from her face to her belly. "You're pregnant? We're having another baby? How? Oh, I know how. Is this real, Celeste? A baby?"

"It's about the size of a chocolate chip, but I can feel him or her in there. Giovanni Baldwin Armstrong if it's a boy or a girl."

Chris hugged her as he quoted James Baldwin, "Perhaps home is not a place but simply an irrevocable condition."

"Our baby's home is definitely an irrevocable condition." She sensed the wonderment of cells dividing and multiplying.

"Thoreau's going to be a big brother," Chis said. "I can't wait for them to meet."

Over the next few months, while Thoreau perfected his toddling, and Chris worked on his political cartoons, Celeste curled on the couch to needlepoint. With each cross-stitch and tug of thread creating stars and planets and the ring around Saturn, she reflected on struggles past and struggles to come. Was she prepared for the difficulties they'd face? Chris gay in a world of homophobia. Thoreau black in a world of racism. Giovanni fitting into a family unlike those of any of their friends. If love is a kind of warfare, Celeste and Chris would face the battle, swords and daggers raised. Only people capable of expressing and reciprocating honest and mature and healthy and loving emotions would be allowed into their lives. She settled on this simple truth of romantic love: Tumble and fall and thrive.

Her finished needlepoint tapestry depicted a galaxy swirling around a quote by Henry David Thoreau: "This whole earth which we inhabit is but a point in space."

Abandoning her former need for Waldenesque solitude, she preferred the boisterous life of raising Thoreau, gestating Giovanni and adoring Chris.

Her world. Her celestial sphere.

Acknowledgments

When I showed up to Ellen Bass' writing workshop with the characters Celeste and Chris in my mind, and little writing experience, she encouraged me to keep going with the story. The manuscript has changed since those days over a decade ago, but Ellen was tremendous in teaching me the poetry of language and the value of perseverance.

Writing conferences have been crucial to the work. The teachers and participants' critique and praise transformed an idea into a novel. I'm beyond grateful for the help and the friendships I developed.

Ernesto Mestre, and his expert developmental edit, made the work infinitely better. Many thanks to him for looking at the book with an editor's eye. I'm grateful for his wisdom and clarity and guidance.

Sincere thanks to Scott Heim for his valued commentary on the story, and his support.

Coverkitchen's artistic intuition resulted in this gorgeous cover. Much praise to them.

Ann Hood for her beautiful self.

Without my dearest friends and family who've listened to me talk about how much I love writing, and have given me support, I'd still be carrying Celeste and Chris around in my head instead of putting them on paper, and letting them grow.